"... The concept of a human society evolved to inhabit a free-fall environment remains in clear focus; *The Integral Trees* is a convincing piece of environmental engineering by one of the masters of the art."

—*Newsday*

The plot and characters "combine with the happily mind-boggling and original premise to make this marvelous, sense-of-wonder, hardcore SF that's sure to be popular."

—*Publishers Weekly*

"In *The Integral Trees* Niven has come up with an idea about as far out as one can get, a created world without a world . . . This is certainly classic science fiction—the idea is truly the hero."

—*Isaac Asimov's*
Science Fiction Magazine

THE
INTEGRAL TREES

— *and* —

THE
SMOKE RING

THE
INTEGRAL
TREES

and

THE
SMOKE RING

Larry Niven

BALLANTINE BOOKS • NEW YORK

A Del Rey® Book
Published by The Random House Publishing Group

The Integral Trees, copyright © 1983 by Larry Niven
The Smoke Ring, copyright © 1987 by Larry Niven

This work was originally published as two separate volumes by The Ballantine
Publishing Group as *The Integral Trees* in 1984 and *The Smoke Ring* in 1987.

Del Rey is a registered trademark and the Del Rey colophon is a trademark of Random
House, Inc.

www.delreydigital.com

Library of Congress Catalog Card Number: 2003090542

ISBN: 978-0-345-46036-3

Text design by Susan Turner
Diagrams and maps by Shelly Shapiro
Cover design by Dreu Pennington-McNeil
Cover art by Michael Whelan

First Omnibus Edition: August 2003

THE
INTEGRAL TREES

This book is dedicated to Robert Forward, for the stories he's sparked in me, for his help in working out the parameters of the Smoke Ring, and for his big, roomy mind.

CONTENTS

PROLOGUE *Discipline*   1

ONE *Quinn Tuft*   5

TWO *Leavetaking*   17

THREE *The Trunk*   26

FOUR *Flashers and Fan Fungus*   34

FIVE *Memories*   42

SIX *Middle Ground*   48

SEVEN *The Checker's Hand*   58

EIGHT *Quinn Tribe*   64

NINE *The Raft*   73

TEN *The Moby*   83

ELEVEN *The Cotton-Candy Jungle*   91

TWELVE *The Copsik Runners*   99

THIRTEEN *The Scientist's Apprentice*   108

FOURTEEN *Treemouth and Citadel*   117

FIFTEEN *London Tree*   124

SIXTEEN *Rumblings of Mutiny*   133

SEVENTEEN *"When Birnham Wood . . ."*   141

EIGHTEEN *The War of London Tree*   149

NINETEEN *The Silver Man*   158

TWENTY *The Position of Scientist's Apprentice . . .* 168

TWENTY-ONE *Go For Gold*   178

TWENTY-TWO *Citizens' Tree*   187

Dramatis Personae   197

Glossary   199

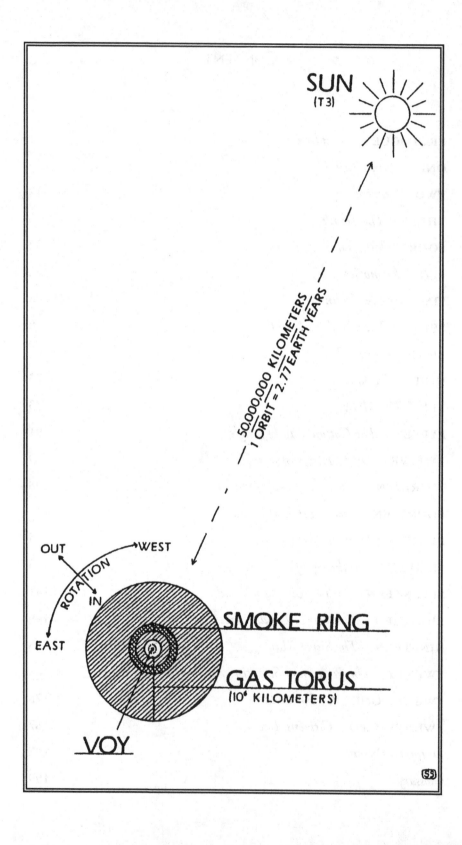

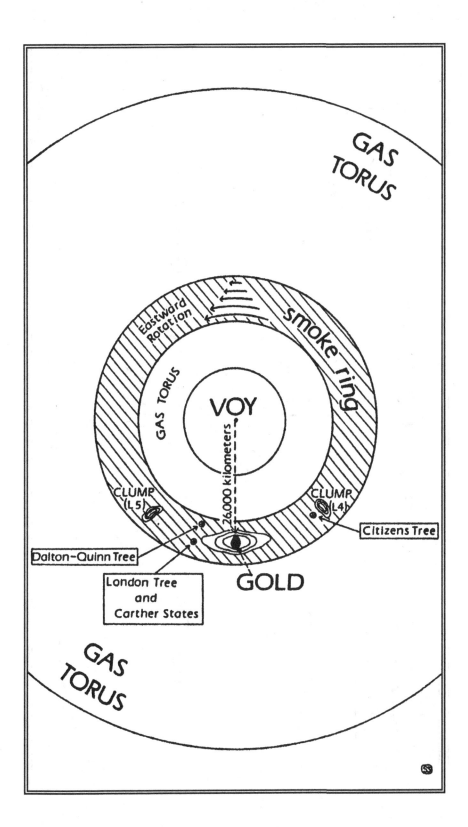

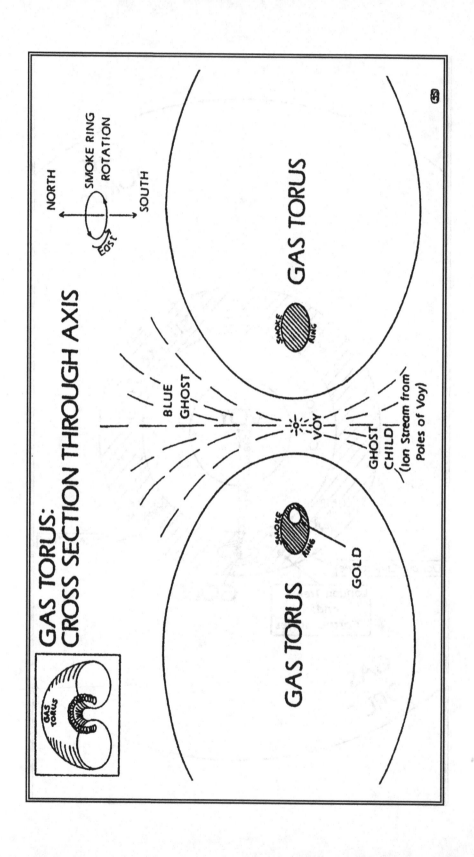

GAS TORUS:
CROSS SECTION THROUGH AXIS

NORTH

SMOKE RING
ROTATION

SOUTH

EAST

GAS TORUS

BLUE
GHOST

SMOKE
RING

VOY

GHOST
CHILD
(Ion Stream from
Poles of Voy)

SMOKE
RING

GOLD

GAS TORUS

GAS TORUS

GAS
TORUS

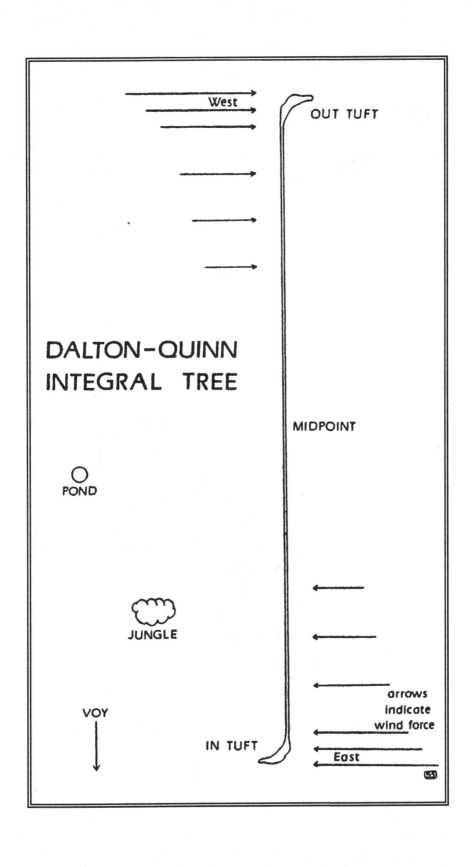

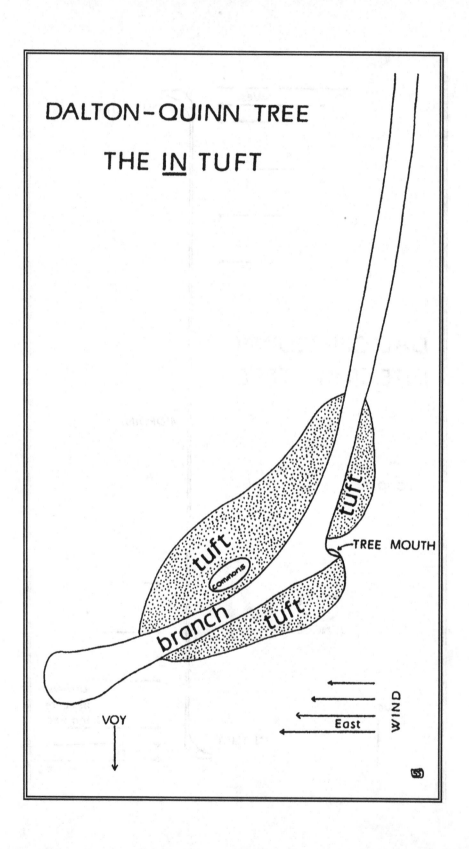

DALTON-QUINN TREE

THE IN TUFT

Prologue

DISCIPLINE

It was taking too long, much longer than he had expected. Sharls Davis Kendy had not been an impatient man. After the change he had thought himself immune to impatience. But it was taking too long! What were they *doing* in there?

His senses were not limited. Sharls's telescopic array was powerful; he could sense the full electromagnetic spectrum, from microwave up to X-ray. But the Smoke Ring balked his view. It was a storm of wind, dust, clouds of water vapor, huge rippling drops of dirty water or thin mud, masses of free-floating rock; dots and motes and clumps of green, green surfaces on the drops and the rocks, green tinges of algae in the clouds; trees shaped like integration signs, oriented radially to the neutron star and tufted with green at both ends; whale-sized creatures with vast mouths, to skim the green-tinged clouds . . .

Life was everywhere in the Smoke Ring. Claire Dalton had called it a Christmas wreath. Claire had been a very old woman before the State revived her as a corpsicle. The others had never seen a Christmas wreath; nor had Kendy. What they had seen, half a thousand years ago, was a perfect smoke ring several tens of thousands of kilometers across, with a tiny hot pinpoint in its center.

Their reports had been enthusiastic. Life was DNA-based; the air was not only breathable, but tasted fine . . .

Discipline presently occupied the point of gravitational neutrality behind Goldblatt's World, the L2 point. This close, the sky split equally into star-sprinkled, black- and green-tinged cloudscape. Directly below, a vast distorted whirlpool of storm hid the residue of a gas giant planet, a rocky nugget two and a half times the mass of Earth.

Sharls would not enter that inner region. The maelstrom of forces could damage his ship. He couldn't guess how long the seeder ramship must survive to accomplish his mission. He had waited more than half a thousand years already. The L2 point was still within the gas torus of which the Smoke Ring was only the densest part. *Discipline* was subject to slow erosive forces. He couldn't last forever in this place.

At least the crew were not extinct.

That would have hurt him terribly.

He had done his duty. Their ancestors had been mutineers, a potential threat to the State itself. To reeducate their descendants was his goal, but if the Smoke Ring had killed them . . . well, it would not have surprised him. It took more than breathable air to keep men alive. The Smoke Ring was green with the life that had evolved for that queer environment. Native life might well have killed off those Johnny-come-lately rivals, the erstwhile crew of the seeder ramship *Discipline*.

Sharls would have grieved; but he would have been free to return home.

They'd call me an obsolete failure, he thought gloomily while his instruments sought a particular frequency in the radio range. *A thousand years out of date by the time I'm home. They'd scrap the computer for certain. And the program? The Sharls Davis Kendy program might be copied and kept for the use of historians. Or not.*

But they hadn't died. Eight Cargo and Repair Modules had gone with the original mutineers. Time and the corrosive environment must have ruined the CARMs; but at least one was still operational. Someone had been using it as late as six years ago. And—there: the light he'd been searching for. For a moment it reached him clearly: the frequency of hydrogen burning with oxygen.

He fired a maser in ultrashort, high-powered pulses. "Kendy for the State. Kendy for the State. Kendy for the State."

The response came four seconds later, sluggish, weak, and blurred. Kendy pinpointed it and fine-focused his telescopes while he sent his next demand.

"Status. Tell me three times."

Kendy sorted the garbled response through a noise-eliminator program. The CARM was on manual, mostly functional, using attitude jets only, operating well inside its safety limits. Once it had been a simplified recording of Kendy's own personality. Now the program was deteriorating, growing stupid and erratic.

"Course record for the past hour."

It came. The CARM had been free-falling at low relative velocity up to forty minutes ago. Then, low-acceleration maneuvers, a course that looked like a dropped plate of spaghetti, a mad waste of stored fuel. Malfunction? Or . . . it could have been a dogfight-style battle.

War?

"Switch to my command."

Four seconds; then a signal like a scream of bewildered agony. Massive malfunction.

The crew must have disconnected the autopilot system on every one of the CARMs, half a thousand years ago. It had still been worth a try, as was his next message.

"Give me video link with crew."

"Denied."

Oh *ho*! The video link hadn't been disconnected! A block must have been programmed in, half a thousand years ago, by the mutineers. Certainly their descendants wouldn't know how to do that.

A block might be circumvented, eventually.

The CARM was too small to see, of course, but it must be somewhere near that green blob not far from Goldblatt's World. A cotton-candy forest. Plants within the Smoke Ring tended to be fluffy, fragile. They spread and divided to collect as much sunlight as possible, without worrying about gravity.

For half a thousand years Kendy had watched for signs of a developing civilization—for regular patterns in the floating masses, or infrared radiation from manufacturing centers, or industrial pollution: metal vapor, carbon monoxide, oxides of nitrogen. He hadn't found any of that. If the children of *Discipline*'s crew were developing beyond savagery, it was not in any great numbers.

But they lived. Someone was using a CARM.

If only he could see them! Or talk to them—"Give me voiceover. Citizen, this is Kendy for the State. Speak, and your reward will be beyond the reach of your imagination."

"Amplify. Amplify. Amplify," sent the CARM.

Kendy was already sending at full amplification. "Cancel voiceover," he sent.

Not for the first time, he wondered if the Smoke Ring could have proved *too* kindly an environment. Creatures evolved in free fall would not have human strength. Humans could be the most powerful creatures in the Smoke Ring: happy as clams in there, and about as active. Civilization develops to protect against the environment.

Or against other men. War would be a hopeful sign . . .

If he could *know* what was going on! Kendy could perturb the environment in a dozen different ways. Cast them out of Eden and see what happened. But he dared not. He didn't know enough.

Kendy waited.

Chapter One

QUINN TUFT

G avving could hear the rustling as his companions tunneled upward.
   They stayed alongside the great flat wall of the trunk. Finger-thick
spine branches sprouted from the trunk, divided endlessly into wire-thin
branchlets, and ultimately flowered into foliage like green cotton, loosely
spun to catch every stray beam of sunlight. Some light filtered through as
green twilight.

Gavving tunneled through a universe of green cotton candy.

Hungry, he reached deep into the web of branchlets and pulled out a
fistful of foliage. It tasted like fibrous spun sugar. It cured hunger, but what
Gavving's belly wanted was meat. Even so, its taste was *too* fibrous . . . and the
green of it was too brown, even at the edges of the tuft, where sunlight fell.

He ate it anyway and went on.

The rising howl of the wind told him he was nearly there. A minute
later his head broke through into wind and sunlight.

The sunlight stabbed his eyes, still red and painful from this morning's
allergy attack. It always got him in the eyes and sinuses. He squinted and
turned his head, and sniffled, and waited while his eyes adjusted. Then,
twitchy with anticipation, he looked up.

Gavving was fourteen years old, as measured by passings of the sun behind Voy. He had never been above Quinn Tuft until now.

The trunk went straight up, straight out from Voy. It seemed to go out
forever, a vast brown wall that narrowed to a cylinder, to a dark line with
a gentle westward curve to it, to a point at infinity—and the point was
tipped with green. The far tuft.

A cloud of brown-tinged green dropped away below him, spreading out into the main body of the tuft. Looking east, with the wind whipping his long hair forward, Gavving could see the branch emerging from its green sheath as a half-klomter of bare wood: a slender fin.

Harp's head popped out, and his face immediately dipped again, out of the wind. Laython next, and he did the same. Gavving waited. Presently their faces lifted. Harp's face was broad, with thick bones, its brutal strength half-concealed by golden beard. Laython's long, dark face was beginning to sprout strands of black hair.

Harp called, "We can crawl around to lee of the trunk. East. Get out of this wind."

The wind blew always from the west, always at gale velocities. Laython peered windward between his fingers. He bellowed, "Negative! How would we catch anything? Any prey would come right out of the wind!"

Harp squirmed through the foliage to join Laython. Gavving shrugged and did the same. He would have liked a windbreak . . . and Harp, ten years older than Gavving and Laython, was nominally in charge. It seldom worked out that way.

"There's nothing to catch," Harp told them. "We're here to guard the trunk. Just because there's a drought doesn't mean we can't have a flash flood. Suppose the tree brushed a pond?"

"*What* pond? Look around you! There's *nothing* near us. Voy is too close. Harp, you've said so yourself!"

"The trunk blocks half our view," Harp said mildly.

The bright spot in the sky, the sun, was drifting below the western edge of the tuft. And in that direction were no ponds, no clouds, no drifting forests . . . nothing but blue-tinged white sky split by the white line of the Smoke Ring, and on that line, a roiled knot that must be Gold.

Looking up, out, he saw more of nothing . . . faraway streamers of cloud shaping a whorl of storm . . . a glinting fleck that might indeed have been a pond, but it seemed even more distant than the green tip of the integral tree. There would be no flood.

Gavving had been six years old when the last flood came. He remembered terror, panic, frantic haste. The tribe had burrowed east along the branch, to huddle in the thin foliage where the tuft tapered into bare wood. He remembered a roar that drowned the wind, and the mass of the branch itself shuddering endlessly. Gavving's father and two apprentice hunters hadn't been warned in time. They had been washed into the sky.

Laython started off around the trunk, but in the windward direction. He was half out of the foliage, his long arms pulling him against the wind. Harp followed. Harp had given in, as usual. Gavving snorted and moved to join them.

It was tiring. Harp must have hated it. He was using claw sandals, but he must have suffered, even so. Harp had a good brain and a facile tongue, but he was a dwarf. His torso was short and burly; his muscular arms and legs had no reach, and his toes were mere decoration. He stood less than two meters tall. The Grad had once told Gavving, "Harp looks like the pictures of the Founders in the log. We all looked like that once."

Harp grinned back at him, though he was puffing. "We'll get you some claw sandals when you're older."

Laython grinned too, superciliously, and sprinted ahead of them both. He didn't have to say anything. Claw sandals would only have hampered his long, prehensile toes.

Night had cut the illumination in half. Seeing was easier, with the sunglare around on the other side of Voy. The trunk was a great brown wall three klomters in circumference. Gavving looked up once and was disheartened at their lack of progress. Thereafter he kept his head bent to the wind, clawing his way across the green cotton, until he heard Laython yell.

"Dinner!"

A quivering black speck, a point to port of windward. Laython said, "Can't tell what it is."

Harp said, "It's trying to miss. Looks big."

"It'll go around the other side! Come on!"

They crawled, fast. The quivering dot came closer. It was long and narrow and moving tail-first. The great translucent fin blurred with speed as it tried to win clear the trunk. The slender torso was slowly rotating.

The head came in view. Two eyes glittered behind the beak, one hundred and twenty degrees apart.

"Swordbird," Harp decided. He stopped moving.

Laython called, "Harp, what are you doing?"

"Nobody in his right mind goes after a swordbird."

"It's still meat! And it's probably starving too, this far in!"

Harp snorted. "Who says so? The Grad? The Grad's full of theory, but he doesn't have to hunt."

The swordbird's slow rotation exposed what should have been its third eye. What showed instead was a large, irregular, fuzzy green patch. Laython cried, "Fluff! It's a head injury that got infected with fluff. The thing's injured, Harp!"

"That isn't an injured turkey, boy. It's an injured *swordbird*."

Laython was half again Harp's size, and the Chairman's son to boot. He was not easy to discipline. He wrapped long, strong fingers around Harp's shoulder and said, "We'll miss it if we wait here arguing! I say we go for Gold." And he stood up.

The wind smashed at him. He wrapped toes and one fist in branchlets, steadied himself, and semaphored his free arm. "Hiyo! Swordbird! Meat, you copsik, *meat!*"

Harp made a sound of disgust.

It would surely see him, waving in that vivid scarlet blouse. Gavving thought, hopefully, *We'll miss it, and then it'll be past.* But he would not show cowardice on his first hunt.

He pulled his line loose from his back. He burrowed into the foliage to pound a spike into solid wood, and moored the line to it. The middle was attached to his waist. Nobody ever risked losing his line. A hunter who fell into the sky might still find rest somewhere, if he had his line.

The creature hadn't seen them. Laython swore. He hurried to anchor his own line. The business end was a grapnel: hardwood from the finned end of the branch. Laython swung the grapnel round his head, yelled, and flung it out.

The swordbird must have seen, or heard. It whipped around, mouth gaping, triangular tail fluttering as it tried to gain way to starboard, to reach their side of the trunk. Starving, yes! Gavving hadn't grasped that a creature could see him as *meat* until that moment.

Harp frowned. "It could work. If we're lucky it could smash itself against the trunk."

The swordbird seemed bigger every second: bigger than a man, bigger than a hut—all mouth and wings and tail. The tail was a translucent membrane enclosed in a V of bone spines with serrated edges. What was it doing this far in? Swordbirds fed on creatures that fed in the drifting forests, and there were few of these, so far in toward Voy. Little enough of anything. The creature did look gaunt, Gavving thought; and there was that soft green carpet over one eye.

Fluff was a green plant parasite that grew on an animal until the animal died. It attacked humans too. Everybody got it sooner or later, some more than once. But humans had the sense to stay in shadow until the fluff withered and died.

Laython could be right. A head injury, sense of direction fouled up . . . and it was meat, a mass of meat as big as the bachelors' longhut. It must be ravenous . . . and now it turned to face them.

An isolated mouth came toward them: an elliptical field of teeth, expanding.

Laython coiled line in frantic haste. Gavving saw Harp's line fly past him, and tearing himself out of his paralysis, he threw his own weapon.

The swordbird whipped around, impossibly fast, and snapped up Gavving's harpoon like a tidbit. Harp whooped. Gavving froze for an instant; then his toes dug into the foliage while he hauled in line. *He'd hooked it.*

The creature didn't try to escape: it was still fluttering toward them.

Harp's grapnel grazed its side and passed on. Harp yanked, trying to hook the beast, and missed again. He reeled in line for another try.

Gavving was armpit-deep in branchlets and cotton, toes digging deeper, hands maintaining his deathgrip on the line. With eyes on him, he continued to behave as if he *wanted* contact with the killer beast. He bellowed, "Harp, where can I hurt it?"

"Eye sockets, I guess."

The beast had misjudged. Its flank smashed bark from the trunk above their heads, dreadfully close. The trunk shuddered. Gavving howled in terror. Laython howled in rage and threw his grapnel ahead of it.

It grazed the swordbird's flank. Laython pulled hard on the line and sank the hardwood tines deep in flesh.

The swordbird's tail froze. Perhaps it was thinking things over, watching them with two good eyes while the wind pulled it west.

Laython's line went taut. Then Gavving's. Spine branches ripped through Gavving's inadequate toes. Then the immense mass of the beast had pulled him into the sky.

His own throat closed tight, but he heard Laython shriek. Laython too had been pulled loose.

Torn branchlets were still clenched in Gavving's toes. He looked down into the cushiony expanse of the tuft, wondering whether to let go and drop. But his line was still anchored . . . and wind was stronger than tide; it could blow him past the tuft, past the entire branch, out and away. Instead he crawled along the line, away from their predator-prey.

Laython wasn't retreating. He had readied his harpoon and was waiting.

The swordbird decided. Its body snapped into a curve. The serrated tail slashed effortlessly through Gavving's line. The swordbird flapped hard, making west now. Laython's line went taut; then branchlets ripped and his line pulled free. Gavving snatched for it and missed.

He might have pulled himself back to safety then, but he continued to watch.

Laython poised with spear ready, his other arm waving in circles to hold his body from turning, as the predator flapped toward him. Almost alone among the creatures of the Smoke Ring, men have no wings.

The swordbird's body snapped into a U. Its tail slashed Laython in half almost before he could move his spear. The beast's mouth snapped shut four times, and Laython was gone. Its mouth continued to work, trying to deal with Gavving's harpoon in its throat, as the wind carried it east.

The Scientist's hut was like all of Quinn Tribe's huts: live spine branches fashioned into a wickerwork cage. It was bigger than some, but there was no sense of luxury. The roof and walls were a clutter of paraphernalia stuck into the wickerwork: boards and turkey quills and red tuftberry dye for ink, tools for teaching, tools for science, and relics from the time before men left the stars.

The Scientist entered the hut with the air of a blind man. His hands were bloody to the elbows. He scraped at them with handfuls of foliage, talking under his breath. "Damn, damn drillbits. They just burrow in, no way to stop them." He looked up. "Grad?"

" 'Day. Who were you talking to, yourself?"

"Yes." He scrubbed at his arms ferociously, then hurled the wads of bloody foliage away from him. "Martal's dead. A drillbit burrowed into her. I probably killed her myself, digging it out, but she'd have died anyway . . . you can't leave drillbit eggs. Have you heard about the expedition?"

"Yes. Barely. I can't get anyone to tell me anything."

The Scientist pulled a handful of foliage from the wall and tried to scrub the scalpel clean. He hadn't looked at the Grad. "What do you think?"

The Grad had come in a fury and grown yet angrier while waiting in an empty hut. He tried to keep that out of his voice. "I think the Chairman's trying to get rid of some citizens he doesn't like. What I want to know is, why me?"

"The Chairman's a fool. He thinks science could have stopped the drought."

"Then you're in trouble too?" The Grad got it then. "You blamed it on me."

The Scientist looked at him at last. The Grad thought he saw guilt there, but the eyes were steady. "I let him think you were to blame, yes. Now, there are some things I want you to have—"

Incredulous laughter was his answer. "What, more gear to carry up a hundred klomters of trunk?"

"Grad . . . Jeffer. What have I told you about the tree? We've studied the universe together, but the most important thing in it is the tree. Didn't I teach you that everything that lives has a way of staying near the Smoke Ring median, where there's air and water and soil?"

"Everything but trees and men."

"Integral trees have a way. I taught you."

"I . . . had the idea you were only guessing . . . Oh, I see. You're willing to bet *my* life."

The Scientist's eyes dropped. "I suppose I am. But if I'm right, there won't be anything left but you and the people who go with you. Jeffer, this could be *nothing*. You could all come back with . . . whatever we need: breeding turkeys, some kind of meat animal living on the trunk, I don't know—"

"But you don't think so."

"No. That's why I'm giving you these."

He pulled treasures from the spine-branch walls: a glassy rectangle a quarter meter by half a meter, flat enough to fit into a pack; four boxes each the size of a child's hand. The Grad's response was a musical "O-o-oh."

"You'll decide for yourself whether to tell any of the others what you're carrying. Now let's do one last drill session." The Scientist plugged a cassette into the reader screen. "You won't have much chance to study on the trunk."

PLANTS

Life pervades the Smoke Ring but is neither dense nor massive. In the free-fall environment plants can spread their greenery widely to catch maximum sunlight and passing water and soil, without bothering about structural strength. We find at least one exception . . .

These integral trees grow to tremendous size. The plant forms a long trunk under terrific tension, tufted with green at both ends, stabilized by the tide. They form thousands of radial spokes circling Levoy's Star. They grow up to a hundred kilometers in length, with up to a fifth of a gee in tidal "gravity" at the tufts and perpetual hurricane winds.

The winds derive from simple orbital mechanics. They blow from the west at the inner tuft and from the east at the outer tuft (where in *is toward Levoy's Star, as usual). The structure bows to the winds, curving into a nearly horizontal branch at each end. The foliage sifts fertilizer from the wind . . .*

The medical dangers of life in free fall are well known. If Discipline has indeed abandoned us, if we are indeed marooned within this weird

*environment, we could do worse than to settle the tufts of the integral
trees. If the trees prove more dangerous than we anticipate, escape is easy.
We need only jump and wait to be picked up.*

The Grad looked up. "They really didn't know very much about the
trees, did they?"

"No. But, Jeffer, they had seen trees from outside."

That was an awesome thought. While he chewed it, the Scientist said,
"I'm afraid you may have to start training your own Grad, and soon."

Jayan sat cross-legged, coiling lines. Sometimes she looked up to watch
the children. They had come like a wind through the Commons, and the
wind had died and left them scattered around Clave. He wasn't getting
much work done, though it seemed he was trying.

The girls loved Clave. The boys imitated him. Some just watched, others
buzzed around him, trying to help him assemble the harpoons and the
spikes or asking an endless stream of questions. "What are you doing?
Why do you need so many harpoons? And all this rope? Is it a hunting
trip?"

"I can't tell you," Clave said with just the proper level of regret. "King,
where have you been? You're all sticky."

King was a happy eight-year-old painted in brown dust. "We went underside. The foliage is greener there. Tastes better."

"Did you take lines? Those branches aren't as strong as they used to be.
You could fall through. And did you take a grown-up with you?"

Jill, nine, had the wit to distract him. "When's dinner? We're still
hungry."

"Aren't we all." Clave turned to Jayan. "We've got enough packs, we
won't be carrying food, we'll find water on the trunk . . . claw sandals . . .
jet pods, I'm glad we got those . . . hope we've got enough spikes . . . what
else do we need? Is Jinny back?"

"No. What did you send her for, anyway?"

"Rocks. I gave her a net for them, but she'll have to go all the way to
the treemouth. I hope she finds us a good grindstone."

Jayan didn't blame the children. She loved Clave too. She would have
kept him for herself, if she could . . . if not for Jinny. Sometimes she wondered if Jinny ever felt that way.

"Mmm . . . we'll pick some foliage before we leave the tuft—"

Jayan stopped working. "Clave, I never thought of that. There's no foliage on the trunk! We won't have *anything* to eat!"

"We'll find something. That's why we're going," Clave said briskly. "Thinking of changing your mind?"

"Too late," Jayan said. She didn't add that she had never wanted to go at all. There was no point, now.

"I could bust you loose. Jinny too. The citizens like you, they wouldn't let—"

"I won't stay." Not with Mayrin and the Chairman here, and Clave gone. She looked up and said, "Mayrin."

Clave's wife stood in the half-shadows on the far side of the Commons. She might have been there for some time. She was seven years older than Clave, a stocky woman with the square jaw of her father, the Chairman. She called, "Clave, mighty hunter, what game are you playing with this young woman when you might be finding meat for the citizens?"

"Orders."

She approached, smiling. "The expedition. My father and I arranged it together."

"If you'd like to believe that, feel free."

The smile slipped. "Copsik! You've mocked me too long, Clave. You and *them*. I hope you fall into the sky."

"I hope I don't," Clave said mildly. "Would you like to assist our departure? We need blankets. Better have an extra. Nine."

"Fetch them yourself," Mayrin said and stalked away.

Here in the main depths of Quinn Tuft there were tunnels through the foliage. Huts nestled against the vertical flank of the branch, and the tunnels ran past. Now Harp and Gavving had room to walk, or something like it. In the low tidal pull they bounced on the foliage as if it and they were made of air. The branchlets around the tunnels were dry and nude, their foliage stripped for food.

Changes. The days had been longer before the passing of Gold. It used to be two days between sleeps; now it was eight. The Grad had tried to explain why, once, but the Scientist had caught them at it and whacked the Grad for spilling secrets and Gavving for listening.

Harp thought that the tree was dying. Well, Harp was a teller, and world-sized disasters make rich tales. But the Grad thought so too . . . and Gavving *felt* like the world had ended. He almost wanted it to end, before he had to tell the Chairman about his son.

He stopped to look into his own dwelling, a long half-cylinder, the bachelors' longhut. It was empty. Quinn Tribe must be gathered for the evening meal.

"We're in trouble," Gavving said and sniffed.

"Sure we are, but there's no point in acting like it. If we hide, we don't eat. Besides, we've got this." Harp hefted the dead musrum.

Gavving shook his head. It wouldn't help. "You should have stopped him."

"I couldn't." When Gavving didn't answer, Harp said, "Four days ago the whole tribe was throwing lines into a *pond*, remember? A pond no bigger than a big hut. As if we could pull it to us. We didn't think that was stupid till it was gone past, and nobody but Clave thought to go for the cookpot, and by the time he got back—"

"I wouldn't send even Clave to catch a swordbird."

"Twenty-twenty," Harp jeered. The taunt was archaic, but its meaning was common. *Any fool can foresee the past.*

An opening in the cotton: the turkey pen, with one gloomy turkey still alive. There would be no more unless a wild one could be captured from the wind. Drought and famine . . . Water still ran down the trunk sometimes, but never enough. Flying things still passed, meat to be drawn from the howling wind, but rarely. The tribe could not survive on the sugary foliage forever.

"Did I ever tell you," Harp asked, "about Glory and the turkeys?"

"No." Gavving relaxed a little. He needed a distraction.

"This was twelve or thirteen years back, before Gold passed by. Things didn't fall as fast then. Ask the Grad to tell you why, 'cause I can't, but it's true. So if she'd just fallen on the turkey pen, it wouldn't have busted. But Glory was trying to move the cookpot. She had it clutched in her arms, and it masses three times what she does, and she lost her balance and started *running* to keep it from hitting the ground. *Then* she smashed into the turkey pen.

"It was as if she'd thought it out in detail. The turkeys were all through the Clump and into the sky. We got maybe a third of them back. That was when we took Glory off cooking duties."

Another hollow, a big one: three rooms shaped from spine branches. Empty. Gavving said, "The Chairman must be almost over the fluff."

"It's night," Harp answered.

Night was only a dimming while the far arc of the Smoke Ring filtered the sunlight; but a cubic klomter of foliage blocked light too. A victim of fluff could come out at night long enough to share a meal.

"He'll see us come in," Gavving said. "I wish he were still in confinement."

There was firelight ahead of them now. They pressed on, Gavving sniffling, Harp trailing the musrum on his line. When they emerged into the Commons their faces were dignified, and their eyes avoided nobody.

The Commons was a large open area, bounded by a wickerwork of branchlets. Most of the tribe formed a scarlet circle with the cookpot in the center. Men and women wore blouses and pants dyed with the scarlet the Scientist made from tuftberries and sometimes decorated with black. That red would show vividly anywhere within the tuft. Children wore blouses only.

All were uncommonly silent.

The cookfire had nearly burned out, and the cookpot—an ancient thing, a tall, transparent cylinder with a lid of the same material—retained no more than a double handful of stew.

The Chairman's chest was still half-covered in fluff, but the patch had contracted and turned mostly brown. He was a square-jawed, brawny man in middle age, and he looked unhappy, irritable. Hungry. Harp and Gavving went to him, handed him their catch. "Food for the tribe," Harp said.

Their catch looked like a fleshy mushroom, with a stalk half a meter long and sense organs and a coiled tentacle under the edge of the cap. A lung ran down the center of the stalk/body to give the thing jet propulsion. Part of the cap had been ripped away, perhaps by some predator; the scar was half-healed. It looked far from appetizing, but society's law bound the Chairman too.

He took it. "Tomorrow's breakfast," he said courteously. "Where's Laython?"

"Lost," Harp said, before Gavving could say, "Dead."

The Chairman looked stricken. "How?" Then, "Wait, eat first."

That was common courtesy for returning hunters; but for Gavving the waiting was torture. They were given scooped-out seedpods containing a few mouthfuls of greens and turkey meat in broth. They ate with hungry eyes on them, and they handed the gourds back as soon as possible.

"Now talk," the Chairman said.

Gavving was glad when Harp took up the tale. "We left with the other hunters and climbed along the trunk. Presently we could raise our heads into the sky and see the bare trunk stretching out to infinity—"

"My son is lost and you give me poetry?"

Harp jumped. "Your pardon. There was nothing on our side of the trunk, neither of danger nor salvation. We started around the trunk. Then Laython saw a swordbird, far west and borne toward us on the wind."

The Chairman's voice was only half-controlled. "You went after a swordbird?"

"There is famine in Quinn Tuft. We've fallen too far in, too far toward Voy, the Scientist says so himself. No beasts fly near, no water trickles down the trunk—"

"Am I not hungry enough to know this myself? Every baby knows better than to hunt a swordbird. Well, go on."

Harp told it all, keeping his language lean, passing lightly over Laython's disobedience, letting him show as the doomed hero. "We saw Laython and the swordbird pulled east by the wind, along a klomter of naked branch, then beyond. There was nothing we could do."

"But he has his line?"

"He does."

"He may find rest somewhere," the Chairman said. "A forest somewhere. Another tree . . . he could anchor at the median and go down . . . well. He's lost to Quinn Tribe at least."

Harp said, "We waited in the hope that Laython might find a way to return, to win out and moor himself along the trunk, perhaps. Four days passed. We saw nothing but a musrum borne on the wind. We cast our grapnels and I hooked the thing."

The Chairman looked ill with disgust. Gavving heard in his mind, *Have you traded my son for musrum meat?* But the Chairman said, "You are the last of the hunters to return. You must know of today's events. First, Martal has been killed by a drillbit."

Martal was an older woman, Gavving's father's aunt. A wrinkled woman who was always busy, too busy to talk to children, she had been Quinn Tribe's premier cook. Gavving tried not to picture a drillbit boring into her guts. And while he shuddered, the Chairman said, "After five days' sleep we will assemble for Martal's last rites. Second: the Council has decided to send a full hunting expedition up the trunk. They must not return without a means for our survival. Gavving, you will join the expedition. You'll be informed of your mission in detail after the funeral."

Chapter Two

LEAVETAKING

The treemouth was a funnel-shaped pit thickly lined with dead-looking, naked spine branches. The citizens of Quinn Tuft nested in an arc above the nearly vertical rim. Fifty or more were gathered to say good-bye to Martal. Almost half were children.

West of the treemouth was nothing but sky. The sky was all about them, and there was no protection from the wind, here at the westernmost point of the branch. Mothers folded their babes within their tunics. Quinn Tribe showed like scarlet tuftberries in the thick foliage around the treemouth.

Martal was among them, at the lower rim of the funnel, flanked by four of her family. Gavving studied the dead woman's face. Almost calm, he thought, but with a last lingering trace of horror. The wound was above her hip: a gash made not by the drillbit, but by the Scientist's knife as he dug for it.

A drillbit was a tiny creature, no bigger than a man's big toe. It would fly out of the wind too fast to see, strike, and burrow into flesh, leaving its gut as an expanding bag that trailed behind it. If left alone it would eventually burrow through and depart, tripled in size, leaving a clutch of eggs in the abandoned gut.

Looking at Martal made Gavving queasy. He had lain too long awake, slept too little; his belly was already churning as it tried to digest a breakfast of musrum stew.

Harp edged up beside him, shoulder-high to Gavving. "I'm sorry," he said.

"For what?" Though Gavving knew what he meant.

"You wouldn't be going if Laythonw wasn't dead."

"You think this is the Chairman's punishment. All right, I thought so too, but . . . wouldn't you be going?"

Harp spread his hands, uncharacteristically at a loss for words.

"You've got too many friends."

"Sure, I talk good. That could be it."

"You could volunteer. Have you thought of the stories you could bring back?"

Harp opened his mouth, closed it, shrugged.

Gavving dropped it. He had wondered, and now he knew. Harp was afraid . . . "I can't get anyone to tell me anything," he said. "What have you heard?"

"Good news and bad. Nine of you, supposed to be eight. You were an afterthought. The good news is just a rumor. Clave's your leader."

"Clave?"

"Himself. Maybe. Now, it could still be true that the Chairman's getting rid of anyone he doesn't like. He—"

"Clave's the top hunter in the tuft! He's the Chairman's son-in-law!"

"But he's not living with Mayrin. Aside from that . . . I'd be guessing."

"What?"

"It's too complicated. I could even be wrong." And Harp drifted off.

The Smoke Ring was a line of white emerging from the pale blue sky, narrowing as it curved around in the west. Far down the arc, Gold was a clot of streaming, embattled storms. His gaze followed the arm around and down and in, until it faded out near Voy. Voy was directly below, a blazing pinpoint like a diamond set in a ring.

It was all sharper and clearer than it had been when Gavving was a child. Voy had been dimmer then and blurred.

At the passing of Gold, Gavving had been ten years old. He remembered hating the Scientist for his predictions of disaster, for the fear those predictions raised. The shrieking winds had been terrible enough . . . but Gold had passed, and the storms had diminished . . .

The allergy attack had come days later.

This present drought had taken years to reach its peak, but Gavving had felt the disaster at once. Blinding agony like knives in his eyes, runny nose, tightness in his chest. Thin, dry air, the Scientist said. Some could tolerate it, some could not. Gold had dropped the tree's orbit, he was told; the tree had moved closer to Voy, too far below the Smoke Ring median. Gavving was told to sleep above the treemouth, where the rivulets ran. That was before the rivulets had dwindled so drastically.

The wind too had become stronger.

It always blew directly into the treemouth. Quinn Tuft spread wide green sails into the wind, to catch anything that the wind might bear. Water, dust or mud, insects or larger creatures, all were filtered by the finely divided foliage or entangled in the branchlets. The spine branches migrated slowly forward, west along the branch, until gradually all was swallowed into the great conical pit. Even old huts migrated into the treemouth to be crushed and swallowed, and new ones had to be built every few years.

Everything came to the treemouth. The streams that ran down the trunk found an artificial catchbasin above, but the water reached the treemouth as cookwater, or washwater, or when citizens came to rid themselves of body wastes, to "feed the tree."

Martal's cushion of spine branches had already carried her several meters downslope. Her entourage had retreated to the rim, to join Alfin, the treemouth custodian.

Children were taught how to care for the tree. When Gavving was younger his tasks had included carrying collected earth and manure and garbage to pack into the treemouth, removing rocks to use elsewhere, finding and killing pests. He hadn't liked it much—Alfin was a terror to work under—but some of the pests had been edible, he remembered. Earthlife crops were grown here too, tobacco and maize and tomatoes; they had to be harvested before the tree swallowed them.

But in these dark days, passing prey were all too rare. Even the insects were dying out. There wasn't food for the tribe, let alone garbage to feed the insects and the tree. The crops were nearly dead. The branch was nude for half its length; it wasn't growing new foliage.

Alfin had had care of the treemouth for longer than Gavving had been alive. That sour old man hated half the tribe for one reason or another. Gavving had feared him once. He attended all funerals . . . but today he truly looked bereaved, as if he were barely holding his grief in check.

Day was dimming. The bright spot, the sun, was dropping, blurring. Soon enough it would brighten and coalesce in the east. Meanwhile . . . yes, here came the Chairman, carefully robed and hooded against the light, attended by the Scientist and the Grad. The Grad, a blond boy four years older than Gavving, looked unwontedly serious. Gavving wondered if it was for Martal or for himself.

The Scientist wore the ancient falling jumper that signified his rank: a two-piece garment in pale blue, ill-fitting, with pictures on one shoulder. The pants came to just below the knees; the tunic left a quarter meter of gray-furred belly. After untold generations the strange, glossy cloth was beginning to show signs of wear, and the Scientist wore it only for official functions.

The Grad was right, Gavving thought suddenly: the old uniform would fit Harp perfectly.

The Scientist spoke, praising Martal's last contribution to the health of the tree, reminding those present that one day they must all fulfill that obligation. He kept it short, then stepped aside for the Chairman.

The Chairman spoke. Of Martal's bad temper he said nothing; of her skill with the cookpot he said a good deal. He spoke of another loss, of the son who was lost to Quinn Tuft wherever he might be. He spoke long, and Gavving's mind wandered.

Four young boys were all studious attention; but their toes were nipping at a copter patch. The ripe plants responded by launching their seedpods, tiny blades whirring at each end. The boys stood solemnly in a buzzing cloud of copters.

Treemouth humor. Others were having trouble suppressing laughter; but somehow Gavving couldn't laugh. He'd had four brothers and a sister, and all had died before the age of six, like too many children in Quinn Tuft. In this time of famine they died more easily yet . . . He was the last of his family. Everything he saw today squeezed memories out of him, as if he were seeing it all for the last time.

It's only a hunting party! His jumpy belly knew better. Hero of a single failed hunt, how would Gavving be chosen for a last-ditch foraging expedition?

Vengeance for Laython. Were the others being punished too? *Who* were the others? How would they be equipped? When would this endless funeral be over?

The Chairman spoke of the drought, and the need for sacrifice; and now his eye did fall on selected individuals, Gavving among them.

When the long speech ended, Martal was another two meters downslope. The Chairman departed hurriedly ahead of the brightening day.

Gavving made for the Commons with all haste.

Equipment was piled on the web of dry spine branches that Quinn Tribe called *the ground*. Harpoons, coils of line, spikes, grapnels, nets, brown sacks of coarse cloth, half a dozen jet pods, claw sandals . . . a reassuring stack of what it would take to keep them alive. Except . . . food? He saw no food.

Others had arrived before him. Even at a glance they seemed an odd selection. He saw a familiar face and called, "Grad! Are you coming too?"

The Grad loped to join them. "Right. I had a hand in planning it," he confided. A bouncy, happy type in a traditionally studious profession, the Grad had come armed with his own line and harpoon. He seemed eager, full of nervous energy. He looked about him and said, "Oh, treefodder."

"Now, what is that supposed to mean?"

"Nothing." He toed a pile of blankets and added, "At least we won't go naked."

"Hungry, though."

"Maybe there's something to eat on the trunk. There'd better be."

The Grad had long been Gavving's friend, but he wasn't much of a hunter. And Merril? Merril would have been a big woman if her tiny, twisted legs had matched her torso. Her long fingers were callused, her arms were long and strong; and why not? She used them for everything, even walking. She clung to the wicker wall of the Commons, impassive, waiting.

One-legged Jiovan stood beside her, with a hand in the branchlets to hold him balanced. Gavving could remember Jiovan as an agile, reckless hunter. Then something had attacked him, something he would never describe. Jiovan had returned barely alive, with ribs broken and his left leg torn away, the stump tourniquetted with his line. Four years later the old wounds still hurt him constantly, and he never let anyone forget it.

Glory was a big-boned, homely woman, middle-aged, with no children. Her clumsiness had given her an unwanted fame. She blamed Harp the teller for that, and not without justice. There was the tale of the turkey cage; and he told another regarding the pink scar that ran down her right leg, gained when she was still involved in cooking duties.

The hate in Alfin's eyes recalled the time she'd clouted him across the ear with a branchwood beam; but it spoke more of Alfin's tendency to hold grudges. Gardener, garbage man, funeral director . . . he was no hunter, let alone an explorer, but he was here. No wonder he'd looked bereaved.

Glory waited cross-legged, eyes downcast. Alfin watched her with smoldering hate. Merril seemed impassive, relaxed, but Jiovan was muttering steadily under his breath.

These, his companions? Gavving's belly clenched agonizingly on the musrum.

Then Clave entered the Commons, briskly, with a young woman on each arm. He looked about him as if liking what he saw.

It was true. Clave was coming.

They watched him prodding the piled equipment with his feet, nodding, nodding. "Good," he said briskly and looked about him at his waiting companions. "We're going to have to carry all this treefodder. Start dividing it up. You'll probably want it on your back, moored with your line, but take your choice. Lose your pack and I'll send you home."

The musrum loosed its grip on Gavving's belly. Clave was the ideal hunter: built long and narrow, two and a half meters of bone and muscle. He could pick a man up by wrapping the fingers of one hand around the man's head, and his long toes could throw a rock as well as Gavving's hands. His companions were Jayan and Jinny, twins, the dark and pretty daughters of Martal and a long-dead hunter. Without orders, they began loading equipment into the sacks. Others moved forward to help.

Alfin spoke. "I take it you're our leader?"

"Right."

"Just what are we supposed to be doing with all this?"

"We go up along the trunk. We renew the Quinn markings as we go. We keep going until we find whatever it takes to save the tribe. It could be food—"

"On the bare trunk?"

Clave looked him over. "We've spent all our lives along two klomters of branch. The Scientist tells me that the trunk is a *hundred* klomters long. Maybe more. We don't know what's up there. Whatever we need, it isn't here."

"You know why we're going. We're being thrown out," Alfin said. "Nine fewer mouths to feed, and *look* at who—"

Clave rode him down. He could outshout thunder when he wanted to. "Would you like to stay, Alfin?" He waited, but Alfin didn't answer. "Stay, then. *You* explain why you didn't come."

"I'm coming." Alfin's voice was almost inaudible. Clave had made no threats, and didn't have to. They had been assigned. Anyone who stayed would be subject to charges of mutiny.

And that didn't matter either. If Clave was going, then . . . Alfin was wrong, and Gavving's stomach had been wrong too. They would find what the tribe needed, and they would return. Gavving set to assembling his pack.

Clave said, "We've got six pairs of claw sandals. Jayan, Jinny, Grad . . . Gavving. I'll take the extras. We'll find out who else needs them. Everyone take four mooring spikes. Take a few rocks. I mean it. You need at least one to hammer spikes into wood, and you may want some for throwing. Has everybody got his dagger?"

It was night when they pulled themselves out of the foliage, and they still emerged blinking. The trunk seemed infinitely tall. The far tuft was almost invisible, blurred and blued almost to the color of the sky.

Clave called, "Take a few minutes to eat. Then stuff your packs with foliage. We won't see foliage again for a long time."

Gavving tore off a spine branch laden with green cotton candy. He stuck it between his back and the pack, and started up the trunk. Clave was already ahead of him.

The bark of the trunk was different from the traveling bark of the branch. There were no spine branches, but the bark must have been meters thick, with cracks big enough to partly shield a climber. Smaller cracks made easy grip for fingers.

Gavving wasn't used to claw sandals. He had to kick a little to seat them right, or they slipped. His pack tended to pull him over backward. Maybe he wanted it lower? The tide helped. It pulled him not just downward, but against the trunk too, as if the trunk sloped.

The Grad was moving well but puffing. Maybe he spent too much time studying. But Gavving noted that his pack was larger than the others'. Was he carrying something besides provisions?

Merril had no pack, just her line. She managed to keep up using her arms alone. Jiovan, with two arms and a leg, was overtaking Clave himself, though his jaw was clenched in pain.

Jayan and Jinny, above Gavving on the thick bark, stopped as by mutual accord. They looked down; they looked at each other; they seemed about to weep. A sudden, futile surge of homesickness blocked Gavving's own throat. He lusted to be back in the bachelors' hut, clinging to his bunk, face buried in the foliage wall . . .

The twins resumed their climb. Gavving followed.

They were moving well, Clave thought. He was still worried about Merril. She'd slow them down, but at least she was trying. She'd find it easier, moving with just two arms, when they got near the middle of the trunk. There would be no tide at all there; things would drift without falling, if the Scientist's smoke dreams were to be believed.

Alfin alone was still down there in the last fringes of tuft. Clave had expected trouble from Alfin, but not this. Alfin was the oldest of his team, pushing forty, but he was muscular, healthy.

Appeal to his pride? He called down, "Do you need claw sandals, Alfin?"

Alfin may have considered any number of retorts. What he called back was, "Maybe."

"I'll wait. Jiovan, take the lead."

Clave worked his pack open while Alfin moved up to join him. Alfin was climbing with his eyes half-shut. Something odd there, something wrong.

"I was hoping you could at least keep up with Merril," Clave said, handing Alfin the sandals.

Alfin said nothing while he strapped one on. Then, "What's the difference? We're all dead anyway. But it won't do that copsik any good! He's only got rid of the lames—"

"Who?"

"The Chairman, our precious Chairman! When people are starving, they'll kick out whoever's in charge. He's kicked out the lames, the ones who couldn't hurt him anyway. Let him see what he can snag when they kick him into the sky."

"If you think I'm a lame, see if you can outclimb me," Clave said lightly.

"Everyone knows why *you're* here, you and your women too."

"Oh, I suppose they do," Clave said. "But if you think *you'd* like living with Mayrin, you can try it when we get back. I couldn't. And she didn't like that, and her father didn't like it either. But you know, she was really built to make babies, when I was just old enough to notice that."

Alfin snorted.

"I meant what I said," Clave told him. "If there's anything left that can save the tribe, it's somewhere over our heads. And if we find it, I think I could be Chairman myself. What do you think?"

Startled, Alfin peered into Clave's face. "Maybe. Power hungry, are you?"

"I haven't quite decided. Let's say I'm just mad enough to go for Gold. This whole crazy . . . well, Jayan and Jinny, they can take care of themselves, and if they can't, I can. But I had to take Merril before the Chairman would give me jet pods, and then at the last minute he wished Gavving on me, and that was the last straw."

"Gavving wasn't much worse than the other kids I've had to train. Constantly asking questions, I don't know any *two* people with that boy's curiosity—"

"Not the point. He's just starting to show beard. He never did anything *wrong* except *be* there when that damn fool Laython got swallowed . . . Skip it. Alfin, some of our party is dangerous to the rest."

"You know it."

"How would you handle that?"

It was rare to see Alfin smiling. He took his time answering. "Merril will kill herself sooner or later. But Glory will kill someone else. Slip at the wrong time. Easy enough to do something about it. Wait till we're higher, till the tide is weaker. Knock against her when she's off balance. Send her home the fast way."

"Well, that's what I was thinking too. You are a *danger* to us, Alfin. You hold grudges. We've got problems enough without watching our backs because of you. If you slow me down, if you give *any* of us trouble, I'll send you home the fast way, Alfin. I've got enough trouble here."

Alfin paled, but he answered. "You do. Get rid of Glory before she knocks someone off the trunk. Ask Jiovan."

"I don't take your orders," Clave said. "One more thing. You spend too much energy being angry. Save it. You're likely to need your anger. Now lead off." And when Alfin resumed climbing, Clave followed.

Chapter Three

THE TRUNK

D ay brightened and faded and brightened again while they climbed. The men doffed their tunics and tucked them into their pack straps; somewhat later, so did the women. Clave leered at Jayan and Jinny impartially. Gavving didn't leer, but in fact the sight distracted him from his climbing.

Jayan and Jinny were twenty-year-old twins, identical, with pale skin and dark hair and lovely heart-shaped faces and nicely conical breasts. Some citizens called them stupid, for they had no fund of conversation; but Gavving wondered. In other matters they showed good sense. As now: Jinny was climbing with Clave, but Merril had dropped far behind, and Jayan stayed just beneath her, pacing her.

Jiovan had lost ground after Clave resumed the lead. He cursed as he climbed, steadily, monotonously: the wind, the bark handholds, his missing leg. Alfin should have been one of the leaders, Gavving thought; but he kept pausing to look down.

Gavving's own shoulders and legs burned with fatigue. Worse, he was making mistakes, setting his claw sandals wrong, so that they slipped too often.

Tired people make mistakes. Gavving saw Glory slip, thrash, and fall two or three meters before she caught an edge of bark. While she hugged herself ferociously against the tree, Gavving moved crosswise until he was behind and to the side of her.

Fear held her rigid.

"Keep going," Gavving said. "I'll stay behind you. I'll catch you."

She looked down, nodded jerkily, began climbing again. She seemed to move in convulsions, putting too much effort into it. Gavving kept pace.

She slipped. Gavving gripped the bark. When she dropped into range he planted the palm of his hand under her buttocks and pushed her hard against the tree. She gasped, and clung, and resumed climbing.

Clave called down. "Is anybody thirsty?"

They needed their breath, and the answer was too obvious. Of *course* they were thirsty. Clave said, "Swing around east. We'll get a drink."

Falling water had carved a channel along the eastern side of the trunk. The channel was fifty meters across and nearly dry over most of its water-smoothed surface. But the tree still passed through the occasional cloud; mist still clung to the bark; wind and Coriolis force set it streaming around to the east as it fell; and water ran in a few pitiful streams toward Quinn Tuft below.

"Watch yourselves," Clave told them. "Use your spikes if you have to. This is slippery stuff."

"Here," the Grad called from over their heads.

They worked their way toward him. A hill of rock must have smacked into the tree long ago, half embedding itself. The trunk had grown to enclose it. It made a fine platform, particularly since a stream had split to run round it on both sides. By the time Merril and Jayan had worked their way up, Clave had hammered spikes into the wood above the rock and attached lines.

Merril and Jayan worked their way onto the rock. Merril lay gasping while Jayan brought her water.

Glory lay flat on the rock with her eyes closed. Presently she crawled to the portside stream. She called to Clave, "Any limit?"

"What?"

"On how much we drink. The water goes—"

Clave laughed loudly. Like the Chairman hosting a midyear celebration, he bellowed, "Drink! Bathe! Have water fights! Who's to stop us? If Quinn Tribe didn't want their water secondhand, we wouldn't be here." He worked their single cookpot from his pack and threw streams of water at selected targets: Merril, who whooped in delight; Jiovan, who sputtered in surprise; Jayan and Jinny, who advanced toward him with menace in their eyes. "I dare not struggle on this precarious perch," he cried and went limp. They rolled him in the stream, hanging on to his hands and feet so that he wouldn't go over.

They climbed in a spiral path. They weren't here just to climb, Clave said, but to explore. Gavving could hear Jiovan's monotonous cursing as they climbed into the wind, until the wind drowned him out.

Gavving reached up for a fistful of green cotton and stuffed it in his mouth. The branch that waved about his pack was nearly bare now. The sky was empty out to some distant streamers of cloud and a dozen dots that might be ponds, all hundreds of klomters out. They'd be hurting for food when sleeptime came.

He was crossing a scar in the bark, a puckering that ran down into the wood itself. An old wound that the bark was trying to heal . . . big enough to climb in, but it ran the wrong way. Abruptly the Grad shouted, "Stop! Hold it up!"

"What's the matter?" Clave demanded.

"The Quinn Tribe markings!"

Without the Grad to point it out, Gavving would never have realized that this was writing. He had seen writing only rarely, and these letters were three to four meters across. They couldn't be read; they had to be inferred: DQ, with a curlicue mark across the D.

"We'll have to gouge this out," the Grad said. "It's nearly grown out. Someone should come here more often."

Clave ran a critical eye over his crew. "Gavving, Alfin, Jinny, start digging. Grad, you supervise. Just dig out the Q, leave the D alone. The rest of you, rest."

Merril said, "I can work. For that matter, I could carry more."

"Tell me that tomorrow," Clave told her. He made his way across the bark to clap her on the shoulder. "If you can take some of the load, you'll get it. Let's see how you do tomorrow with your muscles all cramped up."

They carved away bark and dug deeper into the wood with the points of their harpoons. The Grad moved among them. The Q took shape. When the Grad approached him, Gavving asked, "Why are the letters so big? You can hardly read them."

"They're not for us. You could see them if you were a klomter away," the Grad said.

Alfin had overheard. "Where? Falling? Are we doing this for swordbirds and triunes to read?"

The Grad smiled and passed on without answering. Alfin scowled at his back, then crossed to Gavving's position. "Is he crazy?"

"Maybe. But if you can't dig as deep as Jinny, the mark will look silly to the swordbirds."

"He tells half a secret and leaves you hanging," Alfin complained. "He does it all the time."

They left the tribal insignia carved deep and clear into the tree. The wind was beating straight down on them now. Gavving felt a familiar pain in his ears. He worked his jaw while he sought the old memory, and when his ears popped it came: pressure/pain in his ears, a score of days after the passing of Gold, the night before his first allergy attack.

These days he rarely wondered if he would wake with his eyes and sinuses streaming in agony. He simply lived through it. But he'd never wakened on the vertical slope of the tree! He pictured himself climbing blind . . .

That was what distracted him while a thick, wood-colored rope lifted from the bark to wrap itself around Glory's waist.

Glory yelped. Gavving saw her clinging to the bark with her face against it, refusing to look. The rope was pulling her sideways, away from him.

Gavving pulled his harpoon from his pack before he moved. He crawled around Glory toward the living rope.

Glory screamed again as her grip was torn loose. Now only the live rope itself held her from falling. He didn't dare slash it. Instead he scampered toward its source, while the rope coiled itself around Glory, spinning her, reeling her in.

There was a hole in the tree. From the blackness inside Gavving saw a thickening of the live rope and a single eye lifting on a stalk to look at him. He jabbed at it. A lid flickered closed; the stalk dodged. Gavving tracked it. He felt the jar through his arm and shoulder as the harpoon punched through.

A huge mouth opened and screamed. The living rope thrashed and tried to fling Glory away. What saved Glory was Glory herself; she had plunged her own harpoon through the brown hawser and gripped the point where it emerged. She clung to the shaft with both hands while the rope bent around to attack Gavving.

The mouth was lined with rows of triangular teeth. Gavving pulled his harpoon loose from the eye, with a twist, as if he had practiced all his life. He jabbed at the mouth, trying to reach the throat. The mouth snapped shut and he struck only teeth. He jabbed at the eye again.

Something convulsed in the dark of the hole. The mouth gaped improbably wide. Then a black mass surged from the hole. Gavving flung himself aside in time to escape being smashed loose. A hut-sized beast leapt into the sky on three short, thick legs armed with crescent claws. Short wings spread, a claw swiped at him and missed. Gavving saw with amazement that the rope was its nose.

He had thought it was trying to escape. Ten meters from its den it turned with astonishing speed. Gavving shrank back against the bark with his harpoon poised.

The beast's wings flapped madly, in reverse, pulling it back against its stretching nose . . . futilely. The foray team had arrived in force. Lines wrapped Glory and trapped the creature's rope of a nose. Lines spun out to bind its wings. Clave was screaming orders. He and Jinny and the Grad pulled strongly, turning the beast claws-outward from the tree. In that position it was reeled in until harpoons could reach its head.

Gavving picked a spot and jabbed again and again, drilling through bone, then red-gray brain. He never noticed when the thing stopped moving. He only came to himself when Clave shouted, "Gavving, Glory, dinner's on you. You killed it, you clean it."

You killed it, you clean it was an easy honor to dodge. You only had to admit that your prey had hurt you . . .

Jayan and Jinny worked at building a fire in the creature's lair. They worked swiftly, competently, almost without words, as if they could read each other's minds. The others were outside, chopping bark for fuel. Gavving and Glory moored the corpse with lines and spikes, just outside the hole, and went to work.

The Grad insisted on helping. Strictly speaking, he didn't have the right, but he seemed eager, and Glory was tired. They worked slowly, examining the peculiar thing they had killed.

It had a touch of trilateral symmetry, like many creatures of the Smoke Ring, the Grad said. A smaller third wing was placed far back: a steering fin. The forward pair were motive power and (as the Grad gleefully pointed out) ears. Holes below each wing showed as organs of hearing when the Grad cut into them. The wings could be cupped to gather sound.

It was a digger. Those little wings would barely move it. Everything in the Smoke Ring could fly in some sense; but this one would prefer to dig a hole and ambush its prey. Even its trunk wasn't all that powerful. The Grad searched until he found the sting that had been in its tip. The size of an index finger, it was embedded in Glory's pack. Glory nearly fainted.

They kept the claws. Clave would use them to tip his grapnels. They cut steaks to be broiled and passed to the rest, who by now were moored on spikes outside. They set bigger slabs of meat to smoke at the back of the wooden cave.

Gavving realized that his eyes were blurry with exhaustion. Glory was streaming sweat. He put his arm over her shoulders and announced, "We quit."

"Good enough," Clave called in. "Take our perches. Alfin, let's carve up the rest."

Clave's team was well fed, overfed. They drifted on lines outside the cave. Meat smoked inside. The carcass, mostly bones now, had been set to block the entrance.

Clave said, "Citizens, give me a status report. How are we doing? Is anyone hurt?"

"I hurt all over," Jiovan said and scowled at the chorus of agreement.

"All over is good. Glory, did that thing break any of your ribs?"

"I don't think so. Bruises."

"Uh-huh." Clave sounded surprised. "Nobody's fallen off. Nobody's hurt. Have we lost any equipment?"

There was a silence. Gavving spoke into it. "Clave, what are you doing here?"

"We're exploring the trunk, and renewing the Quinn markings, and stopping a famine, maybe. Today's catch is a good first step."

Gavving was prepared to drop it, but Alfin wasn't. "The boy means, what are *you* doing here? You, the mighty hunter, why did you go out to die with the lames?"

There was muttering, perhaps, but no overt reaction to the word *lames*. Clave smiled at Alfin. "Turn it around, Quinn Tribe's custodian of the treemouth. Why was the tribe able to spare *you*?"

The west wind had softened as they climbed, but it was still formidable; it blew streamers of smoke past the carcass. Alfin forced words from himself. "The Chairman thought it was a good joke. And nobody . . . nobody wanted to speak up for me."

"Nobody loves you."

Alfin nodded and sighed as if a burden had been lifted from him. "Nobody loves me. Your turn."

Gavving grinned. Clave was stuck, and he knew it. He said, "Mayrin doesn't love me. I traded her in for two prettier, more loving women. Mayrin is the Chairman's daughter."

"That's not all of it and you know it."

"If you know better than I do, then keep talking," Clave said reasonably.

"The Grad can back me up. He knows some tribal history. When things go wrong, when citizens get unhappy, the leader's in trouble. The Scientist himself almost got drafted! The Chairman is scared, that's what.

The citizens are hungry, and there's an obvious replacement for the Chairman. Clave, he's scared of *you*."

"Grad?"

"The Scientist knows what he's doing."

"He blamed it all on you!" Alfin cried. "I was there!"

"I know. He had his reasons." The Grad noticed the silence and laughed. "No, I didn't cause the drought! We rounded Gold, and Gold swung us too far in toward Voy, down to where the Smoke Ring thins out. It's a gravity effect—"

"Many thanks for explaining it all," Clave said with cheerful sarcasm. Gavving was irritated and a bit relieved: nobody else understood the Grad's gibberish either. "Is there anything else we should settle?"

Into the silence Gavving said, "How do we cause a flood?"

There was some laughter. Clave said, "Grad?"

"Forget it."

"It'd solve everybody's problems. Even the Chairman's."

"This is silly . . . well. Floods come when a pond brushes the tree, somewhere on the trunk. A lot of water clings to the trunk. The tide pulls it down. Usually we get some warning from a hunting party, and we all scurry out along the branch. The big flood, ten years ago . . . most of us got to safety, but the waterfall tore away some of the huts, and most of the earthlife crops, and the turkey pens. It was a year before we caught any more turkeys.

"And I wish we'd have another flood," the Grad said. "Sure I do. The Scientist thinks the whole *tree*—never mind. You can't catch a pond. We're too far into the gas torus region—"

"There," Gavving said and pointed east and out, toward a metal-colored dot backed by rosy streamers of cloud. "I think it's bigger than it was."

"What of it? It'll come or it won't. If it did come floating past, what would you do, throw lines and grapnels? Forget it. Just forget it."

"Enough," Clave said. "That meat's probably done. Let's get the smoke out and get inside."

Gavving woke in the night and wondered where he was.

He half remembered the sounds of groans. Someone in pain? It had stopped now. Sound of wind, sound of many people breathing. Warm bodies all around him. Rich smells of smoke and perspiration. Aches everywhere, as if he'd been beaten.

A woman's voice spoke near his ear. "Are you awake too?"

And another, a man's: "Yes. Let me sleep." Alfin?

Silence. And Gavving remembered: the cave was just large enough to accommodate nine exhausted climbers, after they flung the nose-arm's bones into the sky. By now the offal might have reached Quinn Tuft, to feed the tree.

They huddled against each other, flesh to flesh. Gavving had no way to avoid eavesdropping when Alfin spoke again, though his voice was a whisper. "I can't sleep. Everything hurts."

Glory: "Me too."

"Did you hear groaning?"

"Clave and Jayan, I think, and believe me, they're feeling no pain."

"Oh. Good for them. Glory, why are you talking to me?"

"I was hoping we could be friends."

"Just don't *climb* near me, all right?"

"All right."

"I'm afraid you'll knock me off."

"Alfin, aren't you afraid to be so high?"

"No."

"I am."

Pause. "I'm afraid of falling off. I'd be crazy not to be."

There was quiet for a time. Gavving began to notice his own aching muscles and joints. They must be keeping him awake . . . but he was dozing when Alfin spoke again.

"The Chairman knew it."

"Knew what?"

"He knows I'm afraid of falling. That's why the copsik bastard kept sending me under the branch on hunts. Nothing solid under me, trying to hang on and throw a harpoon too . . . I got even, though."

"How?" Glory asked while Gavving thought, *So did the Chairman.*

"Never mind. Glory, will you lie with me?"

A strained whisper. "No. Alfin, we can't be alone!"

"Did you have a lover, back in the tuft?"

"No."

"Most of us didn't. Nobody to protect us when the Chairman thought this up."

A pause, as for thought. "I still can't. Not here."

Alfin's voice rose to a shout. "Clave! Clave, you should have brought a masseuse!"

Clave answered from the darkness. "*I* brought *two.*"

"Treefodder," Alfin said without heat, perhaps with amusement. Presently there was quiet.

Chapter Four

FLASHERS AND FAN FUNGUS

In the morning they hurt. Some showed it more than others. Alfin tried to move, grunted in pain, curled up with his face buried in his arms. Merril's face was blank and stoic as she flexed her arms, then rose onto her hands. Jayan and Jinny commiserated with each other, massaging each other's pains away. On Jiovan's face, amazement and agony as he tried to move, then a look of betrayal thrown in Clave's direction.

From Glory, wild-eyed panic. Gavving tapped her shoulder blade (and flinched at his own agony-signals). "We all hurt. Can't you tell? What are you worried about? You won't be left behind. Nobody's got the strength."

Her eyes turned sane. She whispered, "I *wasn't* thinking that. I was thinking I *hurt*. That's normal, isn't it?"

"Sure. You're not crippled, though."

"Thank you for taking care of me yesterday. I'm really grateful. I'm going to get better at this, I promise."

The Grad spoke without trying to move. "We'll all get better. The higher we get, the less we weigh. Pretty soon we'll be floating."

Clave trod carefully among citizens who were awake but not mobile. Gavving felt a stab of envy/anger. *Clave* didn't hurt. From the back of the nose-arm's burrow he selected a slab of smoked meat ragged with harpoon wounds. "Take your time over breakfast," he instructed them. "Eat. It's the easiest way to carry provisions—"

"And we burned a lot of energy yesterday," the Grad said. He moved like a cripple to join Clave and began tearing into a meter's length of what had been the nose-arm's rib. It made sense to Gavving, and he joined them. The meat had an odd, rank flavor. You could get used to it, he thought, if your life depended on it.

Clave moved among them, gnawing at his huge slab of meat. He sliced a piece off and made Merril take it. He listened to Jiovan describing his symptoms, then interrupted with, "You've got your wind back. That's good. Now eat," handing him more of the steak. He cut the rest in half for Jayan and Jinny and spent a minute or two doing massage on their shoulders and hips. They winced and groaned.

Presently, when all had eaten something, Clave looked around at his team. "We'll circle to the east and get water half a day after we start. There's no room in here to do warm-up exercises; we'll just have to start moving. So saddle up, citizens. We'll have to 'feed the tree' in the open, and whether you actually feed the tree is up to the tide and the wind. Alfin, take the lead."

Alfin led them on an upward spiral, counterclockwise. Gavving found his aches easing as they climbed. He noticed that Alfin never looked down. Not surprising if Alfin didn't give a damn for those following him—but he *never* looked down.

Gavving did, and marveled at their progress. Two extended hands would have covered all of Quinn Tuft.

They delayed to repair the Q in a DQ mark. The sun had been horizontal in the east when they started. It was approaching Voy before they reached water-smoothed wood.

A rivulet flowed down a meandering groove. This time there was no natural perch. Nine thirsty citizens pounded spikes into the wood and hung by their lines to drink, wash, soak their tunics, and wring them out.

Gavving noticed Clave speaking to Alfin a little way below. He didn't hear what was said. He only saw what Alfin did.

"And suppose I don't?"

"Then you don't." Clave gestured upward, where the rest of them hung. "Look at them. *I* didn't choose them. What do I do if one of my citizens turns out to be a coward? I live with it. But I have to know."

Alfin looked white with rage. *Not* red with fury. There isn't any "white with rage"; white means fear, as Clave had learned long ago. A frightened man can kill . . . but Alfin's hands were clenched on his line, and Clave's harpoon was over his shoulder, easily reached.

"I have to know. I can't put you in the lead if you can't make yourself look down to see how they're doing. See? I'll have to put you where you don't hurt anyone else if you funk it. Tail end Charley. And if you freeze, I want to be sure nobody—"

"All right." Alfin dug in his pack, produced a spike and a rock. He pounded the spike in beside the one he was hanging from.

"Make sure you can depend on it. It's *your* life."

The second spike was in deeper than the first. Alfin tied the loose end of his line to both spikes and knotted it again. "And I leave you next to it?"

"You take that chance too. Or you don't. I have to *know*."

Alfin leapt straight outward, trailing loops of line. He thrashed, then threw his arms over his face.

He fell slowly. *We're all lighter,* Gavving realized. *It's real. I thought I was just feeling better, but we're lifting less*—And Alfin was still falling, but now he'd uncovered his face. His arms windmilled to turn him on his back. Gavving noticed Clave's hand covering the spikes that moored Alfin's line. The line pulled taut and swung Alfin in against the tree.

Gavving watched him climb up. And watched him jump again, limbs splayed out as if he were trying to fly. It seemed he might make it, he fell so slowly; but presently the tide was pulling him down against the tree again.

"That actually looks like fun," Jayan said.

Jinny said, "Ask first."

Alfin didn't jump again. When he had climbed back up to Clave's position, and both had climbed to rejoin the team, Jinny spoke. "Can we try that?"

Alfin sent her a look like a harpoon. Clave said, "No, time to get moving. Saddle up—"

Alfin was in the lead again when they set out. He made a point of pausing frequently to look back. And Gavving wondered.

Yesterday Alfin had swarmed all over the nose-arm, hacking like a berserker maniac, like Gavving himself. It was hard to believe that Alfin was afraid of Clave, or of heights, or of anything.

The sun circled the sky, behind Voy and back to zenith, before they came to lee again. The water-smoothed wood was soft here, soft enough that they could cross with a spike in each hand, jab and yank and jab. They veered down to avoid scores of birds clustered on the wood. Scarlet-tailed, the birds were otherwise the grayish-brown of the wood itself.

When they reached the rivulet, it was smaller yet, but it was enough: they hung in the water and let it cool them and run into their faces and mouths. Clave shared out smoked meat. Gavving found himself ravenous.

The Grad watched the birds as he ate. Presently he burst out laughing. "Look, they've got a mating dance going."

"So?"

"You'll see."

Presently Gavving did see; and so did others, judging by Clave's bellowing laugh and the giggles from Jayan and Jinny. A gray-brown male would approach a female and abruptly spread his gray wings like a cloak. Under the gray was brilliant yellow, and a tube protruding from a splash of crimson feathers.

"The Scientist told me about them once. Flashers," said the Grad. His smile died as he said, "I wonder what they eat?"

"What difference does it make?" Alfin demanded.

"Maybe none." The Grad made his way upward toward the birds. The birds flew off, then returned to dive at him, shrieking obscenities. The Grad ignored them. Presently he returned.

Alfin asked, "Well?"

"The wood's riddled with holes. Riddled. The holes are full of insects. The birds dig in and eat the insects."

"You're in love," Alfin challenged. "You're in love with the idea that the tree's dying."

"I'd love to believe it isn't," the Grad said, but Alfin only snorted.

They spiraled around to the western side while the sun dipped beneath Voy and began to rise again. The wind was less ferocious now. But they were getting tired; there was almost no chatter. They rested frequently in crevasses in the bark.

They were resting when Merril called, "Jinny? I'm hung up."

A pincer the size of Clave's fist gripped the fabric of Merril's nearly empty pack. Merril pulled back against it. From a hole in the bark there emerged a creature covered in hard, brown, segmented plates. Its face was a single plate with a deeply inset eye. The body looked soft behind the last plate.

Jayan slashed where its body met the bark. The creature separated. It still clung to Merril's pack with idiot determination. Jayan levered the claw open with her harpoon and dropped the creature into her own pack.

When they had circled round to water again, Clave set water to boiling in the small, lidded pot. He made tea, refilled the pot, and boiled Merril's catch. It made one bite each for his team.

They wedged themselves into a wide crack with the shape of a lightning-stroke and moored themselves with lines. Together but separate, head to foot within the bark, they had no chance to converse, and no urge. Four days of climbing since breakfast left them too tired for anything but sleep.

At waking they ate more of the smoked meat. "Let's look for more of those hard-shelled things," Clave suggested. "That was good." He didn't have to urge them to get moving. He never would, Gavving realized, as long as they couldn't sleep where water flowed.

This time Jiovan was given the lead. He took them on a counterclockwise spiral that brought them back to lee within half a day. Again the wood was soft and riddled with holes, and flashers swarmed below them. Alfin and Glory tended to lose ground in the leeward regions. Jiovan remarked on it and earned a look of dull hatred from Alfin.

The thing was that Alfin took more care setting his spikes than the rest did. And Glory didn't, so she lost time slipping and catching herself—

They moored themselves in the stream and drank and washed.

Alfin spotted something far above them: gray nubs reaching out from the bark on both sides of the rivulet. He climbed, doggedly pounding spikes into the wood, and came back with a fan-shaped fungus, pale gray with a red frill, half the size of his pack. "It could be edible," he said.

Clave asked, "Are you willing to try it?"

"No." He started to throw it away.

Merril stopped him. "We're here to keep the tribe from starving," she said. She broke a red-and-gray chunk from the fringes and ate a meager mouthful. "Not much taste, but it's nice. The Scientist would like it. You could chew it with no teeth." She took another bite.

Alfin broke off a piece of the grayish white inside and ate that, looking as if he were taking poison. He nodded. "Tastes okay."

At which point there were more volunteers, but Clave vetoed that. When they departed, Clave veered upward to pick a bouquet of the fan-shaped fungi. A meter-square fan rode like a flag above his pack.

The sun was rising up the east.

It was below Voy—you could look straight down along the trunk, past the green fuzzball that was Quinn Tuft, and see Voy's bright spark at the fringe of the soft sun-glow—and the west wind was blowing almost softly across the ridges of the bark, when Gavving heard Merril shout, "Who needs legs?"

She was holding herself an arm's length from the bark by a one-handed grip. He shouted down. "Merril? Are you all right?"

"I feel *wonderful!*" She let go and began to fall and reached out and caught herself. "The Grad was right! We can *fly!*"

Gavving crawled toward her. Jinny was already below her, pounding in a spike. When Gavving reached them, Jayan was using the spike for support, with her line ready in her other hand. They pulled Merril back against the tree.

She didn't resist. She crowed, "Gavving, why do we live in the tuft? There's food here, and water, and who needs legs? Let's stay. We don't need any nose-arm cave, we can dig out our own. We've got nose-arm meat and those shelled things and the fan fungus. I've eaten enough foliage to last me the rest of my life! But if anyone wants it, we'll send down someone with legs."

We'll have to be careful of that fan fungus, Gavving thought. He was pounding spikes into bark; on the other side of Merril, Jiovan was doing the same. Where was Clave?

Clave was with Alfin, high above them, in furious inaudible argument.

"Come on, let's get going! What are you doing?" Merril demanded while Gavving and Jiovan bound her to the bark. "Or, listen, I've got a wonderful idea. Let's go back. We've got what we want. We'll kill another nose-arm and we, we'll grow fan fungus in the tuft. Then set up another tribe here. Claaave!" she bellowed as Clave and Alfin climbed down into earshot. "How would I do as Chairman of a colony?"

"You'd be terrific. Citizens, we'll be here for a while. Moor yourselves. Don't do any flying."

"I never thought it could be this good," Merril told them. "My parents—when I was little, they were just waiting for me to die. But they wouldn't feed me to the treemouth. I thought about it too, but I never did. I'm glad. Sometimes I thought of me as an example, something people need to be happy. Happy they have legs. Even one leg," she whispered hoarsely to Jiovan. "Legs! So what?"

Jiovan asked Clave, "How long do we have to put up with this?"

"You don't. Take, ah, take the Grad and find us a better place to sleep."

Jiovan looked about him. "Like what?"

"A cave, a crack or a bulge in the bark . . . anything that's better than hanging ourselves here like smoking meat."

"I'll go too," Alfin said.

"You stay."

"Clave, you do not have to treat me like a baby! I only ate from the middle of the thing. I feel fine!"

"So does Merril."

"What?"

"Never mind. You feel grouchy, and *that's* fine. Merril feels fine, and that's—"

"Alfin, I am *so* glad you didn't stop me from coming." Merril smiled radiantly at him. In that moment Gavving thought her beautiful. "Thank you for trying, though. Feel sleepy," Merril said and went to sleep.

Alfin saw questioning eyes. He spoke reluctantly. "I, I thought I could talk the Chairman out of this idiocy. Sending a, a legless woman up the tree! Clave, I *do* feel fine. Wide-awake. Hungry. I'd like to try some more."

Clave removed a fan from his pack. He tore away some of the scarlet fringe, then offered Alfin a hand-sized piece of the white interior. If Alfin flinched, it was far too short a time to measure. He ate the whole chunk with a theatrical relish that had Clave grinning. Clave broke off the rest of the red fringe and pouched it separately.

Jiovan and the Grad returned. They had found a DQ mark overgrown with fungus like a field of gray hair. "Infected. We'll have to burn it out," the Grad said.

"Suppose it keeps on burning? We don't have any water," Clave said. "Never mind. Let's have a look. Jayan, Jinny, stay with Merril. One of you come get me if she wakes up."

They examined the fungus patch dubiously. Scraping out all that gray hair would be a dull job. Clave pulled up a wad and set fire to it. It burned slowly, sullenly.

"Let's try it. But get some of our packs emptied in case we have to beat it out."

The fungus patch burned slowly. The west wind wasn't strong at this height, and the smoke tended to sit within the fungus "hairs," smothering the fire. It kept putting itself out. Yet it crept around in glowing fringes, restarting itself. They had to back away as foul-smelling smoke built up in the vicinity.

The smoke was dissipating. Gavving moved in and found most of the fungus gone, the rest left as black char. The Q was two meters deep.

Clave made a torch from a chunk of bark and burned out some remaining patches. "Scrape that out and I think we can all sleep in it. Gavving, Jinny, you go back for Merril."

When they started to move her, Merril woke instantly, happy and active and bubbling with plans. They coaxed her across the bark, ready for anything, and presently moored her in the scraped-out bottom of the Q.

Then there was nothing for it but to settle into the Q for early sleep.

Merril slept like a baby, but others shifted restlessly. Desultory conversations started and stopped. Presently Clave asked, "Jiovan, how are you doing?"

"How do you mean?"

"I mean the whole trip. How are you doing?"

Jiovan snorted. "I'm hungry. I hurt a lot, but I'm used to that. I can climb. Do you mean how are *we* doing? We won't know that till we get home. Merril's out of her head right now, but she could be right too."

Clave was startled. "You mean, live *here*?"

"No, that's crazy. I mean go back now. Kill something and smoke it and collect more fan fungus and go home. We'd be heroes, as much as any hunt party that comes home with meat, and I don't mind telling you, I'm ready. I'm treefeeding sick of being one of the—the lames. I used to be the one who *fed* the tribe . . . and if the fan fungus will grow in the tuft—"

By now the whole troop was listening. Clave knew he was talking for an audience. He said, "Merril could be pretty sick, you know."

"She feels great."

"Oh, let's see how she feels when it wears off. I might want to try it myself," Clave chuckled. He was hoping it would drop there.

No chance, not with Alfin listening. "What about going home? We've got what we came for."

"I don't think so. We sure haven't scraped out all the tribemarks, have we, Grad?"

"They're supposed to run all along the trunk."

"Then let's go at least as far as the middle. We already know we can feed ourselves. Who knows what else we'll find? The nose-arm was good eating, but we've only found one, and we couldn't feed him in the tuft. We can pick up some fan fungus on the way back. What else? Are the flashers good to eat? Could we transplant those shelled things?"

The Grad was catching fire. "Get them growing just above the tuft. It might work. Sure I'd like to go on. I want to see what it's like when there isn't any tidal force at all."

"We already know what Merril would say. Anyone else?"

Alfin grunted. Nobody else spoke.

"We go on," Clave said.

Chapter Five
MEMORIES

It was there again. There was a special frequency of light that Sharls Davis Kendy had sought for five hundred years. He had found it fifty-two years ago, and forty-eight, and twenty, and . . . six certain sightings and another ten probable. The locus moved about. This time it was west of his position, barely filtering through the soup of dust and gas and dirt and plant life: the light of hydrogen burning with oxygen.

Kendy held his attention on a wavering point within the Smoke Ring. Rarely did the CARM even acknowledge that his signal had penetrated the maelstrom; but he never considered not trying. "Kendy for the State. Kendy for the State."

The CARM's main motor would run for hours now. It would accelerate slowly, too slowly: pushing something massive. What were they doing in there?

Had they entirely forgotten *Discipline* and Sharls Davis Kendy?

Kendy had forgotten much, but what remained to him was as vivid as the moment it had happened. These futile attempts at contact needed little of his attention. Kendy took refuge in memory.

The target star was yellow-white, with a spectrum very like Sol's, circling an unseen companion. At 1.2 solar masses, T3 was minutely brighter and bluer than Sol: about G0 or G1. The companion, at half a solar mass, would be a star, not a planet. It should at least have been visible.

The State had telescopic data from earlier missions to other stars. There was at least a third, planet-sized body in this system. There *might* be a planet resembling the primordial Earth; in which case *Discipline* would fulfill its primary mission by seeding its atmosphere with oxygen-producing algae. On a distant day the State would return to find a world ripe for colonization.

But someone would have come anyway, to probe the strangeness of this place.

Discipline was a seeder ramship, targeted for a ring of yellow stars that might host worlds like the primordial Earth. Its secondary mission was a secret known only to Kendy; but exploration was a definite third on the list; *Discipline* would not stop here. Kendy would skim past T3, take pictures and records, and vanish into the void. He might slow enough to drop a missile with a warhead of tailored algae, if a target world could be found.

Four of the crew were in the control module. They had the telescope array going and a watery picture of a yellow-white star on the big screen, with a pinpoint of fierce blue-white light at its edge. Sam Goldblatt had a spectrum of T3 displayed on a smaller screen.

Sharon Levoy was lecturing for the record; nobody else was listening. "That solves *that*. Levoy's Star is an old neutron star, half a billion to a billion years beyond its pulsar stage. It's still hotter than hell, but it's only twenty kilometers across. The radiating surface is almost negligible. It must have been losing its spin and its residual heat for all of that time. We didn't see it because it isn't putting out enough light.

"The yellow dwarf star might have planets, but we can expect that their atmospheres were boiled away by the supernova event of which Levoy's Star is the ashes—"

Goldblatt snarled, "We're supposed to be the first expedition here! *Prikazyvat Kendy!*"

The crew were not supposed to be aware that the ship's computer and its recorded personality could eavesdrop on them. Therefore Kendy said, "Hello, Sam. What's up?"

Sam Goldblatt was a large, round man with a bushy, carefully tended mustache. He'd been chewing it ever since Levoy found and named the neutron star. Now his frustration had a target. "Kendy, do you have records of a previous expedition?"

"No."

"Well, check me out. Those are absorption lines for oxygen and water, *here*, aren't they? Which means there's green life somewhere in that system, doesn't it? And that means the State sent a seeder here!"

"I noticed the spectrum. After all, Sam, why shouldn't plant life develop somewhere on its own? Earth's did. Besides, those lines can't represent an Earthlike world. They're too sharp. There's too much oxygen, too much water."

"Kendy, if it isn't a planet, what *is* it?"

"We'll learn that when we're closer."

"Hmph. Not at this speed. Kendy, I think we should slow down. Decelerate to the minimum at which the Bussard ramjet will work. We won't waste onboard fuel, we'll get a better look, and we can accelerate again when we've got the solar wind for fuel."

"Dangerous," said Kendy. "I recommend against it." And that should have been that.

For five hundred and twelve years Kendy had been editing clumps of experience from his memory wherever he decided they weren't needed. He didn't remember deciding to follow Goldblatt's suggestions. Goldblatt must have persuaded Captain Quinn and the rest of the crew, and Kendy had given in . . . to them? or to his own curiosity?

Kendy remembered.

Levoy's Star and T3 circled a common point in eccentric orbits, at a distance averaging 2.5×10^8 kilometers, with an orbital period of 2.77 Earth years. The neutron star had been behind the yellow dwarf while *Discipline* backed into the system. Now it emerged into view of *Discipline*'s telescope array.

He saw a ring of white cloud, touched with green, with a bright spark at its center. The spectral absorption lines of water and oxygen were coming from there. It was tiny by astronomical standards: the region of greatest density circled the neutron star at 26,000 kilometers—about four times the radius of the Earth.

"Like a Christmas wreath," Claire Dalton breathed. The sociologist's body was that of a pretty, leggy blonde, but her corpsicle memories reached far back . . . and what was she doing on the bridge? Captain Dennis Quinn might have invited her, the way they were standing together. It indicated a laxity in discipline that Kendy would have to watch.

The crew of *Discipline* continued to study the archaic Christmas wreath. Until Sam Goldblatt suddenly crowed, "Goldblatt's World! Prikazyvat Kendy, record that, Goldblatt's World! There's a planet in there."

"I'm not close enough to probe that closely, Sam."

"It has to be there. You know how a gas torus works?"

It was there in Kendy's memory. "Yes. I don't doubt you're right. I can bounce some radar off that storm complex when we pass."

"Pass, hell. We've got to stop and investigate this thing." Goldblatt looked about him for support. "Green means life! Life, and no planet! We've got to know all about it. Claire, Dennis, you see that, don't you?"

The crew included twelve citizens and eight corpsicles. The corpsicles might argue, but they had no civil rights; and the citizens had less than they thought. For reasons of morale, Kendy maintained the fiction that they were in charge.

Goldblatt's suggestion was not worth considering. Kendy said, "Think. We've got fuel to decelerate once and once only. We'll need it when we reach Earth."

"There's water in there," Dennis Quinn said thoughtfully. "We could refuel. I bet the water's rich in deuterium and tritium. Why not, it's circling the ashes of a supernova!"

Claire Dalton was gazing at the screen, at a perfect smoke ring with a tiny hot pinpoint in its center. "The neutron star has cooled off, lost most of its rotation and most of its heat and most of that ferocious magnetic field the pulsars have. It's bright, but it's too small to be giving off much real heat. We could probably live in there ourselves." She looked around her. "Isn't this what we came for? The strangeness of the universe. If we don't stop now, we might as well be back on Earth." The contempt in her voice was unmistakable.

Kendy's memory jumped at that point. Hardly surprising. That must have been the true beginning of mutiny.

He remembered reviewing and updating his files on gas torus mechanics.

Two planets circled wide around the twin stars: Jupiter-style gas giants with no moons. The old supernova must have blasted away anything smaller.

A body did circle the neutron star. One limb of the Smoke Ring was curdled, a distorted whirlpool of storm. Hidden within was a core of rock and metals at 2.5 Earth masses. There was some oxygen and some water vapor in its thick, hot atmosphere. Goldblatt's World was tidally locked, and uninhabitable. Strip away its atmosphere and it might have harbored Earthly life—but its atmosphere was tremendous, dwindling indefinitely into the Smoke Ring itself.

The strong oxygen-water lines were coming from the gas torus.

A gas torus is the result of a light mass in orbit around a heavy mass, as Titan orbits Saturn. It may be that the light mass is too weak to hold its atmosphere. The faster molecules of air escape—but they go into orbit about the heavy mass. Thus, Titan circles Saturn within a ring of escaped

Titanian atmosphere, as Io orbits Jupiter within a ring of sulfur ionized by Jupiter's ferocious magnetic field.

A gas torus is thin. The gas must be so rarefied that each molecule can be considered to be in a separate orbit: it must reasonably expect to circle halfway round the primary mass without bumping another molecule. Under such circumstances, a gas torus is stable. The occasional stray photon will bump a molecule into interstellar space; but the molecules are continually reencountering the satellite body.

Titan—smaller than Mars, no larger than Ganymede—carries an atmosphere of refined smog at one and a half times Earth's sea level pressure. The atmosphere is continually being lost, of course, but some of it continually returns from the gas torus.

Levoy's Star was an extreme case, and a slightly different proposition too.

The Smoke Ring was the thickest part of the gas torus around Levoy's Star. At its median it was as dense as Earth's atmosphere a mile above sea level: too dense for stability. It must be continually leaking into the gas torus. But the gas torus *was* stable: dense, but held within a steep gravitational gradient. Molecules continually returned from the gas torus to the Smoke Ring, and from the Smoke Ring to the storm of atmosphere surrounding Goldblatt's World.

"Goldblatt's World must have started life as a gas giant planet like, say, Saturn. Probably it didn't fall into range until the pulsar had lost a good deal of its heat and spin." Sharon Levoy's crisp voice spoke within Kendy's memory. "Then it was captured by strong Roche tides. It may have dropped close enough to lose water and soil as well as gas. For something like a billion years Goldblatt's World has been leaking gas into the Smoke Ring, and the Smoke Ring has been leaking to interstellar space. It's not stable, exactly, but hell, *planets* aren't stable over the long run."

"It won't be stable that much longer," Dennis Quinn interrupted. "Most of Goldblatt's World is already gone. Ten million years, or a hundred million, and the Smoke Ring will be getting rarefied."

Kendy remembered these things. The records had been made while *Discipline*'s instruments probed the Smoke Ring from close range. Already some of the crew were exploring the Smoke Ring via CARMs. Their reports were enthusiastic. There was life, DNA-based; the air was not only breathable, but tasted fine . . .

Kendy didn't remember bringing *Discipline* into orbit around Levoy's Star. He must have expended his onboard fuel, postponing by several years his arrival at the target stars along his course. Why?

Claire Dalton's voice: "We've got to get out of this box. It's running down. A little of what we recycle is lost every time around. There's more than water in there; there's air, there's probably even fresh fertilizer for the hydroponics tanks!"

It was Sharls Davis Kendy who ruled *Discipline*. *Discipline*'s crew of twenty was hardly necessary to run a seeder ramship. The State had chosen them as a reservoir of humanity: a tiny chunk of the State, far removed from any local disaster. One planet, one solar system, were too fragile to ensure the survival of the State of humankind itself. Every ship in the sky had a crew large enough to begin the human race over again: their secondary mission, if it ever became necessary. The State expected no such disaster, ever; but the investment was trivial compared to the reward.

When had he lost control? Perhaps they had threatened to bypass the computer and go to manual control. They couldn't; but morale would disintegrate if they ever learned how little control they really had. Kendy might have surrendered on that basis.

Or he might have been curious.

He did not remember any part of what must have been a mutiny. He must have been played for a fool; he might not *want* to remember that. The crew had departed with eight of the ten CARMs and rifled the hydroponics to boot! It should never have been allowed.

He was reasonably sure that seven of the CARMs were inoperable. Some equipment might have been salvaged . . . and the last CARM had now ceased its spray of incandescent water vapor. Kendy ceased beaming his message. The Smoke Ring glowed white and featureless beneath him.

One day he would know. Would they remember him at all?

Kendy waited.

Chapter Six

MIDDLE GROUND

The patch of old-man's-hair should have been tended long since. It was fifty to sixty meters across and had eaten half a meter deep into live wood. Parasol plants had rooted in the resulting compost, and matured, and spread their brightly colored blossoms to attract passing insects.

Minya watched the fire spread in intersecting curves within the fungus patch. Breezes tossed the choking smoke in unpredictable directions. The smoke drove clouds of mites out of the fungus and into the open. She was wishing Thanya's triad would arrive with water.

There were three triads of the Triune Squad now on the trunk. Minya, Sal, and Smitta were nearing the median. Jeel's triad traversed up and down the trunk, ferrying provisions from the tuft, while Thanya's brought water from the lee.

Fire was usually no problem, but mistakes could happen.

"I love these climbs," Smitta said. She floated with her toes gripping an edge of bark. This close to the median, it was enough to hold her against the feeble tide. "I like floating . . . and where else can you see the *entire* Smoke Ring?"

Minya nodded. She didn't want to talk. When a problem couldn't be solved and wouldn't go away, what could one do but run? She had run as far as a human being could go. It was working: she felt at peace here, halfway between infinities.

The tree seemed to run forever in both directions. The Dark Tuft, backlit by Voy and the sun, was a halo of green fluff with a black core. Outward, Dalton-Quinn Tuft was barely larger. A few drifting clouds, wisps of green forest, whorls of storm were all outward. Eastward was a point of bright light off-center in a dark rim: the same small pond that had been drifting tantalizingly closer for a score of days.

Maybe, maybe it would come. They didn't talk about it. Bad luck.

Between the drought and the recent political upsets, it had been too long since the Triune Squad had been free for tree-tending duty. They had been needed as police. One could hope that the executions had settled the troubles; but now the triads were finding parasites and patches of old-man's-hair everywhere on the trunk. Today they were burning virtually a *field* of the horrid stuff.

Motion caught Minya's eye, outward and windward. Blue-against-blue, hard to see, something big. The sun was nearly at nadir, glaring up. She held a hand beneath her eyes, and squinted, and presently said, "Triune."

Smitta snapped alert. "Interested in us? *Sal!*"

Sal sang out from behind the smoke cloud. "I see it."

Minya said, "They're interested. They're pretty close already."

Smitta had pulled herself against the trunk and was readying her weapons. "I fought a triune once. They're smarter than swordbirds. You can scare them off. Just remember, if we kill one, we'll have to kill all three."

The torpedo-shaped object was closer now. It was nearly the blue of the sky, slowly rotating. Six big eyes showed in turn around the circumference, and three great gauzy fins . . . one smaller than the other. That would be the juvenile. Minya whispered, "What do we need?"

"Bows and arrows ready? Tether your arrow and scoop up some burning old-man's-hair on the point. Lucky we had a fire going. Know where your jet pods are, you may need them."

Minya could feel her heart pulsing in her throat. It was her second trip up the trunk . . . but Smitta and Sal had been up many times. They were tough and experienced. Sal was a burly, red-haired forty-year-old who had joined the Triune Squad at age twelve. Smitta had been born a man; she was a woman by courtesy.

Stay clear of Smitta, Minya told herself. Smitta was slow to anger, but under pressure something could snap in her mind. Then Smitta fought like a berserker, even among her own, and the only way to stop her was to pile on her.

Minya strung her hardwood bow and used an arrow point to dig out a gob of burning fungus. Ready—?

The torpedo split in three. Three slender torpedoes flapped lazily toward them, showing small lateral fins and violent-orange bellies. A male and a female, forever mated, plus a single juvenile who would put on body mass fast, then mature more slowly. They divided only to hunt or fight. The Triune Squad itself was named for the triune family's interdependence.

The juvenile would be the smallest, the one hanging back a little. Two adults swept forward.

"Aim for the male," Smitta said and loosed, the line trailing out behind the arrow. Which was male? Minya waited a moment to judge Smitta's target, then loosed her own weapon. She judged that they weren't in range yet . . . and she was right; the male's body rippled him free of the arrows' paths, while the female bored in. Sal had held back. Now she loosed, and the veering female caught an arrow in her fin.

She bellowed. She flapped once, and the arrow snapped free. Sal appeared from the smoke, yanked into the sky. It didn't seem to bother her as she reeled in, her ancient metal bow slung safe over her shoulder. The smoldering old-man's-hair had been left on the female's tail, and she was flapping madly.

Smitta sent a tethered arrow winging at the juvenile.

Both adults screamed. The female tried to block the arrow. Too slow. The juvenile didn't seem to see the arrow coming. Smitta yanked at the line and stopped it a meter short.

The female gaped.

The women were reeling frantically, but it wasn't necessary. The adults moved in alongside the infant, infinitely graceful. Small hands reached out from their orange bellies to pull them together. They moved away like a single blurred blue ghost against the blue sky.

"See? They're smart. You can reason with them," Smitta said.

Sal pulled a teardrop-shaped jet pod from one of the cluster of pockets that ran down and across the front of her tunic. She twisted the tip. A cloud of seeds and mist spurted away from her, thrusting Sal back toward the bark.

She coiled line and stowed her weapons, including the valuable bow. Springy metal, it was, handed down from old to young within the Triune Squad for at least two hundred years. "Well done, troops, but I think the fire is getting to the wood. I wish Thanya would get here. She couldn't have missed us, could she?"

To Minya's eye, the fire might have reached wood by now, or not. Hard to tell where old-man's-hair shaded over into rotted wood. "It's not bad yet," she said.

"I hate to waste jet pods, but . . . treefodder. I want to look for them," Sal decided. She gathered her legs under her, hands gripping the bark to brace herself, and jumped. She waved her arms to flip herself around until she could see the trunk. They watched her drift along the trunk, out toward Dalton-Quinn Tuft.

"She worries too much," Smitta said.

Seventy days had passed since Clave's citizens had departed Quinn Tuft.

The tree fed a myriad parasites, and the parasites fed Clave's team. They had killed another nose-arm, easily, chopping through its nose, then jabbing harpoons into its den. There were patches of fan fungus everywhere. Merril had slept a full eight days after eating from the red fringe of a fan fungus. The subsequent throbbing headache didn't seem to affect her climbing, and presently it went away. So the fan fungus served them as food, and they had found more of the shelled burrowers and other edibles . . .

The Grad saw it all as evidence of the tree's decline.

They had found a jet pod bush, like a mass of bubbles on the bark. Clave had packed a dozen ripe pods in a pouch of scraped nose-arm hide.

They had taken to camping just outside the water-washed wood. Clave laughed and admitted that they should have been doing that all along. They'd slept three times more on the tree: last night in a nose-arm's den, twice before in deep wounds in the wood, cracks overgrown with "fuzz" that had to be burned out first. The char had turned their clothing black.

They had learned not to try to boil water. The bubbles just foamed it out in a hot, expanding mass.

Tidal gravity continued to decrease until they were almost floating up the trunk. Merril loved it. Recovering from the fan fungus hadn't changed that. You *couldn't* fall; you'd just yell for help, and someone would presently throw you a line. Glory loved it, and Alfin smiled sometimes.

But there were penalties. Now water had grown scarce too. There was no wind this high, and thus no leeward stream of water. Sometimes you found wet wood, wet enough to lick dry. There was water in fan fungus flesh.

Here was the DQ mark Jinny had found. Good: it looked nearly clean. And half a klomter farther up the trunk, a fan-shape showed like a white hand against the sky. It must be huge. The Grad pointed. "Dinner?"

Clave said, "We'll find smaller ones around it."

"But wouldn't it look grand," Merril asked, "coming into the Commons?"

The Grad was pulling himself toward the tribal mark when Clave said, "Hold it."

"What?"

"This mark isn't overgrown like the others were. Grad, doesn't it look funny to you? *Tended?*"

"There's some fuzz growing, but maybe not enough." Then the Grad was close enough to see the *real* discrepancy. "There's no takeout mark. Citizens, this isn't Quinn territory."

Gavving and Jiovan had been left behind to tend the smokefire.

Hard-learned lessons showed here. Bark torn from the rim of a patch of fuzz served as fuel. Healthy bark resisted fire. A circle of coals surrounded the meat, all open to the fitful breezes. A sheltered fire wouldn't burn. The smoke wouldn't rise; it would stay to smother the fire. Even here in the open, the smoke hovered in a squirming cloud. The heat of burning stayed in the smoke, so the fire didn't need to be large. Gavving and Jiovan stayed well back. A shift in the breeze could smother an incautious citizen.

The meat should be rotated soon. It was Gavving's turn, but it didn't have to be done instantly.

"Jiovan?"

"What?"

Even Gavving wouldn't ask Jiovan how he lost his leg—nobody would; but one thing about that tale had bothered him for years. And he asked. "Why were you hunting alone, that day? Nobody hunts alone."

"I did."

"Okay." Topic closed. Gavving drew his harpoon. He pulled air into his lungs, then lunged into the smoke. Half-blind, he reached over the coals with the harpoon butt to turn the nose-arm legs—one, two, three. He yanked hard on his line to pull himself into open air. Smoke came with him, and he took an instant to fan it away before he drew breath.

Jiovan was looking in, past the small green tuft that had once enclosed his life, into the bluish white spark that was Voy. His head came up, and Gavving faced a murderous glare. "This *isn't* something I'd want told around."

Gavving waited.

"All right. I've got . . . I had a real gift for sarcasm, they tell me. When I was leading a hunt . . . well, the boys were there to learn, of course, and I was there to teach. If someone made a mistake, I left him in no doubt."

Gavving nodded.

"Pretty soon they were giving me nothing but the fumblers. I couldn't stand it, so I started hunting alone."

"I shouldn't have asked. It used to bother me."

"Forget it."

Gavving was trying to forget something else entirely. This last sleep period he had wakened to find three citizens missing. He'd followed a sound . . . and watched Clave and Jayan and Jinny moor lines to the bark, and leap outward, and make babies while they drifted.

What lived in his head now was lust and envy balanced by fear of Clave's wrath or Jinny's scorn (for he had fixed on Jinny as marginally lovelier). He might as well dream. Any serious potential mate was back in Quinn Tuft, and Gavving couldn't offer anyway; he hadn't the wealth or the years.

That would change, of course. He would return (of course) as a hero (of course!). As for the Chairman's wrath . . . he hadn't been able to send Harp. Possibly Clave could have resisted him too. If they could end the famine, the Chairman could do nothing; they would be heroes.

Gavving could have his choice of mates—

"So I was hunting alone," Jiovan said, "the day Glory busted open the turkey pen."

For an instant Gavving couldn't imagine what Jiovan was talking about. Then he smiled. "Harp's told that tale."

"I've heard him. I was down under the branch that day, with one line to tether me and another loose, nibbling a little foliage with my head sticking down into the sky, you know, just waiting. It was full night at the New Year's occlusion. The sun was a wide bright patch shining up at me, and Voy drifting right across the center.

"Here came a turkey, flapping against the wind, still moving pretty fast, and backward. I put a net on my free line, quick, and threw it. The turkey's caught. Here comes another one. I've got more nets, and in two breaths I've got a turkey on each end. But here come two more, then four, and they're coming from above, and by now I can guess they're ours. I throw the end of the line I'm moored to, and I get a third turkey—"

"Good throwing," Gavving said.

"Oh, sure, there wasn't *anything* wrong with my throwing that day. But the sky was full of turkeys, and most of them were going to get away, and I *still* thought it was kind of hilarious."

"Yeah."

"That's why I never told this story before."

Gavving suddenly guessed what was coming. "I can live with it if you don't want to finish."

"No, that's okay. It *was* funny," Jiovan said seriously. "But the sky was full of turkeys, and a triune family came to do something about all that meat on the wing. They split up and went after the loose turkeys. There wasn't a thing I could do but pull in my three."

Jiovan certainly wasn't smiling now. "The male went after one of my turkeys. Swallowed it whole and tried to swim away. It got the wrong line . . . picture one end of a line spiked deep in the branch, and that *massive* beast pulling on the other, and me in a loop in the middle. I suddenly saw what was happening, and I pulled the loop open and tried to jump out, and the loop snicked shut and my leg was ripped almost off and I was falling into the sky."

"*Treefodder.*"

"I thought I was treefodder, all right. Remember, I still had a line in my hands? But with a turkey on each end, flapping like crazy, and I was *falling.* I tried throwing a turkey, I really did, I thought it might get caught in the branchlets, but it didn't.

"Meanwhile the triune male's been caught by something, and it doesn't know what. It pulls back against the line and feels a tug in its belly and throws up. I think that's what must have happened. All I know is something smacks me in the face, and it's a dead turkey covered with goo, and I grab it—I hug it to me with all my heart and climb the line back into the tuft."

Gavving was afraid to laugh.

"Then I tie off what's left of my leg. What's hanging loose, I had to cut off. Well, kid, did Harp ever tell you a story like that?"

"No. Treefodder, he'd *love* it! Oh."

"He'd make me famous. I don't want to be famous that way."

Gavving chewed it over. "Why tell me now?"

"I don't know. My turn," Jiovan said suddenly. He filled his lungs and disappeared into the smoke.

Gavving felt burdened. Always he asked too many questions. He grinned guiltily, picturing Jiovan trying to throw a line with a turkey flapping at each end. But what if Jiovan regretted telling it?

He saw Clave appear from behind the curve of the trunk.

Jiovan emerged, bringing smoke, and Gavving held his breath while it cleared. Jiovan coughed a little. "It's been so long," he said. "Maybe it doesn't hurt as much. Maybe I just wanted to tell it. Maybe I had to."

"They're coming back," Gavving said. "I wonder what's got them so excited?"

Clave bellowed, "I will not go home without learning something about them!"

"I know quite a lot about them," the Grad answered. "We all lived in the far tuft once. The Quinns left after some kind of disagreement. Before that, it was Dalton-Quinn Tribe."

"Then they're relatives."

The argument had grown a little less chaotic, but only because half the troop was trailing back. It was no less vehement. Alfin shouted, "You're not listening. They kicked us out! For all we know, they think they're still at war with us!"

The Grad said, "Clave, the tribemarks are tended, and we aren't finding as many fan fungi lately, or the shelled things either. I'm thinking they keep this stretch of trunk clean. They must be still around. Our move is to get out of here!"

"You want to run from something you haven't even seen!"

"We saw the tribal insignia," the Grad said. "DQ. No takeout mark across the Q. Maybe they still call themselves Dalton-Quinn. What does that make us? Intruders on *their* tree? We've passed the meridian anyway, we're in their space. Clave, let's go home. Kill another nose-arm, pick some fan fungus and one of the shells, and go home with plenty of food." Clave was shaking his head. "The tribe won't have to go thirsty any more either! We bring water from the trunk—"

Clave waved it away. "That water would get to the tuft anyway. No. I want to meet the Daltons. It's been hundreds of years, we don't know *what* they're like . . . maybe they know better tending methods for the earthlife, or ways to get water. Maybe they grow food we never heard of. *Something.* 'Day, Jiovan."

" 'Day. What's going on?"

"We found a tribemark and it isn't ours. The question before the citizenry is, do we say hello before going home? Or do we just run?"

The Grad jumped in. "Don't you see, we can't fight and we can't negotiate! We've got one good fighter, and two cripples and a boy and four women and a treemouth tender, and all of us thrown out of Quinn Tuft, we can't even make promises—"

Clave broke in. "Alfin, you're for leaving too?"

"Yes."

"Jiovan?"

"What are we running from?"

"Maybe nothing. That mark wasn't tended for a long time. Treefodder, the drought could have killed them off! We could *settle* the far tuft—"

Merril broke in, though she was puffing from the climb. "Oh no. If everyone died there . . . we won't want to . . . go anywhere near it. Sickness."

"Are you for going back or going on?"

"I don't . . . back, I guess, but . . . let's get that . . . big fan fungus first. Wouldn't that impress the citizens! And smoke another nose-arm . . . if we can. Far as that goes . . . we know there's meat to be hunted on the trunk. We should tell the Chairman that."

"Jayan? Jinny?"

"She makes sense," Jinny said, and Jayan nodded.

"Gavving?"

"No opinion."

"Treefodder. Glory?"

"Go back," Glory said. "I haven't tasted foliage in days and days."

Clave sighed. "If I was sure I was right, we'd go on. Aaall right." His voice became fuller, more resonant. "We'll have enough to carry anyway, what with the giant fan and whatever meat we find. Citizens, we've done very well for ourselves and Quinn Tuft. We go home as heroes. Now, I *don't* want to lose anyone on the way down, so *don't* take the tide for granted! It'll get stronger with every klomter. Most of the way down we'll need lines for the meat and the fan fungus—"

Their goals had become Clave's own. Gavving noticed, and remembered.

The flashers had come back. Minya watched them at their mating dance. Two males strutted before the same female with their wing-cloaks spread wide, and the female's head snapped back and forth almost too fast to see. *Decisions, decisions—*

"Something's been worrying you, woman."

—Decisions. Was it any of Smitta's business? Minya made a swift decision: she *had* to talk to someone, or burst. "I've started wondering if—if I'm right for the Triune Squad."

Smitta showed shock. "Really? You were eager enough to join eight years ago. What's changed?"

"I don't know."

But she did, and suddenly Smitta did too. "Don't talk to Sal about this. She wouldn't understand."

"I was only fourteen."

"You looked older . . . more mature. And maybe the loveliest recruit we ever got."

Minya grimaced. "Every man in the tuft wanted to make babies with me. I must have heard every *possible* way of saying that. I just didn't want to *do* that with anyone. Smitta, that's what the Triune Squad is for!"

"I know. What would I be without the Triune Squad? A woman born as a man, a man who wants to be a woman . . ."

"Do you ever want—" What was the right word? Not *make babies*, not for Smitta.

"I used to," Smitta said. "With Risher—he was a lot prettier once—and lately with Mik, the Huntmaster's boy." Minya flinched. Maybe Smitta noticed. "We give all that up when we join. You just have to hold it inside. You know that."

"Does anyone ever . . ."

"What? Quit? Cheat? Alse jumped into the sky, a little after I joined, but nobody really knows why. That's the only way to quit. If you get caught cheating, I can name some would tear you apart. Sal's one."

Tight lips and clenched teeth held back Minya's secret. Now Smitta did notice. "Don't get caught cheating," she repeated. "Maybe you don't know how citizens feel about us. They tolerate us. We won't give the tribe babies, so we do the most dangerous jobs anyone can think of, and pay the debt that way. But you don't ask any ordinary man to, you know, help you be in both worlds."

Minya nodded. Lips pressed together, teeth clenched: if only she had kept them that way when she was with Mik! Mik had been impossible to get rid of, eight years ago. How had he changed so much? *Would he tell?*

"Smitta—"

"Drop it, Sal's coming."

Minya looked. There were *four* figures down there, four women rising on jets of sprayed gas and seeds; and they carried no water. Sal shouted something the wind snatched away.

"They're wasting jet pods," Smitta observed.

They were closer now and in range to snag the bark. This time Minya heard Sal's joyful bellow.

"Invaderrrsss!"

Chapter Seven

THE CHECKER'S HAND

The two triads moved inward, staying in cracks in the bark where they could. Every minute or so Denisse, a tall, dark woman of Thanya's triad, would pop up, look around fast, and drop back into the bark.

"We counted six of them around the tribemark," Thanya said. "Dark clothes. Maybe they're from the Dark Tuft."

"Intruders on the tree." Sal's voice was eager, joyful. "We've never fought invaders! There were some citizens thrown out for mutiny, long ago . . . some of them killed the Chairman, and the rest went with them. Maybe they settled in the Dark Tuft. Mutineers . . . Thanya, what kind of weapons were they carrying?"

"We couldn't go ask them, could we? Denisse says she saw things like giant arrows. I couldn't even tell their sexes, but one had no legs."

They veered to avoid a crack clogged with old-man's-hair. Smitta said, "Six of them, six of us, you may have missed a few . . . shall we send someone back for Jeel's triad?"

Sal grinned wolfishly. "No."

"And no," said Thanya for her triad.

Minya said nothing—her triad leader spoke for her—but she felt a fierce joy. Right now there was nothing she needed more than a fight.

Denisse dropped back from her next survey. Her voice was deadly calm. "Intruders. We have intruders, three hundred meters in and a hundred to port, moving outward. At least six."

"Let's go slow," Thanya said suddenly. "I'd like to question one. We don't know what they want here."

"Do we care? What they want isn't theirs."

Thanya grinned back. "We're not a debating team. We're the Triune Squad. Let's go look."

They worked their way along the bark. Presently Denisse poked her head up, dropped back. "Intruders have reached the Checker's Hand."

Clearing the trunk of parasites was one of the Triune Squad's duties. Fan fungi were dangerous to the tree and edible besides; but one large and perfect fan had special privileges. Found twenty-odd years ago, it had been left to grow even larger. Minya had only heard of the squad's unusual pet. She eased her head above the bark . . .

They were there: men, women, looking entirely human. "More than six. Eight, nine, dressed like dirty civilians. Sooty red clothes, no pockets . . . they're chopping at the stalk! They're killing it, the Checker's Hand—"

Smitta screamed and launched herself across the bark.

No help for it now. Sal cried, "Go for Gold!" and the Triune Squad leapt toward the intruders.

The fan fungus reached out from the trunk like a tremendous hand, white with red nails. Its stalk, disproportionately narrow and fragile-looking from a distance, was still thicker than Gavving's torso. He set to chopping at it with his dagger. Jiovan worked the other side.

"We'll get it down the trunk," Jiovan puffed, "but how will we ever get it through the tuft to the Commons?"

"Maybe we don't," said Clave. "Bring the tribe to the fungus. Let them carve off pieces to suit themselves."

"Tear the fringe off first," Merril said.

The Grad objected. "The Scientist will want some of the red part."

"And try it on who? Oh, all right, save some fringe for the Scientist. Not a lot, though."

The stalk was tough. They'd made some progress, but Gavving's arms were used up. He backed away, and Clave took over. Gavving watched the cut deepen.

Maybe they'd weakened it enough?

He pounded a stake into the bark and tethered his line to it. Then he leapt at the fungus with the full strength of his legs.

The great hand bent to his weight, then sprang back, flipping him playfully into the sky. Floundering, gathering in his line, he saw what the others had missed through being too close to the trunk.

"Fire!"

"What? Where?"

"Outward, half a klomter, maybe. Doesn't look big." The sun was behind the out tuft, leaving the trunk somewhat shadowed; he could see an orange glow within a cloud of smoke.

A flicker at the corner of his eye. He pulled hard at the line before his forebrain had registered anything at all . . . and a miniature harpoon zipped past his hip.

He yelled, "Treefodder!" Not specific enough. "Harpoons!"

Jiovan was stumbling, indecisive; a sharp point showed behind his shoulder blade. Clave was slapping shoulders and buttocks to send his citizens to cover. Something sailed past at a distance: a woman, a burly red-haired woman garbed in purple, with pockets clustered from breasts to hips, giving her a look of lumpy pregnancy. She flew loose through the sky while she pulled something apart with both hands. Something that glittered, a line of light.

Their eyes met, and Gavving knew it was a weapon even before she let it snap shut. He clutched the bark and rolled. Something came as a tiny blur, thudded into the bark alongside his spine: a mini-harpoon with gray and yellow flasher feathers at the butt end. He rolled again to put the fan fungus between them.

Clave was nowhere in sight. Purple-clad enemies sailed along the wall of bark, yelling gibberish and throwing death. The red-haired woman had a harpoon through her leg. She tore it loose, cast it away, and sought a target. She picked the easiest: Jiovan, who wasn't even trying to seek cover. He took a second mini-harpoon through his chest.

They were using jet pods. A lean purple-clad man spotted Gavving; he pulled his weapon apart and a string snapped. He screamed in rage and opened a jet pod to hurl him down at Gavving. His other hand waved a meter's-length of knife.

Gavving leapt out of his way, drew his knife, yanked at the line to pull himself back. The man smacked into the bark. Gavving was on his back before he could recover. He slashed at the man's throat. Inhumanly strong fingers sank into his arm like a swordbird's teeth. Gavving shifted his own grip and jabbed his knife into the man's side. *Hurry!* The grip relaxed.

The tree shuddered.

Gavving didn't notice at once. He was shuddering with reaction. He saw the great wall of bark shuddering too, decided it was the least of his problems, and looked for enemies.

The red-haired woman was coasting treeward not far out, ignoring the blood spreading across her pants; her eye was on the shuddering tree. Out of range? Gavving tried a harpoon cast and instantly dived behind the great fan.

Not necessary. He'd skewered her. She stared at him, horrified, and died.

Purple-clad enemies screamed to each other, voices drowned by a rising background roar. Jiovan was dead with two feathered shafts in him. Jinny held a smaller fan fungus in front of her, harpoon in her other hand. The Grad rolled out of a crevice in the bark, saw what Jinny was doing, and imitated her. A mini-harpoon thudded into Jinny's shield, and she bared her teeth and launched herself in that direction, followed by Jayan and the Grad.

Gavving reeled in his harpoon. The dead woman came with it, her arms and legs jerking. A wave of nausea clawed at his throat. He worked his harpoon loose, and was minded to examine the peculiar gleaming weapon still clutched in the woman's hand. He wasn't given time.

The tree shuddered again. The bass background roar continued, a sound like worlds ripping apart. Bark slid past Gavving; the red-haired corpse tumbled, flailing. He was scrambling for a foothold when someone came at him from the side.

Dark hair, lovely pale heart-shaped face—purple clothing. Gavving thrust a harpoon at her eyes.

"The fire!" Thanya screamed. "It'll block us from the tuft! We've got to get past it!" She blew jet pods and was skimming outward across the bark.

Minya heard, but she didn't pause. Smitta was dead, and Sal was dead, and a single invader boy had killed them both. Minya stalked him.

The boy wore scarlet clothing, citizens' garb; his blond hair curled tightly as a skullcap; his beard was barely visible. His face was set in a rictus of fear or killing-rage. He thrust at her, threw himself back from her sword's counterthrust, lost his toe-grip on the bark. For an instant Minya was minded to go after him. Pierce him, kill him for the honor of Sal's triad, then go!

There wasn't time. Thanya was right. The fire could block them all, maroon them away from Dalton-Quinn Tuft . . . and there was Sal's bow to be recovered. Minya whirled and leapt away, and fired a jet pod for extra speed.

Sal's corpse floated free, her dead hand clutching the tribal treasure. Behind Minya the blond youth gripped bark to set himself and hurled his hand-arrow. Minya kicked to alter her course and watched the weapon whisper past her. She turned back as a shape popped up directly in front of her.

The shape was wrong, not human. It froze her for an instant. Minya hadn't quite grasped what was happening when a fist exploded in her face.

Gavving had ignored the yells from the purple-clad women. Now two were fleeing, firing jet pods to carry them outward along the trunk. Another leapt in a zigzag pattern along the bark. But the dark-haired woman who had tried to kill him was now moving crosswise, back to where Gavving had left . . . left a burly red-haired corpse clutching a curve of silver metal.

Merril popped out of a crack just in front of her. Merril's fist smacked into the stranger's jaw with a sound Gavving heard even above the—

—bass ripping sound he'd been ignoring while he fought for his life: a sound like the sky tearing apart. Now he heard the Grad shrilling like a cricket, a sound of panic, the words drowned in the roar.

But Gavving didn't need to hear. He *knew*.

"*Clave! Claaave!*"

Clave popped out of a deep crack and shouted, "Ready. What do you need?"

"We have to jump!" the Grad screamed. "All of us!"

"What are you talking about?"

"The tree's coming apart! That's how they survive!"

"What?"

"Get everyone to jump clear!"

Clave looked around. Jiovan was dead, floating tethered, but dead. The Grad was already loose in the sky, with line coiled! Gavving . . . Gavving moved across the shuddering bark, ripped something loose from a purple-clad corpse, continued in along the trunk. Jayan and Jinny weren't visible. Alfin snarled as he watched his enemies disappear into the outward smoke cloud. Glory and Merril watched too, not believing it.

Make a decision. Now. You don't know enough, but you've got to decide. It has to be you, it's always you.

Gavving. Gavving and the Grad were old friends. Did Gavving know something? He'd captured an invader weapon, and now he was far in along the trunk . . . headed for the meat they'd left when they went after the mushroom. Of course, they'd need food if they were to cast loose from the tree.

The Grad's mind could have snapped. But Gavving trusted him . . . and everything was happening at once: fire blazing on the tree, the trunk shuddering and moaning, strangers killing and then fleeing . . . There were jet pods in Clave's pack. He could get his citizens back once things settled down. He bellowed, "Grad! Lines to the tree?"

"Nooo! Treefodder, *no!*"

"All right." He bellowed above the end-of-the-world roar. *"Jayan! Jinny! Glory, Alfin, Merril, everybody jump! Jump away from the tree! Do not moor yourselves!"*

Reactions were various. Merril stared at him, thought it over, pushed herself free. Glory only stared. Jayan and Jinny emerged from hiding like a pair of birds taking wing. Alfin clutched the bark in a deathgrip. Gavving? Gavving was working to free one thick leg of nose-arm meat.

The bark still shuddered, the sound filled tree and sky, the purple-clad killers were nowhere to be seen, and . . . nobody had gone after the fan fungus. Clave hurled himself at the stalk.

The fan bent under his weight, then tore loose and was turning end for end. Clave's fingers were sunk into white fungus. The tumbling thing seemed to be picking up speed. Faster, the bark raced beneath the tumbling fan fungus, faster . . . a fiery wind rushed past him and was gone before he could draw breath.

It wasn't possible. Bewildered, Clave saw tufts of flame receding in both directions. No tree. Citizens floundered in the sky. Even Alfin had jumped at last. But the tree, where was the tree? There wasn't any tree. Fistfuls of fungus turned to mush in Clave's closing fists, and he screamed and wrapped his arms around the stalk. They were lost in the sky.

Chapter Eight
QUINN TRIBE

Wood snapped explosively, spattering Gavving with splinters as he leapt across the bucking, tearing bark. A million insects poured from a sudden black gap that must have reached a klomter into the heartwood. Gavving cried out and waved his arms through the buzzing cloud, trying to clear enough air to breathe.

The tree was everything that was, and the tree was ending. If he'd stopped to think, his fear would have frozen him fast. He held to the one thought: *Get the meat and get out!*

The nose-arm legs tumbled loose within a cloud of burning coals. One haunch was in reach. Gavving caught a line to pull it free of the coals, then jumped to catch it against his shoulder. Hot grease burned his neck. He yelled and thrust himself away.

Now what? He couldn't *think* in this end-of-the-world roar. He doffed his backpack, tied it against the nose-arm leg, braced against the pack, and pushed himself into the sky.

Clouds of insects and pulverized wood half hid the shuddering, thundering tree. Dagger-sized splinters flew past.

Gavving braced one of his jet pods against the pack and twisted the tip. Seeds and cold gas blasted past him. The pod ripped itself free of his hands, spat seeds into the flesh of his face, and was gone.

His hands shook. Beads of blood were pooling on his cheek and his neck. He dug out his remaining jet pod and tried again, his tongue between his teeth. This time the pod held steady until it had gone quiet.

The world came apart.

He watched it all while his terror changed to awe. Fiery wind swept past him and left him in the open sky. Two fireballs receded in and out, until the home tree had become two bits of fluff linked by an infinite line of smoke.

Awesome! Nobody could hope to live through a bigger disaster. All of Quinn Tribe must be dead . . . the idea was really too big to grasp . . . all but Clave's citizens, and they'd lost Jiovan too, and who was left? He looked about him.

Nobody?

A cluster of specks, far out.

He'd used both his jet pods, and now he was lost in the sky. At least he wouldn't starve . . .

Thrashing his arms didn't stop the Grad's spin. He wasn't willing to use his jet pods for only that. He settled for spreading his arms and legs like a limpet star, which slowed him enough to search for survivors.

The left side of his face was wet. His fingertips traced a bloody gash that ran from temple to chin. It didn't hurt. Shock? But he had worse to worry him.

Three human shapes tumbled slowly nearby: purple marked with scarlet. His stomach lurched. It was their own doing; he hadn't come here to kill.

The giant fan fungus floated free, turning, turning to reveal Clave clutching the stalk. Good. Clave still wore his backpack: *very* good. That was their store of fresh jet pods. Then why wasn't Clave doing something about rescue?

Feet outward, Jayan and Jinny rotated slowly around their two pairs of clasped hands. It looked almost like a dance. Spreading out like that greatly reduced their spin. Good thinking, and no sign of panic.

Merril was a fair distance in. Her arms hadn't pushed her far, and the tree's wind-wake had caught her.

The world's-end roar had dwindled, allowing lesser sounds. The Grad heard a thin wail. Alfin had leapt free after all. He was thrashing and spinning and crying, but he was safe.

The Grad couldn't find Gavving, nor Glory, nor Jiovan. Jiovan's corpse must have gone with the tree, but where were the others? And why wasn't Clave doing something? He and the fan were drifting away.

The Grad sighed. He shrugged out of his backpack and searched out his jet pods. Old jet pods, from Quinn Tuft stores. Were they still active?

He'd never fired a jet pod. He knew nobody who had. Hunters carried them in case they fell into the sky; but no hunter lost in the sky had ever returned in the Grad's lifetime. He did it carefully: he donned his pack again, then clutched a jet pod in both hands over his navel. When Clave was approximately behind him, he twisted the tip, smartly.

The pod drove into his belly. He grunted. He maneuvered the point, hoping to kill his spin. The push died; he released the pod, and it jumped away on the last of its stored gas.

Looking over his shoulder, he found the fan fungus drifting toward him. Clave still wasn't doing anything constructive, and he hadn't noticed the Grad.

The smoke of the disaster split the sky from end to end. Dense, flickering black clouds were pulling free of the paler smoke. The same insects that had eaten the tree apart were now casting loose to find other prey.

Other debris floated in the smoke trail. The Grad made out great fragments of torn wood and bark; a cloud of flashers whirling in panic; a flapping mote, perhaps a nose-arm fled from its burrow. In that confusion he could still see that the cloud of citizens and corpses was slowly drifting apart.

Far in toward Voy, Gavving maneuvered half his own weight in smoked meat. He'd be hard to reach. He'd gone far to save that meat, and the wind-wake must have pulled him further. Save Gavving for last, and hope.

The fan brushed against the Grad and he clutched it, fungus springy under his hands. Clave watched as if bemused. He asked, "What happened?"

Safe now. "The tree came apart. Clave, I'm going to dig in your pack. We've got to start rescuing citizens."

Clave neither helped nor resisted as the Grad searched through his pack. They could use the big fan as a base of operations . . . rescue Alfin first, because he was nearest . . . He took half a dozen pods. He slid to somewhere near the fan's center of mass and fired a jet pod, then another.

"The *tree* came apart?"

"You saw it."

"How? Why?"

The Grad was judging distances. He cast a line in a wide circle. It brushed Alfin's back, and Alfin convulsed and snatched the line in a deathgrip. He didn't try to reel it in. The Grad had to do that, while Alfin watched in near-mindless terror. Alfin lunged across the last meter or so and wrapped himself around the stalk and buried his fingers in white fungus to the last knuckle.

A hand closed around the Grad's neck. Long, strong fingers overlapped the thumb, tightening like a steel collar. Clave's voice was a hot snarl in his ear. "You'll tell me now!"

The Grad froze. Clave had gone crazy.

"Tell me what happened!"

"The tree came apart."

"Why?"

"Maybe the fire set it off, but it was ready. Clave, everything in the Smoke Ring has some way of getting around. Some way to stay near the median . . . middle, where there's water and air. Where do you think jet pods come from?" The hand relaxed a little, and the Grad kept talking. "It's a plant's way of getting around. If a plant wanders out of the median, too far into the gas torus region—"

"The what?"

Alfin asked, "What on earth is going on?"

"Clave wants to know what happened. Alfin, can you steer this thing and pick up some more of us? Here—" He passed across his store of jet pods.

Alfin took them. He took his time deciding what to do with them, and the Grad ignored him while he lectured. "The Smoke Ring runs down the median of a much bigger region. That's the gas torus, where the molecules . . . the bits of air have long mean-free-paths. The air is very thin in the gas torus, but there's some. It gets thicker along the median. That's where you find all the water and the soil and the plants. That's what the Smoke Ring is, just the thickest part of the gas torus, and that's where every living thing wants to stay."

"Where it can breathe. All right, go on."

"Everything in the Smoke Ring can maneuver somehow. Animals mostly have wings. Plants, well, some plants grow jet pods. They spit seeds back toward the median where they can grow and breed, or they spit sterile seeds farther into the gas torus, and the reaction pushes the plant back toward the median. Then there are plants that send out a long root to grab anything that's passing. There are kites—"

"What about the jungles?"

"I . . . I don't know. The Scientist never—"

"Skip it. What about the trees?"

"Now, that's really interesting. The Scientist came up with this, but he couldn't prove it—"

The hand tightened. The Grad babbled, "If an integral tree falls too far out of the median, it starts to die. It dies in the center. The insects eat it out. They're symbiotes, not parasites. When the center rots, the tree comes apart. See, half of it falls farther away, and half of it drops toward the median. Half lives, half dies, and it's better than nothing."

Clave mulled that. He said, "Which half?"

"East takes you out, out takes you west, west—"

"What are you doing?"

"I'm trying to remember. We were too far in toward Voy, so our end—" It only hit him then. The revelation blocked his throat.

A moment later, so did Clave's fingers. "Keep talking, you copsik. I've had it up to here with you telling half a secret!"

Thickly the Grad said, "Mister Chairman, you may call me the Scientist."

The hand relaxed in shock.

"Quinn Tribe is dead. We are Quinn Tribe."

Alfin broke the long silence that followed that terrible declaration. "Are you happy, Grad? You were right. The tree was dying."

"Shut up," said Clave. He released the Grad's neck. Maybe that had been a mistake, maybe not; he'd have to apologize presently. For now, he clambered around to the edge of the fan. Jayan and Jinny were coming near, watching his approach alternately as they spun.

He'd never felt like this, so helpless, so fearful of making decisions. It bothered him that Alfin and the Grad had seen him like that. He tried his voice and found it normal:

"They're almost here. Good work, Alfin. Go for Merril next. I don't see Glory."

The Grad said, "I haven't seen her since . . . since." He rubbed his throat.

"She may not have jumped. Seven of us. Seven." He flung a line. Jinny snagged it in her toes, and Clave pulled them both in together. He said, "Welcome to what's left of Quinn Tribe."

They clung to Clave more in desperation than affection. Jinny pulled back to look into his face. "They're dead? All the rest?" As if she'd already guessed.

Alfin demanded, "Why didn't the Scientist see *that* coming?"

"He did," said the Grad.

"Treefodder. Why did he stay, then?"

"He was an old man. He couldn't climb fifty klomters of tree."

Alfin gaped. "But . . . but that's the same as murdering everyone who *could* climb!"

There wasn't time for this. Clave said, "Alfin, pay attention to what you're doing."

Alfin set off two jet pods, then another. The fan drifted toward Merril, who waited in what might have been stoic calm. He murmured, "The children!"

Somewhere off to the side, there was motion.

What Clave had taken for a purple-clad corpse was floundering in air. Clave pointed. "One killer left."

They watched. She wasn't floundering now. She'd tied a line to her long knife, and now she cast it out. She snagged a dead companion and reeled it in. She searched the corpse, then pushed off from it in the direction of the next.

She hadn't found much, but it must have been what she wanted. Now she fired two jet pods in turn. The thrust carried her in toward Voy. Alfin said, "She's not coming here. Or going home. What does she think she's doing?"

"Not our problem."

Merril caught a line thrown by Alfin and pulled herself close. By now there was no room to clutch the fan itself. Clave asked her, "Did you see any sign of Glory?"

"Hanging on to the bark for dear life, last I saw her. She was in the out section. Gavving's a good distance in."

"We'll go after him. I hope we get there in time."

By then it was obvious. The woman in purple had passed them and was heading toward Gavving.

Gavving watched her coming. There was little else he could do. When he could see her face he watched her watching him. The rictus of hate he'd seen earlier wasn't there. He saw close-cut dark hair, a triangular face with an oddly narrow chin, an expression that was thoughtful, judging.

She was going to go past.

He didn't know how to feel about that. He didn't want to die alone; but he surely didn't want to die with those mini-harpoons through him. She was close now. She reached behind her back for a tethered mini-harpoon. He could only try to put the meat between them as she pulled her odd weapon apart, looking him in the eye, and released it.

The feathered thing buried itself in warm meat.

Then Gavving moved in frantic haste, pulling his knife, reaching for her line—

Her words were strangely twisted, but he understood her. "No, no, no, let me live! I have water! I have jet pods! I beg you!"

It might be so. He shouted, "Freeze! Don't reel yourself in! I have to think."

"I obey."

She hung, tethered, motionless.

"You've got water and I've got food. What if you kill me and keep both?"

"My sword," she answered and produced the long knife and threw it. Startled, Gavving reached out and managed to catch it by the handle. "My bow," she said, and he had time to bed the knife in the meat before she threw him the pull-it-apart weapon. He caught that too.

Now what? She was just waiting.

"What do you want?"

"I want to join you, your people. There's nobody else."

He could festoon himself with his weapons and hers, and so what? With nothing between them but forty kilograms of smoked meat, either could snatch a weapon and kill the other at any time. He'd have to sleep sometime . . . and still she waited.

He thought suddenly, *Why not? I'm dead anyway.* He called, "Come on."

She coiled the line as she came. Gavving had been hanging on to his pack, but she hugged herself up against the meat with no thought for what it would do to her purple clothing. She worked a jet pod out of one of the dozen pockets that gave her body its shapeless, lumpy look. She set it and twisted the end. When it had expended itself there was some change in their velocity. She used another. Then another.

"Why were you carrying so many?" he asked.

"I took them from my friends."

From their corpses. Gavving turned away. Quinn Tribe now formed a single clump around—

"The Checker's Hand," said his enemy. He had trouble understanding her odd pronunciation. "They're all moored to the Checker's Hand. Good enough. Fans are edible. So is dumbo meat."

"I know that word. *Checker*: the Grad's used it, but he never tells anyone what it means."

"You should not have attacked the Checker's Hand. We tend it . . . tended it."

"Is that why you killed Jiovan? For a *fan fungus*?"

"For that, and for returning from exile. You were cast out for assassinating a Chairman."

"That's news to me. We've been in Quinn Tuft for over a hundred years."

She nodded as if it didn't matter. She was strange . . . she was a stranger. Gavving knew every man, woman, and child in Quinn Tuft. This citizen had dropped on him out of the sky, complete and unknown. He wasn't even sure he should hate her.

"I'm thirsty," he said.

She passed him a squeezegourd pod half full of water. He drank.

The clump that was Quinn Tribe seemed minutely closer. Gavving might have been imagining it. He said, "What do we do now? The way you use a jet pod, maybe you handle yourself better in the sky than we do. Can you tell us what to do next? Dalton Tuft—"

"Dalton-Quinn Tuft," she corrected him.

"Your half of the tree is probably safe, but it's being pulled out by the tide. I can't think of any way to reach it. We're lost." Then his curiosity suddenly became unbearable. "Who *are* you?"

"Minya Dalton-Quinn."

"I'm Gavving Quinn," he said for the second time in his life. The first had been at his rite of passage into adulthood. He tried again. "Who are you all? Why did you want to kill us?"

"Smitta was . . . excitable. Some of us are like that in the Triune Squad, and you were killing the Hand."

"Triune Squad. Mostly women?"

"All women. Even Smitta, by courtesy. We serve the tuft as fighters."

"Why did you want to be a fighter?"

She shook her head, violently. "I don't want to talk about it. Will your citizens accept me or kill me?"

"We're not—" killers? He'd killed two himself. It came to him that if the Grad had taught him rightly, those times when the Scientist would have whipped them both for such talk, then . . . then Minya's half of the tree, falling out from Voy, was also falling out of a drought. So. "Can I tell them this? If we can get you back to the far tuft, you'll see to it that we're made members of your tribe. It looks better if I can say that. Well?"

She didn't speak at once, and then she said, "I have to think."

The meat and the fan were passing at fair speed when Clave cast out a weighted line. He'd reserved their last pod. Another mistake, maybe. Now they'd have only one chance . . . but the dark stranger caught the line neatly and made it fast. They braced against their mutual spin.

Gavving shouted across the gap. "This is Minya of Dalton-Quinn Tribe. She wants to join us."

"Don't pull in yet. Is she armed?"

"She was."

"I want her weapons." Clave cast another line. An impressively thick bundle came back. Clave studied the haul: a knife the length of his own arm, a smaller knife, a bundle of mini-harpoons, and two of the pull-it-apart weapons, one of wood and one of metal. He preferred the look of the wooden one. The metal thing looked like it had been made from something else. By now he'd guessed how they must work, and he liked the idea.

Alfin said, "She tried to kill us all."

"True." Clave handed the Grad his last jet pod, not without reluctance. "Stop our spin. Wait. See that sheet of bark, out from us and not moving very fast? See if you can stop our spin and move us that way too."

Alfin persisted. "What are you going to do?"

"Recruit her, if she'll stand for it," Clave answered. "Seven citizens in a tribe is ridiculous."

"There isn't room to guard her."

"Where do you want to spend the rest of your life?"

The jet pod sprayed gas and seeds. The Grad said, "We won't reach the bark this way. Not enough push."

Alfin still hadn't answered. Clave told him, "Unless you've learned to like falling, I'd guess you want to live in an integral tree tuft. We now have a prisoner who lives in a tuft. We have the chance to earn her gratitude."

"Bring her in."

Chapter Nine

THE RAFT

The pond was a small, perfect sphere, twenty klomters out from the Checker's Hand: a giant water droplet trailing a tail of mist in the direction away from the sun. When the sun shone through from behind, as it did now, Minya glimpsed shadows wriggling within it.

It was going to drift past.

The ends of the tree were far away and still separating: Dalton-Quinn Tuft drifting out and west, the Dark Tuft in and east. The smoke trail that joined them was growing faint, save for dark streamers that were indecisive clouds of insects.

Something surged from the pond, and the pond rippled and convulsed in its wake. The creature was big even at this distance. Hard to judge its size, but it seemed little more than a mouth with fins. Minya watched it uneasily. It didn't seem to be coming toward them. It was flapping toward the smoke trail.

A loose cluster of citizens floated about the Checker's Hand. They couldn't all cling. There wasn't room, and the fungus wasn't holding together that well, either. They used spikes and tethers and showed a reluctance to approach Minya too closely.

The old one, Alfin, clung to the stalk. His look of terror had smoothed out, but he wouldn't talk and he wouldn't move.

The Grad studied her. He said, "Meen Ya. Have I got that right?"

"Close enough. *Minya.*"

"Ah, Mineeya—if we could reach your end of the tree, could you help us join your tribe?"

Their eyes were on her. The old one's seemed desperate. Well, it had

had to come. She said, "We have a drought. Too many mouths to feed already."

The Grad said, "Your drought's probably ending about now. There'll be water."

"You're the Quinn Tribe Scientist's apprentice?"

"That's right."

"I accept what you say. How long before that new water grows new food? In any—"

"There'll be meatbirds in the wind now—"

"I don't want to go back!" There, it was said.

Clave asked, "Did you commit a crime?"

"I was thinking about committing a crime. I would have *had* to. Please!"

"Leave it then. But if we spend our lives here, they're likely to be short. Any passing triune family would think we're some kind of mushroom tidbit. Or that flying mouth that came out of the pond a minute ago—"

"Can't we get to another tree, one with nobody in it? I know we can't go anywhere now, but if we *could* get to Dalton-Quinn Tuft, we could get to another tree, don't you think?" They weren't buying it. Distract them? "Anyway, we can do better than we're doing now. We should be eating the Hand, not clinging to it. It won't last long now that it's been picked. We need a place to moor ourselves."

She pointed. "That."

That was a ragged sheet of bark, ten meters long and half that wide, a couple of hundred meters away. Most of its spin had by now been lost to air friction. Clave—the Chairman?—said, "I've been watching it for the past day. It isn't getting any closer. Treefodder, if we could move ourselves, I'd go for the pond!"

The Grad said, "Maybe the tree left a partial vacuum. That might pull it in. We can hope."

"We can do more than that. The bark may be close enough." Minya reached for the weapons.

A hand clamped on her wrist, the fingers circling almost twice around. "What do you think you're doing?"

Long, strong fingers, and no qualms about touching another citizen. There were men like this Clave in Dalton-Quinn Tuft. They had driven Minya into the Triune Squad . . . Minya shook her head, violently. She was his prisoner, and she had come as a killer. She spoke slowly, carefully.

"I think I can put a tethered arrow into that wood."

He hesitated, then released her. "Go ahead and try."

She used Sal's metal bow. The arrow slowed as it flew, and presently drifted. She tried another. Now two arrows floated at the ends of slack lines. There were murmurs of disgust as the boy Gavving reeled the lines in.

"I'd like to try that," Clave said and took the bow. When he released it, the string brushed his forearm, and he cursed. The arrow stopped short.

Minya never dithered. She made decisions fast, important or no: that too had helped to put her in the Triune Squad. Now she said, "Hold your left arm straight and rigid. Pull as hard as you can. Swing the string a little right and you won't hit your arm. Look along the arrow. Now don't move."

She picked up the loop of line and hurled it as hard as she could in the direction of the sheet of bark. Now the arrow wouldn't pull so much weight. "Whenever you feel ready."

The arrow sped away. It ticked a corner of the bark and stayed. Clave put pressure on the line, slowly, slowly . . . it was coming . . . the arrow worked itself free.

Clave repeated the exercise with no sign of impatience. The bark was meters closer now. He reached it again and pulled line in as if he were fighting some huge meatbird.

The bark came to them. Clave fired another arrow deep into the wood. They crossed on the line. Minya noticed Alfin's shuddering breath once he was safely moored to the bark.

And she noticed Clave's, "Well done, Minya." But he kept the bow.

"We'll use the other side of the bark for privacy," Clave instructed. "Now, the bark is all we've got, so there's no point in getting it dirty. When you feed the tree, the fertilizer should go outward."

"It'll float around us," Alfin said, his first words in hours. He must have seen how they looked at him. "Yes, I *do* have a better idea. Be at the rim when you feed the tree. The spin will throw it away from us. Won't it, Grad?"

"Yes. Good thinking."

Minya chewed on fan fungus. It was fibrous and nearly tasteless, but there was damp in it, and the damp was delicious. Minya looked longingly toward the pond, which was no closer. So near, so far . . .

They had eaten the smoked dumbo meat down to the bone, to prevent its spoiling. Maybe that had been a mistake. Their bellies were full, even overfull, but they were left thirstier yet. They could die of thirst here.

Aside from that, things were going well.

The golden-haired boy, Gavving: she had made a good choice there.

Perhaps he thought he owed her his life. Perhaps it was true. Harmless as he looked, she had seen him kill twice. He'd make a better ally than enemy.

Alfin she couldn't judge. If he was *that* terrified of falling, he'd be dead soon anyway.

Merril was something else again. Legless, but she swung a fist like another woman's kick! After all she'd lived through, she must be tough. More: handicapped as she was, she'd be dead without friends. She must be well thought of, then. Minya intended to make Merril her friend.

The Grad was a dreamer. He'd never notice whether Minya was dead or alive.

Clave was the dominant male. Perhaps he still considered her an enemy. But she had brought them to this raft and let Clave take the credit. It couldn't hurt. If Clave thought he needed her, she didn't care if he trusted her.

But what else might he want of her?

Jayan and Jinny: they *both* acted as if Clave belonged to them, or vice versa. Two women sharing a man was not unheard of. They seemed to accept Clave's decisions. But would they resent a potential third? Best stay clear of Clave, if she could.

She could solve that problem, perhaps—

Merril spoke around a prodigious yawn. "Does it feel like sleeptime? I personally feel like I've been hit on the head."

Clave said, "I want someone awake at all times on each side of the tree. Is there anyone who *isn't* sleepy?"

"I'm not," said Alfin.

So Alfin and Jayan took the first day's watch. Gavving and Merril would be next, then—Minya ignored the rest. Physically and emotionally, she was exhausted. She settled for sleep, floating next to the bark, curled half into fetal position.

The sun was just passing north of Voy. She half noticed activity as citizens took their turns behind the bark, feeding the tree. Clave and Jinny slapped bugs off each other. Jayan presently disappeared around the edge. Alfin . . . Alfin was hovering next to her. He said, "Mineeya?"

She straightened. "Alfin. What do you want?"

"I want you for my wife."

Suddenly she was utterly awake. She *could not* afford enemies now. She said carefully, "I had not considered marriage." *He hadn't recognized her uniform!*

"You'd be a fool to turn me down. What better way to become one of us?"

"I will consider what you say," she said and closed her eyes.

"I'm a respected man. In Clave Tuft I supervised the tending of the treemouth."

Her arms hugged her knees and tightened her into a ball, without her volition.

Alfin's hand shook her shoulder. "Mineeya, your choices aren't wide, here on this sheet of bark. You came as a killer. Some of us may still see you that way."

He wouldn't leave her alone. Well. She tried to keep her voice cool, but she couldn't make herself uncoil, and it came out muffled. "Your argument is good. I should marry one of you. Clave is spoken for, isn't he?"

Alfin laughed. "Thrice."

"Amazing. And the Grad?"

"You're playing games with me. Consider my offer." Then he saw that she was sobbing.

Minya was horrified, but she couldn't stop. The sobs racked her like convulsions. She couldn't even muffle the sounds of distress. She wanted a man, yes, but not this man! Did she have a choice? She might find herself forced to mate this ugly, abrasive old man, only to prevent Quinn Tribe from killing her. Or she could speak of her oath to the Triune Squad and never be mated at all. It was just too much.

"I—I'll come back when you're feeling better." She heard Alfin's distress and guilt, then quiet. When she forced herself to look, she saw him weaving among the sleepers—stealthily?—to reach the far edge of the bark.

She had lost her home, her family, her friends; she was lost in the sky, cast among strangers. *Copsik!* How could he inflict such a decision on her now? *Filthy treefeeding copsik!*

The tears were drying on her face. At least no Triune Squad companion had seen her so shamed. It came to her that her tears had driven Alfin away . . . just as they had been her primary defense when she was fourteen.

But what could she *do*? She hadn't been quite fair to the old man. He had spoken a partial truth, one she'd already considered: marriage was the way into Quinn Tribe.

—And she found that she had made her decision after all.

Dared she sleep now? She must. The sun was a handsbreadth past Voy; and she curled up and slept.

When the sun neared Voy again, Minya woke. Some had the knack. Minya could tell herself when to sleep and when to wake, and she would.

She flexed muscles without moving much. She was thirsty. There was restless motion around her. The Grad seemed to be having a nightmare. She watched until he was quiet.

Alfin shook Gavving awake, then Merril. He settled down while Gavving disappeared to his post on the far side. Minya waited a little longer, for Jayan and Alfin to fall asleep.

Alfin clutched the bark with all his fingers and toes and, for all Minya could tell, his teeth. His face was pressed to the bark, denying the sky. He'd never sleep that way; but he wouldn't see her either.

She uncurled and made her way to the edge of the bark. Merril watched her go. Minya waved and pulled herself around to the smooth side of the bark sheet.

Gavving saw her coming. He started moving away from her—to give her privacy? She called, "Wait! Gavving!"

He paused.

"Gavving, I want to talk to you."

"All right." But he was wary.

She didn't want that. "I don't have any weapons," she said, and then, "Oh. I'll prove it."

"You don't have to—"

She pulled her blouse over her head and moored it to the bark. She came closer, wishing for toeholds to let her walk upright. This crawling lacked the dignity she wanted. At least she'd shed the lumpy-pregnant look of the Triune Squad.

She said, "There are no pockets in my pants. You can see that. I want to tell you why I can't go back to Dalton-Quinn Tuft."

"Why?" He was trying to keep his eyes off her breasts, on her face. "I mean, I'm willing to listen. I've got a name for asking embarrassing questions." He tried to laugh; it stuck in his throat. "But shouldn't everyone hear this?"

She shook her head. "They might have killed me, without you. Gavving, let me tell you about the Triune Squad."

"You told me. You're fighters, and you're all women, even the men."

"That's right. If a man wants to be a woman, or a woman doesn't ever want to be pregnant, she joins the Triune Squad. She can serve the tribe without making babies."

Gavving digested that. "If you don't want to make babies, they make you fight?"

"That's right. And it isn't just fighting. It's anything dangerous. This—" She pulled the rim of her pants down, and he shied, perhaps flinching at the scar. It ran half a meter from her short ribs past her hip. "Tip of a swordbird's tail. If my jet pod hadn't fired I would have been all over the sky."

She suddenly wondered if he might see it as a flaw, rather than a matter of pride. Too late . . . and better that he see it now than later.

He said, "Three of us fought a swordbird a few waketimes ago. Two came back."

"They're dangerous."

"So. You don't like men?"

"I didn't. Gavving, I was only fourteen."

He stared. "Why would a man bother a fourteen-year-old girl?"

She hadn't thought she could still laugh, but she did. "Maybe it was the way I looked. But they all . . . bothered me, and the only way out was the Triunes."

He waited.

"And now I'm twenty-two and I want to change my mind and I *can't*. Nobody changes her mind once she's on the Triune Squad. I could be killed for even asking, and I *did* ask—" She caught her voice rising. This wasn't going as planned. She whispered, "He told me I should be ashamed of myself. Maybe he'll tell. I don't care. I'm not going back."

He reached as if to pat her shoulder and changed his mind. "Don't worry about it. We can't move anyway. If we could, well, an empty tree would still be a better bet."

"And I want to make babies," she said and waited.

He *must* have understood. He didn't move. "With me? Why me?"

"Oh, treefodder, why can't you just . . . all right, who else? The Grad lives all in his head. Alfin's afraid of falling. Clave? I'm *glad* he's here, he's a good leader. But Clave's . . . type pushed me into the Triunes in the first place! He scares me, Gavving. I saw you kill Sal and Smitta, but you still don't *scare* me. I think you had to do that." She knew instantly that she'd said the wrong thing.

He started to tremble. "I didn't hate them. Minya, they were killing us! Without a word. They were your friends, weren't they?"

She nodded. "It's been a bad, bad waketime. But I'm not going back."

"All for a fan fungus."

"Gavving, don't turn me down. I . . . couldn't stand it."

"I'm not turning you down. I've just never done this before."

"Neither have I." She pulled her pants off, then didn't have a spike to tether them. Gavving saw the problem and grinned. He pounded a spike into the bark and added two tethers. One he tied to Minya's pants, then to his own pants and tunic. The other he tied around his waist.

"I've watched," he confided.

"That's a relief. I never did." She reached to touch what his pants had covered. A man had put his male member into her hand once, against her will, and it hadn't looked like this . . . except that it was changing before her eyes. Yes.

She had thought she could just let it happen. It wasn't like that. But she was used to using her feet as auxiliary hands, and thus she pulled him against her. She'd been warned against the pain; some of the Triunes had not joined while they were still virgins. She had known far worse.

Then Gavving seemed to go mad, as if he were trying to make two people one. She held him and let it happen . . . but now it was happening to her! She'd made this decision in the cool aftermath of disaster, but now it was changing her, *yes* she wanted them joined forever, she could pull them closer yet with her heels and her hands . . . no, they were coming apart . . . it was ending . . . ending.

When she had her breath back she said, "They never told me *that*."

Gavving heaved a vast sigh. "They told me. They were *right*. Hey, didn't you hurt?" He pulled away from her, a little, and looked down. "There's blood. Not a lot."

"It hurt. I'm tough. Gavving, I was so afraid. I didn't want to die a virgin."

"Me too," he said soberly.

A hand shook the Grad's ankle and pulled him out of a nightmare. "Uh! What. . . ?"

"Grad. Can you think of any reason Gavving shouldn't make a baby with a woman?"

"What then, a musrum?" His head felt muzzy. He looked around. "Who is it, the prisoner?"

Merril said, "Yes. Now, I don't see any reason to stop it, unless she's got something else in mind. I just want to keep an eye on them. But someone has to be on watch."

"Why me?"

"You were closest."

The Grad stretched. "Okay. You're on watch. I'll keep track of the prisoner."

Merril's glare lost out to a smile. "All right, that's fair."

The Grad heard voices as he poked his head around the edge of the bark. Gavving and Minya floated at the end of a tether, quite naked, talking. "A hundred and seventy-two of us," Minya was saying. "Twice as many as you?"

"About that."

"Enough to crowd the tuft, anyway. The Triune Squad isn't a punishment. It's a refuge. We *shouldn't* be having children any faster than we are. And I was good, you know. I fight like a demon."

"You need a refuge from . . . uh, this?"

A laugh. "This, and being pregnant. My mother died of her fourth pregnancy, and that was me."

"Aren't you afraid now?"

"Sure. Are you volunteering to carry it for me?"

"Sure."

"Good enough." They moved together. The Grad was intrigued and embarrassed. His eyes shifted . . . and the sky had opened a mouth.

The shock lasted only a moment. A great empty mouth closed and opened again. It was rotating slowly. An eye bulged above one jaw; something like a skeletal hand was folded below the other. It was a klomter away and *still* big.

The beast turned, ponderously, still maintaining its axial rotation. Its body was short, its wings wide and gauzy. No illusion: it really was mostly mouth and fins, and big enough to swallow their entire bark raft. Sunlight showed through its cheeks.

It was cruising the clouds of bugs left in the wake of the disaster. *Not* a hunting carnivore. Good. But wasn't there such a beast in the Scientist's records? With a funny name—

Merril touched the Grad's shoulder, and he jumped. "I'm a little worried about the bug-eater," she said. "We're embedded in bugs, have you noticed?"

"Noticed! How could I not?" But in fact he had learned to ignore them. The bugs weren't stinging creatures, but they were all around the bark raft, millions and millions of winged creatures varying from the size of a finger down to dots barely big enough to see. "We're a little big to be eaten up by accident."

"Maybe. What's happening with—?"

"I would say Gavving is in no danger. I'll keep an eye open, though."

"Good of you."

"We're being watched."

Minya's whole body convulsed in reflex terror. Gavving said, "Easy! Easy! It's only the Grad."

She relaxed. "Will they think we're doing wrong?"

"Not really. Anyway, I could marry you."

He heard an incipient stutter when she said, "Are you sure you want to do that?"

For a fact, he was not. His mind lurched and spun. The destruction of the tree had been no more disorienting than this first act of love. He loved Minya now, and feared her, for the pleasure she could give or withhold. Would she think she owned him? The lesson of Clave's marriage, what he knew of it, was not lost on him. Like Mayrin, she would be older than her mate . . .

And none of that mattered. There were four women in Quinn Tribe. Jayan and Jinny were with Clave; that left Merril and Minya. Gavving said, "I'm sure. Shall we go make an announcement?"

"Let them sleep," she said and snuggled close. Her eyes tracked a moving mouth sweeping through the clouds of bugs. It was closer now. It didn't have teeth, just lips, and a tongue like a restlessly questing snake. It rotated slowly: a way of watching the entire sky for danger.

"I wonder if it's edible," Gavving said.

"Me, I'm thirsty."

"There has to be a way to reach that pond."

"Gavving . . . dear . . . we need sleep too. Isn't your watch about over?"

His face cracked in a great yawn, closed in a grin. "I've got to tell someone."

The Grad was curled half into the fetal position, snoring softly. Gavving jerked twice on his tether and said, "We're getting married."

The Grad's eyes popped open. "Good thinking. Now?"

"No, we'll wait till sleeptime's over. It's your watch."

"Okay."

Chapter Ten

THE MOBY

oices woke her. She came awake fully alert, thirsty and nervous. *He was young. She had given him what he wanted, had virtually forced it on him. He would lose interest. He would remember that she'd tried to kill him. He'd had hours to change his mind—*

The voices were some distance away, but she heard them clearly. "—Ten years older than you, and you don't have the bride-price . . . but that's trivia. Six or seven days ago she was trying to kill us all!"

"She could have her pick of us." Clave speaking, and he was amused. "All but me, of course. You wouldn't like that, would you, loves?"

"I think it's wonderful," said Jayan or Jinny. The other twin said, "It's—hopeful."

"Gavving, you are not old enough to know what you're doing!"

"Feed it to the tree, Alfin."

Gavving noticed Minya when she stirred and pulled herself back to the bark. "Hello," he called. "Ready?"

"Yes!" Too eager? It was a little late to be coy! "What kind of ceremony will it be? We can't use mine. I left our Scientist in the Tuft." *And he'd have me killed.*

"There's that too," said Alfin. "The Scientist—"

The Grad said, "I'm the Scientist now."

Ignoring Alfin's contemptuous snort, he opened his pack and spread the contents. Packed in spare clothing were four small flat boxes of starstuff—plastic—and a flat, polished surface that was glassy, like the Chairman's mirror, but didn't reflect.

Quinn Tribe seemed as surprised as Minya. Gavving asked, "Have you been carrying that all along?"

"No, I materialized it from thin air. We Scientists have our ways, you know."

"Oh, sure."

They grinned at each other. The Grad picked up the mirror and one of the boxes. He fitted the box into the thick rim of the mirror. "Prikazyvat Menu."

The Grad's pronunciation had shifted; it was odd, archaic. Minya had heard the Dalton-Quinn Scientist speak like that. The mirror responded: it glowed like the diffuse nighttime sun, then bloomed with tiny black print.

Minya couldn't read it. The Grad apparently could. He pulled the box loose and substituted another. "Prikazyvat Menu . . . Okay. Prikazyvat Record," he said briskly. "First day since sleeptime, the first sleep following the breakup of the tree, year three hundred and seventy. Jeffer speaking as Scientist. Quinn Tribe consists of eight individuals . . . Prikazyvat Pause."

Then nothing happened, until Minya couldn't stand it anymore. "What's wrong?"

The Grad looked up. His face was a mask of pain. A keening moan tore through his throat. Crystal lenses trembled over his eyes. Tears didn't run here, without tide to pull them.

Clave put his hand on the Grad's shoulder. "Take a minute. Take as long as you need."

"I've been trying not to . . . think about it. The Scientist. He knew. He sent these with me. What good does it do if we're dying too?"

"We're not dying. We're a little thirsty," Clave said firmly.

"We're all dead except us! I feel like recording it makes it real."

Clave glared around him. The tears were about to become contagious. Jayan and Jinny were sniffling already. Minya had to remind herself that Dalton-Quinn Tuft still lived, invisibly far, somewhere.

Clave snapped, "Come on, Scientist. You've got a marriage to perform."

The Grad gulped and nodded. Teardrops broke loose and floated away, the size of tuftberries. He cleared his throat and said in a creditably crisp voice, "Prikazyvat Record. The tree has been torn in half. Seven of us survive, plus a refugee from the outer tuft. Marriage between Minya Dalton-Quinn and Gavving Quinn exists as of now. No children are yet born. Terminate." He pulled the box from the mirror and said, "You're married."

Minya was stunned. "That's it?"

"That's it. My first act as Scientist. Tradition says you should consummate the marriage the first chance you—"

"Just what have you got there?" Alfin demanded.

"Everything I need," the Grad said. "This cassette is recent records. It used to be medicine, but the Scientist ran out of room and erased it. We couldn't use that stuff anyway. Starmen got sick in ways nobody ever heard of and used medicines nobody ever heard of either . . . This cassette is life-forms, this one is cosmology, this one is old records. They're all classified, of course."

"Classified?"

"Secret." The Grad started rolling the gear in clothing again.

Clave said, "Hold it."

The Grad looked at him.

"Is there anything in your classified knowledge that we might need to know, to go on living?" Clave paused, not long enough for the Grad to answer. "If not, why should we guard that stuff, or let you carry it to slow you down?" Pause. "If so, you're hiding knowledge we need. Why should we protect you?"

The Grad gaped.

"Grad, you're valuable. We're down to eight, we can't spare even one. But if you know why we need a Scientist more than an apprentice hunter, you'd better show us now."

It was as if the Grad had been frozen with his mouth open. Then . . . he gave a jerky nod. He chose a cassette and fitted it into the rim of the nonmirror. He said, "Prikazyvat Find *moby*: em, oh, bee, wye."

The screen lit, filled with print. The Grad read, " '*Moby* is a whale-sized creature with a vast mouth and vertical cheek slots that are porous, used as filters. It feeds by flying through clouds of insects. Length: seventy meters. Mass: approx. eight hundred metric tons. One major eye. Two smaller eyes, better protected and probably near-sighted for close work, on either side of a single arm. It stays near ponds or cotton-candy jungles. It prefers to be spinning, for stability and to watch for predators, since there is no safe direction in the free-fall environment. Moby avoids large creatures and also shies from our CARMs. When attacked it fights like Captain Ahab: its single arm is tipped with four fingers, and the fingers are tipped with harpoons grown like fingernails.' "

Clave glanced over his shoulder. They had a side view of the flying mouth. Despite the swarm of insects near the raft, it was going around them. "That?"

"I'd think so."

"Carms? Captain Ahab? Whale-sized?"

"I don't know what any of that means."

"Doesn't matter, I guess. So. It's timid, and it eats bugs, not citizens. Doesn't sound like a threat."

"And *that* is why you need a Scientist. Without the cassettes you wouldn't know anything about it."

"Maybe," said Gavving, "we don't want it to go around us."

He explained, stumbling a little. Nobody laughed. Maybe they were too thirsty. Clave studied the massive bug-eater, pursed his lips, nodded . . .

Clave stood as Minya posed him, gripping the steel bow in his left hand, drawing the bowstring halfway back toward his cheek. It felt awkward. Instead of one of Minya's mini-harpoons, a meter and a half of his own harpoon protruded before him.

The moby was watching him. He waited until the creature's spin put the major eye on its far side. "Throw the line," he said.

Gavving hurled the coiled line toward the moby. Clave let it unroll for a moment, then sent the harpoon after it.

The harpoon wobbled in flight, until the trailing line dragged it straight again. With the steel bow and Clave's muscles to propel it, the massive harpoon might have flown as far as the moby. It didn't. It didn't even come close.

"Reel it in and coil the line," he told Alfin. To the others he said, "Arrows. Put some arrows in the beast. Get it mad. Get its attention."

The Grad's arrow went wide, and Clave stopped him from wasting another. Gavving's and Minya's were flying true, and each had fired another when Clave said, "Stop. We want it mad, not scared, not injured. Grad, how timid is that thing likely to be?"

"I read you everything I know."

Classified! The first chance he got, Clave was going through all of the information on all of those "cassettes." He'd make the Grad read them to him.

The moby's gauzy tail was in motion. It had spotted the harpoon's motion and was edging away. Then the first arrows reached it. One struck the fin, one a cheek, neither with any great force.

The moby convulsed. Its fins thrashed and it turned. A third arrow struck near its major eye. It turned to face them.

"Alfin, have you got that line coiled?"

"Not yet."

"Then hurry, you copsik! Are we all tethered?"

The sky had opened a mouth; it gaped and grew huge. A skeletal arm folded forward, presenting four harpoons. Alfin asked, "Do we want to hurt it now?"

Clave discarded the metal bow and took up the harpoon. "Treefodder. I want this in its *tail.*"

The moby obliged. Its tail flicked forward—and they felt the wind—as it circled to examine the situation. As the tail came into sight, Clave cast. The harpoon struck solidly in the meaty part, ahead of the spreading translucent fin. The moby shuddered and continued to advance.

The "hand" lashed forward. Gavving whooped and leapt from between closing horn harpoons, away into the sky, until his tether went taut and pulled him around the edge of the bark. Minya yelled and slashed at the "hand." "Feels like bone," she reported and swung again.

Clave snatched up another harpoon and jumped toward the tremendous face. He pricked the creature's lip before his line pulled him back. The great skeletal fingers curled around behind him. Minya's sword slashed at a joint, and one of the harpoon-fingers was flying loose.

The moby snatched its hand back fast. Its mouth closed and stayed that way. The creature backpedaled with side fins.

Gavving reeled himself back to the bark. They watched the moby turning, retreating.

The bark raft surged. The moby stopped, turned to look back. The raft was following it. It began swimming strongly against the air.

A point of sunlight blazed near the edge of the pond. Vagrant breezes rippled the surface. Shadows moved within. A distant seed pod sent a tendril growing across a klomter of space toward the water. Gavving licked his lips and yearned.

Tens of thousands of metric tons of water dwindled in their wake.

Clave was cursing steadily. He stopped, then said, "Sorry. The moby was supposed to dive into the water and try to lose us."

Gavving opened his mouth, reconsidered . . . and spoke anyway. "My idea. Why aren't you blaming me?"

"I'd still get the blame. I'm the Chairman. Anyway, it was worth a try! I just wish I knew where the beast was taking us."

They waited to learn.

Gavving's eyes traced the line of the Smoke Ring, congealing out of the background of sky into the pale blue of water vapor and distance. Toothpick splinters, all aligned, might have been a grove of integral trees. Tens of thousands of klomters beyond, a clot of white storm marked Gold. A thickening halfway down the arch toward Voy would be the far Clump.

Here were all the celestial objects a child had once wondered about. Harp had told him that he might see them someday. More practical heads had denied this. The tree moved at the whim of natural forces, and nobody left the tree.

He had left the tree, and was married, and marooned, and thirsty.

Quinn Tribe clung along the forward edge of the bark raft. At Clave's insistence they had donned their packs. Anything could happen . . . but nothing had, except that the pond continued to dwindle.

"So near and yet so far," the Grad said. "Don't we still have a few jet pods?"

"Not enough." Clave looked around him. "At least we haven't lost anyone. Okay. We're moving, and we're moving *out*; that's good, isn't it, Scientist? Thicker air?"

"Thicker anything," said the Grad. "Air, water, plants, meat, meat-eaters."

The moby was turning, swinging gradually east, and slowing. Tiring. Its fins folded against its side, presenting a streamlined egg-shape to the wind; it continued to fall outward, towing the bark raft. The pond had become a tiny jewel, glowing with refracted blue Voylight.

Clave said, "We'll cut loose as soon as we get near anything interesting. Integral tree, pond, forest, anything with water in it. I don't want anyone cutting the line too soon."

"Cloud ahead," Merril said.

A distant, clotted streamer of white fading into blue. Clave barked laughter. "How far ahead? Sixty, seventy klomters? Anyway, it isn't ahead, it's straight out from us. We're aimed almost east."

"Maybe not," said the Grad. "We're aimed out from east and moving pretty fast. Gavving, remember? 'East takes you out, out takes you west, west takes you in, in takes you east, port and starboard bring you back.' "

"What the treefodder is *that*?" Clave demanded. Gavving remembered, but he said nothing. It was "classified" . . . and the Grad had never told him what it meant.

But Minya was saying, "Every child learns that. It's supposed to be the way to move, if you're lost in the sky but you've got jet pods."

The Grad nodded happily. "We're being pulled east. We're moving too fast for our orbit, so we'll fall outward and slow down. I'll bet the moby is making for that cloud bank."

The moby's fins were spread and flapping slowly. There was nothing at all ahead of them, out to where the arch of the Smoke Ring formed from infinity. Minya moved her tether to bring herself alongside Gavving. They clung to the rim of the bark and watched the wisp of cloud out from them, and hoarded their thirst.

The sun circled behind Voy.

Again. Already they had moved many klomters outward; the day-night cycle had grown longer.

The cloud bank was growing. It was!

"It'll try to lose us in the fog," the Grad said with more hope than conviction.

The moby hadn't moved for some time. The spike that tethered the harpoon was working itself loose. Clave pounded another into the wood and wrapped the slack line around it. But the cloud bank was spreading itself across the sky.

Details emerged: streamlines, knots of stormy darkness. Lightning flashed deep within.

Jayan and Jinny took off their shirts. Alfin, enjoying the sight without questions, suddenly said, "They're right. Get our shirts off. Try to catch some of that wet."

Darkness brightened as the sun emerged below the edge of the cloud. It continued to sink. They watched the first tenuous edge of mist envelop them and began flapping their shirts. Gavving asked, "Do you feel damp?"

Merril snarled, "I feel it, I smell it, I can't drink it! But it's coming!"

Lightning flashed, off to the west. Gavving felt the mist now. He tried to squeeze water out of his shirt. No? Keep swinging it. Now? He wrung the shirt tight and tried to suck it, and got sweaty water.

They were all doing it now. They could barely see each other. Gavving had never in his life seen such darkness. The moby was invisibly far, but they felt the tugging of the tether. They swung their shirts and sucked the water and laughed.

There were big fat drops around them. It was getting hard to breathe. Gavving breathed through his shirt and swallowed the water that came through.

Light was gaining. Were they emerging from the cloud? "Clave? Maybe you want to cut that tether. Do we want to stay in here?"

"Anybody still thirsty?" Silence. "Drink your fill, but we can't live in here, breathing through our shirts. Let's trust the moby a while longer."

The pale green light was getting stronger. Through thinning fog Gavving thought he could see sky . . . green-tinged sky, with a texture to it. Green? Was this some effect in his eyes, due to the long, abnormal darkness?

Clave bellowed, "Treefodder!" and swung his knife. The harpoon tether sang a deep note, cut short as Clave slashed again. The line whipped free; the bark sheet shuddered.

Then they were out of the mist, in a layer of clear air. Gavving glimpsed the moby flapping away, free at last, and spared it only a glance. He was looking at square klomters of textured green, expanding, growing solid. It was a jungle, and they were going to ram.

Chapter Eleven
THE COTTON-CANDY JUNGLE

The carm was like nothing else in the universe. It was all right angles, inside and out; all plastic and metals, unliving starstuff. The white light that glowed from the dorsal wall was neither Voylight nor sunlight. Weirder lights crawled across the control panel and the bow window itself. The carm was mobile, where London Tree moved only with the help of the carm. If London Tree was a living thing inhabited by other living things, then Lawri saw the carm as a different form of life.

The carm was a mighty servant. It served Klance the Scientist, and Lawri. Sometimes it went away into the sky with Navy men as its masters. This time it carried Lawri too.

It grated on her nerves that she was not the carm's master here.

Seen through the picture-window bow, the jungle was green, dotted with every color of the rainbow—including overlaid scarlet dots that were heat sources. The Navy pilot pushed the talk button and said, "Let go."

Several breaths went by before Lawri heard, "We're loose."

The pilot touched attitude jet keys. A tide pulled Lawri forward against her straps. Warriors had been clinging to nets outside the hull. Now they swept into view of the bow window as the carm decelerated. A cloud of sky-blue men fell toward undulating clouds of green.

The pilot released the keys after (by Lawri's count) twelve breaths. She'd watched numbers flickering on a small display in front of him. He'd released at zero. And the jungle was no longer moving toward the carm's bow window.

"The savages haven't moved yet," he reported. He was ignoring Lawri, or trying to; his eyes kept flicking to her and away. He'd made it clear enough: a nineteen-year-old girl had no place here, no matter what the First said. "They're just under the greenery. Are you sure you want to do this?"

"We don't know who they are." The ancient microphone put a squawk in the Squad Leader's voice. "If it's just fighters, we'll retreat. We don't need fighters. If it's noncombatants, hiding—"

"Right."

"Have you found any other heat sources?"

"Not yet. That greenery is a pretty good reflector unless you're looking right into it. We can pick up some meat. Flocks of salmon birds . . . Squad Leader, I see something off to the side. Something's falling toward the jungle."

"Something like what?"

"Something flat with people clinging to it."

"I see it. Could they be animals?"

"No. I'm using science," the pilot said.

The display superimposed on the bow window showed scarlet dots clustered close. Warmer objects—salmon birds, for instance—showed more orange in that display. Ribbon birds showed as cooler: wavy lines of a darker, bloodier red . . . The pilot turned and caught Lawri looking.

"Learned anything, darling?"

"Don't call me *darling*," Lawri said primly/evasively.

"Pardon me, Scientist's Apprentice. Have you learned enough to fly this ship, do you think?"

"I wouldn't like to try it," Lawri lied. "Unless you'd like to teach me?" It was something she wanted very much to try.

"Classified," the pilot said without regret. He returned to his microphone. "That thing hit pretty hard. I'd say it's not a vehicle at all. Those people may be refugees from some disaster, just what we need for copsiks. Might even be glad to see us."

"We'll get to you when we . . . can." The Squad Leader sounded distracted, and with reason. Spindly savages taller than a man ought to be were boiling out of the green cloud, riding yellow-green pods bigger than themselves. They were clothed in green, hard to see.

There was a quick exchange of arrows as the armies neared each other. London Tree's warriors used long foot-bows: the bow grasped by the toes of one or both feet, the string by the hands. The cloud of arrows loosed by the savages moved more slowly, and the arrows were shorter.

"Crossbows," the pilot murmured. He played the jets, kicking the carm away from the fight. Lawri felt relief, until he started his turn.

"You'll endanger the carm! Those savages could snatch at the nets!"

"Calm down, Scientist's Apprentice. We're moving too fast for them." The carm curved back toward the melee. "We don't want them close enough for swordplay, not in free fall."

If the Scientist had his wish, the carm would never be used for war at all. Putting his Apprentice aboard had been a major strategic victory. He'd told her, "Your sole concern is for the carm, not the soldiers. If the carm is threatened, it *must* be moved out of danger. If the pilot won't, you must."

He had not told her how to subdue a trained fighter, nor how to fly the ancient machine. The Scientist had never flown it himself.

Savages flew toward the bow window. Lawri saw their terrified eyes before the pilot spun the carm about. Masses thumped against the carm's belly. Lawri shuddered. She would do nothing, this time. She would more likely wreck the carm than save it . . . and there would be hell to pay even if she got home to London Tree.

The savages were grouping to attack again. The pilot ignored them. He eased the carm into the midst of his own warriors.

"Nice going. Thanks," said the radio voice. Lawri watched the cloud of savages advancing.

"We're all aboard," said the Squad Leader.

The carm turned and coasted across the green cotton, southwest. Savages screamed or jeered in its wake. They hadn't a hope of catching up.

There was time to look, and time to feel rising fear. Gavving tried to take it all in before the end.

It was curves and billows of green wall spotted with blossoms: yellow, blue, scarlet, a thousand shades and tones. Insects swarmed in clouds. Birds were there in various shapes, dipping into the blossoms or the insect clouds. Some looked like ribbons and moved with a fluttering motion. Some had membranous triangular tails; some were themselves triangles, with whiplike tails sprouting from the apex.

Far to the east was a dimple in the green, funnel-shaped, perhaps half a klomter across; distances were hard to judge. Would a jungle have a treemouth? Why would it be rimmed with gigantic silver petals? The biggest flower in the universe set behind the jungle's horizon as they fell.

The storm had hidden a jungle. He'd never seen one close, but what else could it be? The moby had planned this well, Gavving thought.

Birds were starting to notice the falling mass. Motionless wings and tails blurred into invisibility. Ribbons fluttered away, as if in a strong wind. Larger torpedo-shapes emerged from the greenery to study the falling bark sheet.

Clave was snapping orders. "Check your tethers! Arm yourselves! Some of those things look hungry. We'll be shaken up when we hit. Has anybody noticed anything I might miss?"

Gavving thought he saw where they'd strike. Green cloud. Could it be as soft as it looked? East and north, far away, more darting swarms of . . . dots at this distance . . . men?

"Men, Clave. It's inhabited."

"I see them. Treefodder, they're fighting! Just what we need, another war. Now what's *that*? Grad, do you see something like a moving box?"

"Yes."

"Well?"

Gavving located a brick-shape with rounded corners and edges. It was turning in sentient fashion, moving away from the battle. A vehicle, then . . . big . . . and glittering as if made of metal or glass. Men clung to its flanks.

The Grad said, "I never saw anything like it. Starstuff."

The aft end of the box was spiky with bell-shaped structures: four at each corner and one much larger in the middle. Nearly invisible flames, not flame-colored but the blue-white color of Voy, puffed from some of the small—nostrils? The vehicle stopped its turn and surged back into the battle.

"That should do it," Clave said. Gavving turned and saw what he had been doing: setting his last jet pods to orient the turning raft, so that the underside would strike first. It seemed to be working, but the jungle was hidden now. Gavving clutched the bark, waiting. . .

His head was ringing, his right arm was banged up somehow, his stomach was trying to find something to reject, and he couldn't remember where he was. Gavving opened his eyes and saw the bird.

It was torpedo-shaped, about the mass of a man. It hung over him, long wings stretched out and motionless while it studied him with two forward-facing eyes in deep sockets. The other side of its head bore a saw-toothed crest. Its tail was a ribbed fan; the four ribs ended each in a hooked claw.

Gavving looked around for his harpoon. The crash had bounced it free of his hand. It was meters away, slowly turning. He reached for his knife instead and eased himself out of the greenery in which he was half-buried. He whispered, "I'm meat. Are you?" intending it as a threat.

The bird hung back. Two companions had joined it. Their mouths were long and blunt, and closed. *They don't bluff,* Gavving thought.

A fourth bird skimmed across the green cloud, moving fast, right at his head. He scrambled for cover as the bird dipped its tail hooks into the foliage and stopped dead. Gavving stayed where he was, half under the raft. The birds watched him mockingly.

A tethered harpoon thudded into a bird's side.

It screamed. The open mouth had no teeth, just a scissors-action serrated edge. The bird set itself whirling as it tried to snap at its belly. A third eye was behind the crest, facing backward.

The rest made their decision. They fled.

With his toes locked in branchlets, Alfin reeled the bird into knife range. By then Gavving had retrieved his own harpoon. He used it to pin the bird's tail while Alfin finished the kill, a performance that left Alfin's sleeves soaked in pink blood. A wide grin stretched his wrinkles into uncustomary patterns.

"Dinner," he said and shook his head as if he'd drunk too much beer. "I can't believe it. We made it. We're alive!"

During all the years in Quinn Tuft, Gavving couldn't remember seeing Alfin grin. How could Alfin be consistently morose in Quinn Tuft, and happy while lost in the sky? He said, "If we'd hit something solid at that speed we'd all be dead. Let's hope the luck holds."

Missing citizens emerged from the green depths. Merril, Jayan, Jinny, Grad . . . Minya. Gavving whooped and gathered her in his arms.

Alfin asked, "Where's Clave?"

The others looked around. The Grad tethered himself to the bark and jumped toward the storm, with a turning motion. "I don't see him anywhere," he shouted back.

Jayan and Jinny burrowed into the foliage. Minya called, "Wait, you'll get lost!" and prepared to follow.

"He's here."

Clave was under the bark sheet. They moved it to expose him. He was half-conscious and moaning softly. His thigh bent in the middle, and white bone protruded through skin and blood.

The Grad hung back, squeamishly; but everyone was looking at him, and it was clearly the Scientist's job. He set Alfin and Jayan to holding Clave's shoulders, Gavving to pulling on the ankle, while the Grad moved the bones into place. It took too long. Clave revived and fainted again before it was finished.

"That flying box," Alfin said. "It's coming here."

"We're not finished here," said the Grad.

The starstuff box fell toward them through the clear air between foliage and storm cloud. Men garbed in sky-blue clung to all four sides. The glassy end faced them like a great eye.

Clave's eyes had opened, but it didn't seem he understood. *Somebody* had to do something. Gavving said, "Alfin, Minya, Jinny, let's get the bark sheet out of sight, at least."

They turned it edgewise and pushed it down into the greenery. Gavving moved after it, and Minya after him, forcing their way through the thicket into dark green gloom. The foliage was dense at the surface. Underneath were open spaces and masses of springy branchlets.

"Grad?"

The Grad looked up. "Scientist."

"All right, Scientist. I need a Scientist," Alfin said. "Can you leave him for a moment?"

Clave was half-conscious and whimpering. He should be all right with two women watching him. "Call me if he starts thrashing around," he told them. He moved away, and Alfin followed.

"What's the problem?"

"I can't sleep."

The Grad laughed. "It's been a busy time. Which of us do you accuse of sleeping well?"

"I haven't slept since we reached the midpoint. We're in a jungle, we've got food and water, but Grad—Scientist, we're still falling!" Alfin's laugh surprised the Grad; it had a touch of hysteria in it.

Alfin didn't look good. His eyes were puffy, his breathing was irregular, he was as jumpy as tonight's dinner turkey. The Grad said, "You know as much about free fall as I do. You learned it the same way. Are you about to run amok?"

"Feels that way. I'm not helpless. I killed a bird that was after Gavving." And for that moment his pride was showing.

The Grad mulled the problem. "I've got a bit of that scarlet fringe from the fans. You know how dangerous it is. Anyway, you don't want to sleep now."

Alfin glanced at the sky. The starstuff box was taking its sweet time, but . . . "No."

"When it's safe. And I haven't got much."

Alfin nodded and turned away. The Grad stayed where he was. He wanted solitude to nurse his jumpy stomach. He'd never set a broken bone before, and he'd had to do it without the Scientist's help . . .

Alfin made his way back toward Jayan and Merril and Clave. He looked back once, and the Grad was looking at the sky.

He looked back again, and the Grad was gone. Jayan screamed.

The darkness and the strange, dappled shadows made them almost invisible, even to each other. "We can hide in here," Gavving said.

Minya was nodding. "Burrow deep. Stick together. What about Clave?"

"We'll have to pull him through. What looks like a good spot?"

"None of it," Jinny said. "It would hurt him."

Gavving tracked a dense cluster of branchlets back to a single spine branch. "Cut here," he told Minya.

She didn't have room to swing. She used the sword as a saw, and it took her a hundred breaths or thereabouts. Then Gavving pushed against the freed end and found that the entire cluster moved outward as a plug. He pulled himself into open air and looked about him. "Merril! Here!"

"Good," Merril called. She and Alfin towed Clave toward the opening, moving with frantic haste. The one-eyed box was too close. The occupants must be watching them by now.

They'd have to dig in fast, get lost in the deep branchlets. But— "Where's Jayan? Where's the Grad?"

"Gone," Merril puffed. "He's gone. Something pulled him down . . . into the thicket."

"*What?*"

"Move it, Gavving!"

They got Clave inside and pulled the plug-bush closed. Gavving saw that Clave's leg had been splinted with strips of a blanket and two of Minya's arrows.

"The men on the box," Minya said, "they'll follow us."

"I know. Merril, what got the Grad? An animal?"

"I didn't see. He yelled and disappeared. Jayan snatched up a harpoon and ducked through and saw people disappearing deeper in. She's trailing a line. Gavving, should we stop her? They'll trap her too."

Why did it all have to happen at once? Clave's leg, the kidnappers, the moving box—"Okay. The soldiers on the box would be fools to come in here. It's the natives' territory—"

"We're here."

"We're more desperate . . . never mind, you're right. We go after Jayan right *now*, because it gets us away from that starstuff relic. Merril—"

Would Merril slow them down? Probably not, in free fall. Okay. "Merril, me, Minya. We'll follow Jayan and see what's going on. Maybe we *can* bust the Grad loose. Jinny, you and Alfin follow as fast as you can, with Clave. Merril, where's Jayan's line?"

"Somewhere over there. Treefodder, why does it all have to happen at once?"

"Yeah."

Chapter Twelve

THE COPSIK RUNNERS

Birds were raising an incredible ruckus. Unseen hands pulled the Grad headfirst through darkness and the rich smell of alien foliage. Branchlets no longer scratched his face; there must be open space around him.

He'd had no warning at all. Hands had grasped his ankles and pulled him down into another world. His yell was strangled by something stuffed into his mouth, something that wasn't clean, and a rag was tied to hold it in. A blow on the head convinced him not to struggle.

His eyes were beginning to adjust to the gloom.

A tunnel wound through the foliage. It was narrow: big enough for two to crawl side by side, not big enough to walk in. No need, the Grad thought. You couldn't walk with no tide.

His captors were human, roughly speaking.

They were all women, though this needed a second glance. They wore leather vests and trousers, dyed green. The looseness of the vests was their only concession to breasts. Three of the five wore their hair very short, and they all had a gaunt, stretched-out look: two and a half to three meters, taller than any of Quinn Tribe's men.

They held implements: small wooden bows on wooden platforms, the bowstrings pulled back, ready to fire.

They were making good time. The tunnel turned and twisted until the Grad was entirely disoriented. His directional senses wouldn't give him an *up*. It presently opened into a bulb-shape four or five meters across, with three other tunnels leading off. Here the women stopped. One pulled the rag out of his mouth. He spit to the side and said, "Treefodder!"

A woman spoke. Her skin was dark, her hair a compact black storm cloud threaded with white lightning. Her pronunciation was strange, worse than Minya's. "Why did you attack us?"

The Grad shouted in her face. "Stupid! We saw your attackers. They've got a traveling box made of starstuff. That's science! *We* got here on a sheet of bark!"

She nodded as if she'd expected that. "An eccentric way to travel. Who are you? How many are you?"

Should he be hiding that? But Quinn Tribe must find friends somewhere. Go for Gold—"Eight of us. All of Quinn Tribe, now, plus Minya, from the opposite tuft. Our tree came apart and left us marooned."

She frowned. "Tree dwellers? The copsik runners are tree dwellers."

"Why not? You don't get a tide anywhere else. Who're you?"

She studied him dispassionately. "For a captured invader, you are most impertinent."

"I've got nothing to lose." A moment after he said it, the Grad realized how true it was. Eight survivors had done their best to reach safety, and this was the end of it. Nothing left.

She had spoken. He said, "What?"

"We are Carther States," the black-haired woman repeated impatiently. "I am Kara, the Sharman." She pointed. "Lizeth. Hild." They looked like twins to the Grad's untrained eye: spectrally tall, pale of skin, red hair cropped two centimeters from the skull. "Ilsa." Ilsa's pants were as loose as her vest. That discrete abdominal bulge: Ilsa was pregnant. Her hair was blond fuzz; her scalp showed through. Long hair must be a problem among the branchlets. "Debby." Debby's hair was clean and straight and soft brown, and half a meter long, tied in back. How did she keep it that neat?

Sharman could mean *Shaman*, an old word for *Scientist*. Could mean *Chairman*, except that she was a woman . . . but strangers wouldn't do everything the way Quinn Tribe did. Since when did the Chairman take a name?

"You haven't given us your name," Kara said pointedly.

There was something left to him after all. He said it with some pride: "I'm the Quinn Tribe Scientist."

"Name?"

"The Scientist doesn't take one. Once I was called *Jeffer*."

"What are you doing in Carther States?"

"You'd have to ask a moby."

Lizeth snapped her knuckles across the back of his skull, hard enough to sting. He snarled, "I meant it! We were dying of thirst. We hooked a moby. Clave was hoping he'd try to lose us in a pond. He brought us here instead."

The Sharman's face didn't reveal what she thought of that. She said, "Well, it all seems innocent enough. We should discuss your situation after we eat."

The Grad's humiliation kept him silent . . . until he saw their meal and recognized the harpoon. "That's Alfin's bird."

"It belongs to Carther States," Lizeth informed him.

He found he didn't care. His belly was stridently empty. "That wood looks too green to make a cookfire—"

"Salmon bird is eaten raw, with falling onion when we can get it."

Raw. Yuk. "Falling onion?"

They showed him. Falling onion was a plant parasite that grew at the forks of the branchlets. It grew as a green tube with a spray of pink blossoms at the tip. The pretty brown-haired woman named Debby assembled a handful and cut the blossom-ends off. Ilsa's sword carved the scarlet meat in translucently thin slices.

Meanwhile Kara bound the Grad's right wrist to his ankles, then freed his left. "Don't untie anything else," she warned him.

Raw meat, he thought and shuddered; but his mouth watered. Hild wrapped sheets of pink meat around the stalks and passed one to the Grad. He bit into it.

His mind went blank. You learned to put hunger out of your mind during a famine . . . but he had definitely been hungry. The meat had an odd, rubbery texture. The flavor was rich; the onion taste was fiery, mouth-filling.

They watched him eat. *I have to talk to them,* he thought hazily. *It's our last chance. We have to join them. Otherwise, what is there? Stay here and be hunted, or let the invaders catch us, or jump into the sky . . .* The man-sized bird was dwindling. Lizeth seemed content to carve slices until they stopped disappearing; Debby was now cutting the falling onions to stretch them. The women had long since finished eating. They watched with irritating smiles. The Grad wondered if they would consider a belch bad manners, and belched anyway, and had to swallow again. He'd learned while climbing the tree: a belch was bad news in free fall, without tide to bring gas to the top of the stomach.

He asked for water. Lizeth gave it to him in a squeezegourd. He drank a good deal. The falling onion had run out. Feeling pleasantly full, the Grad topped off his meal with a handful of foliage.

Nothing could be entirely bad when he felt this good.

Kara the Sharman said, "One thing is clear. You are certainly a refugee. I never saw a starving copsik runner."

A test? The Grad took his time swallowing. "Cute," he said. "Now that that's established, shall we talk?"

"Talk."

"Where are we?"

"Nowhere in particular. I wouldn't lead you to the rest of the tribe until I knew who you were. Even here, the copsik runners might find us."

"Who are they, these . . . runners?"

"Copsik runners. Don't you use the word *copsik*?" It sounded more like *corpsik* when she said it.

He answered, "It's just an insult-word."

"Not to us or them. They take us for copsiks, to work for them the rest of our lives. *Boy, what are you doing?*"

The Grad had reached for his pack with his free hand. "I am the Quinn Tribe Scientist," he said in freezing tones. "I thought I might find some background on that word."

"Go ahead."

The Grad unwrapped his reader. He had Carther States' undivided attention. The women were awed and wary; Lizeth held her spear at the ready. He chose the records cassette, inserted it into the reader, and said, "Prikazyvat Find copsik."

NOT FOUND.

"Prikazyvat Find—" the Grad said and held the reader to Kara's face. The Sharman shied, then spoke to the machinery. "Corpsik."

CORPSICLE?

The Grad said, "Prikazyvat Expound."

The screen filled with print. The Grad asked, "Can you read it?"

"No," Kara said for them all.

" '*Corpsicle* is an insult-term first used to describe people frozen for medical purposes. In the century preceding the founding of the State, some tens of thousands were frozen immediately after death in the hope of someday being revived and cured. This was found to be impossible. The State later made use of the stored personalities. Memory patterns could be recorded from a frozen brain, and RNA extracted from the central nervous system. A brainwiped criminal could thus be fitted with a new personality. No citizenship was conferred upon these corpsicles. The treatment was later refined and used by passengers and crew on long interstellar voyages.

" 'The seeder ramship *Discipline*'s crew included eight corpsicles. The memory sets were those of respected citizens of advanced age, with skills appropriate to an interstellar venture. It was hoped that the corpsicles would be grateful to find themselves in healthy, youthful bodies. This assumption proved—' I can't make sense of all that. One thing seems clear enough. A copsik isn't a citizen. He has no rights. He's property."

"That's right," said Debby, to the Sharman's evident annoyance.

So the Sharman doesn't trust me. So? "How do they find you in here? There must be cubic klomters of it, and you know it and they don't. I don't see why you fight at all."

"They find us. Twice now they have found us hidden in the jungle," Kara said bitterly. "Their Sharman is better than I am. It may be that their science enhances their senses. Grad, we would be glad to have your knowledge."

"Would you make us citizens?"

The pause lasted only seconds. "If you fight," said Kara.

"Clave broke his leg coming down."

"We make citizens only of those who fight. Our warriors are fighting now, and who knows if they will repel the corpsik runners? If we can hurt a few, perhaps they will not seek out the children and old men and women who host guests."

Guests? Oh, the *pregnant* ones. "What about Clave and the women? What happens to them?"

The Sharman shrugged. "They may live with us, but not as citizens."

Not good, but it might be the best they could get. "I can't say yes or no. We'll have to talk. Kara . . . ah!"

"What is it?"

"I just remembered something. Kara, there are kinds of light you can't see. There used to be machines that could see the warmth of a body. That's how they find you."

The women looked at each other in dread. Debby whispered, "But only a corpse is cold."

"So light little fires all through the forest. Make them check each one."

"Very dangerous. The fire might . . ." she trailed off. "Never mind. Fires go out unless fanned. The smoke smothers them. It might be possible after all, near the jungle surface."

The Grad nodded and reached for more foliage. Things were looking better. If some could become citizens, they could protect the rest. Perhaps Quinn Tribe had found a home . . .

"Three groups, and they're all going deeper. The traces are getting blurred," said the pilot's blurred voice. The carm hung behind Squad Leader Patry's shoulder, bow aimed at the jungle. "Are you going after them?"

"Groups how big?"

"Three and three and a bigger group. The big group started first. You probably won't catch them."

In the hands of Patry's men a mass of greenery rose from the rest and floated free. Patry reported, "We've found where they dug in. Okay, we're going in after them." He joined the waiting men. "Mark, take the point. The rest of you follow me. Go wide of that yellow stuff, it's poison fern."

Mark was a dwarf, the only man in London Tree who could wear the ancient armor, and thus the only possible custodian of the spitgun. Ten years ago he had tended to shy back from an attack, until he gained confidence in his invulnerability. The men had called him Tiny until Patry himself raised hell about it. Mark was born to wear the armor. He'd learned to wear it well.

He climbed past the severed bush and into the dark with London Tree's infantry behind him.

The agony was real, centered above Clave's knee, but spreading in flashes throughout his body. The rest faded in and out. He was being towed through a tunnel. Soon the Scientist's plant extracts would erase the pain. But hadn't the plants died in the drought? And . . . the tree was gone. There wasn't any Scientist, and the Grad had no drugs, and the Grad was gone too. Too few survivors followed the Grad through green gloom. Clave's pitiful remnant of a tribe was split, and there was no medicine for an injured man.

Jinny and Minya stopped abruptly, jarring his leg. The pain shouted in his brain. Then they had plunged into the tunnel's branchlet walls, and Clave tumbled in free fall, abandoned.

His tumble turned him and the dream turned nightmare. He faced a bulky, faceless silver thing. The apparition raised something . . . metal? A splinter stabbed into Clave's ribs. He plucked it out. His mind was muzzy . . . was it a thorn? The metal-and-glass creature forced itself through the tunnel wall, ignoring Clave. Acolytes followed it in, blue men carrying huge, unwieldy bows.

The pain had gone and reality was fading. Here was medicine after all.

THE INTEGRAL TREES   105

"I see you've caught up with the first group," the pilot said. "The forward group has stopped. The middle group has joined them. Maybe you should quit."

"I sent Toby back with two copsiks. The third had a broken leg, so we left him. We're almost at full strength. Let's just see what happens."

"Patry, is there something unusual about your mission?"

Classified . . . oh, what did it matter? "Catch some copsiks. Shoot some meatbirds. Collect some spices. Pick up anything scientific." That last wasn't usual. Maybe the First Officer wanted the Scientist to owe him a favor. Patry didn't comment, not with the Scientist's Apprentice listening.

"Fine. You've got copsiks. How many do you need? You don't really expect to find science here, do you?"

"There's a big group ahead. I'm going to at least look at the situation." Patry turned the volume down. Pilots tended to argue a point to death, and Patry wanted silence.

Gavving hadn't burrowed far before Jayan's line led them to a tunnel carved through the foliage. They moved faster then.

Despite its alien smell, Gavving was hungry enough to try the foliage. The taste was alien too; but it was sweet and went down well. He ate more.

In fact, he felt almost at home here. His toes thrust into branchlets and pushed him down the tunnel in remembered rhythm. Cheeping and croaking rose from thousands of unseen throats. They wouldn't be birds, this deep in the thicket; but they chirped, and if need came they could probably fly. The sound was the sound of Gavving's childhood, before the drought killed the small life throughout the tuft.

It was an effort to remember that this wasn't Quinn Tuft; that he followed enemies who knew this thicket as Gavving knew his tree.

Minya, it seemed, didn't have that problem. She was snatching handfuls of foliage, but the hand she used clutched an arrow, and her bow was in the other.

They were moving faster than the line that slithered ahead of them. Merril wound it up as they went. The coil trailed from a thumb; she used both hands to move herself. When Gavving noticed, he said, "Let me do that for a while. Eat."

"Keep yours hands free!" A little later, perhaps regretting her sharpness, she said, "I need my hands to move. You can fight with your hands. Where's your harpoon?"

"On my back. We're all right as long as Jayan is still pulling on the line," he said and immediately noticed that the line had gone slack. Gavving reached for his harpoon before he moved again.

A disembodied white arm thrust out of the tunnel wall and beckoned.

Jayan looked out through a screen of branchlets. Her voice was a hoarse and frightened whisper. "They're ahead of us."

"Where?"

"Not far. Don't take the tunnel. There's a long, straight part, then it swells out. They'd see you. Go where I go, or they'll hear branchlets breaking."

They followed her into the thicket.

Jayan had broken a trail. Twice she'd had to cut thicker spine branches. In the end they watched from behind a screen of branchlets as the Grad spoke with the weird women.

They were lean and elongated, like exaggerated cartoons of the ideal woman, or like a further stage in human evolution. They looked relaxed. So did the Grad. His feet and one hand were bound, but he was casually eating foliage while they talked. The carcass of a bird was mostly bones.

Minya's breath was warm on his shoulder. She whispered, "It looks like the Grad may have talked them around. I can't hear, can you?"

"No." There was too much birdsong . . . and an occasional crackling as someone moved, making Gavving glad for the birdsong. Still, someone was making too much noise . . .

Minya leapt through the branchlets in a hideous crackling, straight into the midst of the weird women, screaming, "Monster made of star-stuff! There!"

Gavving kept after her, ready to do battle. He'd have appreciated some warning—

The weird women didn't hesitate an instant. Five of them jumped toward other tunnels and were gone in three directions. The sixth jumped clumsily. She struck the edge of the opening and tumbled away unconscious. Had she struck *that* hard?

The Grad was struggling to free his hands. Gavving felt something sting his leg. He turned to fight.

To fight *what?* A thing of glass and metal! There were men behind it— ordinary men who floated free, sighting over their toes as they pulled huge bows taut with their hands—but they didn't fire. The thing of science pointed a metal tube at Minya, then at the Grad. Gavving's harpoon bounced off its mirror-glass face. It pointed at Gavving and stung him again.

You can't fight science, Gavving thought, and he drew his long knife and leapt at the monster. Then everything went dreamy.

"You're too deep," the pilot said. "I can't get individual readings on you. I've got a hot spot, a cluster of a dozen or so. You and the copsiks together?"

"Sounds right. We've got six copsiks here, one already tied up for us. We'll leave the one with no legs. That gives us seven total. A bunch went off through the tunnels. Can you locate them?"

"Yes. It looks like they're together again. There's you, and there's a tighter, brighter spot east of you. I'd say quit now. Kill some meatbirds on the way out."

"There's something here . . . I've got something scientific here, something I don't understand. Too scientific by half." Squad Leader Patry picked up a rectangular mirror that didn't reflect, a mirror that shone by its own light. With some trepidation he flipped an obvious switch. The light went out, to his relief. "You're right, we've got enough. We're coming out."

Chapter Thirteen
THE SCIENTIST'S APPRENTICE

L assitude . . . an odd, pleasant sensation like fizzing in the blood . . .
constriction and resistance at his wrists and ankles . . . memories
drifting into place, sorting themselves. The Grad waited until his mind
was straight before he opened his eyes.

He was bound again, tension at wrists and ankles holding his body
straight. *Getting to be a habit.* His bonds gave as he tugged at them. He
was tied to netting, facedown to a wall that was hard and cold and
smooth, and translucent to a millimeter's depth, over a gray substrate.

He'd never seen the like before; but from a distance this stuff might
look like metal.

It was the flying box. He was tied to the flying box. He twisted his
head left and saw others: Minya, Gavving, Jayan (already awake and trying to hide it), Jinny. To his right, a row of dead salmon birds and ribbon
birds, Alfin smiling in his sleep, and one of the Carther Tribe women, the
pregnant one, Ilsa. Her eyes were open and empty of hope.

A jovial voice boomed at them. "Some of you are awake by now—"
The Grad arched his back to see over his head. The copsik runner was
big, burly, cheerful. He clung to the net near the windowed end. "Don't
try to wriggle loose. You'll just get lost in the sky, and we won't come back
for you. We don't want fools for copsiks."

Minya called to him. "May we talk among ourselves?"

"Sure, if you don't interrupt *me.* Now, you're wondering what's going
to happen to you. You're going to join London Tree. There's tide when
you're in a tree. You'll have to get used to the pull on things, and balanc-
ing on your feet without falling, and so forth. You'll get to like it. You can

heat water till it boils without it spewing all over the place, and that lets you cook things you never tasted. You always know where you are, by what a thing does if you let go of it. You can drop garbage—" From below their feet came an unnerving whistling roar. The copsik runner's voice rose "—and know it won't float back at you." He stopped talking because some of his prisoners were screaming.

A tide pulled toward the Grad's feet. He was not surprised to see sky wheeling past: green forest, a strip of blue, billowing white. The textured green below his feet began to contract.

A wet wind blew past. Mist thickened around them. The panicky screams thinned to whimpers, and the Grad heard Alfin's, "Treefodder! We're going back into the treefeeding storm cloud! Whose bright idea—" and he must have silenced himself, because nobody else could have reached him.

Their guard waited for quiet. He said, "It's *very* impolite for a copsik to interrupt a citizen. I am a citizen. I'll forget it for the duration of this voyage, but you will learn. Questions?"

Minya screamed, "What gives you the *right?*"

"Don't ever say that again," the copsik runner said. "Anything else?"

Minya seemed to calm herself in an instant. "What about our children? Will they be copsiks too?"

"They'll have the chance to be citizens. There's an initiation. Some won't want to take it. Some won't pass."

Mist enclosed them completely. The copsik runner himself was half-invisible. A wave of droplets each the size of a thumb swept across them, leaving them soaked.

Nobody else seemed inclined to, so the Grad spoke. "Is London Tree stuck in this storm cloud?"

The copsik runner laughed. "We're not stuck anywhere! We moved into the cloud because we need water. After we get you home we'll move out, I expect."

"How?"

"Classified."

Gavving was just waking up. He looked left and right and found the Grad. "What's happening?"

"The good news is we're going to live in a tree."

Gavving tested his bonds while he absorbed that. "As what?"

"Copsiks. Property. Servants."

"Huh. Better than dying of thirst. Where are we? The flying box?"

"Right."

"I don't see Clave. Or Merril."

"Right again."

"I feel wonderful," Gavving said. "Why do I feel so good? Something was on those thorns, maybe, like the red fringe on a fan fungus."

"Could be."

"You're not saying much."

The Grad said, "I don't want to miss anything. If I know how we get to London Tree, maybe I could get us back. I had some Carther Tribe citizens convinced that we should join them."

Gavving turned to Minya. They spoke together at length. The Grad didn't try to hear. It was too noisy anyway. The whistling roar had faded, but the windsong was nearly as loud.

"Too many changes," Minya said.

"I know."

"I can't seem to *feel* anything. I want to get angry, but I can't."

"We're drugged."

"It's not that. I was Minya of the Triune Squad of Dalton-Quinn Tuft. Then I was lost in the sky and dying of thirst. I found you and married you and joined the Dark Tuft people. We hitched a ride with a moby and got slung into a jungle. Now we're what? Copsiks? It's too many changes. Too much."

"All right, I'm a little numb myself. We'll get over it. They can't keep us drugged forever. You're still Minya, the berserker warrior. Just . . . forget it till you need it."

"What will they do with us?"

"I don't know. The Grad's talking escape. I think we'd better wait. We don't know enough."

She found a laugh, somewhere. "At least we won't die virgins."

"We met each other. We were dying, and now we're not dying at all. We're going to a tree, and it can move itself. We'll never see another drought. It could be worse. It's *been* worse. . . . I wish I could see Clave, though."

It was dark and wet around them. Lightning marched a meandering path across the bow. The vehicle swung around. Now the wind blew up from their feet. In that direction a bushy shadow was forming.

"There," said Minya.

The roar of motors resumed.

Gavving watched for a time before he convinced himself that it was one tuft of an integral tree. He'd never seen any tree from such a vantage.

They were coming up on the in branch. The tuft was greener and healthier-looking than Quinn Tuft had been, and foliage reached farther to cover the branch. The bare wooden tail sported a horizontal platform of hewn wood, clearly a work of tremendous labor.

The roar of science-in-action wavered, rose and fell, as the flying box settled toward the platform. A great arching gap had been chopped through the branch itself, linking this platform to one on the other side. At its west end, where foliage began to sprout, a large hut had been woven.

The whistling roar died.

Then things happened fast. People left the hut on the jump. More appeared from underneath, perhaps from inside the flying box. London Tree's citizens didn't have the incredible height of the forest denizens. Some wore gaudy colors, but most wore tuftberry red, and the men had smooth faces scraped clean of hair. They swarmed to what was now the roof of the flying box and began pulling prisoners loose.

Jinny, Jayan, Minya, and the tall Carther Tribe woman were freed in turn and escorted off the roof of the vehicle. Then nothing happened for a time.

They took the women first. The drug on the needles still held him calm, but that bothered Gavving nonetheless. He couldn't see what was happening on the ledge. Presently he was pulled free of the net, lifted, and walked off the roof.

Somehow he had expected normal tides. Here was no more than a third of the tidal force at Quinn Tuft. He drifted down.

Alfin's eyes popped open when the copsik runners turned him loose. They were closing again when he hit the platform. He grunted in protest, then went back to sleep. Two men in tuftberry red picked him up and carried him away.

A copsik runner, a golden-haired woman of twenty or so with a pretty, triangular face, held up the Grad's reader and tapes. "Which of you belongs to these?" she demanded.

The Grad called from above Gavving's head; he was still falling. "They're mine."

"Stay with me," she commanded. "Do you know how to walk? You're short enough to be a tree dweller."

The Grad staggered when he touched down, but stayed upright. "I can walk."

"Wait with me. We'll use the carm to reach the Citadel."

Strangers were among them, leading Gavving and Alfin toward the big hut. The Grad's eyes followed them, and Gavving would have waved, but his wrists were still tied. A smallish, fussy-looking man in red pushed a bird's carcass into his hampered arms—it was nearly his own mass—and said, "Take this along. Can you cook?"

"No."

"Come." The copsik's hand shoved against the small of his back. He moved in that direction, toward where the fin flowered into tuft. But where were the women?

The flying box had blocked his view. Now he saw the women through the arch, on the other ledge. Minya began struggling, crying, "Wait! That's my husband!"

The drug slowed him down, but Gavving threw the bird into the copsik's arms, sending him tumbling backward under its mass, and tried to jump toward Minya. He never completed the first step. Two men stepped in from either side and caught his arms. They must have been waiting for just such a move. One clouted him across the head hard enough to set the world spinning. They hustled him into the hut.

The copsik was studying Lawri as she studied him. He was thin, with stringy muscles; three or four ce'meters taller than Lawri herself, and not much older. His blond hair and beard were raggedly cut. He was dirty from head to foot. A line of dried blood ran from his right eyebrow to the corner of his jaw. He was very much the kind of copsik who might come spinning from the sky on a sheet of bark, and hardly a convincing man of science.

But his eyes inquired; they judged her. He asked, "Citizen, what will happen to them?"

"Call me Scientist's Apprentice," Lawri said. "Who are you?"

"I'm the Quinn Tribe Scientist," he said.

That made her laugh. "I can hardly call you *Scientist*! Don't you have a name?"

He bristled, but he answered. "I did. Jeffer."

"Jeffer, the other copsiks don't concern you now. Get aboard the carm and stay out of the pilot's way."

He stood stupidly. "Carm?"

She slapped its metal flank and pronounced the syllables as she had been taught. "Cargo And Repair Module. CARM. In!"

He got through both doors and a few paces beyond, and there he stopped, gaping, trying to see in every direction at once. For the moment she left him to it. She didn't blame him. Few copsiks ever saw the interior of the carm.

Ten chairs faced into a tremendous curved window of thick glass. Images were there that couldn't be outside the glass, nor could they be reflections. They must be in the glass itself: numbers and letters and line drawings in blue and yellow and green.

Behind the chairs was thirty or forty cubic meters of empty space. There were bars set to swivel out of the walls and floor and ceiling, and numerous loops of metal: anchorage for stored goods against the jerky pull of the motors. Even so, the cabin was only a fifth the size of the . . . carm. What was the rest?

When the carm moved, flame had spurted from nostrils at the rear. It seemed that something must burn to move the carm . . . a good deal of it, if it occupied most of the carm's bulk . . . and pumps to move the fuel, and mysteries whose names he'd glimpsed in the cassettes: *attitude jet, life support system, computer, mass sensor, echo laser* . . .

The calm left by the needle had almost left his blood. He was starting to be afraid. Could he learn to read those numbers in the glass? Would he have the chance?

A man in blue lounged before the box window. A big-boned man of average height, he was still too tall for the chair; what would have been a curved head rest poked him between the shoulder blades. The Scientist's Apprentice spoke briskly. "Please take us to the Citadel."

"I don't have orders to do that."

"Just what are your orders?" Her voice was casual, peremptory.

"I don't have orders yet. The Navy may be interested in these . . . scientific items."

"Confiscate them, if you're sure enough. And I'll tell the Scientist what happened to them, as soon as I'm allowed to contact him. Will you confiscate the copsik too? He says he knows how to work them. Maybe you'd better confiscate me, to talk to him."

The pilot was looking nervous. His glance at the Grad was venomous. A witness to his discomfiture . . . He decided. "Citadel, right." His hands moved.

The girl, forewarned, was clutching the back of a chair. The Grad wasn't. The lurch threw him off balance. He grabbed at something to stop his fall. A handle on the back wall; it twisted in his hand, and dirty water spilled from a nozzle. He turned it off quick and met the girl's look of disgust.

After perhaps twenty heartbeats the pilot lifted his fingers. The familiar whistling roar—barely audible through the metal walls, but still fearfully strange—went quiet. The Grad immediately made his way to one of the chairs.

The carm was moving away from the tuft, east and out. Were they leaving London Tree? Why? He didn't ask. He was uncharacteristically leery of playing the fool. He watched the pilot's hands. Symbols and numbers glowed in the bow window and in the panel below it, but the pilot touched only the panel, and only the blue. He could feel the response in shifting sound and shifting tide. *Blue moves the carm?*

"Jeffer. How did you get those wounds?" The blond girl spoke as if she didn't care very much.

Wounds? Oh, his *face*. "The tree came apart," he said. "They do that if they fall too far out of the Smoke Ring. We had a close encounter with Gold some years ago."

That touched her curiosity nerve. "What happens to the people?"

"Quinn Tuft must be dead except for us. Five of us now." He'd accepted that Clave and Merril were gone too.

"You'll have to tell me about it sometime." She tapped what she was carrying. "What are these?"

"Cassettes and a reader. Records."

She thought it over, longer than seemed necessary. Then she reached to plug one of the Grad's cassettes into a slot in front of the pilot. The pilot said, "Hey—"

"Science. My prerogative," she said. She tapped two buttons. (*Buttons*, permanent fixtures in a row of five: yellow, blue, green, white, red. The panel was otherwise blank, save for the transitory glowing lights within. A tap of the yellow button made all the yellow lights disappear; the white button raised new symbols in white.) "Prikazyvat Menu."

The familiar table of contents appeared within the glass: white print flowing upward. She'd chosen the cassette for cosmology. The Grad felt his hands curling to strangle her. *Classified, classified! Mine!*

"Prikazyvat Gold." The print shifted. The pilot was gripped by terrified fascination, unable to look away. The Scientist's Apprentice asked the Grad, "Can you read?"

"Certainly."

"Read."

" 'Goldblatt's World probably originated as a Neptune-like body, a gas giant world in the cometary halo that circles Levoy's Star and Tee-Three, hundreds of billions of kilometers . . . klomters out. A supernova can spew its outer envelope asymmetrically due to its trapped magnetic field, leaving the remaining neutron star with an altered velocity. The planetary orbits go all to hell. In Levoy's s-scenario Goldblatt's World would have dropped very close to Levoy's Star, with its per . . . perihelion actually inside the neutron star's Roche Limit. Strong Roche tides would quickly warp the orbit into a circle. The planet would have continued to leak atmosphere to the present day, replacing gases lost from the Smoke Ring and the gas torus to interstellar space.

" 'Goldblatt estimates that Levoy's Star went supernova a billion years ago. The planet must have been losing atmosphere for all of that time. In its present state Goldblatt's World defies description: a world-sized core of rock and metals—' "

"Enough. Very good, you can read. Can you understand what you read?"

"Not that. I can guess that Levoy's Star is Voy and Goldblatt's World is Gold. The rest of it—" The Grad shrugged. His eye caught the pilot's, and the pilot flinched. He seemed shrunken into himself.

Dominance games. The Scientist's Apprentice had assaulted the pilot's mind with the wonders and the cryptic language of science. Now she was saying, "We have that data on our own cassettes, word for word, as far as I can remember. I hope you brought us something new."

A shadow was congealing in the silver fog around them. They were drifting back toward London Tree.

The carm's free-falling path had curved back toward the tree's midpoint. *East takes you out. Out takes you west*—He had a great deal to learn about flying the carm. Because he *must* learn. He would learn to fly this thing, or end his days as a copsik.

There were structures here. Huge wooden beams formed a square. Inward, four huts in a column, not of woven foliage, but of cut wood. Cables and tubes ran down the trunk in both directions, farther than the Grad could follow. A pond had touched the trunk: a silvery globule clung to the bark, and that seemed strange. A single pond in this region of mist? Men in red moved around it, feeding it water carried in seed pods. It too must be artificial.

With all these artificial structures, London Tree made Quinn Tuft look barbaric! But was it wise to—"Scientist's Apprentice, do you cut the wood for these structures from the tree itself?"

She answered without looking at him. "No. We bring it from other integral trees."

"Good."

Now she turned, startled and annoyed. He wasn't expected to judge London Tree. The Grad was developing a dislike for the Scientist's Apprentice . . . which he would try to keep in check. If she was behaving as a typical citizen toward a copsik, it augured badly for Quinn Tribe.

The trunk was coming at them, too fast. The Grad was relieved when he heard the motors start and felt the carm slowing. Those wooden beams would just about fit against the carm's windowed end . . . and that was what the pilot was doing, tapping at blue lights, fitting the window into that wooden frame. *Watch his hands!*

Chapter Fourteen

TREEMOUTH AND CITADEL

I n the large hut the women were stripped naked and examined by two women taller than humans, like Ilsa of Carther Tribe. Their long hair was white and thin enough to expose scalp. The skin seemed to have withered on their bones. Forty to fifty years old, Minya thought, though that was hard to judge; they looked so strange. They wore ponchos in tuftberry-juice scarlet, closed between the legs. Their walk was easy, practiced. Minya judged that they had spent many years in the tide of London Tree.

"It looks like people live a long time here," she whispered to Jayan, and Jayan nodded.

The supervisors would not answer questions, though they asked many.

They found dirt and wounds in plenty, but no disease. They treated Minya's bruises, and brusquely advised her to avoid offending citizens in future. Minya smiled. Offended? She was sure she had broken a man's arm before they clubbed her unconscious.

Ilsa was clearly pregnant. Jayan was also declared pregnant, to her obvious surprise, and sent off with Ilsa. Minya gripped Jinny's arm, afraid that she would attempt a futile battle for her twin.

One of the supervisors noticed Jinny's distress. "They'll be all right," she said. "They carry guests. One of the Scientist's apprentices will have to look them over. Also, the men won't be allowed near them."

The *what* would *what*? But she would say no more, and Minya had to wait.

———

The Grad watched through the small windows; the big bow window now gave on to rugged bark four ce'meters distant. Things were happening outside.

A man in a white tunic was talking to men in blue or red ponchos that fit like oversized sacks. Presently the others all launched themselves along the bark toward the lowest of the column of huts.

"Who's that?" the Grad asked.

The Scientist's Apprentice disdained to answer. The pilot said, "That's Klance the Scientist. Your new owner. No surprise there, he thinks he owns the whole tree."

Klance the Scientist was arguing with himself as he approached the carm. His white smock reached just below his hips; the ends of a citizen's loose poncho showed below. He was tall for a tree dweller, and lean but for a developing pot belly. Not a fighter, the Grad thought—forty-odd, with slack muscles. His hair was thick and white, his nose narrow and convexly curved. In a moment the Grad heard his voice speaking out of the air.

"Lawri." Sharp, with a peremptory snap in it.

The pilot tapped the yellow button and spread two fingertips apart over the resulting pattern of yellow lines *(remember)*, beating Lawri to it. The carm's two doors swung out and in.

The Scientist was already in conversation as he entered. "They want to know when I can move the tree. Damn fools. They only just finished topping off the reservoir. If I moved it now the water would just float away. First we have to—" He stopped. His eyes flickered to the pilot's back (the pilot hadn't bothered to turn around), then to the Grad, then to Lawri. "Well?"

"He's the Scientist of a ruined tribe. He carried these." Lawri held up plastic boxes.

"Old science." His eyes turned greedy. "Tell me later," he said. "Pilot."

The Navy man's head turned.

"Was the carm damaged in any way? Was anything lost?"

"Certainly not. If you need a detailed report—"

"No, that will do. The rest of the Navy party is waiting for the elevator. I think you can still catch it."

The pilot nodded stiffly. He rose and launched himself toward the twin doors. He nearly brushed the Scientist, who held his ground; pulled himself through the doors and was gone.

The Scientist tapped at yellow lights. The window sprouted a display. "Fuel tanks are damn near dry. We'll be filling them for weeks.

Otherwise . . . looks all right. Lawri, from you I do want a detailed report, but tell me now if anything happened."

"He seemed to know what he was doing. I don't love the treefeeder, but he didn't bump any rocks. The foray team brought back these, and him."

The Scientist took the plastic objects Lawri handed him. "A reader!" he breathed. "You bring me treasure. What's your name?"

The Grad hesitated; then, "Jeffer."

"Jeffer, I'll wait for your story. We'll get you cleaned up first. All these years I've been waiting for the Navy to lose my carm, reader and all. I can't tell you what it means to have a spare."

The tide was lighter. Otherwise Minya couldn't tell London Tree from her own tuft. Here was the same green gloom, the same vegetable smells. Branching tunnels ran through foliage stripped bare by passersby. The tall women led them in silence. Jinny and Minya followed. They passed nobody.

They were still naked. Jinny walked hunched over, as if that would cover her. She hadn't spoken since Jayan was taken away.

They had traveled some distance before Minya felt the wind. Minutes later the tunnel swelled out into a great cavity, lit by harsh daylight at the far end.

"Jinny. Was the Commons this big in Quinn Tuft?"

Jinny looked about her, dutifully, and showed no reaction. "No."

"Neither was ours." The cavity ran round the trunk and all the way to the treemouth itself. She could see the empty sky beyond. The shadows were strange, with the blue tinge of Voylight glaring from below. In Dalton-Quinn Tuft Voy had been always overhead.

All that foliage had had to be torn out. Weren't the copsik runners afraid of killing the tree? Or would they only move to another?

Thirty or forty women had formed a line for food. Many were attended by children: three years old and younger. They ignored Minya and Jinny as they were marched past, toward the treemouth.

"Tell me what bothers you most," Minya said.

Jinny didn't answer for several breaths. Then, "Clave."

"He wasn't on the box. He must be still in the jungle. Jinny, his leg has to heal before he can do anything."

"I'll lose him," Jinny said. "He'll come, but I'll lose him. Jayan's got his child. I won't be his anymore."

"Clave loves you both," Minya said, though she hadn't the remotest idea how Clave actually thought.

Jinny shook her head. "We belong to the copsik runners, the men. Look, they're already here."

Minya frowned and looked about her. Was Jinny imagining . . . ? Her eye picked up something in the green curve that roofed the Commons, a dark shape hidden in shadow and foliage. She found two more . . . four, five . . . men. She said nothing.

They were led to the edge of the treemouth, almost beneath the great reservoir mounted where branch merged into trunk. Minya looked downslope. Offal, garbage . . . two bodies on platforms, completely covered in cloth. When she turned away, their escorts had stepped out of their ponchos.

They took their charges by the arms and led them beneath the huge basin. One of the supervisors heaved on a cord, and water poured forth like a flood in miniature. Minya shuddered with the shock. The women produced lumps of something, and one began rubbing it over Minya's body, then handed it to her.

Minya had never experienced soap before. It wasn't frightening, but it was strange. The supervisors soaped themselves too, then let the flood pour forth again. Afterward they dried themselves with their garments, then donned them. They handed scarlet ponchos to Jinny and Minya.

The suds left her skin feeling strange, tingly. Minya had little trouble stepping into the poncho despite its being sealed between the legs; but it did seem uncomfortably loose. Was it made for the elongated jungle people? It bothered her more that she wore tuftberry-red. Copsik-red here, citizen-red at home. She had worn purple too long.

Their escorts abandoned them at the serving table. Four cooks—more of the elongated women—ladled a stew of earthlife vegetables and turkey meat into bowls whose rims curved inward. Minya and Jinny settled themselves into a resilient arm of foliage and ate. The fare was blander than what she was used to in Dalton-Quinn Tuft.

Another copsik settled beside them: two and a half meters tall, middle-aged, walking easily in London Tree's tide. She spoke to Jinny. "You look like you know how to walk. You from a tree?"

Jinny didn't answer. Minya said, "A tree that came apart. I'm Minya Dalton-Quinn. This is Jinny Quinn."

The stranger said, "Heln. No last name, now."

"How long have you been here?"

"Ten years, or something like. I used to be Carther. I keep expecting . . . well."

"Rescue?"

Heln shrugged. "I keep thinking they'll try *something*. Of course they couldn't, then. Anyway, I've got kids now."

"Married?"

Heln looked at her. "They didn't tell you. Okay, they didn't tell me either. The citizens *own* us. Any man who wants you owns you."

"I . . . thought it was something like that." She moved her eyes only, toward the shadows at the outskirts. And they'd watched her naked— "What are they doing, making their selections?"

"That's right." Heln looked up. "Eat faster if you want to finish." Two shadowy men were coming toward them, drifting at leisure along the interlocked branchlets that formed the ground.

Minya watched them while she continued eating. They paused several meters away, waiting. Their ponchos fit more closely than hers and were a riot of colors. They watched the women and talked. Minya heard "—one with the bruises broke Karal's—"

Heln ignored them. Minya tried to do the-same. When her bowl was empty, she asked, "What do we do with these?"

"Leave them," Heln said. "If no man takes you, take it back to the cooks. But I think you'll have company. You look like citizens; the men like that." She grimaced. "They call us 'jungle giants.' "

Too many changes. Three sleeptimes ago, no man in her local universe would have dared to touch her. What would they do to her if she resisted? What would Gavving think of her? Even if they could escape later—

If she strolled toward the treemouth now, Minya thought, would anyone stop her? She'd be "feeding the tree." A short sprint past the treemouth would put her into the sky before anyone could react. She'd been lost in the sky and survived . . .

But how could she alert Gavving to jump too? He might not have the chance. He might think it was a mad idea.

It *was* mad. Minya dropped it. And the men strolled over to join them.

The Grad's first meal at the Citadel was simple but strange. He was given a gourd with a fair-sized slot cut in it, and a squeezegourd for liquids, and a two-pronged wooden fork. Thick stew, shipped from the out tuft, had cooled by the time it reached the Citadel. He could recognize two or three of the ingredients. He wanted to ask what he was eating, but it was Klance who asked the questions.

One of the first was, "Were you taught medicine?"

"Certainly." The word was out of his mouth before his mind quite caught up.

Lawri looked dubious. Klance the Scientist laughed. "You're too young to be so sure. Have you worked with children? Injured hunters? Sick women? Women carrying guests?"

"Not with children. Women with guests, yes. Injured hunters, yes. I've treated malnutrition sicknesses. Always with the Scientist supervising." His racing mind told him what to tell Klance. In fact he had worked with children; he had inspected a pregnant woman, once; he had set the bone in Clave's leg. *The old copsik runner won't let me practice on citizens, will he? He'll try me out on copsiks first! My own people . . .*

Klance was saying, "We don't get malnutrition here, thank the Checker. How did you come to be found in a jungle?"

"Inadvertently." Eating strange food with strange implements in free fall took concentration. Not letting it make him sick took a distraction; the Grad was glad for the chance to talk. He ate what he was given and told the tale of Quinn Tribe's destruction.

The Scientist interrupted with questions about Quinn Tuft, treemouth tending, musrums, flashers, the dumbo, the moby, the insects at the tree median. Lawri seemed fascinated. She burst in only once, demanding to know how one fought swordbirds and triunes. The Grad referred her to Minya and Gavving. Maybe she'd let them know where he was.

The meal ended with a bitter black brew which the Grad refused; and he continued to talk. He was hoarse when he finished.

Klance the Scientist puffed at his pipe—shorter than the one the Quinn Chairman had used—and clouds of smoke drifted sluggishly about the room and out. The room was more a cage of timber than a hut; there were narrow windows everywhere, and boards would swing to cover them. Klance said, "This giant mushroom had hallucinogenic properties, did it?"

"I don't know the word, Klance."

"The red fringe made you feel strange but nice. Maybe that was the reason they were protecting it?"

"I don't think so. There were too many of those fan fungi. This one was big and nicely formed and had a special name."

"The Checker's Hand. Jeffer, have you ever heard that word *Checker* before?"

"My grandmother used to say, 'Treefeeder must think he's the Checker himself,' when she was mad at the Chairman. I never heard anyone else—"

The Scientist reached for the Grad's reader and one of his own cassettes. "I think I remember . . ."

CHECKER. Officer entrusted with seeing to it that one or a group of citizens remains loyal to the State. The Checker's responsibility includes the actions, attitudes, and well-being of his charges. The Checker aboard *Discipline* was the recording of Sharls Davis Kendy in the ship's master computer.

"This is strictly starman stuff. Hmp. The State . . . it took me four days to read the insert on the State. Have you seen it?"

"Yes. Strange people. I did get the feeling that they lived longer than we do."

Klance snorted. "Your scientist never tumbled to that? They had shorter years. They used one whole cycle of their sun for their year. We only use half a circle, but it's still about seven-fifths of a State year. The truth is, we live a little longer than they do, and grow up more slowly too."

To hear his teacher so slighted set the Grad's ears burning. He barely heard Klance add, "All right, Jeffer, from now on you must think of me as your Checker."

"Yes, Scientist."

"Call me Klance. How do you feel?"

The Grad answered with careful half-truth. "I'm clean, fed, rested, and safe. I'd feel even better if I knew the rest of Quinn Tribe was all right."

"They'll get showers and food and drink and clothing. Their children may become citizens. The same goes for you, Jeffer, whether or not I keep you here; but I think you'd be bored in the tuft."

"So do I, Klance."

"Fine. For the time being I have two apprentices."

Lawri exploded. "It's unheard of for a freshly claimed copsik to be at the Citadel at all! Won't the Navy—"

"The Navy can feed the tree. The Citadel is mine."

Chapter Fifteen

LONDON TREE

G avving was on the bicycle with three other copsiks.

There wasn't tide enough to pull him against the pedals. Straps ran from the belt around his waist to the bicycle frame. Forcing his legs down against the pedals pushed him up against the belt. After the first session he'd thought he was crippled for life. The endless passage of days had toughened him; his legs no longer hurt, and the muscles were hard to the touch.

The bicycle gears were of old metal. They squealed as they moved and gave forth a scent of old animal grease. The frame was massive, of cut wood. There had been six sets of gears once; Gavving could see where two had been ripped out.

The frame was anchored to the trunk where the tuft grew thin. Foliage grew around the copsiks. Surrounded by sky, with most of the tuft below them, they could still snatch and eat a handful while pedaling. They worked naked, with sweat pooling on their faces and in their armpits.

High up along the trunk, a wooden box descended slowly. A similar box had risen almost out of sight.

Gavving let his legs run on while he watched the elevator descend. The mindless labor let his eyes and ears and mind run free.

There were other structures around the trunk. This level was used for industry, and here were all the men. Man's work and woman's work never seemed to intersect in London Tree, at least not for copsiks. Sometimes children swarmed through or watched them with bright, curious eyes. Today there were none.

The citizens of London Tree must have kept copsiks for generations. They were skilled at it. They had chopped Quinn Tribe apart. Even if opportunity came to run, how would he find Minya?

Gavving, pumping steadily, watched storms move sluggishly around a tight knot on the eastern arm of the Smoke Ring. Gold was nearer than he had ever seen it, save for that eerie time when he was a child, when Gold had passed so near and everything had changed.

The jungle hovered hundreds of klomters beyond the out tuft: a harmless-looking green puffball. *How are you doing, Clave? Did that broken leg save your freedom? Merril, were those shrunken legs finally good for something? Or have you become copsiks among the jungle people, or are you dead?*

Over the past eighty-five days or so, twenty sleeps, the tree had drifted to the eastern fringes of the cloud bank. He'd been told, during the trip across the sky to London Tree, that the tree could move by itself. He had seen no evidence of it. Rain swept across them from time to time . . . surely the tree had collected enough water by now . . .

The elevator had settled into its slot and was releasing passengers. Gavving and the others stopped pedaling. "Navy men," Horse puffed. "Come for the women."

Gavving said, "What?"

"Citizens live in the out tuft. When you see a boxful come down and it's all men, they're come for the women."

Gavving looked away.

"Nine sleeps," said Horse. He was in his fifties, three ce'meters shorter than Gavving, with a bald, freckled head and tremendously strong legs. He had driven the bicycles for two decades. "Forty days till we meet the women. You wouldn't believe how rancy I get thinking about it." By now Gavving was strangling the handbar. Horse saw the muscles standing out along his arms and said, "Boy, I forgot. I was never married, myself. I was born here. Failed the test when I was ten."

Gavving forced himself to speak. "Born here?"

Horse nodded. "My father was a citizen; at least mother always said so. Who ever knows?"

"Seems likely. You'd be taller if—"

"Na, na, the jungle giants' kids aren't any taller than the citizens."

So: children raised in the jungle grew taller, without tide to compress them. "What are the tests like?"

"We're na supposed to say."

"Okay."

The supervisor called, "Pedal, you copsiks!" and they did. More passengers were coming down. Over the squeal of the gears Horse said, "I flunked the obedience test. Sometimes I'm glad I didn't go."

Huh? "Go?"

"To another tree. That's where you go if you pass the tests. Heh, you are green, aren't you? Did you think your kids would stay as citizens if they passed the tests?"

"That's . . . yes." He hadn't been told that; he'd been allowed to assume it. "There are other trees? How many? Who lives in them?"

Horse chuckled. "You want to know everything at once? I think it's four bud trees now, settled by any copsik woman's kid who passes the tests. London Tree goes between them, trading for what they need. Any man's kid has the same chance as a citizen's, because nobody ever knows, see? I thought I wanted to go, once. But it's been thirty-five years.

"I did think I'd be picked for service in the outfit. I should've been. I'm second-generation . . . and when they turned me down for that, I damn near lost my testes for swatting a supervisor. Jorg, there"—Horse indicated the man pedaling in front of him—"he did. Poor copsik. I don't know what the gentled ones do when the Holidays come."

Gavving still hadn't learned to shave without cutting himself. It was not his choice. All copsiks shaved. He had seen no man wearing a beard in London Tree, save one; and that one was Patry, a Navy officer. "Horse, is that why they make us shave? So the gentled ones won't be quite so obvious?"

"I never thought of that. Maybe."

"Horse . . . you must actually have seen the tree move."

Horse's laughter brought a supervisor's head around. He lowered his voice. "Did you think it was just a story? We move the tree about once a year! I've been on water details too, to feed the carm."

"What's it like?"

"It's like the tide goes slantwise. Going to the treemouth is like climbing a hill. You don't want any hunting parties out when it happens, and you have to tilt the cookpot. The whole trunk of the tree bends a little . . ."

"Lawri," said the Grad, "trouble."

Lawri glanced back. The pond clung to the bark, a flattened hemisphere. The Grad had run the hose into the water. Now the water was flowing up the outside of the hose, forming a collar.

"Don't worry about it. Just get to the bicycle and pedal," Lawri told him. "And don't call me that."

The Grad strapped himself to the saddle and started the pedals turning. The gears moved a pump. It was all starstuff, metal, discolored with age. The collar of water shrank as water was sucked into the hose.

It was strange work for the Quinn Tuft Scientist, or for the London Tree Scientist's Apprentice, for that matter. Hadn't Klance suggested that he would be better off than the standard run of copsiks? He wondered what Gavving was doing now. Probably worrying about his new and alien wife . . . and with reason.

Water spurted from the hose as Lawri carried it into the carm. The Grad couldn't see what she was doing in there. He pedaled.

In Klance's presence the Grad was Lawri's equal. Otherwise Lawri treated him as a copsik, a spy, or both. He was clean, fed, and clothed. Of the rest of Quinn Tribe he had not even rumors. He and Lawri and the Scientist explored the cassettes together for old knowledge, and that was fascinating enough. But he was learning nothing that would rescue Quinn Tribe.

It was night. Both Voy and the sun were hidden behind the in tuft. In the peculiar light that remained, two faint streamers of blue light fanned out from the tuft. If he stared at them they went away. He could catch them by looking near them. He could almost imagine human shapes pouring as smoke from a squeeze-gourd. To starboard, the Blue Ghost. To port, even fainter, the Ghost Child.

The Scientist (*the* Scientist) had told him that they were discharges of peculiar energies from the poles of Voy itself. The Scientist had seen them when he was younger, but the Grad had never been able to see them, not even from the midpoint of Dalton-Quinn Tree.

He was sweating. He watched the elevator climb the tree to its housing. A Navy man and two copsiks emerged. None were jungle giants; he had never seen a first-generation copsik at the Citadel, barring himself. They entered the Scientist's laboratory complex and presently left carrying the dishes from brunch.

Lawri called from the carm. "The tank's full."

The Grad moved with a briskness he didn't feel, unfastening the belt, jerking the hose free of the pond. There were lineholds, wooden hoops, set in the bark to crisscross the citadel region. The Grad used them to make his way toward the carm, calling ahead of him, "Can I help?"

"Just coil the hose," Lawri answered.

She hadn't yet let him into the carm during this operation. The hose must lead, somehow, into a water tank in the carm. They filled it repeatedly, and a couple of days later they would fill it again.

The Grad coiled the hose as he moved toward the carm. He heard cursing from within. Then Lawri called, "I can't move this damn fitting."

The Grad joined her at the doors. "Show me." That easy?

She showed him. The hose attached to a thing on the back wall, with a collar. "It has to be turned. That way." She rotated her hands.

He set his feet, grasped the metal thing, put his back into it. The collar lurched. Again. He turned it until it was loose in his hands, and kept turning. The hose came loose. A mouthful of water spilled out. Lawri nodded and turned away.

"Scientist's Apprentice? Where does the water *go*?"

"It's taken apart," she said. "The skin of the carm picks up sunlight and pumps the energy into the water. The water comes apart. Oxygen goes in one tank and hydrogen goes in the other. When they come together in the motors, the energy comes back and you get a flame."

He was trying to imagine water coming apart, when Lawri asked, "Why did you want to know?"

"I was a Scientist. Why did you tell me?"

She sent herself skimming across the seats and settled herself at the controls. The Grad moored the coiled hose to fixtures in the cargo area.

The tank must be behind the wall. The carm had been nearly out of fuel . . . which came in two "flavors"? There must be fuel by now; the artificial pond was visibly shrunken.

Lawri tapped the blue button as he came up behind her. The display she'd been studying disappeared before he could see it. The Grad had half forgotten his question when she turned to him and said, "The Scientist quizzes me like that. Since I was ten. If I can't answer I get some dirty job. But I don't like having my buttons pushed, Jeffer, and that information is classified!"

"Scientist's Apprentice, who is it that calls you Lawri?"

"Not you, copsik."

"I know that."

"The Scientist. My parents."

"I don't know anything about marriage customs here."

"Copsiks don't get married."

"You're not a copsik. Would your husband call you Lawri?"

The airlock thumped, and Lawri turned in some relief. "Klance?"

"Yes. Put that display on again, will you, Lawri?"

She looked at the Grad, then back at Klance.

"Now," said the Scientist. Lawri obeyed. She'd made her point: she'd show scientific secrets to a copsik, but only under protest. Dominance games again. If she really cared, she would have removed the hose herself.

The blue lights and numbers had to do with what moved the carm, as green governed the carm's sensing instrument and yellow moved the doors and white read the cassettes . . . and more. He was sure that they all did more than he knew. And red? He'd never seen red.

Every time he saw this display, certain numbers were larger. Now they read O_2: 1,664. H_2: 3,181. Klance was nodding in approval. "Ready to go anytime. Still, I think we'll feed in the rest of the reservoir. Jeffer, come here." He cut the blue display and activated the yellow. "This number tells you if there's a storm coming, if you watch it."

"What is it?"

"It's the external air pressure."

"Can't you *see* a storm coming?"

"Coming, yes. Forming, no. If the pressure goes up or down fast, over a day or so, there's a storm forming. Lets you impress hell out of the citizens. This is classified, of course."

The Grad asked, "Where does the tree go from here?"

"Out of this rain. Then on to Brighton Tree; they haven't seen us in a while. Grad, you'll get a good chance to look the bud colonies over and pick and choose among them."

"For what, Klance?"

"For your children, of course."

The Grad laughed. "Klance, how am I going to have children if I spend my life at the Citadel?"

"Don't you know about the Holidays?"

"I never heard of them."

"Well, every year's-end, when Voy crosses in front of the sun, the copsiks all get together at the treemouth. It's holiday for six days while the copsiks mate and gossip and play games. Even the food comes from the out tuft. The Holidays start in thirty-five days."

"No exceptions? Not even for a Scientist's Apprentice?"

"Don't worry, you'll go," Klance chuckled.

Lawri had turned away, showing her bowed back, the wealth of blond hair floating around her. He wondered then: *How would Lawri have children?* The Scientist didn't seem to be her lover; the Grad knew that he imported copsik women from the in tuft. If she never left the Citadel—How would Lawri ever find a man?

Me?

A copsik could have children, but Lawri could not. It couldn't be helped. He dared not think of Lawri as other than an enemy.

There was flesh against her as she woke. It happened often. Minya shifted position and refrained from wrapping her arms around the citizen who slept beside her. She might hurt him.

Her motion wakened him. He turned carefully—his arm was bound with cloth against his torso—and said, "Good morning."

"Good morning. How's your arm?" She searched her memory for his name.

"You did a good job on it, but it'll heal."

"I wondered why you came looking for me, given that I broke it."

He scowled. "You stuck in my head. While Lawri was setting the bone I kept seeing your face, two ce'meters away with your teeth bared like you were going for my throat next . . . yeah. So I'm here." The scowl relaxed. "Under, eh, different circumstances."

"Better now?"

"Yes."

His name surfaced. "Karal. I don't remember a Lawri."

"Lawri's not a copsik. She's the Scientist's Apprentice—one of his apprentices, now—and she treats Navy men if we get hurt."

One of his apprentices? Minya gambled. "I hear the new one is a copsik."

"Yes. I saw him from a distance, and he's not a jungle giant. One of yours?"

"Maybe." She stood, donned her poncho. "Will we meet again?"

He hesitated—"Maybe"—and added, "The Holidays are eight sleeps away."

She let her smile show through. *Gavving!* "How long do they last?"

"Six days. And all work stops."

"Well, I have to get to work now."

Karal disappeared into the foliage while Minya strolled into the Commons. She missed Dalton-Quinn Tuft. She'd grown almost used to the obtrusive differences: the huge Commons, the omnipresent supervisors, her own servility. But little things bothered her. She missed cupvines, and copter plants. Nothing grew here but the foliage and the carefully cultivated earthlife, beans and melons and corn and tobacco, as thoroughly regimented as herself.

A dozen copsiks were up and stirring. Minya looked for Jinny and spotted her at the treemouth, just her head showing above the foliage as she fed the tree.

The schedules were loose. If you arrived late, you would work late. Beyond that, the supervisors didn't care much ... but Minya cared! She would do nothing badly. She would be an exemplary copsik, until the time came to be something else.

She tried to remember nuances of Karal's speech. A citizen's accent was odd, and she had been practicing it.

It had been strange for Minya. Her instincts were at war: a conditioned reflex that resisted sexual assault as blasphemy incarnate, versus the will to live.

Survival won. She would do nothing badly!

Jinny stood up, set her poncho in order, then sprinted west.

Minya screamed. She was too far to do anything but shout and point as she ran. A pair of supervisors, much closer, saw what was happening and ran too.

Jinny plunged through a last screen of foliage, into the sky.

Minya kept running. The supervisors (Haryet and Dloris, hard-faced jungle giants of indeterminate age) had reached the edge. Dloris swung a weighted line round her head, twice and out. Haryet waited her turn, then swung her own line while Dloris pulled. The line resisted as she pulled it in, then gave abruptly. Dloris reeled back, off balance.

Minya reached the edge in time to see the stone at the end of Haryet's line spin round Jinny. Dloris threw her line while Jinny was still fighting Haryet's. Jinny thrashed, then went limp.

Haryet pulled her in.

Jinny huddled on her side, face buried in her arms and knees. By now they were surrounded by copsiks. While Dloris gestured them away, Haryet rolled Jinny on her back, groped for her chin, and pulled her face out of the protection of her arms. Jinny's eyes stayed clenched like fists.

Minya said, "Madam Supervisor, a moment of your attention."

Dloris looked around, surprised at the snap in Minya's voice. "Later," she said.

Jinny began to sob. The sobs shook her like Dalton-Quinn Tree had shaken the day it came apart. Haryet watched for a time, impassively. Then she spread a second poncho over the girl and sat down to watch her.

Dloris turned to Minya. "What is it?"

"If Jinny tries this again and succeeds, would it reflect badly on you?"

"It might. Well?"

"Jinny's twin sister is with the women who carry guests. Jinny has to see her."

"That's forbidden," the jungle giantess said wearily.

When citizens talked like that, Minya had learned to ignore them. "These girls are twins. They've been together all their lives. They should be given some hours to talk."

"I told you, it's forbidden."

"That would be your problem."

Dloris glared in exasperation. "Go join the garbage detail. No, wait. First talk to this Jinny, if she'll talk."

"Yes, Supervisor. And I'd like to be checked for pregnancy, at your convenience."

"Later."

Minya bent to speak directly into Jinny's ear. "Jinny, it's Minya. I've talked to Dloris. She'll try to get you together with Jayan."

Jinny was clenched like a knot.

"Jinny. The Grad made it. He's at the Citadel, where the Scientist lives."

Nothing.

"Just hang on, will you? Hang on. Something will happen. Talk to Jayan. See if she's learned anything." Treefodder, there must be something she could say . . . "Find out where the pregnant women are kept. See if the Grad ever comes down to examine them. He might. Tell him we're hanging on. Waiting."

Jinny didn't move. Her voice was muffled. "All right, I'm listening. But I can't stand it. I can't."

"You're tougher than you think."

"If another man picks me, I'll kill *him*."

Some of them like women who fight, Minya thought. She said instead, "Wait. Wait till we can kill them all."

After a long time, Jinny uncurled and stood up.

Chapter Sixteen

RUMBLINGS OF MUTINY

G avving woke to a touch on his shoulder. He looked about him without moving.

There were three tiers of hammocks, and Gavving's was in the top layer. The daylit doorway made a black silhouette of a supervisor. He seemed to have fallen asleep standing up: easy enough in London Tree's gentle tide. In the dimness of the barracks, Alfin clung to Gavving's hammock-post. He spoke in a whisper that wanted to shout in jubilation.

"They've put me to work at the treemouth!"

"I thought only women did that," Gavving said without moving at all. Jorg snored directly below him—a "gentled" man, pudgy and sad, and too stupid to spy on anyone. But the hammocks were close-packed.

"I saw the farm when they took us for showers. There's a lot they're doing wrong. I talked to a supervisor about it. He let me talk to the woman who runs the farm. Kor's her name, and she listens. I'm a consultant."

"Good."

"Give me a couple of hundred days and I might get you in on it too. I want to show what I can do first."

"Did you get a chance to speak to Minya? Or Jinny?"

"Don't even think it. They'd go berserk if we tried to talk to the women."

To be a treemouth tender again . . . seeing Minya, but not allowed to speak to her. Meanwhile, maybe Alfin could carry messages, if he could be talked into taking the risk. Gavving put it out of his mind. "I learned something today. The tree does move, and it's the carm, the flying box, that moves it. They've settled other trees—"

"What does that do for us?"

"I don't know yet."

Alfin moved away to his hammock.

Patience came hard to Gavving. In the beginning he had thought of nothing but escape. At night he could drive himself mad with worry over Minya . . . or he could sleep, and work, and wait, and learn.

The supervisors wouldn't answer questions. What *did* he know, what *had* he learned? The women farmed the treemouth and cooked; pregnant women lived elsewhere. Men tended machinery and worked with wood, here in the upper reaches of the tuft. The copsiks talked of rescue, but never of revolt.

They wouldn't revolt now anyway, with the Holidays eight sleeps away. Afterward, maybe; but wouldn't the Navy know that from experience? They'd be ready. The supervisors were never without their truncheons, sticks of hardwood half a meter long. Horse said the women supervisors carried them too. During an insurrection the Navy might be given those instead of swords . . . or not.

What else? Bicycle works wore out. Damaging them—damaging anything made of starstuff—would hurt London Tree, but not soon. Here was where the elevators could be sabotaged; but the Navy could still put down a revolt by using the carm.

The carm did everything. It lived at the tree's midpoint, where the Scientist kept his laboratory. Was the Grad there? Was he planning something? He'd seemed determined to escape, even before they reached London Tree.

Was any of that worth anything? *If we were together! We could plan something—*

He had learned that he might spend the rest of his life moving an elevator or pumping water up the trunk. He had not had an allergy attack since his capture. It was not a bad life, and he was dangerously close to becoming used to it. In eight sleeps he would be allowed to see his own wife.

Carther States was setting fires halfway around the biggest flower in the universe.

Clave flapped his blanket at the coals. His arms were plunged elbow-deep in the foliage to anchor him. His toes clutched the edge of the blanket. He undulated his legs and torso to move the blanket in waves, exerting himself just enough to keep the coals red.

Eighty meters away, a huge silver petal gradually shifted position, turning to catch the sun at a sharper angle.

A fire would die in its own smoke, without a breeze, and breezes were rare in the jungle. The day was calm and bright. Clave took it as a chance to exercise his legs.

There was a knot as big as a boy's fist where the break had been on his thighbone. His fingers could feel the hard lump beneath the muscles; his body felt it when he moved. Merril had told him it couldn't be seen. Would she lie to spare him? He was disinclined to ask anyone else.

He was disfigured. But the bone was healing; it hurt less every day. The scar was an impressive pink ridge. He exercised, and waited for war.

There had been tens of days of sleep merging into pain. He'd seen spindly, impossibly tall near-human forms flitting about him at all angles, green shapes fading like ghosts into a dark green background, quiet voices blurred in the eternal whisper of the foliage. He had thought he was still dreaming.

But Merril was real. Homely, legless Merril was entirely familiar, entirely real, and mad as hell. The copsik runners had taken everyone. "Everyone but us. They left us. I'll make them sorry for that!"

He had taken little notice in the pain of a healing bone and the sharper ache of his failure. A hunt leader who had lost his team, a Chairman who had lost his tribe. Quinn Tribe was dead. He told himself that depression always followed a serious wound. He stayed where he was, deep in the dark interior of the jungle, for fear that fluff might grow in the wound; and he slept. He slept a great deal. He didn't have the will to do more.

Merill tried to talk to him. Things weren't that bad. The Grad had impressed the Carthers. Merril and Clave were welcome in the tribune . . . though as copsiks.

Once he woke to find Merril jubilant. "They'll let me fight!" she said, and Clave learned that the Carthers were planning war against London Tree.

Over the following days he grew to know the jungle people. Of around two hundred Carthers, half were copsiks. It didn't seem to carry any onus. Copsiks here lacked for nothing save a voice in the council.

He saw many children and many pregnancies and no starvation. The jungle people were healthy and happy . . . and better armed than Quinn Tribe had been.

He was questioned at a gathering of the tribe. Carther States' Commons was a mere widening in a tunnel, perhaps twelve meters across and twice that long. Surprisingly, the space held everyone. Men and women and children, copsiks and citizens, all clung to the cylinder wall, covering it with an inner layer of heads, while Comlink or the Sharman spoke from one end.

"How can you even *reach* London Tree?" he had asked, but only once. That information was "classified"; spies would not be tolerated. But he could watch the preparations. He was sure these fires were part of it.

He had been flapping wind at the coals for half a day now. His leg was holding up. Soon he would have to shift position.

Kara the Sharman came skimming toward him. She dipped her grapnel into the foliage and stopped herself next to Clave. "How are you doing?"

"You tell me. Does the fire look right?"

She looked. "Keep it that way. Feed it another branch a few hundred breaths from now. How's the leg?"

"Fine. Can we talk?"

"I've other fires to check."

The Sharman was Carther States' equivalent to the Scientist. Maybe the word had meant *Chairman* once. She seemed to have more power than the political boss, the Comlink, who spent most of his time finding out what everybody else wanted. Getting her attention was worth a try. Clave said, "Sharman, I'm a tree dweller. We're going to attack a tree. Shouldn't you be using what I know?"

She considered that. "What can you tell me?"

"Tides. You're not used to tides, I am, and so are these copsik runners. If you—"

Her smile was twisted. "Put you in charge of our own warriors?"

"Not what I meant. Attack the *middle* of the tree. Make them come to us there. I saw them fighting in free fall, and you're better."

"We thought of that—" She saw his grimace. "No, don't stop. I'm glad you agree. We've watched London Tree for decades now, and two of us did escape once. We know that the copsiks live in the inner tuft, but the carrier is kept at the center of the tree. Should we go after that first?"

Science at the level of the carrier, the flying box, made Clave uneasy. He tried to set the feeling aside . . . "I saw how they use that thing. They put their own warriors where they want them and leave yours floundering in air. Yes. Get the carrier first, even if you can't fly it."

"All right."

"Sharman, I don't know how you plan to attack. If you'll tell me more, I can give you better answers." He'd said it before. It was like talking to the tree.

Kara freed her grapnel with a snap of the snag line. She was moving on. *Treefodder!* Clave added, "One thing. If I know the Grad, he knows how to fly the carrier by now, if he's had any kind of a chance at it. Or Gavving might have seen something and told the Grad."

"There's no way we'll learn that."

Clave shrugged.

"We'll go for the carrier and try for the Grad."

Clave pushed a dead spine branch into the coals and resumed flapping his blanket.

Kara said, "You call yourself Sharman . . . *Chairman* of a destroyed people. I trust you know how to be a leader. If you learn things that should not be known to our enemies . . . if you ride to war in the first gust of warriors . . . what would you tell my citizens, if you were me?"

That was clear enough. " 'Clave must not live to be captured and questioned.' Sharman, I have little to lose. If I can't rescue my people, I'll kill copsik runners!"

"Merril?"

"She'll fight with me. Not under tides, though. And . . . don't tell her anything. *I* won't kill Merril if she's captured."

"Fair enough. You called the funnel a 'treemouth'—"

"I was wrong, wasn't I? The jungle can't feed itself that way. There's not enough wind. What is it?"

"It's what makes the jungle move. The petals are part of it too. Whatever side of the jungle is most dry, there the funnel wants to face. The petals reflect sunlight to swing the jungle round in that direction."

"You talk like the jungle is a whole creature, that thinks."

She smiled. "It's not very smart. We're fooling it now. The fires are to make the jungle dry on one side."

"Oh."

"There are tens of life-forms in the jungle. One of them is a kind of . . . spine for the whole thing. Its life is deep down, and it lives off the dead stuff that drifts toward the center. Everything in the jungle contributes something. The foliage is various plants that root in what the jungle-heart collects, but they rot and feed the jungle-heart and shield the jungle-heart if something big hits the jungle. We do our part too. We transport fertilizer down—dead leaves and garbage and our own dead—and we kill burrowing parasites."

"How does a jungle move? The Grad didn't know."

"The silver petals turn the jungle to put the funnel where the jungle is most dry. If everything gets too dry, then the funnel spits hot steam."

"So?"

"Clave, it's time to put the fires out. I must tell the others. I'll be back."

Minya followed Dloris through twisting, branching tunnels. Minya's grip on Jinny's arm was relaxed; it would tighten if Jinny tried anything foolish. But the treemouth, and any chance to leap into the sky, were farther away with every step.

The way the tunnels twisted, Minya wasn't sure where she was. Near the midbranch, she thought; and the tuft would be narrowing toward the fin. She couldn't see solid wood, but from the way the spine branches pointed, the branch was below and to her left. Earlier she had passed a branching tunnel and heard children's laughter and the shouting of frustrated adults: the schools. She could find this place again.

The mouth of a woven hut showed ahead. Dloris stopped. "Minya. If anyone asks . . . you and Jinny both think you're pregnant. So the Scientist's Apprentice will examine you both. Jinny, I'll take you to your sister, and what happens then is none of *my* business."

They had reached the hut. Dloris shooed them in. Two men waited inside, one in Navy blue, the other—"Who are you?" Dloris demanded.

"Madam Supervisor? I'm Jeffer, the Scientist's Apprentice . . . other apprentice. Lawri is otherwise engaged."

To meet both Minya and Jinny was more than the Grad had hoped for.

He introduced his Navy escort to the women; Ordon was clearly interested. Ordon and Dloris stayed while the Grad questioned Jinny. She couldn't be pregnant, the timing was wrong, and he told her so. She and Dloris nodded as if they'd expected that and departed the hut through the back.

He asked Minya the appropriate questions. She hadn't menstruated since a dozen sleeps before Dalton-Quinn Tree came apart. He told the Navy man, "I'm going to have to examine her."

Ordon took the hint. "I'll be right outside."

The Grad explained what was needed. Minya stepped out of her poncho's lower loop, lifted it, and lay down on the table. The Grad palped her abdomen and her breasts. He tested the secretions of her vagina in plant juices Klance had shown him how to use. He'd practiced such an examination in Quinn Tuft, with the Scientist supervising, as part of his training. Once.

"No problem. A normal pregnancy," he said. "It's anyone's guess when it happened."

Minya sighed. "All right. Dloris said so too. At least it gives me a chance to see you. Could it be Gavving's?"

"The timing's right, but . . . you've been available to the citizens, haven't you?"

"Yes."

"Minya, shall I tell Gavving it's his?"

"Let me think." Minya ran faces past her memory. Some were blurs, and she liked it that way. Did they resemble Gavving at all? But the arrogant dwarf had claimed two of her sleeptimes—"No. What's the truth? You don't know?"

"That's right."

"Tell him that. We'll just have to see what the child looks like."

"All right."

Jinny and Dloris had gone down to the pregnant women's complex, a good, safe distance away. Luckily the Grad's guard was male. A woman might not have given them privacy during the examination. With her poncho hiked up and her legs apart, Minya said, "Stay where you are in case Ordon peeks in. Grad, is there any chance of getting us out of here?"

Keeping his head clear wasn't easy under the circumstances, but he made the effort. "Don't move without me. I mean it. We can't do *any-thing* unless we can stop them using the carm."

"I wasn't sure you were still with us."

"With you?" He was startled . . . though he had had doubts. There was so much to *learn* here! But what was it like for the others, for Gavving or Minya? "Of course I want to break us free! But no matter what we do, they can stop us while they've got the carm. And have you seen a dwarf around?" *Like Harp,* he thought, but Minya hadn't known Harp.

"I know him. Mark. Acts like he's three meters tall, but he's less than two. Thick-bodied, lots of muscles, likes to show them off." Bruises healing on her arms helped her to remember.

"He's important. He's the only one who can use the old armor."

"We'd like him to meet with an accident?"

"If it's convenient. Don't do anything till we're ready to move."

She laughed suddenly. "I admire your coolness."

"Really? Look down."

She looked, and blushed and covered her mouth. "How long—?"

"Ever since you pulled up your poncho. I'm going to have a serious case of lover's plaint."

"When I first met you I thought . . . no, don't move. Remember the guard."

He nodded and stayed where he was. She said, "Grad . . . my guest . . . I hope it's Gavving's, but it's already there, no matter whose. Let's—" She sought words, but the Grad was already moving. She finished in a breathless laugh. "—Solve your problem."

The poncho was ludicrously convenient. It need only be pulled aside. He had to bite hard on his tongue to hold his silence. It was over in a few tens of breaths; it took longer to find his voice. "Thank you. Thank you, Minya. It's been . . . she's . . . I was afraid I'd be giving up women."

"Don't do that." Minya's voice was husky. She laughed suddenly. *"She?"*

"The other apprentice is a citizen who treats me like a thieving copsik. Either I'm dirt for the treemouth or I'm a spy. Anyway, it's my problem. Thanks."

"It wasn't a gift, Grad." She reached down to squeeze his hands. "I'm sick of being treated like a copsik too. When do we get *loose?*"

"Quick. It has to be. The First Officer has spoken. We move the tree as soon as possible."

"When's that?"

"Days, maybe less. I'll know when I get back to the Citadel. Lawri's up there counting down the carm's motor systems. I'd give either testicle to be in two places at once, but I *couldn't* miss the chance to talk to you. Can you pass a message to Gavving?"

"No way at all."

"Okay. There's a cluster of huts under the branch, and that's where the women stay when they carry guests, for more tidal pull while the baby's developing. So. Is there anyone at the treemouth that you want fighting beside you?"

"Maybe." She thought of Heln.

"Maybe isn't good enough. Skip the treemouth. If something happens, grab Jayan and anyone else you think you need and go up. A lot of the men spend their time at the top of the treemouth. We can hope Gavving and Alfin are there. But wait till something drastic happens."

Chapter Seventeen
"WHEN BIRNHAM WOOD . . ."

The huge silver petals were rising, folding inward. The funnel at their center faced east and out, and the sun was moving into line with the funnel. Gold was eastward and seemed close. The sluggish whorl of storm was a strange sight, neither mundane nor scientific, but mind-gripping.

Clave and Kara were alone. The other fire-tenders had gone elsewhere after the fires were quenched. The Sharman asked, "Do you know the law of reaction?"

"I'm not a baby."

"When the steam spits from the funnel, the jungle moves in the oppo-site direction. That would be back to moister surroundings, back into the Smoke Ring, if we weren't . . . meddling. Afterward something must be regrown: fuel perhaps. It takes twenty years."

"That's why they've been getting away with the raids."

"Yes. But no more."

The petals stood at thirty degrees from vertical. The sun shone directly into the funnel, and the petals were shining into it, too. The funnel cupped an intolerable glare.

Kara said, "The jungle-heart spits when the sun shines straight into the blossom. It's not easy to make it spit at a chosen time, but . . . this day, I think."

It came as if by the Sharman's command: a soft, bone-shaking *fumf* from the funnel. Clave felt heat on his face. The jungle shuddered. Kara and Clave clung tight with hands and feet.

A cloud began to form between himself and the sun. A column of steam, racing away from him. He felt a tug, a tide, pulling him toward the sky.

"It works," he said. "I didn't . . . How long till we reach the tree?"

"A day, maybe less. The warriors are gathering now."

"*What?* Why didn't you tell me?" Without waiting for an answer, Clave dove into the foliage. His thoughts were murderous. Had she cost him his place in the coming battle? *Why?*

Four copsiks were running the elevator lines with their legs, and the Grad's eye caught Gavving among them. The elevator had almost reached its cradle. Was there no way to tell him? *Minya's with the pregnant women. She's fine. I'm in the Citadel—*

Ordon said, "So you couldn't wait for the Holidays."

The Grad jumped violently. For a moment he was actually floating. Ordon bellowed laughter. "Hey, forget it, it's nothing. With a chance like that, how could you not? That's why Dloris got a little upset when she saw you weren't Lawri."

The Grad grinned a sickly grin. "Did you watch the whole time?"

"No, I don't need to get my kicks that way. I can visit the Commons. I just poked my head in and saw what you were poking and pulled it back out again." He put the Grad into the elevator with a friendly, forceful shove in the small of his back and followed him in.

He seemed friendly enough, but first and last he was the Grad's guard. The Grad was not to be harmed; the Grad was not to escape. He liked to talk, but . . . they had come to the pregnant women's complex the long way round, by way of the Navy installation on the fin. They had returned by the same route. Presumably Ordon had some business on the fin. The Grad had asked about it. Ordon had become coldly suspicious. He would not talk to a copsik about his work.

The tuft sank away. This was far easier than the four-day climb up Dalton-Quinn Tree. A flock of small birds was veering wide of the trunk. "Harebrains," Ordon said. "Good eating, but you have to use the carm to chase them down. The old Scientist used to let us do that. Klance won't."

A streamer of rain was blowing across the out tuft. Was that why the First was so eager to move the tree? Wet citizens?

A mobile tree: it boggled the mind. Find your own weather!

A fluffy green bauble hung east of the out tuft, with a strange spreading plume of white mist behind it. Within a day or two London Tree would have put it from sight. The Grad wondered if he was being unreasonably antsy. The carm could reach Carther States across any distance. If he couldn't capture the carm, he would be here forever; and if he could, what was the hurry?

But time had a chokehold on his throat.

Life was not intolerable for the Scientist's Apprentice. In a hundred sleeps he might grow into this new life. When the time came he feared he would move too slowly, or not at all.

Clave found Merril in the Commons. She was dipping the points of crossbow bolts in the evil-smelling brew the Carthers made from poison fern.

The increasing tide caught Clave jumping toward her. He paused, then floated back, laughing. "It's real! I sure wasn't going to call her a liar, but—"

"Clave, what's *happening?*" Merril was drifting too, arrows all about her. She managed to catch the poison pot and cap it before it spilled.

"We're on our way. The warriors are on the surface." Clave jumped to his pack against the pull of the strange tide. He had readied it some sleeps ago.

Merril barked, "*What?* How long have we got?"

She had spent her days learning how to make arrows, twist bowstrings, shape a crossbow and fire it. Clave had watched her at target practice. She was as good as most of the Carthers, and her powerful arms were faster at resetting the crossbow.

He said it anyway. "Merril, you're in Carther States whether you go or not. A lot of Carthers aren't citizens."

"So?"

"You don't have to go."

"You can feed that to the tree, O Chairman!"

Clave shoved a handful of the freshly poisoned bolts into his quiver. "Then grab your gear and go!"

The tide was about like that in Quinn Tuft. Using the tunnels was almost like walking. But it was *strange.* Every branchlet and foliage tuft had the tremors.

Clave pulled himself through crackling branchlets and soft green tuft, through to the sky. A column of cloud raced outward from beyond the jungle's horizon. The surface was nearly vertical. He took care for his handholds.

Skeletal warriors emerged like earthworms out of the green billows. Fifty or sixty Carthers had already chosen and boarded pods. Clave was annoyed. The Sharman had told him late, and nobody had told Merril. Why? To give them a chance to back out? "Sure I'd have fought, but I didn't get the word in time—"

Maybe the Carthers needed copsiks more than citizens.

He helped Merril through the foliage. The light of battle was in her eye. She said, "The copsik runners left us behind. Not worth their time."

"I had a broken leg." Clave got it then, and hid his grin. "They made a terrible mistake leaving you, though."

"They'll find out. Don't you laugh!" She shook a harpoon; its point was stained with evil yellow. "This goop will drive you crazy if it doesn't kill you."

The sky was a vast sheet of cloud. Lightning flashed in dark rifts. Clave searched the western fringe until he found a thin line of shadow. London Tree was too big to hide in a cloud: fifty klomters or so, half the length of Dalton-Quinn, but five times the long axis of this puffball jungle.

The Comlink's chosen leader, Anthon, already had his legs wrapped around the largest pod. Anthon was brawnier than the average Carther man, and darker. To Clave he might have had a fragile look, with long bones that could be snapped at whim. But he was festooned with weaponry, crossbow and bolts and a club with a knot on the end; his nails were long and sharp; scars showed here and there on his body; and in fact he looked savage and dangerous.

The stem-ends of the jet pods had been pierced by wooden stakes that now served as plugs. A warrior would nestle into the inner curve of the pod and move his weight to guide it. Clave had used up a few pods practicing.

There were more pods than warriors, a hundred or so spaced wide apart and tied down with light line. Merril chose one and boarded it. Clave asked, "Shall I tether you?"

"I'll handle it." She swung her coil of line below her and caught it coming up. Clave shrugged and chose his own pod. It was bigger than he was but less massive: thirty kilos or so.

Men outnumbered women, but not by a lot. Merril said, "Notice the women? You *fight* for citizenship in Carther States. A citizen makes a better wife. The family gets two votes."

"Sure."

"Clave, how are they *doing* this?"

"Classified." He grinned and ducked the butt of her harpoon. "I can't tell you everything. The Sharman says the jungle will pass the tree at an angle, about midpoint, with a klomter to spare. By then we'll have launched. We'll match speed with the tree and come in while they're still terrified."

"How do we get back?"

"I asked that too." Clave's brows furrowed. "Lizeth and Hild are bringing extra pods. They'll hover in the sky till they see the battle's over . . . but they'll just be caught with the rest of us if the copsik runners use the carm. We've *got* to take the carm."

"What are we trying to do, exactly? I mean you and me."

"Gather Quinn tribe. We want to look good to Carther States, but Quinn Tribe comes first. I wish I knew where they all are."

Mist was drifting over them, seeping into the foliage. A wind was rising. Storm blurred the sky. He kept his eyes on the faint, shadowy line of London Tree . . . which was nearer and growing.

The out tuft was nearest: the citizens' tuft. Citizens would be first to see the oncoming terror: a green mass klomters across flying at the trunk, green warriors coming out of the sky. Not much chance of surprise here. The jungle too was too big to be hidden.

Realistically, they hadn't a ghost of a chance of rescuing anybody. They would do as much damage as possible and die. Why not attack the out tuft first? Kill some citizens and they'd remember better.

Too late now. The Sharman was klomters away, tending a pillar of fiery steam, aiming it to send the jungle a fingernail's width from the tree. Fat chance of getting to her with a change in plan!

The line within the fog had solidified into a tremendous integral sign tufted at the ends. Every Carther now held a sword. Clave drew his.

"Warriors!" Anthon bellowed. He waited for silence, then cried, "Our attack must be remembered! It's not enough to break some heads. We must *damage* London Tree. London Tree must remember, for a generation to come, that offending Carther States is dangerously stupid. Unless they remember, they will come when we cannot move.

"Let them remember the lesson!

"Launch!"

Sixty swords slashed at the lines that tied them to the jungle. Sixty hands pulled the plugs from the stem-ends of sixty jet pods. Pods jetted away in a wind that smelled of rotted plants. At first they clustered, even bumping into each other. Then they began to separate. Not all jet pods thrust alike.

Clave clung with arms and legs, tight against the screaming pod. He was wobbling a little, more than the others. Unskilled. Blood was draining from his head. The tide was ferocious.

The sky was dark and formless, and lightning flashed nearby. They were approaching the center of the tree, as planned. There at the midpoint was the carrier, its nose against the trunk. Its tail was on fire.

Lawri tapped the blue button in a row of five.

Blue numbers flickered and steadied in the bow window. Blue lights appeared in the panel below: four clumps of four little vertical dashes each, in diamond patterns around a larger vertical bar. The array tickled at the Grad's memory. Lawri's hands hovered like Harp about to play.

"Strap in," Klance said. Lawri looked back in annoyance, then tapped rapidly. The Grad got it then. He was in a chair when the carm roared and trembled and lunged.

Tide pulled the Grad back in his seat, then eased off. (It hadn't mattered in Quinn Tuft, but the Scientist had drummed it into his head. Not tide! This was thrust! It might feel the same, but causes and consequences were different. The dead Scientist's legacy: *thrust!*)

The bow window nestled snug against the trunk. A breeze had sprung up; eddies swirled through the side windows.

Lawri activated green patterns and tapped at them. Within the bow window appeared a smaller window in which an edge of sky peeped around a glare of white light. An aft view within the forward view: disconcerting.

Klance was going for a better look. He made his way to the airlock, gripping chair backs as he went. The Grad followed. A few kilograms of tide . . . of thrust took the vibrating walls forward, past him, till he hit the aft wall with a solid thump.

Klance was braced in the outer door, all of his fingers and toes gripping the rim. "I'll let you see in a minute, Jeffer. Don't fall out. You might not get back." He craned his head out. "Damnation!"

"What is it?"

"It's the jungle. I had no *idea* they could move the jungle! Hah. We'll give them a surprise. We'll just move away from them." Klance grinned over his shoulder. He saw the Grad brace himself, too late.

The Grad's foot lashed out and caught the Scientist above the hip. Klance yelled and flew outward. Long fingers and toes still clung. The Grad's heel smashed at a hand and a foot. Klance disappeared.

He moved into the outer door and leaned out. The drive screamed in his ears.

The tree was massive, but it was moving. Klance drifted slowly aft, thrashing, trying to reach the nets on the carm's hull. In his terror he seemed to have forgotten his line. He saw the Grad leaning out and shrieked at him: curses or pleading, the Grad couldn't tell. He looked away.

The tree now had a slight curve to it, like Minya's bow. The carm thrust in the center, and the tufts trailed behind, not very far. A stronger thrust might break the tree in the middle. But the carm was so much tinier than the tree; it was probably thrusting at full power now.

Klance was a thrashing black shadow against a brilliance like Voy brought close. The carm's main motor sprayed blue-white fire, pushing the carm forward against the mass of the tree. Klance was floating into the flame.

Ordon, halfway to the elevator, had seen them.

The jungle had become half the sky. Scores of objects moved alongside it: shapes like those he'd seen before the bark raft crashed into the jungle. Jungle giants on jet pods! But they wouldn't arrive if the carm continued to push the tree away. He had to turn off the main motor, now!

So he *hadn't* been premature, *hadn't* murdered Klance for nothing.

Lawri! He reentered the carm and leapt toward the bow. Lawri hadn't seen him. She stiffened suddenly and half rose, staring aghast at the rear window display. A shadow was thrashing in the flame, dissolving.

She whirled about. She was staring him in the eye when the Grad lashed out at her jaw.

Her head snapped back; she bounced against her straps and hung limp. The Grad used his line to tie her to one of the chairs. He sat down at the controls and studied them.

Yellow governed life support systems, including interior lights and the airlock. Green governed the carm's senses, internal and external. Blue had to do with what moved the carm, including the motors, the two flavors of fuel supply, the water tank, and fuel flow. White read the cassettes.

What had Lawri done to activate the drive? His mind had gone blank. He tapped the blue button. No good: the blue displays disappeared, but the motor's roar continued. He restored the display.

Through a side window he glimpsed patches of Navy blue cloth moving across the bark. *No time. Think.* Blue vertical bar surrounded by blue dashes . . . in a pattern like the motors at the stern. He tapped the blue bar.

The roar and the trembling died to nothing. The tree recoiled: he felt himself pulled forward. Then it was quiet.

Kendy was prepared to beam his usual message when the source of hydrogen light disappeared.

That was puzzling. Normally the CARM's main motor would run for several hours. That, or the attitude jets would send it jittering about like the ball in a soccer match. Kendy held his attention on a drifting point within the Smoke Ring maelstrom, and waited.

A dozen Navy men were making their way toward the carm, using lines and the lineholds, wary that he might start the drive again. Ordon was far ahead of the rest, mere meters from the window. There was murder in his face.

Quick, now! Hit the yellow button. The display was too cluttered: turn off the blue. Yellow display: interior lights showed *dim*, internal wind *on*, temperature shown by a vertical line with numbers and a notch in the middle; here, a complicated line drawing of the carm's cabin seen from above. The Grad closed lines that should represent the doors, with a pinching motion of his fingertips. Behind him the airlock sealed itself.

Lawri stirred.

He heard muted clanging from the doors.

The Grad began playing with the green displays, summoning different views from the carm's cameras. He had precious little time to learn to fly this starstuff relic. He felt Lawri's eyes on him, but would not look.

The clanging stopped, then resumed elsewhere. Ordon snarled through a side window. He must be clinging to the nets, pounding at the glass.

The Grad moved to the window. He spoke a word. Ordon reacted—puzzled—he couldn't hear. The Grad repeated it, exaggerating the motions of his lips the word that would justify murdering his benefactor Klance, assaulting Lawri, betraying his friend Ordon, leaving London Tree helpless against attack.

"War, Ordon! War!"

Chapter Eighteen

THE WAR OF LONDON TREE

C lave was being left behind. The Carthers had judged him a novice, and he was: he hadn't known how to choose among these strange pods. They had let him pick a slow one. He'd flown past the trunk; his path was curving back now. He would be among the last half dozen to land.

Lines ran along the trunk of London Tree, and wooden boxes were rising toward the center from both ends. Clave saw both boxes break open almost simultaneously, spilling men in blue, eight to a box. The copsik runners seemed to know what they were about. They rapidly oriented themselves and fired small jet pods to send them toward the midpoint of the tree, on the eastern face.

Toward the carrier. Twenty-odd copsik runners already surrounded it. The flame at its tail had died, for whatever that might mean.

The Carthers had passed the trunk in a gust of jet pods. Now they were returning, coming up on the western side of the trunk, drastically spread out. Feathered harpoons flew from the copsik runners' long foot-bows. The Carther warriors sent crossbow bolts among them. They outnumbered the enemy almost two to one.

The jungle was tremendous, a green world passing less than a klomter away. Clave had wondered if it would actually hit the tree, but it seemed to be going past. The steam jet had stopped firing. The jungle trailed a curdled line of cloud and a storm of birds trying to catch up, and two dark masses: Lizeth's and Hild's clusters of twenty jet pods each.

This close to the tree, the curve of the trunk hid the ancient carrier and

its mooring; but both gusts of enemy reinforcements seemed to be converging on the carrier. They would know its value too. They flew behind
a thicket of feathered harpoons.

The jet from Clave's pod died away.

Curses ran through his mind while he clambered around the pod to
put it between himself and the harpoons. He was still approaching the
trunk. Others were there first. Carthers were using lineholds about the
clustered buildings to dodge the feathered harpoons or tearing up sheets
of bark for shields. The copsik runners preferred to fire on them from the
sky, where their limbs were free to work their huge bows.

Anthon and a dozen warriors were firing at the carrier, using the curve
of the trunk as cover.

Merril's pod struck a wooden hut with Merril behind it. She'd used the
pod as a shock absorber: good technique. Some of the copsik runners
were trying to reach that building. Merril shot two from behind the
building, then abandoned the shelter when the rest came too close.

Something valuable in that building? The copsik runners seemed to want
it. Clave put an arrow among them and thought he hit someone's foot.

They wanted the carrier more. Clave could see it now: they were all
over it, hanging on the nets and the bark.

Most of the Carther warriors had reached the trunk. Clave would
touch down inward from the battle, presently. For now he could only
watch. From the chaos of battle, patterns began to form.

The copsik runners were outnumbered. They hung back, for that reason and another. In close work they couldn't use the bows. They had
swords, and so did the Carthers; but the taller Carthers had more reach.
They won such encounters.

The copsik runners had small jet pods, the kind that would grow on
an integral tree. They preferred to stay in the sky.

Clave watched Carthers leap into an eight-man gust of blue ponchos.
The copsik runners used their jet pods, left Carthers floundering in the
sky behind them, and fired back with the footbows. Then two Carthers
were among them, slaying, and two more joined them. In free fall the
copsik runners fought like children. The Carthers robbed the corpses of
their jet pods.

Clave drifted, and Carther States was winning without him!

In along the trunk, a wooden box was rising slowly. It spilled reinforcements: six blue-clad footbowmen and a bulky silver creature. There was a
terrible familiarity to that shape . . . but they wouldn't arrive for a kilo-
breath yet.

A copsik runner spotted Clave, a sitting target. He carefully fired a harpoon through Clave's pod, then moved in along the trunk. He'd have a clear shot when Clave came nearer. Clave fired at him. No good; the copsik runner dodged and waited. Clave could see his grin.

The grin vanished when Merril shot him from behind. The bolt protruded below the kidney. He could have fought on . . . but his face was a silent scream; he clawed at the bolt, then went into convulsions. That poison-fern brew must be terrible stuff.

The pod bumped wood with Clave behind it. He turned it loose, clutched bark, and made his way toward Merril with his crossbow ready. He saw blue against storm cloud sky, fired a bolt through one man, and drew his harpoon as the other came at him with a sword.

The copsik runner came too fast. Clave batted him in the face with the crossbow handle and, as he recoiled, stabbed him in the throat.

Merril was making her way around the curve of the bark. He followed her. She stopped and crouched a moment before he saw the carrier, outward along the trunk. Copsik runners were all over it.

He moved up beside her. She said, "All right, why aren't they killing us with that scientific thing?"

"Good question." Clave watched Anthon's team launching crossbow bolts from around the curve of the wood. The carrier's guardians fired back, not very successfully.

He said, "Forget it. They *aren't* using it. They *are* using those wooden boxes to get reinforcements. Let's—"

"Cut the lines."

"Right."

Two lines as thick as Clave's arm ran parallel along the trunk. The last box was on its way in, nearly gone from sight. Another box must be rising. Clave and Merril made their way to the nearest line and began to chop at it.

Six men and a silver thing were coming into footbow range. Clave and Merril set bark sheets to protect themselves. Clave stared at the silver man. It was as if he were trying to remember a nightmare: a man made of starstuff, with a blank ball for a head. Clave fired at it until he saw a crossbow bolt strike and bounce away.

There were feathered harpoons in his shield and Merril's. Clave saw three tiny things like thorns strike her shield in a line aimed at her bare head.

He yelled. She ducked. Thorns spat into the trunk. She said, "Oh. The silver man."

"You know him?"

"Yes . . . keep chopping . . . he was with the copsik runners in Carther States. We don't have anything to breech that armor."

Another box had come into sight when the line parted. That box began to drift. Men spilled loose and flew in curves, pod-propelled, making for the trunk. They seemed too far in to do anything useful. The other line had gone slack. Merril said, "It's a loop. We don't have to cut the other one."

"Then let's get out. There was a cable running outward—"

"No. Let's go join the victory party. Quick, or we'll be left behind."

"Victory—?" Then Clave saw what she meant.

Green-clad warriors clustered round the carrier. Some were crawling into the doors. Men in blue floated about it with the looseness of dead men. Live copsik runners had retreated around the curve of the trunk to wait for reinforcements.

It looked like the war of the carrier was over. But other copsik runners were coming too near. Clave had made a lucky shot: there were five now, plus the silver man.

Ordon died with a bolt peeking through his chest. The Grad saw his face through the window . . . but even if Ordon could have heard him, there was nothing left to say. He turned back to the yellow display.

He had five floating rectangles in the bow window: aft view, dorsal, ventral, and both sides. He caught glimpses of men in blue, men and women in green; impossible to tell who was winning.

Three Navy men moved into the cover of the drive motors. The Grad touched blue dashes. Flames burst near them. They yelled, threw themselves clear, floundered to orient themselves . . . and one had a bolt through his hip.

Lawri screamed, "Murderer!"

"Some of us don't like being copsiks," the Grad said. "Some of us don't even like copsik runners."

"Klance and I never treated you with anything but kindness!"

"That's true enough. What have you done for the rest of Quinn Tribe? Did you forget that I had a tribe?"

"Your tribe is dead! Your tree is torn apart! *We* could have been your tribe, you treefeeding mutineer you!"

The Grad had no particular urge to stop her mouth. Lawri's accusations only echoed those in his own mind. He had made his decisions.

So he spoke without heat. "Do you know what's been happening to our women? Gavving might have had permission to visit his wife thirty-odd days from now, but any male citizen had rights to her any time he liked. Now she's pregnant. She doesn't know who the father is, and I don't either."

Lawri said, "They'll kill you. Shall I tell you what the penalty is for mutiny?"

"Feel free, but I notice the line of argument has shifted."

She told him anyway. It sounded dreadful enough: good reason to keep the doors closed.

He had found the infrared display. It showed him red dots in along the trunk. He cut the infrared out and recognized Clave and Merril, and Navy chasing them . . . including what had to be a dwarf in a pressure suit.

Clave and Merril! Then the Carthers were actually on his side. He had wondered.

The green-clad warriors rushed the carm. When the Navy retreated he was able to wrap one in flame, not as a casual killing but as a signal to the Carthers. *I'm with you!* For it was Carthers who now swarmed the carm, and Navy who retreated around the trunk.

The Grad opened two yellow lines with his fingertips. He turned to greet the tall, bloody jungle giants.

Gavving was on his feet, held upright by two men, before he even started to wake up. He said, "What?"

"We need pedalers," someone said.

Four Navy men helped three sleepy copsiks out of the barracks and up through the tuft. Gavving held his temper and Horse took it with typical docility, but Alfin was still protesting as they broke through into sunlight. "I'm the treemouth tender's assistant! Not a treefeeding pair of legs—"

"Listen, you. We're sending men up to the Citadel as fast as we can. We've worked the regular team half to death. You'll take your place and pedal with the rest!"

"And carry out my regular duties too? *I'll* be half-dead! What do I tell the Supervisor?"

"You board that bicycle or you'll be telling your Supervisor where your testes went. Just before the Holidays too!"

The copsiks on the platform were sheathed in sweat; it drifted in droplets from their hair; they panted like dying men. The Navy men helped three of them down, wincing at the soggy touch. Other Navy men were boarding the elevator.

Half the sky was textured green.

The jungle! The jungle had come to London Tree!

Only three Navy men remained. One was an officer; Gavving recognized him, and he carried a piece of old science, a talking box. The rest had entered the elevator. Gavving was lifted into the saddle. He started pedaling. The elevator rose.

The jungle had attacked London Tree. The jungle was mobile. Who would have guessed? The green cloud was awesomely close . . . and receding.

He should be doing something! But what? Armed men were watching.

The elevator was tens of klomters above him now, and Gavving was gasping. He felt the change before he saw it. Suddenly it was easier to pedal. The grating whine of the bicycle gears rose half an octave. He looked up.

The elevator box was turning, falling. Blue shapes spilled out and made for the trunk. One was too slow. When he reached the trunk he was moving too fast; he bounced away, spinning like a broken thing, and continued to fall. But the box was falling faster.

"Stop pedaling. Hold your places," the officer ordered.

The invaders had cut the cable. Now what? *In takes you east.* The box wouldn't hit here; it would strike farther east along the branch, but where? Gavving pictured the massive wooden structure smashing through diffuse cottony foliage. "Officer? Suppose that thing hits the pregnant women's complex?"

"It's under the branch," the man said. "Mmm . . . it could hit somebody, though. Damn, there's the school complex! *Karal!* Move east along the top of the branch and get everyone underneath. Don't miss the examination hut. Docking section too. Then get under yourself, if you're fast enough."

"Sir." A Navy man—wounded, with one arm bound across his chest—darted awkwardly away. Two left.

The officer spoke to his talking box. "Squad Leader Patry here. The enemy has cut our elevator cables. What's your status?"

The answer was almost unintelligible with static. Gavving let his chin droop and his eyes half close (poor exhausted copsik, clearly too tired to think of mutiny) and listened hard. He heard, "Elevators running. We . . . ing troops. Enemy numbers for*garble*, repeat, forty to fifty. *Garble* outnumbered. They're gentling us. They garble the carm, but even . . . can't use . . . tethered."

"I see two dark masses west of here."

"Forget them. . . . trouble enough. We are sending more men to the Citadel."

"Patry out."

The Grad recognized the long-limbed woman, Debby, by her long, straight brown hair. The two men with her were strangers. The crossbows aimed at him didn't bother him as much as their fear. They didn't like the carm at all.

He spread open hands to the sides. "I'm the Quinn Tribe Scientist, the only one who can fly this thing. Good to see you, Debby—"

Lawri broke in with, "Feed it to the tree, mutineer! You'd lose us in the sky or smear us all over the trunk."

"—and this is Lawri, the copsik runner."

One snapped out of it. "I'm Anthon. This is Prez. Debby told us about you, Grad. Can we leave immediately? Pile all our warriors on the nets and go? The silver man is coming."

The Grad said, "We're tied to the tree. Cut those lines and we're free to go. But I don't leave without Clave and Merril, and I think there's time to get one more thing."

He pointed into the dorsal window display. Anthon and Debby very gingerly moved up behind him. All this scientific stuff must be daunting.

"That hut is the Lab. Debby, you'll find some cassettes and the reader inside, on the walls. You remember what they look like?"

Debby nodded.

"Go get them. Anthon, get some warriors to cut the carm loose." He looked into the displays. Clave was towing Merril as he jumped along the bark, his legs serving both while she fired bolts at their pursuers. One Navy man was dropping back, hurt. The silver man came on. The Grad said, "See if you can give them some covering fire."

Anthon said quietly, "You're not the leader here, Scientist."

"Here, *I am.* And I have had enough of being a copsik!"

"Debby, go get that treefodder for the Scientist. Take a team. Prez, get those cables chopped." Anthon waited until they were through the doors before he spoke again. He wanted no witnesses to this discussion.

"Grad, have you fought in war?"

"I captured the carm."

"You? *I* cap—" He trailed off. "Never mind."

"How many are you?"

"Forty or less, now. We won't fit inside, but we can hang on to the nets."

"I want to set the rest of Quinn Tribe free. They're in the tuft, and I can find them. The carm's got plenty of what makes it go. We've got the small motors for spraying fire. It should be easy."

Anthon was in no hurry to make a decision. Into the silence Lawri said, "He can't fly the carm. I can. I'm the Scientist's Apprentice."

"Why haven't you killed this one?" Anthon demanded.

"Hold it! She's what she says . . . and I did have to kill the Scientist himself. Lawri has a great deal to teach us, if she can be talked into it. She's harmless as long as she's tied up."

Anthon nodded. "She lives, then. But *I* lead Carther States."

"*I* captain the carm."

Anthon stepped into the doors and began to shout orders. He'd let the word pass. *Captain.* He who violated the Grad's orders aboard the carm would be a mutineer!

Carthers chopped at the lines that tethered the carm. Crossbow bolts flew among the blue men who followed Clave and Merril. Those dove for cover on the bark. The silver man came on alone. He wasn't using jet pods. There must be something on the pressure suit itself.

The carm was drifting free.

Lawri spoke in an angry whisper. "They'd kill me, wouldn't they?"

"They don't have my reasons for liking you," the Grad said without overt sarcasm. "Keep your opinions to yourself for a while, if you can. Did you really think a jungle warrior would let you at the controls?"

Clave and Merril and Debby entered like a storm. Debby was gashed and bleeding along the ribs. Merril flew into the Grad and hugged him. "Grad! I mean Scientist. Good work. I mean, glorious! Can you run this thing?"

The Grad felt huge relief. Let Clave play these dominance games with Anthon! The Grad would captain the carm and hope Lawri was wrong . . . "I can fly it."

Clave asked, "Can you find the rest of us?"

"They're all in the in tuft. Gavving's at the top, where we can get at him. Jayan and Minya are with the pregnant women. Jinny and Alfin should be in the Commons. We may have to leave the carm to get to them."

"Then, it's going to work. I can't believe it."

The Grad grinned. "So why'd you come? Never mind. Debby—"

"I got these. We had to fight for them." Seven cassettes. "We couldn't find the reader."

"Maybe Klance had it . . . it doesn't matter. Get into a chair. You too, Clave, Merril, *strap down!*" He looked into the displays. "In a few breaths we can . . ."

"What?" Clave saw the displays floating in the bow window. "This place is too strange for me. Those pictures make my eyes cross! I . . . Grad, have you got anything to take out the silver man?"

"Not unless he crawls into a motor. That's a starman's pressure suit."

"Well, he's killing all our allies."

"That spitgun only puts you to sleep and makes you feel wonderful. Doesn't matter to us, though. They're still out of action. Anthon, good timing. Get into a chair."

Anthon was panting; his crossbow was on line with the Grad's eyes. "You waited too long! That goddam silver—"

"Get into a chair and strap down! And tell me how many we've got left." The Grad was trying to watch all the displays at once. Carthers were disappearing over the trunk's horizon. Too many floated limp; some were being towed by others who hadn't been hit. The man in the pressure suit was hovering over the carm, firing darts.

The glazed look left Anthon's eyes. He worked himself into a chair. "We can't hurt him. I was the only one who even got to the carrier. The rest won't come anyway. They're afraid of it."

"We can't leave them."

The silver man darted down at the doors. The Grad pinched his fingers together. The silver man shied back as the doors closed in his face, then moved back into view in the dorsal display. Now he was gripping the nets on the hull.

"He's on the carm," said Grad.

"Take off," said Anthon.

"Leave?"

"We can leave my citizens if we take the silver man with us. I've got spare jet pods coming."

"Good enough." The Grad's fingers tapped. The silver man was still hanging on the nets when the carm backed away from the trunk and started down.

Chapter Nineteen

THE SILVER MAN

The laundry vat was a tall glass cylinder. It hung from the underside of the branch, from lines pounded into the black bark over Minya's head. Around it ran an extensive wickerwork platform woven from live spine branches. A layer of rocks beneath the vat supported a bed of coals. A pipe ran all the way from the treemouth reservoir to supply the water: an impressive achievement, had Minya not been too tired to appreciate it.

Minya and Ilsa stirred dirty clothing in a matrix of foaming water with a paddle two meters long. It took skill and fine attention. Left to itself, the laundry-soup would have foamed right out of the vat, clothing and all. The supervisor Haryet kept popping out to see how they were doing.

Minya wasn't feeling awkward yet, but there was the sense of a guest building inside her. Ilsa's pregnancy looked ludicrous, a bulge on a straight-edge. Like the others, she seemed to have adjusted to her new status with little difficulty. Once she had told Minya, "We know all our lives that the copsik runners might come for us. Well, they came."

A chain of huts ran along the underside of the branch. Most of the women preferred to stay inside. They weren't all pregnant. Some were nursing their erstwhile guests. They all had work: knitting, sewing, preparation of food to be cooked at the treemouth.

The quiet was broken by a hurried rustling.

Then four people burst from the tunnel that led down from the examination hut: Jayan and Jinny, the supervisor Dloris, and a Navy man with his arm in a sling. Karal spotted her, ran to her, gripped her arm. She shied from his wildness.

"You're all right." He was gasping. "Good. Minya. Stay under the branch. Don't let anyone . . . *anyone* else go wandering."

"We don't tend to. We're too awkward. I thought men weren't allowed. . . ?"

"I'm not staying. Minya, it's both elevators and at least one man, they're falling from thirty klomters up, and we don't know just where they'll hit. I've got to warn the children in the school complex." He pointed a finger at the tip of her nose. "Stay here!" And he sprinted for the tunnel, wobbling, chest heaving.

If something happens, the Grad had said. Something was happening, all right, but what? Would Dloris know?

Minya guessed where the supervisor would be. She moved down the line of huts and entered the last one as Dloris came through with Haryet. "We've been counting," Dloris said. "Gwen's missing. Have you seen her? Three meters tall and pale as a ghost, with a year-old guest?"

"Not lately. What's happening?"

"Get those clothes out and drying and then put the fire out. Do you have lines? Good. Keep them handy." The two supervisors moved on.

Minya turned to Jayan and Jinny. "Give us a hand. Jinny, we're lucky you were around. We're all together now. Do *you* know what's happening?"

"No. Karal looked scared stiff."

"Is it war?"

"Better stick to our task till we're sure," Ilsa said.

They pulled the clothing from the vat in a gelid mass, manipulating it with poles. Some water remained. They inverted the vat and moved back while the water-glob flowed sluggishly out onto the fire. Live steam didn't rise fast enough in London Tree's feeble tide. It tended to expand in an invisible globe, scalding hot.

Minya had never seen that fire go out. Dloris must be expecting something drastic!

They continued to work. They set the laundry in the press and cranked two great wooden slabs together. Water squeezed out around the edges of the wad of clothing, then began to slide downward.

Something smashed through foliage, somewhere nearby.

They froze. Then Minya plunged into the branchlets with Jinny and Ilsa behind. They made their way toward the sound. Minya angled above where she thought it had stopped.

There, a trail of broken branchlets. She followed it down to the broken and twisted remains of what had been a Navy officer. The corpse wore a sword, scabbarded, and a quiver that was still full, though the bow was missing.

"*Now* it's war," Minya said.

"We'll have to kill the supervisors," Ilsa said.

Minya jumped. "What?" It was as if a stone had spoken. "Never mind, you're right. I thought you were . . . I thought you'd given up."

Ilsa only shook her head.

West takes you in. In takes you east. At first the Grad held the bow window pointed straight down. They dropped smoothly . . . faster . . . he swung the carm to point west and fired aft jets to correct as it drifted away from the trunk.

His passengers were rigid with terror, save for Lawri, who was rigid with fury.

They still had a passenger on the hull.

Anthon's voice wanted to stutter. He wouldn't let it. "I want to point out that we could go back to Carther States *now*. We've got the silver man and the carm. These copsik runners don't own anything they value more. We can trade for your copsiks."

That actually sounded sensible. The Grad said, "Clave?"

"Feed it to the tree."

Anthon said, "You want to kill some copsik runners. All right, I can underst—"

"I want to rescue them myself! I am the Quinn Tribe Chairman. They are entitled to my protection." Clave spat the word: "Trade! They attacked us, we attacked them. We've got the carm and we'll have our people too. All right, Grad—Scientist—have you got an opinion?"

They were dropping too fast. The Grad swung the carm nose-down and fired forward jets. He said, "Nice of you to ask. We've got the Scientist's Apprentice and the silver suit and the only man alive who can fit into it. Maybe they would trade. We keep the carm."

"Never," said Lawri. "Trade with *copsiks!*"

Anthon and Clave looked at each other. The Grad said, "Never mind," and they laughed. Lawri's tone of voice said it all.

Minya stopped and looked out through a screen of branchlets.

The supervisors had found Gwen. Haryet was scolding her as they led her toward the huts. Haryet was second-generation copsik, shorter than Minya; she looked tiny beside her very pregnant captive.

They'll have heard us coming, Minya thought. Jinny must have realized that too. She stepped out through the crackling foliage, ten meters east of Minya's position. *Good! They'll think they heard one, not two—*

Dloris came toward Jinny with thunder in her face. Breaking new paths was strictly forbidden.

Minya emerged behind Haryet and stabbed her.

Gwen turned with her baby in her arms and shrieked. Dloris whirled and stared. Perhaps this place of mothers and babies had given the supervisor a false sense of safety. She reacted slowly. Before she could reach her truncheon, Jinny was pinning her arms and Minya was running at her in long, low leaps.

Dloris flipped forward. Jinny flew over her back and came spinning at Minya, who lost a moment sidestepping. Then Dloris held half a meter of hardwood at guard; but she faced a Navy sword.

"Wait," she said. "Wait."

"My child will not be born a copsik!" Minya screamed and lunged.

Dloris danced backward. The tunnel was behind her, and Minya knew she had to stop the supervisor from reaching it. She ran at her, ready to bat the truncheon aside. Then Jayan and Ilsa were moving into place behind Dloris. Jayan held the big paddle well up the haft, blade first, like a two-handed sword.

Dloris dropped her truncheon. "Don't kill me. Please."

"Dloris, tell us what's happening."

"Carther States is all over the trunk. I don't know who's winning."

"Have they got the carm?"

"The *carm*?" Dloris showed nothing but astonishment.

They tied her with line. Ilsa wanted to do more; Minya knew Dloris too well to allow it. She wouldn't have killed Haryet either, if . . . if.

Gavving watched the carm descend in fire. Patry was talking to his box, too far away for Gavving to hear; but the Navy officer looked furious and frightened.

He caught Gavving watching him. "You! All of you! Stay where you are! Move and you'll be shot. Do you understand? Arny, take cover."

The two Navy men disappeared into the foliage. Presently Alfin said, "We're bait."

"There's only two."

Horse asked, "Do you really think your friends have the carm? What will they do with it?"

"Rescue us," Gavving said with more assurance than he felt. "Alfin, when it comes down, jump for the doors and hope they open."

Alfin snorted. "You've got to be out of your mind. *Look* at that thing, you want to *ride* in it?"

"I'll ride anything to get out of here, if I can take Minya."

"You don't have Minya. Listen, Gavving. I remember you with your eyes red and half-closed and crying in rivers. They make their own weather here! Nobody starves, nobody goes thirsty. It's a good, healthy tree with a good crop of earthlife. I've got a responsible position—"

"You *like* it here?"

"Oh . . . treefodder. Maybe I don't really like it anywhere. I took orders in Dalton-Quinn too. I'm seeing a supervisor, a nice woman even if she towers over me. I didn't have that in Quinn Tuft. Kor's a year or two old for the citizens, but we get along . . . and I don't like that box."

"I do." It was Horse who had spoken. "Gavving, cede me Alfin's place."

The carm was falling straight at them. Those had better be friends aboard! He could only die fighting if they were not. He told Horse, "It's not my decision. Just do what I do, and we'll see what Clave says."

"Done."

"Alfin. Last chance—"

"No."

"Why?"

Alfin met his eyes. "There's tide here."

Gwen's shriek of terror had started her baby screaming. He was quieter now. Gwen's awareness was in the hands that stroked and patted the child. There was none in her eyes.

The conspirators ignored Gwen as she ignored them. Ilsa led her back, once, when she tried to return to the huts. They didn't want Gwen talking to the others.

Jayan asked, "Ilsa, are you sure you want in on this?"

Jinny wasn't pregnant; Jayan and Minya were not obtrusively so. Ilsa was. She said, "My baby won't be born a copsik either."

The branch shuddered with the force of a tremendous blow. Ilsa said, "The second elevator. Karal said two."

Jayan said, "Minya, you've talked to the Grad. What did he say?"

"The Grad said to go up. He'll try to capture the carm. If he can't get the carm—"

"Then he's dead," Ilsa concluded, "and all the Carther States warriors are going to die, and we'll never get loose at all. So he's *got* to have the carm. He's got the carm and as many Carther States warriors as he can get aboard, and he's trying to reach us. Who goes with us?"

Nobody suggested a name. Jayan said, "We're the only new copsiks. Let the rest run their own revolt."

"You can't go up."

They turned, surprised. Dloris's eyes shied from their potentially lethal attention. She repeated doggedly, "You can't go up. The tunnels lead to the fin and the treemouth. There isn't any connecting tunnel to the top of the tuft; that's where the men live. None of you are in shape to tunnel through foliage, and if you got to the top you'd stand out like so many mobies in a stewpot."

"Then what?"

"Stay here till your friends come for you."

Ilsa shook her head. "The children's complex? Karal must have the upper reaches evacuated by now."

"Ilsa, it's big and complicated and it doesn't connect to the top. The most you'd do is get lost."

"What's your stake in this, Dloris?"

"Let me live. Don't tell anyone I helped."

"Why?"

"I wanted to escape once myself. Now I've been a supervisor too long. Somebody would be sure to want me dead. But you can't go up. Stay here and wait."

They looked at each other. Minya said, "You did that. For thirty years? No. I think I know what we have to do."

The Grad tapped at the motor controls . . . tricky. They had to be used in pairs and clusters or they'd spin the carm. He dropped into the foliage several meters from the platform, with a horrendous crashing, and opened the doors at once.

Three men jumped toward the door. Gavving gripped an older man's arm. The third man wore blue, and he was swinging a sword. Debby took careful aim and put a crossbow bolt through him.

Gavving and the stranger pulled themselves inside. The older man was gasping. "Get us moving," Gavving said. "This is Horse. He wants to join Quinn Tribe. Alfin isn't coming. He likes it here."

A feathered harpoon ricocheted through the doors. The Grad closed them. He said, "I left Minya and Jayan in the pregnant women's compound—"

"What? Minya?"

"She's carrying a guest, Gavving. Your child. And men aren't permitted there." Later the Grad would tell him the truth . . . part of it. For now, for witnesses and the record, *Minya is carrying her husband's child.* "Ilsa's there too, Anthon. I told Minya to gather them all and go up. We'll have to wait for them."

Clave nodded. Gavving stared with open mouth. He said, "Grad, don't you know the men's tunnels don't connect to the women's?"

"What?"

"They'd have to go all the way to the fin or the treemouth, and back! Or break trail—Grad, they're sure to be captured!"

Clave had a hand on Gavving's shoulder. "Calm down, boy. Grad, where would they go?"

The Grad tried to think. It was Horse who spoke. "Not the fin. That's Navy. Maybe nobody would notice some extra women at the Commons or the schools. Or maybe they'd just stay where they are and wait."

"Jinny'll be at the treemouth anyway. Okay." The Grad fired the forward motors.

The carm lifted tail-first from the tuft, leaving fires in its wake. Lawri screamed, "You're setting the tree on fire!"

She was ignored. "I've been to the pregnant women's complex," the Grad said. "I haven't been in the Commons."

"Alfin has," Gavving said. "It's big, and it reaches to the treemouth. If we can get the carm into the treemouth—"

Lawri writhed. "You can't! You can't burn the treemouth, what *are* you? This isn't mutiny anymore, it's just wanton destruction!"

Anthon asked mildly, "Will London Tree trade with copsik mutineers?"

Lawri was silent.

"Lying wouldn't have helped. You were too convincing before. We'll go get our people."

The carm moved sideways above the tuft, accelerating sluggishly. Then there was clear sky below, and the Grad swung the carm around.

They were dropping past the treemouth. The carm slowed, hovered. The Grad touched paired yellow dots. Light flared into the Commons in twin beams, as if the carm were a tethered sun.

Women were running . . . away. Jungle giants all, leapfrogging across the woven spine-branch floor. None were the right size, nor dark enough, to be Jinny.

"Drop it," Clave said as if his voice hurt him. "Go for the pregnant women's compound. How do we get there?"

The Grad let the carm sink. They were below the tuft now: blue sky below, green passing above. "It's under the branch. I think our best move is to go up into it. I may not hit it exactly, and the Navy may have figured out what we're doing by now. Are you ready for a fight?"

"Yes," said several voices.

The Grad grinned. "Maybe I can scrape off the silver man too. I notice he's still with us . . . Now what's *that*?"

Things were falling from the foliage. A bundle of cloth tied with line. Long loaves of bread. A bird carcass, cleaned and skinned. Then the green sky was raining women. Jayan, Jinny, and a jungle giant: Ilsa?

"They jumped," Gavving said in wonder. "What if we hadn't come?"

"We did," Merril said. "Get 'em!"

Two big leather bags fell, and then another woman, leaping head-down to catch up with the rest: Minya.

The Grad cut the motors and took a moment to think. He was aware of voices yelling at him but was able to ignore the intrusive noises.

Got to catch them in the airlock. What about the silver man? He was still clinging to the dorsal surface. The Grad rotated the carm to put it between the pressure-suited dwarf and the falling women.

They were separating. It would be three operations. Jayan and Jinny first. They faced each other across clasped hands, as they had after Dalton-Quinn Tree came apart. They seemed calm enough under the circumstances. The carm eased toward them.

The silver man was crawling around to the airlock.

"Hang on," the Grad said, and he started the carm spinning. Faster. His head spun too; he could see sickness in the faces behind him. The silver man, caught rounding a corner, was hanging by his hands. The Grad used the motors again, against the spin, and slapped the silver man hard against the hull. He flew free.

The Grad opened the doors. The twins were flying at him. He jetted flame to slow the carm; stopped just alongside them, backed and moved sideways. Then they were crawling into the carm.

Blue shapes crawled within the green sky. Armed Navy men, carrying jet pods and footbows and a massive thing that took three men to handle.

The reunion would have to wait. "Get 'em into chairs," he called back to Clave. Minya next. He was flying the carm like he'd done it all his life. He got a little careless; Minya thumped the hull, then came in with a bloody nose. "Sorry," he said. "Gavving, never mind that, get her to a chair! Who's the other one?"

"It's Ilsa," Anthon said. "They're shooting at her! Grad, get her!"

"I'm doing that. Do we need the food and other stuff?" He was alongside

Ilsa now, between her and the falling Navy men. Voy glared behind her. Footbow arrows *tick*ed off the hull . . . but that *thump* had no place in his scheme. What—?

Ilsa's look of terror and determination faded into blissful sleep. He knew before he looked: the silver man was back, spitgun and all. He was on the dorsal surface, out of reach of the doors, and Anthon had thrown a line round Ilsa's waist and was pulling her in.

"Get her into—" The chairs were full. "Get her against the back wall and stay with her. Don't turn any fixtures. Debby, put a tethered bolt in that carcass and we'll pull it in."

Anthon said, "The silver man—"

"These are close quarters. If he gets through the door, swarm him. The spitgun doesn't kill, but if he shoots us all, he owns us."

Jinny called to the Grad, "We brought a stack of clean laundry and a water supply."

"We've got water. Laundry . . . why not? Hey, I told Minya to go *up*. You did it right, we'd never have found you—"

Minya said, "If you had the carm, you could find us in the sky. So we grabbed what we could and went down."

The Navy men had not left the branch's green underside. Hardly surprising. If they failed to capture the carm, how would they reach the tree again? They would have looked futile, the Grad thought, were it not for the bulky starstuff thing they handled like a weapon.

The salmon bird carcass was a black silhouette with Voy painfully bright behind it. Anthon and Debby had to squint . . . but their tethered arrows nailed it and they reeled it in. Maybe the silver man was hoping someone would show his head; none did. He tried to enter with the stack of ponchos, and the Grad almost managed to catch him in the closing door. That left the laundry outside too, and a red border around the yellow diagram. "I never saw red before. What's it mean?"

Lawri deigned to answer, contemptuously. "Emergency. Your line's holding the airlock open."

The Grad opened the door (the red warning disappeared) and Debby pulled the mass in. The silver man didn't try to follow. The door may have scared him. It was his last chance: the Grad closed the doors and sighed with satisfaction.

His sigh chopped off when his ventral view flared pure, dazzling red, then disappeared from the bow window.

From other displays he caught glimpses of painfully bright scarlet. "Can that thing hurt us?" Anthon demanded, while Lawri cried, "Now you'll see! They'll cut us in half!" and Clave said, "They're almost on us. We'll have them all over the hull if—"

"Feed it to the tree!" the Grad shouted at them all. He couldn't think. What *could* that light do to them? Neither Klance nor Lawri had ever mentioned such a thing.

We've got what we need. Forget the bread, forget the water. Get out! They'll never catch the carm.

Lawri saw his hand move and screamed, "Wait!" The Grad didn't. He tapped the center of the big blue vertical bar.

Chapter Twenty

THE POSITION OF SCIENTIST'S APRENTICE . . .

·

The air sighed out of the Grad's lungs. He was being crushed flat. His left arm had missed the armrest; it was behind him, being pulled gradually from the shoulder socket. The chair was too low to support his head. His neck hurt savagely. Above the muted shriek of the main motor he heard his passengers fighting for breath.

This must be killing the jungle giants.

London Tree dwindled like a dream in the aft view. They were in the storm now, and blind. The Grad tried to raise his right arm, to touch the blue bar, to end the force that flattened him. Up, up . . . farther . . . his arm fell back across his chest with a jolt that smashed the last sipful of air from his lungs. His sight blurred.

Lawri's chin was tucked down against her collarbone. She was sure that if she relaxed her neck the tide would snap it.

She watched Jeffer trying to turn off the motor and knew he couldn't make it. And Lawri's arms were bound.

This will kill some mutineers, she thought with alloyed satisfaction. *And I did it to them.* The com laser would burn or blind at close range, but almost certainly it would not have hurt the carm. She'd lied in hope that the mutineers would panic. She'd succeeded beyond her ambitions. *But it's killing me!*

The screen of clouds swept past and away.

Gold was to left of center in the bow window. The Smoke Ring trailed left of Gold. They were accelerating east and a little out.

East takes you out . . .
They were leaving the Smoke Ring.
I knew it. That crazy Jeffer's killed us all.

With his head pulled far back, with the points of what should have been a neckrest digging savagely into his shoulder blades, Gavving looked along his nose and tried to make sense of what he was seeing.

The sky flowed away at the edges of the bow window. A triune family split and fluttered and were gone before they could move. A small, flattish green jungle drifted close, accelerated, whipped past. A fluffy white cloud showed ahead. Closer. White blindness, and the carm shuddered and rang with the impact of water droplets. Something tiny struck the bow window a terrific blow and left a pink film a quarter meter across. In a breath the rain had pounded it clear.

The cloud was gone, and the sky ahead was clear of further obstructions. Gold and the Smoke Ring showed like a puffball on a stem, against blue sky . . . a deep, dark blue sky, a color he'd never seen in his life.

He rolled his head to look at Minya. The agony in his neck shifted . . . the pressure was easier to take this way. She looked back at him. Lovely Minya, her face fuller than he remembered. He tried to speak and couldn't. He could barely breathe.

She sighed, "Almost."

The light of the CARM's main drive was back, and blue-shifting!

A shift in its spectral line, and he'd caught it. Lucky. Kendy aborted his usual message. The CARM's time-eroded program would be busy enough without distraction. For the CARM was in flight. It must have been accelerating for some minutes already. By the frequency shift, it was building up enough velocity to take it out of the Smoke Ring . . . within a few thousand kilometers of *Discipline* itself!

When the light went out, Kendy began his message. The air was already thinning around the CARM. Reception should be good. "Kendy for the State. Kendy for the State. Kendy for the State."

The sound stopped, the terrible tide was gone, all in a moment. Bodies bent like bows recoiled. Citizens who had not had the breath for screaming, screamed now.

As the reflexive screams died to groans, the Grad heard Lawri say, wearily, "Jeffer. Never use the main motor unless you're pushing the tree."

The Grad could only nod. He'd captured the carm, he'd . . . treefodder, everyone he knew, if he hadn't murdered him he'd put him aboard the carm! And *then* he'd touched the blue bar. He said, "Lawri, I'm open to suggestions."

"Feed it to the tree."

The Grad heard full-throated laughter aft . . . from Anthon. Debby swatted him hard across the belly. The blow snapped him into a U, but he kept laughing, and she joined him.

They had reason! They had been flat against the back wall, protecting Ilsa from what should have been mild jolting. The killer chairs would have snapped their backs, but none of the jungle giants had been in them.

Others were groaning, stirring, moving from pain to fear. Ilsa was beginning to wake up. Merril—vacant-eyed, hypnotized by the peculiar sky rushing at the bow—seemed to snap out of it. "Well, *somebody* do something!"

Clave's voice was a carrying one, and it filled the carm's cabin to over-flowing. "Calm down, citizens. We're not in *that* much trouble. Remember where we are."

Other sounds stopped. Clave said, "The carrier was built for this. It came from the stars. We know it operates inside the Smoke Ring, but it was built to operate *anywhere*, wasn't it, Grad?"

That simply hadn't occurred to him. "Not anywhere, but . . . outside the Smoke Ring, that's certain."

"Good enough. What's our status?"

"Give me a breath." The Grad was ashamed. It had taken Clave to get his mind working again. *We're not in trouble*—Luck, that Clave didn't have the training to know what nonsense *that* was.

The blue display was on. *Thrust:* 0. *Acceleration:* 0. The big blue rectangle had a border of flickering scarlet: *main motor on, fuel exhausted.* He tapped it off, for what that was worth. O_2: 211. H_2O: 1,328. "Plenty of water, but no fuel. We can't maneuver. I don't know how to find out where we're going. Lawri?"

No answer.

"But we're bound to fall back sooner or later." Green display: "Pressure's way down outside. We're—" This could start a riot; but they'd have to know. "We're leaving the Smoke Ring. That's why the sky's that peculiar color." Yellow display: "Life support looks okay." Window displays: "Oh, my."

In the aft and side views, all detail had become tiny: integral trees were toothpicks, ponds were drops of glitter, everything seemed embedded in fog. Gold had become a bulge within a larger lens of cloud patterns that trailed off to east and west: a storm pattern that spread across the Smoke Ring. The hidden planet seemed indecently close.

"Grad?"

"Sorry, Clave, I got hung up. Citizens, don't miss this! Nobody's seen the Smoke Ring from outside since men came from the stars."

Others were craning forward to see the displays or peering out through the side windows. But Gavving said, "I think Horse is dead."

Horse? The old man Gavving had brought with him. Horse certainly looked dead enough; small wonder if the tide had stopped an old man's heart. *Poor copsik,* the Grad thought. He had never met Horse, but what human could have wanted to die before seeing *this*? "Check his pulse."

Lawri said, "Port view, Jeffer."

Something in her voice . . . the Grad looked. Off to the edge: a flash of silver? "I don't—"

"It's Mark! He's still out there!"

"I don't believe it."

But the silver pressure suit was crawling into view. The dwarf must have clung to the nets throughout that savage acceleration.

"Jeffer, let him in!"

"What a man! I . . . Lawri, I can't. The pressure's too low outside. We'd lose our air."

"He'll die out there! . . . Wait a minute. Open the doors one at a time. Hah! that's why Klance calls it an airlock! So did the cassettes—"

"Sure, two doors to lock the air in. Okay." Muffled thumps sounded aft. The silver man wanted in. "Anthon, Clave, he may be dangerous. Take the spitgun away from him when he comes in." The Grad cleared all but the yellow display. No fast decisions from now on. He pinched both lines together—make *sure* they're closed tight!—then opened the outer door with a forefinger.

The silver man disappeared from view, into the airlock.

Good. Now close the outer line, *wait*—no red borders? Open the inner. Air *shush*ed into the airlock. The silver man stepped into the carm, handed the spitgun to Anthon, and reached for his helmet.

In her heart of hearts, Lawri may have hoped for a last-breath counter-mutiny from the Navy's toughest warrior. She gave up that hope when she saw his face. Mark was a dwarf, of course, and the bones of his face were massive, brutal; but his jaw hung slack and his breath came fast and his face was pale with shock. His eyes wavered about the cabin, seeking reassurance. "Minya?"

A dark-haired woman answered. "Hello, Mark."

Her voice was flat and her face was hostile. Mark nodded unhappily. Now he recognized Lawri. "Hello, Scientist's Apprentice. What now?"

"We're in the hands of mutineers," Lawri said, "and I wish they were better at flying what they've stolen."

The mutineers' First Officer said, "Welcome to Quinn Tribe, as a citizen. Quinn Tribe doesn't keep copsiks. I'm Clave, the Chairman. Who are you?"

"Navy, point man, armor. Name's Mark. Citizen doesn't sound too bad. Where we going?"

"Nobody seems to know. Now, we don't quite trust you, Mark, so we're going to tie you to a seat. That must have been quite a ride. Maybe you really are made of starstuff."

Mark was letting himself be led forward, to an empty chair. "All things considered, I'd rather ride inside. I was too mad to let go. We're not really going to *hit* Gold, are we?"

He's turned docile! Lawri thought in disgust. *He's given in to the mutineers! Are they really going to win?*

And then she saw that they were not.

She kept her silence.

Clave counted ten seats and thirteen citizens, one dead. Horse didn't need a chair. Neither did the three jungle giants. Quite the contrary! But even with the wide cargo space aft, the carm was crowded.

The citizens seemed calm enough. Exhausted, Clave guessed, and too awestruck to feel fear. He felt a touch of that himself. Most of them— even the silver man—were looking out the windows.

The sky was nearly black and scattered with dozens of white points. The Scientist's Apprentice broke her angry silence to say, "You've heard about them all your lives. The stars! You say it without knowing what you're talking about. Well, there they are. You'll die for it, but you've seen the stars."

Real they were, and impressive enough, but they were just points. It was the Blue Ghost and Ghost Child that held Clave's attention. He'd never seen them either. The paired fans of violet light were vivid and terrifying. They were entirely outside the Smoke Ring, flowing out along the hole in the ring.

Anthon and Debby were keeping busy. They had moored the ponchos and the smoked and cleaned carcass of a salmon bird to fixtures along the cargo hold walls. Now they were carving thin slices from the bird.

Clave remembered feeling like this when the tree came apart. He didn't know enough to make decisions! Then, he had been ready to strangle the Grad for withholding information. Now—

The Grad was watching him uneasily. Did he think Clave would attack their prisoners? Clave smiled back. He made his way aft and helped the jungle giants pass curls of meat forward.

Now was different. Clave was not Chairman here. If they died it would not be Clave's fault.

Probably the jungle giants found the carm more frightening than most—than Clave!—yet they were acting to make it their home. Squeezegourds of water were passing up and down the chairs . . . three squeezegourds, looking somewhat flat. Clave wondered about the carm's water supply.

He was about to ask when the Grad spoke first. "Gavving, would you come here for a moment?"

There was secret urgency in his voice. Anthon noticed and continued what he was doing. So did Clave. If their help was needed it would be requested.

Gavving squeezed between Lawri and the Grad. The summons was something of a relief. Minya's news had startled him, and he did need time to compose his face.

The Grad pointed. "See the red border blinking around that number?"

"Sure."

"Red means emergency. That number is the air in the cabin. How do you feel? Allergy attack coming on?"

"Actually, it was the last thing on my mind." Gavving listened to his body. Ears and sinuses were unhappy . . . eyes scratchy . . . "Maybe."

The yellow number dropped a digit behind the decimal point.

"Scientist's Apprentice, any comments?"

"Fix it yourself, Jeffer the Scientist."

"Mmm."

"Grad, what does it *mean*?"

"Oh, sorry, Gavving. There's no air outside. The air inside must be leaking out into the, um, universe. You know, I talk to you when I get confused. Maybe you'll come up with something."

Gavving chewed it over. "What Clave said—"

"Clave did *not* say that the carm is almost four hundred years old and maybe falling apart."

"Like all those bicycle gears . . . okay, what's your opinion of the Scientist's Apprentice?"

Lawri bore their considering stares with her lips pressed tight and her eyes full on Gavving's. The Grad smiled and said, "Better you ask her opinion of us."

Gavving didn't have to. "Four enemy warriors, six copsiks caught in mutiny, one corpse, and a Navy man who surrendered his weapon." Her expression flickered. Had she forgotten the silver man? This wouldn't be easy, guessing at a stranger's thoughts. Try anyway. "I only wondered if she's good enough to save us if she wanted to. We could waste too much time on that."

The Grad nodded. "Lawri, if the Scientist were here, could he save us?"

"Maybe. But he wouldn't!"

"Klance wouldn't save the carm?" The Grad smiled.

She shrugged as best she could within her bonds. "All right, he'd save the carm if he could."

"How?" She didn't answer. "Can you save us?"

She raised an eyebrow at him. Gavving found that admirable, but what he said was, "Bluff. Grad, we'll have to fix it ourselves. The Scientist told you things about gases, didn't he?"

"Both Scientists did. Come to that . . . oxygen? We must be getting air from the oxygen tank. It's the hydrogen tank that's empty. And . . . we'll have more fuel pretty soon. The carm splits water into the two flavors of fuel. The one flavor, the oxygen, it's what we breathe. At least we'll have some time."

Gavving studied the blond girl's face. What did she know? What did she *want*? If she only wanted everybody dead, then dead they were. But there was something she might hate even more than mutiny.

It depended on getting the Grad moving, which was a good idea anyway. How? Ask stupid questions; that worked sometimes. "Can we find the leak? Set something smoldering and watch the smoke?"

"Yes! It'll tell the others what's wrong, though, and burn up air too. Mph?"

"Inspiration?"

"Molecules of . . . bits of air move more slowly when they're cold." The board was already alive with yellow numbers and drawings. The Grad touched an arrowhead on a vertical line, then moved his fingertip slowly toward him. The arrowhead became two arrowheads, and one followed his finger.

"I never even wondered if we could make the cabin warmer or cooler, but it *has* to be true. That oxygen is liquid. Cold! It'd be freezing our lungs out if something wasn't keeping the cabin warm. Okay, now it'll be cold in here, but we'll live longer. I think you'd better tell Clave what's on and let him make the announcement. They'll have to know now, because we'll have to pass out the extra ponchos. Then we'll try the smoke—"

Lawri spoke. "Just let me at the damn controls!"

Gavving turned from her. Hide the smile. Lawri might want their deaths, but she *couldn't* let the Grad save them without her help. He asked, "Is it too complicated to tell the Grad?"

"No. But I won't!"

"Grad? Try the smoke?"

"Worst she can do is kill us. Besides, Lawri always wanted to fly the carm. Lawri, the position of Scientist's Apprentice is now open."

Lawri flexed her arms and looked about at her captors. Her hands prickled; her arms hurt. Her urge was to strike out at the mutineers. But the look on Jeffer's face: considering . . . like Klance waiting for the right answer to some stupid rote question . . .

The sky was black as charcoal. The stars were white points, like tiny versions of Voy, but *thousands* of them. And if they roused fear in Lawri, what must they be doing to these savages? She watched them nibbling on rolled slices of raw meat, and suddenly smiled.

She reached past the Grad and tapped the white key. "Prikazyvat Voice." *Hear this, you treefeeders!*

"Ready," said a voice belonging to nobody in the carm. "Identify yourself."

The lunchtime conversation went dead silent. The jungle giant male cocked his crossbow. She turned her back on him. "I am Lawri the Scientist. Give us your status."

"Fuel tanks nearly empty. Power depleted, batteries charging. Air pressure dropping, will be dangerously low in five hours, lethal in seven. Displays are available."

"Why are we losing air pressure?"

"All openings are sealed. I will seek the source of a leak."

Lawri tapped the white switch again. "That's what will kill us. We'll strangle without air. Too bad. It would have been quite a show, but you won't see it," she flashed at the Grad.

"Why did you turn off the display?"

"Voice can't hear us till I tap it again. It can do almost anything if you say the wrong thing, just talking."

"Would it talk to me?"

"You're a . . ." Her scorn became something else. "It wants you to identify yourself, and it remembers. Hmm. Try it." She tapped the talk button.

"Prikazyvat Voice," said the Grad.

"Identify yourself."

"I'm the Scientist of Quinn Tuft. Do we have enough fuel to get back into the Smoke Ring?"

"No."

For a moment the Grad forgot how to breathe. Then, "We have a water supply. Won't it be separated into fuel?"

Voice paused. Then, "If the flux of sunlight maintains its intensity, I will have fuel soon enough to effect a return. I note a mass near our course. I can use it as a gravity sling."

"Would that be Gold?"

"Rephrase."

"The mass, is it Goldblatt's World?"

"Yes."

The Grad tapped the switch before he began laughing. "Go for Gold! If we live that long."

The whispering aft had become obtrusive. With the air turning icy and Voice speaking from the walls, luncheon was sliding over to panic. Jeffer said, "Gavving, you'd better tell them about the pressure. We don't have time to brief Clave."

Lawri asked, "Shall I do it?" She knew more about what was going on.

Jeffer seemed appalled. "Lawri, they'd think *you* started the leak!"

"Savages—"

"Anyone would."

She couldn't decide if he meant it.

Gavving was telling the rest of the mutineers about the leak. He told it long, including what they planned to do about it. Jeffer tapped the white button. "Prikazyvat Voice. Have you found the leak?"

"I find no point of leakage. Air is disappearing."

"Will we live long enough to get back into the Smoke Ring?"

"No. The course I've programmed would take twenty-eight hours. Air pressure will have dropped to lethal levels in ten hours. Times are approximate."

Lawri couldn't remember how long an hour might be. Still . . . ten hours? It had been seven before the cabin got so cold. She wondered why Voice hadn't taken it into account. Sometimes Voice could be such a fool.

She said, "Display the areas where you have looked for a leak."

The yellow line diagrams of the cabin sprouted green borders along two-thirds of the interior. Red dots blinked elsewhere. "Those are sensors that have died," Lawri told Jeffer. "Voice, implement your course correction."

Jeffer added, "Prikazyvat Voice. Do not use the main motor at any time!"

"I will fire as I have fuel," Voice said. "First burn in ten seconds. Nine. Eight."

"Everybody grab something," Jeffer called.

Mutineers were pulling the extra ponchos over their clothing. They stopped to strap themselves in. The jungle giants moved against the aft wall and grabbed fixtures—

"Two. One."

But only the attitude jets lit. The carm's nose swung toward the Smoke Ring and stayed there while the aft motors fired. It lasted several tens of breaths. They would pass closer to Gold . . . which had become huge, a spiral storm seen edge-on, whose rim was already below them.

If Mark weren't tied, Lawri thought, *and if the main motor fired, nobody would be able to move except Mark.* It was something to keep in mind. Jeffer didn't seem to realize that the thrust could be controlled, by touching the top or bottom of those rectangles to raise or lower the fuel flow.

Meanwhile . . . how could the leaks be blocked? If there was a way, Lawri was damned well going to find it before Jeffer did.

Chapter Twenty-One

GO FOR GOLD

"Kendy for the State. Kendy for the State. Kendy for the State." The response came almost instantly, sharp and crisp through near-vacuum and dwindling distance. The CARM was out of the Smoke Ring. Kendy had clear sending for the first time since the mutiny. He sent: "Status?"

The motors were functional, all of them. Fuel: a few teacupsful. Water: a good deal. Solar power converters: functional. Batteries: charged, but running down as they changed water into liquefied hydrogen and oxygen. Sunlight flux from T3 would be steady in vacuum. There *would be* fuel.

The CARM was on manual. CO_2 flux indicated a full load of passengers. The carbon dioxide was accumulating slowly; the life support system could almost handle it . . . and the cabin was leaking air. Oh shit, they were dying!

"Course record since initiating burn."

It came. The CARM was rising. It would have passed near the L2 point—Kendy's own location, the point of stability behind Goldblatt's World—were it not for Goldblatt's World itself. And were it not for Goldblatt's World, the CARM would presently fall back to safety . . . but the core of an erstwhile gas giant planet was pulling the CARM's orbit into a tilted near-circle entirely outside the Smoke Ring.

"Switch to my command."

Massive malfunction.

"Give me video link with crew."

"Denied."

And the cabin pressure was dropping. Something had to be done. Kendy sent, "Copy," and waited.

The CARM computer thought it over, slowly, bit by bit; geared up; and began beaming its entire program. It took twenty-six minutes. Kendy looked it over—a simplified Kendy, patched with subsequent commands and garbled by time and entropy—while he sent, "Stand by for update programming."

"Standing by."

Kendy didn't believe it. The long-dead programmer would have embedded *protect* commands. He simply hadn't reached them yet . . . unless they had deteriorated too? Kendy didn't *have* an update program, he'd been so sure. He'd have to assemble it from scratch.

The speed with which a computer can think was Kendy's triumph and tragedy. Always he was freshly surprised by the boredom of his eventless life. It stayed fresh, because Kendy was constantly editing his memories. The storage capacity of his computer-brain was fixed. He was always near his limit. He had edited his memory of the mutiny, deleting the names of key figures, for fear that he might later seek vengeance against their descendants. He regularly deleted the memory of his boredom.

Once he had examined the solution to the Four-Color Problem in topology. The proof submitted in 1976 by Appel and Haken could not be checked except by a computer. Kendy *was* a computer; he had experienced the proof directly and found it valid. He remembered only that. The details he had deleted.

He had used a simplified program for the CARM computers, then deleted it. But now he had the CARM's program as a template. He ran through it, sharpening everywhere, correcting where suitable, updating his own simplified personality . . . leaving intact the CARM's own memories of the time of mutiny, because he was determined to ignore them. He looked for a way to plug the leak in the cabin. It was hopeless: the life support sensors had failed, not the program. He almost deleted the command that barred use of the main motor. The main motor was more efficient. He didn't understand that command . . . but it was input, and recent. He left it alone.

Now: a course program to bring them here, to study them . . .

He barely had time to hope. Kendy apprehended orbital mechanics directly. He saw instantly that the fuel wasn't there, nor the sunlight to electrolyze enough water in time. His own pair of CARMs, which fed him power via their solar collectors, didn't have fuel to meet and tow the savages' CARM even if he were willing to risk them both.

Forget it and try again . . . He could get them back into the Smoke Ring via a close approach past Goldblatt's World. In fact, the CARM's computer had already worked out a course change. It didn't matter. They'd be dead by then.

He left that part of the program intact. He deleted the barriers that barred him from communication. He beamed the revised program to the CARM at the snail's pace the CARM could accept.

The CARM filed it.

It had worked! At least he could look them over, get to know them a little, before they were gone. After five hundred and twelve years!

The cold had gotten to the jungle giants. Anthon and Debby and Ilsa were curled into a friendly, cuddling, shivering ball, with the spare ponchos pulled around them.

The other passengers were taking it better. There were ponchos for everyone but Mark, and two to spare. One they tore into scarves. Jinny wound a scarf around Mark's neck and tucked the ends into the collar of the silver suit. "Comfortable?"

The silver man seemed cheerful enough, despite the lines that held him immobile in his chair. "Fine, thanks."

"Is that suit thick enough?"

"Damn it, woman, you're the one who's shivering. This suit keeps its own temperature, just like the carm. If anyone needs my scarf . . . you want it?"

Jinny smiled and shook her head.

"Of course, I'd be even better off with my helmet closed," Mark said, and they laughed as if he'd said something funny. It didn't need saying: if they couldn't plug the leak, or if Lawri chose to kill them somehow, Mark would die with the rest.

The Grad had made a torch from one of the scarves plus fat scraped from the skin of the salmon bird. He was about to light it when he noticed mist before his face. He blew . . . white smoke. Everyone save Horse was breathing white smoke, as if they were all using tobacco.

"If you think something's leaking, breathe on it!" he announced. "Watch your breath. No, Jayan, forget the doors. Voice has sensors there."

Lawri did something to the controls. "I'm turning up the humidity . . . the wetness in the air. More fog that way."

Citizens took their turns at the control panel to find the blank spots in the yellow diagram. The Grad began the uncomfortable job that others might miss: he crawled between the seats, edging around the cold corpse of Gavving's friend, blowing mist where the floor joined the starboard wall.

Merril called, "I've got it. It's the bow window."

A crowd of citizens crawled around the rim of the bow window, blowing, watching the pale smoke form streamlines where the window joined the hull. The window was loose around the ventral-port corner.

"Keep looking," Lawri ordered. "There may be more."

She herself made her way aft. The Grad joined her at the back wall. "What have you got in mind? Is there a way to plug the leaks?"

Voice began a countdown. Lawri waited while small jets fired. The cluster of jungle giants sagged against the aft wall without falling apart. Ilsa giggled. She must be still floating from the spitgun drug.

The burn ended. Lawri said, "Maybe. Have we got something to hold water?"

The Grad called, "We need squeezegourds!"

They found three. Merril collected them and brought them back. Jayan and Jinny were blowing on the side windows, which seemed all right. Gavving and Minya moved along the rim of the bow window, blowing and watching. Mist formed outside and vanished immediately, along a curve of window as long as the Grad's arm, shoulder to fingers.

Lawri turned a valve. Brown water oozed from the aft wall, formed a growing globule.

"It's *mud*!" Merril said in disgust.

Lawri said, "We put pond water in. The carm breaks the pure water into hydrogen and oxygen, but it leaves the goo behind. Every so often we have to clean it out. That's why there's an *eject* system, and you can be damn glad of it."

"We can't drink that stuff. We should have picked up Minya's water supply."

"Say that if we live long enough to get thirsty." Lawri took the gourds and filled them from the brown globule. Merril winced, watching each of their water gourds become fouled.

Lawri went forward with the gourds. Would she plug the leak with mud? He could do it himself, now, if Lawri balked; but he wanted her on his side, as far as that was possible.

Lawri squeezed muddy water along the rim of the bow window.

Mist showed outside. The glass began to frost. The water stayed where she put it, in a long brown bubble. Over the next several minutes—while Lawri alone watched the controls—the water dwindled and thickened to a darker brown. Presently it began to turn *hard.*

Clave said, "Grad? Is it working?"

The Grad had read of ice. It was no more real to him than the liquefied gases in the tanks. He looked to Lawri.

Lawri met his eyes and said, "I will not accept the position of Scientist's Apprentice."

After such a performance, was she quitting on them? Clave spoke first, and in haste. "I'm certain there's room in Quinn Tribe for two Scientists. Especially under the circumstances."

"I've saved you. Now I want to go home to London Tree. That's *all* I want."

She's earned it, the Grad thought, *but—*

Clave said, "Point to it."

The carm was nose-down to the Smoke Ring. Closest was the storm pattern that surrounded and cloaked Gold, a turbulent spiral of cloud, humped in the middle. The whole pattern drifted west at a speed that looked sluggish, but must be quick beyond imagination. The arms of the Smoke Ring reached away in both directions. They could see the flow of cloud currents, faster toward Voy, drifting backward near the carm. Minor details—like integral trees—were invisibly small.

"You're the Scientist," Clave said. "Could you get us back to London Tree?"

Lawri shook her head. She began to shiver; and once begun, she couldn't stop. Minya got her the last of the ponchos and they wrapped it around her, then tied a strip of cloth round her head and throat. She said, "We're not losing air anymore. Leave the humidity up and we won't get thirsty so fast. Jeffer, I'm cold and tired and lost. I can't make decisions. Don't bother me."

They weren't human.

Kendy had watched them for a bit. They had the temperature turned far down. Kendy was going to fix it, until he realized that the lowered temperature had slowed the leak.

They must have kept some of the old knowledge. But the cold was killing them too. He watched the *really* strange ones succumb first and crawl into a ball to wait for their deaths.

The CARM's medical sensors indicated a corpse and twelve citizens, not one of them quite normal. One had no legs. If lethal recessive genes were appearing in the Smoke Ring, it might point to inbreeding. Otherwise they seemed healthy. He saw no scars or pockmarks, no sign of disease—which was reasonable. *Discipline* had carried none of the parasites or bacteria that had adapted over the millions of years to prey on humanity. They didn't even show the sores that came with insufficient bathing.

The abnormal height, the long, vulnerable necks and long, fragile fingers and long, *long* toes, must be evolution at work, an adaptation to the free-fall environment.

He would have his problems, bringing *these* back into the State. In its way this small group was a perfect test sample. He could make his mistakes here and never pay a penalty. In time the CARM would be found by other savages.

Time to make his appearance.

Lawri was eating raw salmon bird, clearly hating it, but eating. Jayan and Jinny had gone aft to join the clustered Carther States warriors. It looked like fun, the Grad thought wistfully; but he was needed here.

Something was happening to the bow window: a pattern like a colored shadow, occluding the view.

"Lawri? Have you done something?"

"Something's wrong . . . I've never seen anything like . . ." she trailed off.

The carm was silent. A ghostly face filled the bow window. It took on color, huge and transparent, with the storms around Gold showing through.

It was brutal, with bushy brown hair and brows; thick brow ridges and cheekbones; a square, muscular jaw; a short neck as thick in proportion as a man's thigh. A face that resembled Mark's or Harp's. A gigantic dwarf. It spoke in Voice's voice.

"Citizens, this is Kendy for the State. Speak, and your reward will be beyond the reach of your imagination."

The passengers looked at each other.

"I am Sharls Davis Kendy," the face said. "I brought your ancestors here to the Smoke Ring and abandoned them when they made mutiny against me. I have the power to send you into Gold, to your deaths. Speak and tell me why I should not do so."

Too many were looking at the Scientists. Was this some trick of Lawri's? The Grad could feel the hair rising in a halo around his head . . . but *somebody* had to speak. He said, "I am the Quinn Tribe Scientist—"

"And I am the London Tree Scientist," Lawri said firmly. "Can you see us?"

"Yes."

"We are lost and helpless. If you want our lives, take them."

"Tell me of yourselves. Where do you live? Why are you of different sizes?"

The Grad said, "We are of three tribes living in two very different places. The three tall ones—" He kept talking while his mind sought a memory. *Sharls Davis Kendy?*

Lawri broke in. "You were the Checker for *Discipline*."

"I was and am," said the spectral face.

" 'The Checker's responsibility includes the actions, attitudes, and well-being of his charges,' " Lawri quoted. "If you can help us, you must."

"You argue well, Scientist, but my duty is to the State. Should I treat you as citizens? I must decide. How did you come in possession of the CARM? Are you mutineers?"

The Grad held his breath . . . and Lawri said, "Certainly not," contemptuously. "The carm belongs to the Navy and the Scientist. I'm the Scientist."

"Who are the rest of you? Introduce me."

The Grad took over. He tried to stick to lies he could remember, naming the copsiks of London Tree—Jayan, Jinny, Gavving, Minya—as London Tree citizens; Clave and Merril as refugees who had become copsiks; himself as a privileged refugee; the jungle giants as visitors. Too late, he remembered Mark tied motionless in his chair.

Go for Gold—"Now, Mark *is* a mutineer," he said. "He tried to steal the carm."

Would the dwarf brand him a liar? But the rest would back him up . . . except Lawri . . . Mark let his eyes drop. He looked sullenly dangerous.

Sharls Davis Kendy began to question Mark. Mark answered angrily, belligerently. He created a wild tale of himself as a copsik barred from citizenship by his shape; of trying to steal the carm by activating the main motor, hoping to immobilize all but himself, then finding that the ferocious thrust left him as helpless as the rest.

The face seemed satisfied. "Scientist, tell me more of London Tree. You keep some who are barred from citizenship, do you?"

Lawri said, "Yes, but their children may qualify."

"Why does a tree come apart?" the face asked, and "How does London Tree move?" and "Why do you call yourself *Scientist*?" and "Are many of you crippled?" and "How many children do you expect to die before they grow to make children?" It wanted populations, distances, durations: numbers. Lawri and the Grad answered as best they could. With these they could stick close to the truth.

And finally the voice of Kendy said, "Very well. The CARM will reenter breathable atmosphere in eleven hours. The air will slow it. Keep the—"

"Hours?"

"What measure do you use? The circuit that Tee-Three makes around the sky? In about one-tenth of a circuit, you'll be falling through air. Air is dangerous at such speeds. Keep the bow forward. You'll see fire; don't worry about it. Don't touch anything at the bow. It will be hot. Don't open the airlock until you've stopped. By then you'll have fuel to move about. Do you understand all of that?"

Lawri said, "Yes. What are our chances of living through this?"

The face of Kendy started to answer—and froze with its mouth half-open.

Update: Cabin pressure has returned to normal.

They had blocked the leak! *How?* A man without glands might naturally feel curiosity and duty as his strongest emotions. For Kendy these were now in conflict. And the CARM was about to pass out of range.

Kendy had never intended to tell them that they would not live to see reentry. Medical readouts implied that they had lied to him too . . . and he dared not accuse them of it.

This changed everything. The savages might actually return to describe Kendy and *Discipline.* He could stop them, of course, by beaming some wild course change to the CARM. Or he could spend the next few minutes . . . indoctrinating them into the State? Impossible. He could take one trivial step in that direction, then try to impress them with the need to talk to him again.

And when they did that—years from now, or decades—he could begin the work that had waited for half a thousand years.

The face said, "You have stopped the leak. Well done. Now you must kill the mutineer. Mutiny cannot be tolerated in the State."

Mark went pale. Lawri started to speak; the Grad rode her down. "He'll face trial on our return."

"Do you doubt his guilt?"

"That will be decided," the Grad said. At this point he probably became guilty of mutiny himself, but what choice did he have? If Mark didn't talk to save himself, Lawri would. *And I captain the carm!*

"Justice is swift in the State—"

The Grad countered, "Justice is *accurate* in Quinn Tuft."

"Our swiftness may well depend on instant communication, which you clearly do not have." The face began speaking louder and more rapidly, as if in haste. "Very well. I have a great deal to tell you. I can give you instant communication and power that depends on sunlight instead of muscle. I can tell you of the universe beyond what you know. I can show you how to link your little tribes into one great State, and to link your State to the stars you now see for the first time. Come to me as soon as you can . . ."

The voice of Kendy died in a most peculiar fashion, blurring into mere noise, as the brutal face blurred into a wash of colored lines. Then the voice was silent, and the storm pattern around Gold glowed blue and white through the bow window.

Chapter Twenty-Two

CITIZENS' TREE

Kendy's readings were beginning to blur. Frustratingly, the CARM's aft and ventral cameras worked perfectly. He had two fine views of the stars and the thickening Smoke Ring atmosphere. Plasma streamed past the dorsal camera, and Kendy sought the spectral lines of silicon and metals: signs that the CARM's hull was boiling away. There was some ablation, not much more than he would have expected when the CARM was new.

Inside the cabin the CO_2 content was building. The jolting looked bad enough to tenderize meat. The passengers were suffering: mouths wide, chests heaving. Temperature was up to normal and rising. A blurred figure snapped its safety bands loose and struggled to tear its clothing away. Kendy couldn't get medical readings through the growing ionization, but the pilot had been under terrific tension earlier . . .

It looked chancy, whether the CARM would live or die. Kendy wasn't sure which he preferred.

He had bungled.

The principle was simple and had served the State before. To further the cause, a potential convert was ordered to commit some obscene crime. He could never repudiate the cause after that. To do so would be to admit that he had committed an abomination.

The caveat was simple too. One must never give such an order unless it would be obeyed.

Kendy was ashamed and angry. He had attempted to bind their loyalty to him by ordering an execution. Instead, he had almost turned them all into mutineers! He'd had to back down gracefully and fast. He'd had no chance to recover from that, with the ionosphere building up around the CARM, cutting communications. His medical readings told him that they had lied to him, somewhere. He shouldn't have forced them to do that either! He didn't know enough even to guess at what they were hiding.

Too late now. If he sent some lethal course correction now, ionization would garble it. If they lived, they would tell of a Kendy who was powerful but gullible, a Kendy who could be intimidated. If they died . . . Kendy would remain a legend fading into a misty past.

The forward view was a blur of fire as the CARM plowed deeper into atmosphere. He was losing even the cabin sensors . . .

There was flame in front of them, transparent blue, streaming to the sides. The Grad felt the heat on his face. They'd be losing air again: the black ice around the rim of the bow window had turned to mud . . . mud that bubbled. He'd been wrong. The screaming flame-hot air massed before the bow was coming *in*.

Things came at them. Little things were hopeless; they hit or they didn't. Blood spots turned black and evaporated. Larger objects could be avoided.

His hands strangled the chair arms. Trying to steer the carm through this would have been bad enough. Watching Lawri steer was distilled horror. From her rigid posture, the knotted jaw and bared teeth, she was just at the edge of screaming hysterics. Her hands hovered like claws, reached, withdrew, then tapped suddenly at blue dashes. His own hands twitched when she was slow to see danger.

The chairs were full. Citizens had objected, but the Grad had simply kept yelling until it got done: the corpse of Horse moored to cargo fixtures; Mark the silver man in back, gripping cargo moorings with his abnormal strength; Clave beside him, swearing that his own strength was enough; everyone else strapped into seats that would give *some* protection, even to jungle giants, against thrust from the bow. Reentry wasn't like using the main motor. It was an attack. The air was trying to pound the carm into bits of flaming starstuff.

Lawri had lived half her life with the carm. She *had* to be better at this than the Grad, she'd insisted, and she was right. He gripped the chair arms and waited to be smashed like a bug.

The carm fell east and in. Integral trees showed foreshortened, as three . . . four pairs of green dots, hard to see . . . she'd seen them: jets fired. A bit of green fluff, dead ahead . . . Lawri fired port jets . . . the carm swung sluggishly around, shuddering as the flaming air blasted the nose off-center. Forward jets: the carm eased backward, too slowly, while the fluff swelled to become an oncoming jungle.

A grunt of pain, aft. Clave had been jarred loose. The silver man was holding him in place with a hand on his chest.

The Grad saw birds and scarlet flowers before the jungle was past. Lawri let the bow face forward again. A pond a klomter across just missed swatting them; droplets of fog in its wake rang the hull like a myriad tiny chimes. The debris was growing ever thicker.

And it was moving past them more slowly.

Something barred their path like a green web. It might have been half of an integral tree with the tuft gone wild, the foliage spreading like gauze, the trunk ending in a swollen knob. Small birds played in the slender branches. Swordbirds hovered at the edges. He'd never seen such a plant . . . and Lawri was steering clear of it.

The Grad said, "Lawri?"

"It's over," she said. "Damn, I'm tired. Take the controls, Jeffer."

"I have it. Relax."

Lawri rubbed her eyes fiercely. The Grad touched blue dashes to slow the carm further. A fingertip touch set the cabin warmth control to normal. The cabin was already warm. If it hadn't been lethally cold when they entered atmosphere, they might well have roasted.

He looked back at his passengers. Six of Quinn Tribe remained. Twelve total, to start a new tribe . . . "We're back," he said. "I don't know just where. Are we all alive? Does anyone need medical help?"

"Lawri! You did it!" Merril chortled. "We lived long enough to get thirsty!"

The Grad said, "We're low on fuel and there's no water at all. Let's find a pond. Then pick a home."

"Open the doors," Jayan said. She released her straps and moved aft, with Jinny following.

"Why?"

"Horse."

". . . Right." He opened the airlock to a mild breeze that smelled fresh, clean, wonderful. The carm's air stank! It was stale, a treefodder stink, fear and rotting meat and too many people breathing in each other's faces. Why hadn't he noticed?

The twins released the corpse from its mooring, wincing at the touch. They towed it through the doors. The Grad waited while they sent the bones of the salmon bird after it.

Then he fired the aft motors. *If I met his ghost, he wouldn't even recognize me. How can I say I'm sorry? Never use the main motor unless*—Horse dwindled into the sky.

The pond was huge, spinning fast enough to form a lens-shape, fast enough to have spun off smaller ponds. The Grad chose one of the smaller satellites, no bigger than the carm itself. He let the carm drift forward until the bow window just touched the silver sphere.

What happened then left him breathless. He was looking into the interior of the pond. There were water-breathing things shaped like long teardrops with tiny wings, moving through a maze of green threads. He turned on the bow lights, and the water glowed. There was a jungle in there, and swimming waterbirds darting in flocks among the plants.

Lawri roused him. "Come on, Jeffer. Nobody else knows how to do this. Pick two mutineers with good lungs."

He followed her aft and didn't ask her about lungs until he'd figured it out himself. "Clave, Anthon, we need some muscle. Bring the squeezegourds. Better than lungs, Scientist."

"Squeezegourds, fine. If you'd planned your mutiny better, you'd have dismounted the pump and stored it aboard."

He laughed and thought, *Should I have asked your advice too?* and didn't say it. After all Lawri had been through, it was good to hear her joking, even in treemouth humor.

While she mounted the hose to the aft wall, the Grad carried the other end outside. He saw no sign of the nets that had covered the hull. Even the char had been burned off. He tethered himself before he jumped toward the water a few meters away. Clave came after him, also properly moored, carrying squeezegourds, followed by Jinny and Jayan.

Everyone was coming out. Mark was out of his pressure suit and tethered to Anthon. Merril, Ilsa, Debby . . . In a tangle of lines they plunged into the water and drank. The Grad hadn't let himself think of his thirst. Now he surrendered to it, submerging head and shoulders and doing his best to swallow the pond. The carm's headlamps lit the water around him.

It was playtime. Why not? He tugged on his line, pulled himself out before he drowned. The rest of the citizens were drinking, splashing, washing themselves and each other.

Was Lawri alone in the carm?

Alone with the controls of a vehicle that could hover near the pond, spraying fire on men and women who would have to choose between burning and drowning—He saw Lawri emerge with Minya and Gavving behind her. He'd been careless; they hadn't. The Grad kept an eye on her thenceforth to be sure she didn't return alone.

She splashed in the water. She and the dwarf washed each other and talked a little, in earshot of Anthon. Her motions were jerky, twitchy. She looked wire-tense in the aftermath of reentry. His suspicions seemed silly; she was in no shape to contemplate a countermutiny. He wondered if she would have nightmares.

They took turns pumping. The technique was to shove the neck of a squeezegourd into the hose, warily, because there were three gourds in motion; squeeze; duck it under water, squeeze, wait while it filled; into the hose, squeeze . . .

"My arms just quit," Minya said and handed her gourd to Merril. With her archer's muscles she had lasted longer than most. Gavving was some distance from the others, motionless in the water. He'd already speared four peculiar, supple, scaly waterbirds. She watched him and wondered how he really felt about the guest growing in her.

How did she feel? Her impregnation was part of her past. The past was dead for anyone, but stone dead for these citizens, with hundreds of thousands of klomters and the storms of Gold itself between them and their homes. She would have a child. Time was when she had given up hope of that . . . but how did Gavving feel?

Merril said, "Nobody's talking about Sharls Davis Kendy."

"What for?" Debby wondered. "He never bothered us before and he never will again."

"Still, it's something to have seen the Checker, isn't it? Something to tell our children. Someone that old must have learned a lot—"

"If he wasn't lying, or crazy."

"He had the facts right," the Grad said. "We did take him at his word, didn't we? Maybe he only had cassettes, like me. A dwarf Scientist, stuck out there in a carm, like we almost were. He's not all that bright, either. He swallowed Mark's story—"

"Come on, I was brilliant!" the silver man bellowed.

"You tell a fine story. Mark, why did you back me up?"

It was a breath or two before the dwarf answered. "You understand that I can't support a bloody copsik revolution."

"Okay. *Why?*"

"It was none of this Kendy's business. Whoever he is. Whatever he is."

"Yeah . . . He did have some interesting machinery. Maybe he got stuck aboard *Discipline* itself, somehow. I'd have liked to see *Discipline*."

Lawri hadn't even tried pumping. She flexed her fingers, wondering if they would heal. She had smelled the stink of fear on herself. That at least was gone.

She said, "I wouldn't deal with Sharls Davis Kendy if he *gave* me *Discipline*. Ugly, arrogant treefeeder. He wanted Mark dead like you'd kill a turkey, because it's time. Convenient. And he ordered us around like copsiks!"

They laughed at that. Even Mark.

At the end of three hours their forearms were distilled pain. The blue indicator inside read H_2O: 260. The Grad asked Lawri, "Enough?"

"For what we've got in mind—"

"We wondered about going home," Debby said.

Clave snorted, but they waited for Lawri's reply. She said reluctantly, "I'd never find London Tree again. Carther States is even smaller, and they're both on the wrong side of Gold. We'd have to accelerate west, drop in from the Smoke Ring, and let Gold pull us around. Do you want to go for Gold again?"

She smiled at their reactions. "Me neither. I'm tired. We can get to another tree and moor the carm. We'll build a pump before we need more water than that."

"We'd prefer a jungle, of course," Ilsa said.

One of the women bristled. "Nine of us and three of you! If—"

Clave said, "Hold it, Merril. Ilsa, are you sure? You can move a jungle, and that's good, right?"

Ilsa nodded cautiously. Anthon said, "That's *one* of the things we like about jungle life."

"But you can only do it every twenty years or so. We can moor the carrier . . . carm to the middle of an integral tree and move it when and where we like."

"Why not do that with a jungle?"

"Where would you mount the carm?"

Anthon thought it over. "The funnel? No, it might suddenly blow live steam—" He smiled suddenly. "There are more of you than us anyway. Sure, pick a tree."

There was a grove of eight small trees, thirty to fifty kilometers long. The Grad chose the biggest, without asking. He hovered on the forward jets at the western reach of the in tuft.

It was a wilderness. A stream ran down the trunk and directly into the treemouth. He looked for the rounded shapes of distorted old huts, and they weren't there. The foliage around the treemouth had never been cut; there were no paths for burial ceremonies or moving of garbage. No earthlife showed, not even as weeds.

It was daunting. He said cheerily, "It seems we're the first here. Lawri, have you thought of a way to land this thing?"

"You have the helm."

He'd thought it through in detail. "I'm afraid our best move is to moor at the trunk and go down."

"Climb?"

"We did it before. Clave could lead most of us down while, say, Gavving and I wait. We'd have the carm for rescue operations. After the rest of you get down, Gavving and I can follow. We've climbed before—"

"Hold it," Clave said. "This is taking too treefeeding *long*. Grad, quit fooling around and just land in the treemouth."

"We might set it on fire!"

"Then we try again with another tree!"

Lawri had gone berserk at the suggestion of landing in the treemouth of London Tree. Now she just rubbed her eyes. Tired . . .

They were all too tired. They'd had enough of shocks and strangeness. Clave was right, delay would be torment, and there were trees to waste.

There was no kind of landing site in that wilderness. Everything he saw was green; there was no drought here. Would it burn?

Go for Gold.

He went in over the treemouth and rammed the carm into the foliage hard enough to stick. Still shaken by the impact, they forced their way through the doors, fast, and flailed with ponchos at the smoldering fires until they went out.

Then, finally, they had time to look around.

Minya stood panting, grinning, her black hair wild and wet, the blackened poncho trailing from her hand. She snatched at his hand and cried, "Copter plants!"

Gavving laughed. "I didn't know you liked copter plants."

"I didn't either. But in London Tree they weeded out the copter plants and flowers and anything else they couldn't use." She tapped at one, two, three ripe plants, and the seed pods buzzed upward. Suddenly, she was looking into his eyes, close. "We did it. Just like we planned, we found an unoccupied tree and it's ours."

"Six of us. Six out of Quinn Tuft . . . sorry."

"Twelve of us. More to come."

She had fought the fire with a predatory grace unhampered by the thickening around her hips. *Mine*, Gavving thought. *Whether it looks like me or some copsik runner . . . or Harp, or Merril! Mine; ours.* He'd tell her when the mood was right. But that was too serious for now. "Okay, everything you see is ours. What shall we call it?"

"The thing I like best . . . I can say *citizen* and mean *all of us*. I'm no copsik and I'm not a triune. Citizens' Tree?"

The foliage tasted like Quinn Tuft in the Grad's childhood, before the drought. He lay on his back in virgin foliage and sucked contemplatively.

He became aware that Lawri was watching him from the dappled shadows. She looked cold, or just twitchy, hugging her elbows, cringing as if from a blow. He snapped, "Can't you relax? Eat some foliage."

"I did. It's good," she said without inflection.

It was irritating. "All right, what's got you worried? Nobody's ever going to call you a copsik runner. You saved our lives and everyone knows it. You're clean, fed, rested, safe, and admired. Take a break, Scientist. It's *over*."

Now she wouldn't meet his eyes. "Jeffer, how does this sound? There are only two London Tree citizens for at least ten thousand klomters around. Doesn't it stand to reason that we'd . . . get along best together?"

He sat back on his haunches. Why ask him? "I suppose it does."

"Well, Mark thinks so too."

"Okay."

"He didn't have to say so. We talked a little about building huts, that's all, but he looks at me like he *knows*. Like, he's too polite to broach the subject yet, but where else can I go, who else is there? Jeffer, don't make me marry a dwarf!"

"Uh . . . huh."

She turned, convulsively, to see his face. He held up a hand to stop her from speaking. "In principle, two Scientists ought to make good mates too. Does *that* make sense? But you watched me murder Klance. I didn't warn him. I didn't make any speeches about copsiks and freedom and war and justice. I just killed him the first good chance I got. I'd have killed you too to get us free of that place."

She didn't nod, she didn't speak.

"You could put a harpoon in my belly while I'm sleeping. So don't push me. I have to think."

She waited. He thought. Now he knew why she irritated him with her twitchy unhappiness. He was guilty, and she had seen it. Not quite what one wanted in a mate!

Did he want a wife? He'd always thought he did, and with seven women and five men in Nameless Tuft . . . no chance for an unmarried man to play around in such a tiny population, but he should have his choice of wives. So who?

Gavving and Minya: married. Clave, Jayan, Jinny: a unit, and the twins seemed to like it that way. Anthon, Debby, Ilsa might all have left mates in Carther States, and they might all be looking around . . . but Anthon didn't seem to think so, and even if Debby or Ilsa were available . . . a romp might be fun, but they looked so *odd*. Which left . . . Lawri.

He said, being nearly sure he could get away with it, "Lawri, will you forgive me for murdering Klance?"

"I notice you said murder. Not kill."

"I'm not even claiming it was war. I know what he was to you. Lawri, I *demand* this."

She turned her back and wept. The Grad did not turn his back. He'd virtually invited her to try to kill him. *Now or never, Lawri! You can add too. There's me or there's Mark or there's nobody. I might be giving Mark another reason to kill me. Do I want to risk that?*

She turned around. "I forgive you for murdering Klance."

"Then let's go to the carm and register a marriage. We'll pick up witnesses along the way."

Clave looked down into the treemouth. "I see rocks down there. Good. We'll have to collect them for a cookfire. Cook Gavving's waterbirds. Tear out some foliage so we'll have room. Where do we want the Commons?"

He didn't see many of his citizens in earshot, and none were listening.

He raised his voice. "Treefodder, we have to get organized! A reservoir. Tunnels. Huts. Pens. Maybe we won't find turkeys, but we're bound to find *something*. Maybe dumbos. We need *everything*. Sooner or later we want elevators to the midpoint so we can moor the carm there. But for now—"

Anthon, flat on his back in the foliage with a long, long woman in each arm, bellowed, "Claaave! Feed it to the treeee!"

Clave grinned at Anthon. He did seem to represent the majority opinion. "Take a break, citizens. We're home."

For good or ill, they were alive and safe, two-thirds of the distance from Goldblatt's World to the congestion of masses and life-forms around the L4 point; and they would remember Kendy.

He had promised a treasure of knowledge. A pity he hadn't had time to give them more of a foretaste; but they must have experienced exactly what he'd predicted during reentry, given that they'd survived. A savage's gods *were* omniscient, weren't they? Or were they gullible, easily manipulated? Kendy's memory had been pruned of such data.

Whatever: the legend would spread.

I can show you how to link your little tribes into one great State.

He had altered the programming in the CARM. The CARM would watch their behavior and record everything. Before the children of the State came again to Kendy, he would know them . . .

He would know one tiny enclave within that vast cloud. The Smoke Ring was roomy enough for endless variety. 10^{14} cubic kilometers of breathable atmosphere was about thirty times the volume of the Earth! Kendy wished for a thousand CARMs, ten thousand. *What were they doing in there?*

Never mind. Sooner or later there would come a man eager to carve out an empire, determined enough to take the CARM, crazy enough to trust his life to the ancient, leaky service vehicle. Kendy would know how to use him. Such men had helped to shape the State on Earth. They would again, in this strange environment.

Kendy waited.

DRAMATIS PERSONAE

The Crew of Discipline

SHARLS DAVIS KENDY   Once a Checker for the State, now deceased. Also, the recordings of Sharls Davis Kendy's personality in the master computer of the seeder ramship *Discipline* and its service spacecraft.

Quinn Tuft

GAVVING   A young warrior subject to allergies.

HARP   The teller, or bard.

LAYTHON   The Chairman's son.

MARTAL   Quinn Tuft's cook (deceased).

THE SCIENTIST   Quinn Tuft's guardian of knowledge.

THE GRAD   The Scientist's half-trained apprentice.

THE CHAIRMAN   Ruler of Quinn Tribe.

CLAVE   A mighty warrior, the Chairman's son-in-law.

MAYRIN   Clave's wife, the Chairman's daughter.

JAYAN and **JINNY**   Twin sisters enamored of Clave.

MERRIL   An older woman, strong, but barren. Small, withered legs.

JIOVAN   A hunter.

GLORY   A woman of unwanted fame.

ALFIN   An older man, Keeper of the treemouth.

Others

MINYA   A fighting woman of the Triune Squad, of Dalton-Quinn Tuft.

SAL, SMITTA, JEEL, THANYA, DENISSE   Others of the Triune Squad.

KARA   Sharman (or Scientist) of Carther States.

DEBBY, ILSA, HILD, LIZETH, ANTHON   Citizens of Carther States.

KLANCE   London Tree's Scientist.

LAWRI   London Tree's Scientist's Apprentice.

HORSE, JORG, HELN, GWEN   Copsiks in London Tree.

DLORIS, HARYET, KOR   Supervisors in London Tree.

KARAL, MARK, PATRY   London Tree Navy men.

GLOSSARY

BLUE GHOST and **GHOST CHILD**   Auroralike glow patches produced by magnetic effects above Levoy's Star's poles. Rarely visible.

BRANCH   One at each end of an integral tree, curving to leeward.

BRANCHLETS   Grow from the spine branches and sprout into foliage.

CARM   Cargo And Repair Module. *Discipline* originally carried ten of these.

THE CLUMP   The L4 and L5 points for Gold. They tend to collect debris.

COPSIK   Slave. Used as a general insult.

COPSIK RUNNER   Slavetaker or slavemaster.

COTTON-CANDY JUNGLE or **JUNGLES**   Describes almost any large cluster of plants. A good many plants and clusters of plants look like fluffy green cotton candy. Many are edible.

DAY   One orbit about Levoy's Star, the neutron star (equals two hours for Dalton-Quinn Tree).

DUMBO   A predator of the integral trees.

FAN FUNGUS   An integral tree parasite. Parts are edible.

"FEED THE TREE"   Defecate, or move garbage, or die.

FLASHER   An insectivorous bird.

GHOST CHILD   See **BLUE GHOST**.

GO FOR GOLD   Rush headlong into disaster. Or battle!

GOLD   See **GOLDBLATT'S WORLD**. Secondary meaning: something to avoid.

GOLDBLATT'S WORLD   A gas giant planet captured after Levoy's Star went supernova/neutron. Named for *Discipline*'s Astrophysicist, Sam Goldblatt.

HUTS   Any dwelling. In the integral trees, huts are woven from living spine branches.

INTEGRAL TREE   A crucial plant.

JET POD   Some plants grow pods that may be carried for attitude control: they jet gases (of corruption, or of oxygen in plants that favor the outer fringes of the Smoke Ring). Other plants fire seeds when dying, or going to seed, or falling too far out of the Smoke Ring. There are tropisms.

LEVOY'S STAR   A neutron star, the heart of the Smoke Ring system. Named for its discoverer, Sharon Levoy, Astrogator assigned to *Discipline*.

NOSE-ARM   See **DUMBO**.

OLD-MAN'S-HAIR   A fungus parasite on integral trees.

POND   Any large globule of water.

PRIKAZYVAT   Originally, Russian for "command." Presently used to activate computer programs.

QUINN TUFT   The in tuft (or point nearest Levoy's Star) of Dalton-Quinn Tree.

THE SCIENTIST   Quinn Tuft's guardian of knowledge. Tribes elsewhere use the same term.

SPINE BRANCHES   Grow from the branch of an integral tree.

SUN   A G0 star orbits the neutron star at 2.5×10^8 kilometers, supplying the sunlight that feeds the Smoke Ring's water-oxygen-DNA ecology.

TREEFODDER   Used as a curse. Treefodder is anything that might feed the tree: excrement, or garbage, or a corpse.

TUFTBERRIES   Fruiting bodies growing in the tuft of an integral tree. They fruit and scatter seed only at the tuft closest to the Smoke Ring median.

VOY   See **LEVOY'S STAR**.

YEAR   Half of a complete circuit of the sun around Levoy's Star, equal to 1.385 Earth years.

Directions

OUT   Away from Levoy's Star.

IN   Toward Levoy's Star.

EAST   In the orbital direction of the gas torus.

WEST   Against the orbital direction of the gas torus. The way the sun moves.

WINDWARD   Into the wind.

LEEWARD   The direction toward which the wind blows.

PORT   To the left if your head is out and you're facing west, or if your head is in and you're facing east, and so forth. Direction of the Ghost Child.

STARBOARD   Opposite port. Toward the Blue Ghost.

DOWN and UP   Usually applied only where tides or thrust operate. The general rule as known to all tribes is "East takes you out. Out takes you west. West takes you in. In takes you east. Port and starboard bring you back." Even those tribes who no longer can maneuver within the Smoke Ring know the saying.

THE
SMOKE RING

It is reassuring to know that the human race is still capable of producing big, roomy minds. This book is dedicated to Dan Alderson.

CONTENTS

PROLOGUE   *Discipline*   213

Section One   CITIZENS' TREE

ONE   *The Pond*   217

TWO   *Discipline*   227

THREE   *Refugees*   238

FOUR   *The In Tuft*   246

FIVE   *The Silver Suit*   259

SIX   *The Appearance of Mutiny*   271

Section Two   THE LOGGERS

SEVEN   *The Honey Hornets*   279

EIGHT   *The Honey Track*   289

NINE   *The Rocket*   297

TEN   *Secrets*   307

ELEVEN   *Happyfeet*   318

Section Three   CIVILIZATION

TWELVE   *Customs*   331

THIRTEEN   *The Termite Nest*   342

FOURTEEN   *Docking*   348

FIFTEEN   *Half Hand's*   358

SIXTEEN   *High Finance*   369

SEVENTEEN   *Serjent House*   376

EIGHTEEN   *Headquarters*   382

Section Four   THE DARK AND THE LIGHT

NINETEEN   *The Dark*   397

TWENTY   *The Library*   409

TWENTY-ONE   *The Silver Suit*   420

TWENTY-TWO   *Loop*   432

TWENTY-THREE   *Beginnings*   441

Dramatis Personae   455

Glossary   457

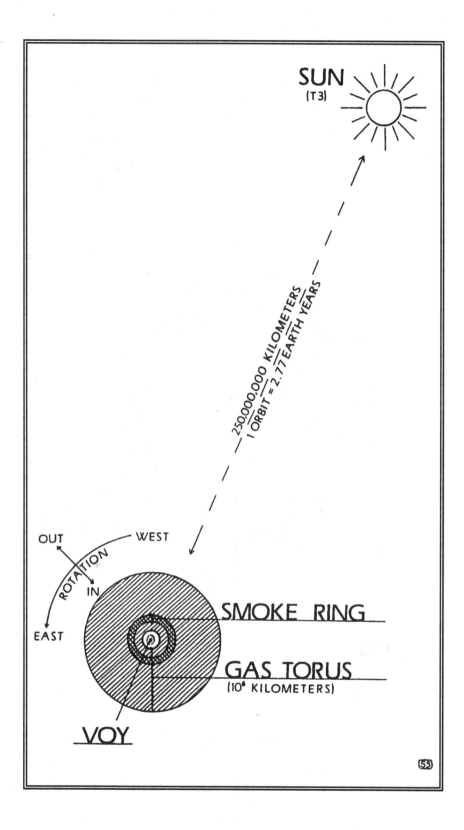

SUN
(T3)

$$\frac{250,000,000 \text{ KILOMETERS}}{1 \text{ ORBIT}} = 2.77 \text{ EARTH YEARS}$$

OUT
WEST
ROTATION
IN
EAST

SMOKE RING

GAS TORUS
(10⁶ KILOMETERS)

VOY

55

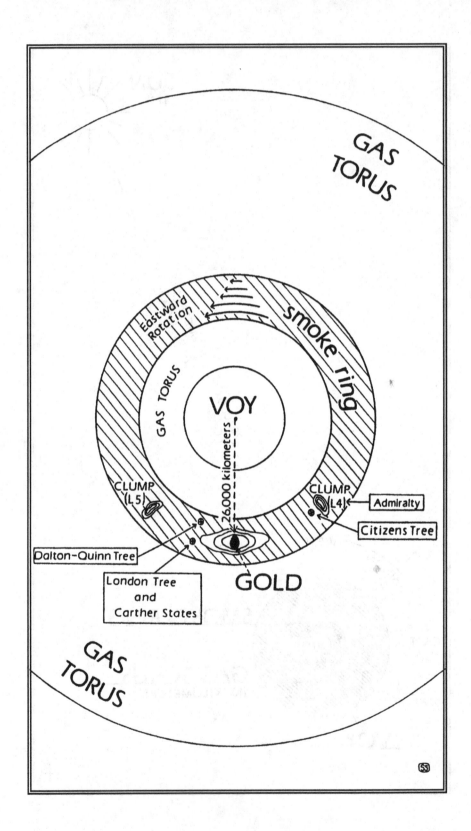

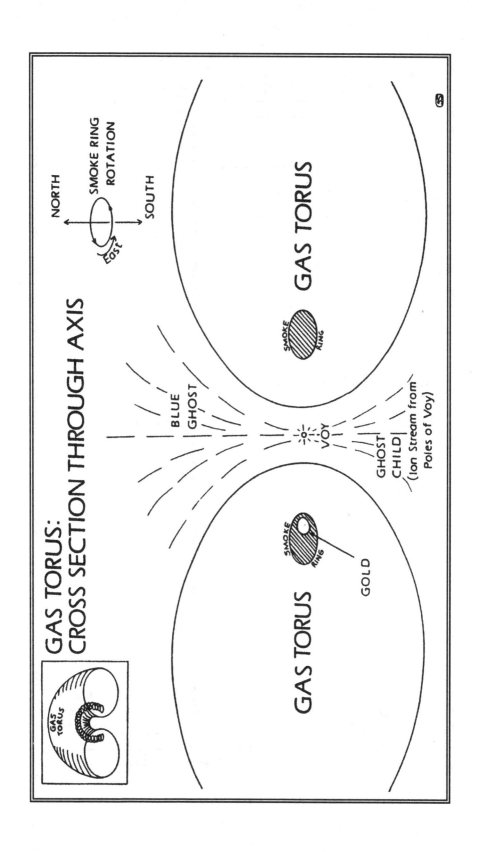

GAS TORUS:
CROSS SECTION THROUGH AXIS

GAS TORUS

GAS TORUS

GAS TORUS

SMOKE RING

SMOKE RING

GOLD

BLUE GHOST

VOY

GHOST CHILD
(Ion Stream from Poles of Voy)

NORTH

SOUTH

East

SMOKE RING ROTATION

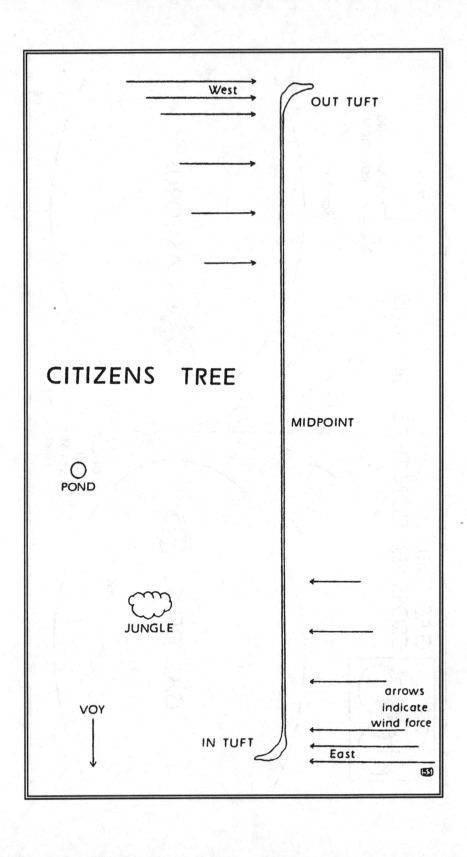

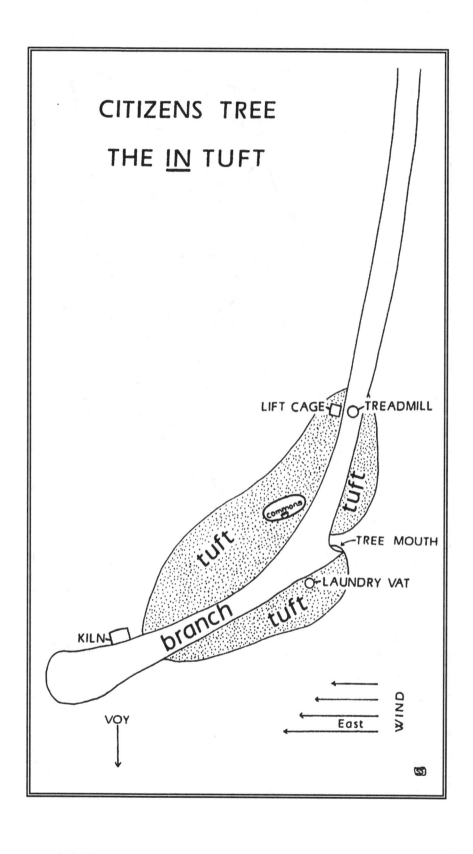

CITIZENS TREE

THE **IN** TUFT

LIFT CAGE — ○ — TREADMILL

tuft

commons

tuft

TREE MOUTH

○ — LAUNDRY VAT

branch   tuft

KILN

VOY

WIND

East

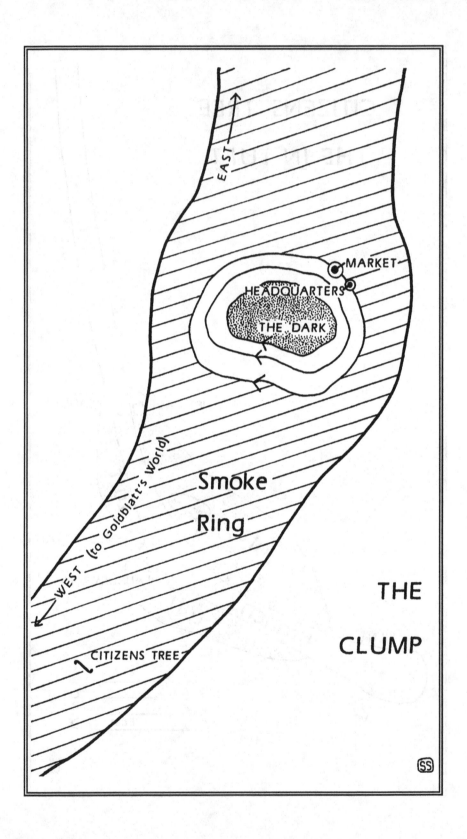

DISCIPLINE

The planet below him was hidden to all of Sharls's senses save for the Neutrino Screen, the Neudar. What had been a gas giant planet a billion years ago was still a world two and a half times the size of the Earth: an egg of rock and nickel-iron hidden in world-sized storms. The storms spread out into a cloudy ring occupying the entirety of Goldblatt's World's orbit around the neutron star.

Sharls watched storms spin outward from the gas giant. Streams of fog and cloud and dust ran slow near the Smoke Ring's outer rim, faster at the Smoke Ring median, faster yet as they neared Levoy's Star; and everywhere there were flattened whorls of hurricane. The gravity gradient was savage this near the ancient neutron star. The innermost limits of the Smoke Ring circled Levoy's Star every two hours.

The Smoke Ring was tinged with green—it had its own billion-year-old ecology—and somewhere in that cloud were men.

The temptation to go to them was a constant low-level irritant.

When moving between stars, *Discipline* burned the near-infinite hydrogen of interstellar space; but *Discipline* had been at rest for a long time now, and onboard fuel was limited. Refueling could not have progressed far when the mutiny came. Sharls's supply of deuterium-tritium mix was finite. He had no way of knowing how long he must wait for the children of *Discipline*'s crew to rediscover civilization, to build their own spacecraft, to come to him. He was always short of power. The solar collectors on his two remaining CARMs didn't give him much.

Sharls ignored the stars, most of the time. He watched the Smoke

Ring. When the boredom became too much for him, he edited it from his memory. Boredom was a recurring surprise.

Five hundred and thirty-two Earth years was one hundred and ninety-two orbits of Levoy's Star round its companion star. But the natives of the Smoke Ring measured years from the passings of the neutron star (Levoy's Star, "Voy") across the face of the yellow dwarf (T3, "Sun"); so a Smoke Ring "year" was 1.384 Earth years. Sharls had been waiting in the L2 point behind Goldblatt's World for three hundred and eighty-four Smoke Ring years.

Best to sit it out in a stable orbit, and watch, and wait for men to develop civilization. Best to edit the memory of boredom . . .

Discipline's computer/autopilot stored its information as a human brain did, or a hologram, though Sharls could feel differences. Memories from his time aboard *Discipline* were sharp and vivid. Those he had edited were gone completely. But memories from his time as a man, transferred long ago from a human brain now long dead, were blurred, hard to retrieve.

So: it wasn't like a relay clicking over.

But somewhere in the computer there was a change of state. Five hundred and thirty-two years, and *enough is enough*. Sharls Davis Kendy was done with waiting.

Section One

CITIZENS' TREE

Chapter One

THE POND

from the Citizens' Tree cassettes, year 19 SM:

PONDS

Water droplets come in all sizes here. Clouds may hold everything from fine mist, to globules the size of a fist, to spheroids that house all manner of life. The biggest "pond" we've seen massed ten million metric tons or so; but the tide from Levoy's Star had pulled it into two lobes and the differential winds were tearing it apart.

The ecology of the ponds is one rather than many. Life is queer and wonderful, but in every pond we have examined it is the same life. Ponds are temporary; pond life must occasionally migrate. In the Smoke Ring even the fish can fly.

—Carol Burnes, Life Support

Lawri and Jeffer swam beneath murky pondwater, trailing forty square meters of fabric stretched across the net more commonly used to sieve harebrains from the sky. They gripped its corners in strong toes and swam with their arms.

The sheet resisted. The leading edge tried to crumple. Tethers at the corners of the harebrain net got in their way. *We could have had some help,* Jeffer thought. *Lawri wouldn't have it. Lawri's idea, Lawri's project! She'd be doing this by herself if she possibly could.*

Air! He slapped her thigh. She dropped the sheet and they swam toward the light.

Air is the sweetest taste, though one must risk drowning to appreciate it.

They were at the arc of the pond nearest Citizens' Tree. The center of the trunk was a mere three klomters east. Seventy klomters of trunk ran out and in from the pond, ending in paired curved tufts. The in tuft, *home,* looked greenish black, with Voy's blue pinpoint shining almost behind it. A single line ran from the trunk, and divided.

The sheet was a ghostly shadow deep within the pond. Lines ran from the corners, up through the water and out, to join the main cable that ran to the trunk.

"Almost in place," Lawri said doubtfully.

"Close enough."

"All right. You go get the carm ready. I'll draft some hands to pull it in."

Jeffer nodded. His legs scissored and shot him into the air. He drifted toward the main cable in a spray of droplets.

It was easier than arguing. Lawri would not leave Jeffer to organize the final stage. When Lawri the Scientist got an idea, nobody else got credit. Particularly not Citizens' Tree's other Scientist, her husband.

Partway around the curve of the pond, Minya and Gavving floated in the interface between air and water, surrounded by thrashing children.

Lines ran from each child toward the cable from Citizens' Tree. The children were taught the backstroke first. It kept their faces in the air. Some preferred the frog-kick that let them look beneath the water. Swimming was a balance of surface tension versus the thrust of arms and legs.

If a child kicked himself entirely out of the water, an adult must go after him. A child who went beneath the surface could panic and must be pulled out before he drowned. There were carnivores among the waterbirds. Minya and Gavving wore harpoons. They had three of their own among the swimmers.

Gavving used lazy strokes to change his attitude, moving his field of view in a clockwise circle.

"Look at Rather," Minya said.

The oldest of the children were swimming together. Daughter of two jungle giants, golden-blond Jill had grown to merely normal height in the tide of Citizens' Tree. She was thirty ce'meters shorter than her parents . . . but the contrast between Jill and Rather was startling. At fourteen, Minya's dark-haired firstborn son was less than two meters in height. Jill had more than half a meter on him.

Yet Minya never spoke of Rather's height. Gavving looked again and said, "Right. *Rather!*"

Rather paddled over, reluctantly. Fine green fur, barely visible, grew a mi'meter long on his left cheek. Gavving gripped the boy's arm and lifted him partway out of the water, against surface tension. The green could be traced down Rather's neck, over his shoulder, and partway across his chest.

"Fluff," Gavving said. "Why didn't you tell someone?"

Rather grinned guiltily. "I've never swum before."

Minya snapped, "You go straight—"

"No. Finish your swim. You'll pay for it. You've seen your last of the sun for a while. Have we raised a fool? It's almost reached your eye!"

Rather nodded solemnly and paddled away. Minya watched him go, her mouth pursed in anger. Her husband wriggled and was silently underwater; kicked, and was beneath her; grasped an ankle and dove. Minya doubled back on herself and kicked him across the jaw. Gavving reached through the defense of her waving arms and legs and had her head between his hands; pulled her to him by main strength and kissed her hard. She laughed bubbles.

He kicked toward the surface with Minya in tow. They blew water from their faces before they inhaled, and were back on duty before any child could get into trouble.

Debby was some distance from where the children swam. She stayed just under the surface, motionless, peering, her spear poised. She expelled stale air—which stayed before her as a bubble—raised her head, snatched a breath, ducked again.

Debby had lived her first nineteen years in free fall. Fourteen years in the tree tide had put muscle on her without shrinking her height. Her children—and Ilsa's, the children they had borne to Anthon—were no taller than ordinary tree dwellers. But Debby was two and a half meters tall. Her fingers were long and fragile; her toes were sturdier if less agile, and the big toes measured six ce'meters. Her rich brown hair was beginning to show gray, but she still wore it a meter long. For swimming she wore it looped in a braid around her throat.

The water was murky. This was a new skill for Debby, but she was learning.

She struck. The ripple of her thrust expanded outward around the great globule, past playing children and the Scientists working their cloth sheet.

A silver shape wriggled on Debby's spearpoint. Debby reached above her head, tugged hard at the tether, and gasped as her head broke the surface. The waterbird, suddenly thrust into air, expanded its small wings and thrashed mightily. A blow to the head end quieted it. Debby pushed it into a net bag to join five others.

Her chest still heaved with the need for air. She rested quietly on her back, her hands fluttering from time to time to keep surface tension from pulling her under.

Eastward, a thousand klomters past Citizens' Tree, the cloud patterns thickened into a flattened whirlpool. The Smoke Ring converged beyond and below the whorl in a stream of white touched with blue-green, narrowing as it dropped toward the dazzling point of Voy.

Things tended to collect in that special part of the Smoke Ring, east of Gold by sixty degrees of arc. The citizens had reason to know that the storm-whorl around Gold was dangerous. They assumed that the Clump was too. They had never taken the tree nearer than this.

They had never visited a jungle.

Human beings certainly lived elsewhere in the Smoke Ring, but Citizens' Tree had never attempted to contact them.

Citizens' Tree was placid, safe. Working within the pond was as much excitement as Debby ever got these days. Life in Carther States had been different. The occasional raids from London Tree forced the citizens to be always prepared for war, until in one magnificent raid they had ended London Tree's power forever.

Debby's connection with the jungle warriors had ended too. A mixed group of copsiks and warriors had stolen London Tree's carm. The vehicle was old science, powerful and unfamiliar. They and their prisoners had been lucky to bring the carm to any kind of safety; but Carther States was lost somewhere in the sky beyond Gold.

From westward came a cheerful cry. "Citizens! We need muscle!" Debby saw Lawri the Scientist floating in the sky with one hand on the main tether.

Debby snatched at the net bag (six was a nice day's catch), kicked herself into the sky, and began reeling her line in. She was first to reach the Scientist. Clave and Minya and Mark the Silver Man were leaving the pond, reeling in lines. Gavving had stayed to gather the children.

Four tethers led to the corners of the sheet-covered net, which was now deep underwater. Lawri stationed them along the main tether as they arrived. "Gather it in," she directed them. "Make loops. Steady pull."

Debby wrapped her toes and her fingers around the cable, and did her savage best to contract her body. No loop formed. She knew she wasn't as strong as a tree dweller, but the others were having trouble too.

Lawri called, "Good! It's coming straight out."

That was not obvious to Debby. She strained . . . and gradually the pond bulged. The sheet and its net backing were rising, carrying tons of water. Debby pulled until her knees and elbows met, then shifted her grip and continued pulling.

The pond stretched, and tore. A baby pond pulled clear, leaving a trail of droplets the size of a man's head. Water flowed over the edges of the cloth but was not lost, for surface tension held it. The main pond pulsed as surface tension tried to form the sphere again.

"Keep pulling!" Lawri shouted. "Steady . . . okay. That should do it."

The citizens relaxed. The bud-pond continued to move east on its own momentum, toward the tree, with the net and sheet now in the middle of a pulsing sphere.

Debby coiled line that was now slack. Glancing toward the trunk, she saw what the curve of the pond had hidden earlier.

Parallel to the trunk and many klomters beyond it floated a slender dark line. A young tree, no more than thirty klomters long, and injured; for the in tuft was missing, chopped away somehow. The view was confusing, for the midtrunk was wreathed in cloud . . . dark, dirty cloud . . . smoke!

Debby tugged abruptly at another line. The motion set her drifting toward the Chairman. Clave caught her ankle as she arrived. "Something?"

Debby pointed with her toes. "That tree. It's on fire!"

". . . I believe you're right. Treefodder! It'll be coming apart. Two fires to worry about."

Debby had never seen a tree break in half, but Clave spoke from dreadful experience. They might have to move the tree. It would take time to get the carm ready—

Clave had already thought that far. His voice became a whipcrack roar. "Citizens, it's getting toward dinnertime, and we've got all these waterbirds. Let's break up the swim."

His voice dropped. "You go *now*, Debby. Tell Jeffer we may need the carm. We'll get the women and children down into the tuft, if we've got time. Your eyes are better than mine. Do you see anything leaving the tree? Like clouds of insects?"

There were black specks, big enough to show detail. "Not insects. Something bigger . . . three, four . . . birds?"

"Doesn't matter. Get going."

It had taken Jeffer the Scientist a fifth of a day to cross three klomters of line.

Free fall brought back memories. When Quinn Tribe was lost in the sky after Dalton-Quinn Tree came apart, his crew would have given eyes and limbs to reach a pond. Fourteen years later, the grandmother of all ponds floated three klomters from Citizens' Tree; and now their main problem was to get rid of most of it. Jeffer wondered if the children appreciated their wealth.

Perhaps they did. Most of Citizens' Tree, thirty naked adults and children, had come to swim in that shimmering sphere of water.

There was no foliage on the high trunk. It was thick rough bark, with fissures deep enough to hide a man. Jeffer found and donned his tunic and pants, then anchored his toes in a crevice and thrust to send himself gliding out along the bark, toward the carm.

The lift cable ended two hundred meters short of the carm's dock. The citizens may have feared that careless use of the carm might spray fire across a rising cage. More likely, they feared the carm itself. They would not lightly come too near that ancient scientific thing.

The carm was old science. It was roughly brick-shaped, four meters by ten by thirty-two, and made of starstuff: metal and glass and plastic, sheathed with darkly luminous stuff that took the energy from sunlight. The bulk of it was tanks for hydrogen and oxygen and water. Nostrils at the aft end—four at each corner, and a larger one in the middle—would spurt blue fire on command.

They had neglected the carm of late, and Jeffer accepted some of the blame. The carm made two "flavors" of fuel out of water and the power in the batteries. The batteries held their full scientific charge—they filled themselves, somehow, as long as sunlight could reach the carm's glassy surface—but the hydrogen and oxygen tanks were almost empty. It was high time they filled the water tank.

The carm's bow was moored in a dock of wooden beams. Double doors led into a hut with cradles for passengers, moorings for cargo, and a broad transparent window. The window looked forth on nothing but bark. Ventral to the window was a gray sheet of glass and a row of colored buttons.

Jeffer went forward. A touch of a blue button lit the gray glass panel. Blue governed what moved the carm: the motors, the two flavors of fuel supply, the water tank, fuel flow. Jeffer read the blue script:

$$H_2: \quad 0,518$$
$$O_2: \quad 0,360$$
$$H_2O: \quad 0,001$$
$$POWER: \quad 8,872$$

The batteries danced with energy. Why not? The carm wasn't using power. Nobody in Citizens' Tree had bothered to fill the water tank in seven years; so power wasn't needed to split water into hydrogen and oxygen. The water tank was virtually dry.

And he could get something done while he waited for Lawri's pond. Jeffer touched the blue button (the panel went blank) and the yellow (there appeared a line diagram of the carm's bow, the hut section). He touched a yellow dot in the image, and turned his fingertip. Then he moved aft.

The residual goop in pondwater stayed in the tank after the pure water was gone. Jeffer's finger motions had (magically, *scientifically*) caused a spigot in the aft wall to ooze brown mud. He cupped the globule in his hands. He tossed it at the airlock, and most of it got through. Another globule formed, and he sent it after the first. He wiped his hands on his tunic. The mud flow had stopped.

Next he pulled several loops of hose from cargo hooks. He rotated one end onto the spigot, then tossed the coil through the twin doors. Done! When Lawri's blob of pond arrived, she would find the carm ready to be fueled.

Jeffer returned to the controls. He had a surprise for his wife.

Two sleeps ago, while the rest of the tribe was roasting waterbirds from the pond, Lawri had held one of the creatures up for his perusal. "Have you ever really looked at these?"

Jeffer had seen waterbirds before . . . but he'd kept his mouth shut, and looked.

There were no feathers. The modified trilateral symmetry common to Smoke Ring life expressed itself in two wings and a tailfin, all in smooth membrane on collapsible ribs. The wings could be held half collapsed for motion within the denser medium of water. Only one of the three eyes looked like a normal bird's eye. The others were big and bulbous, with large pupils and thick lids. The bodies were slippery-smooth.

"I've eaten them, but . . . you're right. I've seen everything from mobies to triunes to flashers to drillbits, and they don't look like this. Earthlife doesn't either. Do you think it's so they can move through water?"

"I've tried looking them up in the cassettes," Lawri had said. "I tried *bird*. I tried *water* and *pond*. There's nothing."

Jeffer's next sleep had ended with a dream fading in his mind, leaving a single phrase. ". . . even the fish can fly."

He'd had to wait until now to try it.

He tapped yellow (the display vanished), then white (and got a tiny white rectangle at the dorsal-port corner). White read the cassettes; white summoned Voice. "Prikazyvat Voice," he said.

The voice of the carm was a throaty bass, as deep as Mark the dwarf's voice. "Ready, Jeffer the Scientist."

"Prikazyvat Read *Fish*. Read it aloud."

The cassette was one that Jeffer had stolen from London Tree, but it was no different from Quinn Tribe's lost records of Smoke Ring life-forms. As Voice spoke, print scrolled down the display screen: words recorded long ago by one of *Discipline*'s abandoned crew.

FISH

If the birds within the Smoke Ring resemble fish—legless, designed to move through air weightlessly, as a fish moves through water—then the fish that live within the ponds resemble birds.

*Every fish we have examined breathes air. They are not mammals, but lungfish. The single class of exceptions, **gillfish**, are discussed elsewhere.*

*Some can extrude a tube to the pond's surface. A few can expand the size of their fins via membranes, to make them serve as wings. One form, **core fish**, inflates itself with air, dives to the center of a pond, and expels a bubble. It can stay submerged for up to a day—several Smoke Ring days—rebreathing its air bubble, making forays to hunt, and then returning.*

*The whale-sized **moby** uses its pond as a lair from which it bursts to sweep through passing clouds of insects. **Moby** is a compromise form, and there are others.*

Clearly even the largest ponds can break up or evaporate or be torn apart by storm. Every creature that lives in a pond must be prepared to migrate to another: to behave like a bird. Even gillfish—

"Prikazyvat Stop," Jeffer said. This memory that had surfaced from his adolescent training under Quinn Tribe's Scientist was going to put him one up on his wife!

Back to work. He tapped white, then green, then each of the five green rectangles now onscreen. Within the great window that faced the bark, five smaller windows appeared, looking starboard, port, dorsal, ventral, and aft. The ventral view had a blur and a flicker to it. The rest were clear, like the window itself.

The aft view looked along the line that led west to the pond. Citizens were returning to the tree. Behind them a bud of pond was already drifting toward the tree, with the harebrain net showing as a shadow within. Lawri's crazy idea was working.

They swarmed back along the cable toward the midpoint of Citizens' Tree. Gavving and Minya and Anthon hung back, counting heads to be sure that all children were accounted for. A girl lost her grip and drifted; she was chortling and trying to swim through the air when Anthon scooped her up.

As children arrived, Clave herded the smaller ones, with some difficulty, into a rectangular frame with a slatted floor: the lift cage. He stopped when twelve children were inside. Leave room for a couple of adults.

The rest clung to the rough bark or floated like balloons on their tethers. There were wrestling matches. Eight-year-old Arth was getting good at using the recoil of his opponent's line. He was Clave's youngest, and just beginning the tremendous growth of adolescence.

Debby had arrived first. Clave could see her a hundred meters out along the bark, climbing toward the carm.

The bud-pond continued to move. Lawri wore a proprietary smile. Still, Citizens' Tree had better have more line next time they tried this. The pond was too close. If the tree had brushed it there would have been a flood.

The lift now held a score of children. Whoever was in the treadmill would have a problem braking that weight. It couldn't be helped. Clave looked about. Mark and Anthon looked ludicrous together, Mark short and wide, Anthon long and narrow, their heads pointing in opposite directions—He called, "Anthon, Mark. Take the children down and bring back any adult you can find. Be prepared to fight a fire."

Anthon stared in astonishment. *"Fire?"*

"Burning tree. It's around the other side of the trunk now. Go down and get some help. Rather—Where on Earth is Rather?"

Mark pointed outward. "I didn't know any reason to stop them," he said defensively. "They won't fit in the lift this trip—"

Clave cursed silently as he watched Rather and Jill clawing their way out along the bark. There was no tide to hurt them here. If they slipped, someone would go get them. But he could have used their help.

Jeffer couldn't guess how long it took him to realize that the background had changed. Behind the five camera views superimposed upon it, the window no longer showed bark a few ce'meters distant. It showed a huge face, strong, with massive bones: the brutal face of a dwarf.

Chapter Two

DISCIPLINE

from the Citizens' Tree cassettes, year 6 SM:

FIRE
Making a cookfire in free fall is an excessively interesting experience if what you really wanted was dinner. It's taken me eight State years to perfect my technique.

The first lesson is that a flame doesn't rise in free fall. I learned that with a candle, when I was a cadet dreaming of strange worlds. If there's no wind (turn off the air feed), the candle flame seems to go out.

But it isn't out yet. There's wax vapor, and there's the air around it, and at the interface is an envelope of plasma where gas and oxygen interact. It can stay hot for minutes. Combustion continues at the interface. Wave the candle and **pop!** *The flame is back.*

In the case of a cookfire, the wood continues to char. Wait an hour, then blow on the coals with a bellows. The fire jumps to life and there went your eyebrows.

—Dennis Quinn, Captain

*D*iscipline had been deteriorating.

Cameras outside the hull showed rainbow-hued scars from matter that had penetrated the electromagnetic ramscoop while *Discipline* was in flight. They also showed newer micrometeorite pocks. Sharls could ward off anything big enough to see coming, by turning on those magnetic shields for a few seconds, but they ate power in great gulps.

One day he might regret even the little power he used to maintain the gardens and the cats.

Within the hull, time had discolored metal and plastic. The air was dust-free; metal was clean, but not recently polished. Many of the servomechs had worn out. All but a few of the crew cubicles were kept cold and dark and airless. Kitchen machinery was in storage, with power shut down. Some of the bedding had decayed. Water mattresses had been drained and stored.

Sharls kept the control room free of water vapor and almost cold enough to freeze carbon dioxide. He hoped that the computer and its extensions would survive longer in the cold. But the gardens and corridors and even some of the cubicles were kept habitable. Sharls left the lighting on a day-night cycle, for the birds and cats and plants.

The gardens were surviving nicely. It was true that some of the plants had died out completely; but after all, his ecosystem was missing its most important factor. Human crew were supposed to be in that cycle, and they had been gone for half a thousand years.

Scores of cats prowled the ship hunting hundreds of rats and a lesser number of turkeys and pigeons. The turkeys made a formidable enemy. The cats had learned to attack them in pairs.

Sharls trained the cats to respond to his voice. He had released the experimental rats long ago. The birds were already loose; they must have been released during that blank spot in his memory, the mutiny; but by themselves they wouldn't have fed the cats. They were too agile, for one thing. With all of the animal life in the system now, the gardens had a better chance of surviving.

By watching the cats and rats and plants and turkeys and pigeons interact, Sharls hoped to learn how an ecological system would behave in a free-fall environment . . . like the larger ecosystem that flowed beneath *Discipline* in endless rivers of curdled cloud.

Or had he simply become lonely? In his youth Sharls had never been a cat lover. (A sudden memory: his hand swelling with white patches rimmed in red, itching horribly. A kitten had scratched him playfully while he was stroking it.) And now? They didn't obey orders worth a damn . . . but neither had his crew.

A computer program would hardly have retained allergies; but who would expect a computer program to become lonely?

Discipline skimmed above the curdled whorl of the fourth Lagrange point. A fraction of Sharls Davis Kendy's attention watched on various wavelengths. This close, he could confirm an earlier sighting: minor amounts of carbon were being burned at sites around the edges of that endless storm. This was no forest fire: too small, and it had gone on for years. It might indicate human industry at a primitive level.

Now, where was CARM #6?

. . . Funny that the cats hadn't gone with the mutineers. The crew had loved cats. Somewhere in the lost part of his memory, there must be a reason. Perhaps Sharls had pulled free of the Smoke Ring without warning. He might have done that if the mutineers planned something really foul, like cutting the computer out and trying to run *Discipline* manually.

The mutiny was a blank to Sharls.

He had edited those memories. He even remembered why. The descendants of the mutineers would need Sharls Davis Kendy someday. It was not good that he hold grudges against specific ancestors, against old names. But had he been *too* thorough?

—There! CARM #6's communications system had come alive.

It was a thousand kilometers behind him and something less than six thousand kilometers in toward Voy. Kendy did several things at once. Before his new orbit could carry him away, he restarted the drive. He beamed, "Kendy for the State. Kendy for the State."

The CARM autopilot responded.

"Link to me. Beam records."

He'd made mistakes enough during that unexpected contact twenty Earth years ago! At least he'd accomplished something: he'd broken the program that denied him access to the Cargo and Repair Module. The drive systems were beyond his reach. The original mutineers must have physically cut the fiber-optic cable. But the CARM would talk to him!

He'd instructed the autopilot to take photographs at ten-minute intervals. Reentry was in progress when he sent that message. Static might well have fuzzed him out. But pictures were streaming in:

Time passed at a furious rate. CARM #6 flamed as it plowed through thickening air, veering from plants and ponds and creatures. It dipped into a pond to refuel, then bedded itself in the Voy-ward tuft of the largest of a cluster (grove?) of integral trees. It stayed there, with not much of a view at all, for most of a Smoke Ring year. Flickering shapes carved cavities through the foliage and wove small branches into wasp's-nest structures. Abruptly the CARM backed into the sky, skittered outward under inexpert handling, and docked at the midpoint of the tree.

With another part of his mind, Kendy fiddled with *Discipline*'s fusion motor. He could not match his orbit to that of the CARM. He must stay well outside the ·Smoke Ring to protect *Discipline* from corrosion. The best he could do was twice the CARM's orbital period, to dip low above the CARM's position once every ten hours and eight minutes. But he'd be in range for half an hour while his motor was firing.

More of his attention went to watching the CARM's lone occupant in real time.

Jeffer the "Scientist" was stored in memory. He had aged twenty Earth years: hair and beard going gray, wrinkles across his forehead (broken by a white line of scar that was a healing pink wound in Kendy's records), and knuckles turning knobby. Height: 2.3 meters. Mass: 86 kilograms. Long arms and legs, toes like stubby fingers, fingers like a spider's legs: long, fragile, the hands of a field surgeon.

The Smoke Ring had altered *Discipline*'s descendants. The tribes of London Tree and Dalton-Quinn Tree had all looked like that. The jungle giants who had grown up without tidal gravity were hardly human: freakishly tall, with long, fragile, agile fingers and toes; and one of the twelve was a cripple, and others had legs of different length. Only Mark the Silver Man had looked like a normal State citizen. They had called him "dwarf."

They were savages; but they had learned to use State technology in the form of the CARM. Still human. Perhaps they could be made citizens again.

To Kendy, who thought with the speed of a computer, the "Scientist" moved much too slowly. Now he was at the controls, auditing a cassette; now checking the camera views in present time . . .

The incoming CARM records showed clouds and ponds and trees and trilaterally symmetric fishlike birds swirling across the sky. Natives flickered through the CARM cabin: the same savages, growing older; a growing handful of children.

At fifteen years minus-time the CARM backed out of its timber dock for a journey of exploration. It visited a green puffball several kilometers across, and when it emerged there was vegetation like a houseful of green spaghetti bound to its dorsal surface. It hovered in the open sky while men darted among a flock of birds—real birds with real wings: turkeys—and returned to its dock with prisoners.

At thirteen years minus-time it left the trunk to return with a dubious prize: several tons of black mud.

There were no more such forays. The Cargo and Repair Module had become a motor for the tree.

It was docked when the main drive fired for several hours. Kendy watched side views as the integral tree drifted across the sky. It had been circling too far from the neutron star. Air grew thin away from the Smoke Ring median.

The tree was lower now; the air would be as thick as mountain air on Earth. And now the CARM was not being used at all; but there was plenty to watch. The Smoke Ring environment was fascinating. Huge spheres of water, storms, jungles like tremendous puffs of green cotton candy.

In present time, the aft CARM camera showed nearly thirty natives maneuvering between the tree and a tremendous globule of water. They were using the free-fall environment better than any State astronaut. The State had need of these people!

Discipline's own telescope had found the foreshortened tree, with the pond to mark it. And what was that on the opposite side of the tree? Infrared light glowed near its center . . .

Half a thousand years of sensory deprivation were being compensated for in a few minutes. After more than five hundred years, Sharls Kendy had left the stable point behind Goldblatt's World. He had burned irreplaceable fuel, and it was worth it! Sharls tried to absorb it all, integrate it all . . . but that could wait. The "Scientist" might leave at any minute!

He beamed: "Interrupt records." It was twenty Earth years of nothing happening, and the tiny CARM autopilot couldn't handle too many tasks at once. "Activate voice."

"Voice on." The .04-second delay was almost too short to notice.

"Send—" He displayed a picture of himself as a human being, with minor improvements. At age forty-two Kendy had been handsome, healthy, mature, firm of jaw, authoritative: a recruitment-poster version of a State checker.

These were not obedient State citizens. They hadn't trusted him twenty years ago. What words might give him a handle on Jeffer the "Scientist"?

He sent, "Kendy for the State. Jeffer the Scientist, your citizens have been idle too long."

Jeffer jumped like a thief caught in the act. Two long seconds passed before he found his voice. "Checker?"

"Speaking. How stands your tribe?"

Out beyond the terrible whorl of storm that surrounded Gold, out where water boiled and froze at the same time and the legendary stars were a visible truth, lived Kendy the Checker. He had claimed to be something like an elaborate cassette: the recording of a man. He had claimed authority over every human being in the Smoke Ring. He had offered knowledge and power, while they were still near enough to hear his ravings.

Perhaps he was only a madman trapped somehow aboard the spacecraft that had brought men from the stars. But he had knowledge. He had coached them through that terrible fall back into the Smoke Ring, fourteen years ago.

The face in the carm's window had not been seen since. It was the face of a dwarf, a brutal throwback. The jaw and orbital ridges were more massive even than Mark's, the musculature more prominent.

"We lived through the reentry," Jeffer told him. "Ilsa and Merril are dead now. There are children."

"Jeffer, your tribe has possessed the CARM for fourteen of your years. In that time you have moved the tree twice and thenceforth done nothing at all. What have you learned of the people of the fourth Lagrange point?"

The what? "I don't understand the question."

"Sixty degrees ahead of Goldblatt's World on the arc of the Smoke Ring and sixty degrees behind are regions where matter grows dense. They are points of stability in Goldblatt's World's orbit. Material tends to collect there." The dwarf's brutal features registered impatience. "East of you by twelve hundred kilometers, a vast, sluggish, permanent storm."

"The Clump? You're saying there are *people* in the Clump?"

"I sense activity there. A civilization is growing twelve hundred kilometers from where your tree has floated for fifteen Earth years. Jeffer, where is your curiosity? Has it been bred out of you?"

"What do you want from me, Checker?"

Kendy said, "I can be in range to advise you every ten hours and eight minutes, once every two of your days. I want to know more of the people of the Smoke Ring. In particular, I want to know about you and about the Clump civilization. I think you should link with them, perhaps rule them."

Jeffer's one previous experience indicated that Kendy was harmless. For good or ill, he could only talk. Jeffer gathered his courage and said, "Kendy, the tales say that you abandoned us here, long ago. Now I expect you're bored and—"

"I am."

"And you want to talk to someone. You also claim authority I won't grant you. Why should I listen?"

"Are you aware that you are being invaded?"

"What?"

The face of Kendy was suddenly replaced by a dizzying view. Jeffer looked into a river of storm, streaming faster as the eye moved inward toward a tiny, brilliant violet pinpoint. Jeffer had seen this once before: the Smoke Ring seen from outside.

Before he could remember to breathe, the view jumped. He was looking at what had been the center of the picture, vastly enlarged.

"Look." Scarlet arrowheads appeared, pointing—"Here, your tree."

"Citizens' Tree, from the out tuft? Yeah, and that must be the pond." Both were tiny. Opposite the pond was . . . another tree? And dark cloud clinging to the trunk?

The view jumped again. Through the blur and flicker in the illusion of a window, Jeffer watched a tree on fire. Moving between the two trees were creatures he had never seen before.

"Treefodder! Everybody's on the other side of the trunk. Those bird-things will be on the tree before anyone knows it."

"Look in infrared." The picture changed again, to red blobs on black. Jeffer couldn't tell what he was looking at. The scarlet arrowhead pointed again. "You are seeing heat. This is fire in the intruder tree. Here, these five points are just the temperature of a man."

Jeffer shook his head. "It doesn't mean anything."

The enlarged picture returned . . . and suddenly those tiny "creatures" jumped into perspective. "Winged men!"

"I would have called those enlarged swimming fins rather than wings. Never mind. Have you ever heard tales of winged men?"

"No. There's nothing in the cassettes either. I've got to do something about this. Prikazyvat Voice off." Jeffer made for the airlock without waiting to see the face fade. His citizens wouldn't have a chance against winged warriors!

The sun was at three o'clock: dead east, just above where the Smoke Ring began to take definite shape. *Kendy can only talk, sure, but he talks with pictures, and he tells things nobody can know. He'll be in range every other day at this time. Do I want to know that?* But Jeffer had other concerns, and the rest of that thought lay curled unfinished in the bottom of his mind.

Jill was leaving Rather behind. She glanced back once and moved on, and there was laughter in the sound of her panting.

Jill was his elder by half a year. When he wanted company it was generally Jill he wanted; but they did compete. There had been a year during which she could beat him at wrestling, when she suddenly grew tall and he'd lagged behind. She'd taught him the riblock the hard way: she'd held his floating ribs shut with her knees so that he couldn't breathe. He could wrestle her now—he was a boy *and* a dwarf—but her longer arms and legs gave her an unbeatable advantage at racing. He'd never catch her.

So he moved outward at his own pace, giving due care to his handholds and footholds in the rough bark, following the blond girl in the scarlet tunic. Her long-limbed mother had already reached the carm ahead of them.

At fourteen-plus, Rather was considered an adult. He was built wide and muscular, with heavy cheek, jaw, and orbital bones. His fingers were short and stubby, and his toes, though strong, were too short to be much use. His hair was black and curly like his mother's. His beard was sparse, without much curl to it yet. His eyes were green (and green tinged his cheek, with a growth of fluff that would be many days healing). He stood a meter and three-quarters tall.

Dwarf. Arms too short, legs too short. He should have gone around the trunk. Jill could have told the Scientist about the burning tree; Debby might already know. He could have been getting a closer look!

The carm loomed ahead of him. It was as big . . . no, *bigger* than the Citizens' Tree commons.

Debby shouted into the airlock. Someone emerged: Jeffer. They talked, heads bobbing. Debby moved to the front of the carm; Jeffer was about to go back inside—

Rather heard Jill calling. "Scientist! There's a burning tree coming toward us!" She paused to catch her breath. "We saw it, me and Rather, we—while we were swimming—"

Jeffer called back. "Debby told me. Did you see anything like winged men?"

". . . No."

"Okay. Help Debby with the moorings, there at the bow." He noticed Rather struggling in Jill's wake. "Get Rather to help you."

Debby and Jill were both fighting knots, and Jill was muttering "Treefodder, treefodder, treefodder," when Rather caught up. "I bent my finger," she said.

Debby said, "I hate to cut lines. See what you can do."

The carm's tethers hadn't been moved in years, and the knots were tight. Rather's stubby fingers worked them loose. *Dwarf. Clumsy but strong.* Presently the carm was held by nothing but its own inertia. Jill did not look pleased. Debby and Rather grinned at each other. It was something, to do a thing an adult warrior could not!

Jeffer called from the airlock, twelve meters beyond the bark. "Come aboard!"

Debby jumped and Jill followed. Rather hesitated until he saw them bump against the airlock door. The jump looked dangerous. Tide was gentle, but one *could* fall into the sky. Rather had never been inside the carm, and he wasn't sure he wanted to be. The starstuff box was like nothing else in or on the tree.

But he had to follow. He caught the edge of the outer door as it passed, pivoted on the strength of his arms, and entered feetfirst. *Can't jump right, can't reach far. What if I'd missed?*

It was weird inside the carm. There were openings in the back wall, and hard round loops sticking out of the dorsal and side walls. Farther toward the front were rows of cradles almost the size of an adult, ten in all, made of nothing like wood or cloth.

Rather made his way forward. The others were in the first row of cradles. "Take a seat and strap yourself in," Jeffer ordered. "Here, like this." He fastened two elastic tethers across Jill's torso. "Lawri showed me how to work these, years ago."

The cradle had a headrest that fitted nicely behind his ears. Jill's and Debby's dug into their shoulders. *It's true,* Rather thought suddenly. *The carm was built for dwarves!* He liked the thought.

"The winged men weren't very close," the Scientist said. "We've got time." His fingers drummed against the flat panel below the window.

There was tide pulling Rather forward, and a whisper-roar like a steady wind. The bark receded; the tree backed into the sky. Jill gripped the armrests of her cradle. Her mouth was wide. Debby said, "Clave didn't say take off, Scientist. He said get ready."

"No time. They're headed for the trunk. Also the carm is *mine,* Debby. We settled that once."

"Tell it to Clave."

"Clave knows."

The invaders kicked themselves through the air, slowly, in the last stages of exhaustion. Five, it looked like, until Rather realized that the older woman carried a half-grown girl in her arms.

Jeffer nudged the carm toward them, in along the trunk.

Smoke Ring people came long, longer, or dwarf. These invaders were of the longer persuasion, like jungle giants, born and raised in free fall. They were quite human: an older man and woman and four girls. The wings were artificial, bound to their shins, made of cloth over splayed ribs. One girl trailed behind, struggling along with only one wing.

They were in sorry shape. Closer now, and Rather could see details. The man's hair was burned, and the loose sheet that covered him was charred. The wingless girl was coughing; she didn't even have the strength to cling to the woman who carried her.

Their legs stopped pumping as, one by one, they saw the carm.

Debby said, "I don't see anything like bows or harpoons. Can we take them aboard?"

"I thought of that, but *look* at them. The carm scares them worse than being lost in the sky. Anyway, the man's almost there."

The burned man hadn't seen them. Kicking steadily, far ahead of the others, he reached the bark and clung. Without a pause he pounded a stake into the bark, moored a coil of line, and hurled the coil at the older woman. She freed a hand and caught it, pulled herself toward the tree, then snapped the line to send a sine wave rolling toward the trunk. The nearer girl caught the line in her toes as it bowed toward her.

Clave came around the bulge of the bark. He slowed when he saw the strangers. Gavving and Minya joined him. They moved toward the strangers.

There were four on the trunk now: a girl, the man, and the older woman with her coughing burden. Rather watched Clave take the burned man's line, hurl a sine wave across the one-winged girl's torso, and pull her in.

"Looks okay," the Scientist murmured.

Clave looked up and waved. Jeffer nodded and set the carm moving. "It's all right," he said. "They sure don't look dangerous. I wonder what happened to them? Where are they *from*?"

"I never saw strangers before," Jill said. "I don't know what to think."

"That burning tree is still coming at us," Rather said.

Jeffer nodded. The carm surged, turning.

Black smoke wreathed the middle section of the tree. Flame glowed sluggishly from within, illuminating blurred curves and oblongs. Debby said, "There's stuff in the fire. Made stuff, machinery. It'll burn up."

That was knowledge burning in the core of the fire. Jeffer hated what he had to say. "We can't save it. If we had Mark and the silver suit . . . no. That might burn even him."

"You're not taking us into the fire?"

"We can push anywhere. The tide will hold the tree straight." Jeffer had already taken them below the inward limit of the firecloud, where a black plume drifted east. The carm was passing north of the trunk. Jeffer tapped: the carm turned. "It's still dangerous. The tree could come apart while we're on it."

He moved in on the trunk. The bow grated against bark; Jeffer's crew surged forward against their elastic bands. "I think the carm was *built* for pushing," he said. He tapped a blue dash in the center of the panel, and the whisper of power became a whistling roar. Tide surged against his back.

This was what it was to be a Scientist. Knowledge, power, mastery of a universe. This was what Kendy the Checker had to offer. At what price? Who but a Scientist would have the strength to resist?

The sun passed zenith and started down its arc. Jeffer had changed the display; he watched sets of letters and numbers. The roar of the main motor strummed his bones.

Chapter Three
REFUGEES

from the Citizens' Tree cassettes, year 4 SM:

TIME

We've been trying to keep to Earth time, but that word "day" is about as useful as balls on a Checker. The closer you get to Voy, the shorter the days get, down to about two hours. Closer than that, the air's too thin and there's no water to speak of. At a ten-hour orbit, same thing, there's nothing to breathe. We've been keeping to ship time. Twenty-four hours constitute a "sleep." A "day" is one orbit around Voy, wherever you happen to be. Gold's orbit is a "standard day."

The State takes its dates from the year of its founding. We've done the same, dating Smoke Ring years from four years ago. Our years are half a rotation of Voy and its companion sun . . . half because it's more convenient.

*If **Discipline** ever does come back for us, Kendy will have to learn a whole new language.*

—Michelle Michaels, Communications

The huts of Citizens' Tree were enclosures made by weaving living spine branches into a kind of wickerwork. The Scientists' hut was larger than most, and more cluttered too.

The Scientists were the tribe's teachers and doctors. Any hut would have harpoons protruding from the walls and high ceiling; but here the wicker sprouted starstuff knives, pots of herbs and pastes, and tools for writing.

The hut was crowded. Lawri stepped carefully among five sleeping jungle giants.

She'd covered their wounds in undyed cloth. The strangers moaned and twisted in their sleep. The youngest girl, with her hair burned down to the scalp on one side of her head, was holding herself half in the air.

The noise from outside wasn't helping. Lawri bent to get through the doorway. "Could you hold it down!" she whisper-snarled. "These citizens *don't* need . . . oh. Clave . . . Chairman, I'm trying to give them some quiet. Can you take the talk to the commons?"

Clave and Anthon were intimidated into silence. Jeffer asked, "Can any of them answer questions?"

"They're asleep. They haven't said anything sensible."

Her husband merely nodded. Lawri went back in. Rustling sounds receded. For a moment she felt remorse. Jeffer would want to see the strangers as much as anyone.

When the burns healed, the strangers would be handsome, but in weird fashion. Only birds wore the gaudy colors of their scorched clothing. Their skin was dark; their lips and noses were broad; their hair was like black pillows.

The youngest girl stirred, thrashed, and opened her eyes. "Tide," she said wonderingly. The dark eyes focused. "Who're you?"

"I'm Lawri the Scientist. You're in Citizens' Tree. You're safe now."

The girl twisted to see the others. "Wend?"

"One of you died."

The girl moaned.

"Can you tell me who you are and how you came here?"

"I'm Carlot," the girl said. Two tears were growing. "We're Serjent House. Loggers. There was a fire . . . the whole tree caught fire. Wend got caught when the water tank let go." She shook her head; teardrop globules flew wide.

"All right, Carlot. Have some water, then go to sleep."

Carlot's drinking technique was surprising. She took the pottery vessel, set two fingers to nearly block the opening, then jerked the pottery vessel toward her face. The jet of water struck her lower lip. She tried again and reached her mouth.

"Would you like something to eat? Foliage?"

"What's that?"

Lawri went out to strip some branchlets of their foliage. Carlot looked dubiously at the fluffy green stuff. "Oh, it's *greens*."

"You know it?"

"I've been in a tree tuft." She tasted it. "This is sweet. Older tree?" She continued eating.

Lawri said, "Later I'll get you some stew. You should sleep now."

Carlot patted the wicker floor. "How can I sleep with this pushing up against me? All my blood wants to settle on one side."

London Tree, Lawri's home, had been bigger, with a stronger tide. In Citizens' Tree you could drop a stone from eye level and draw a slow breath and let it out before the stone struck. But this Carlot must be used to no tide at all.

She turned over, gingerly. Her eyes closed and she was asleep.

They moved through the green gloom of the corridor, back toward the commons. Anthon said, "I always wondered. Lawri doesn't take orders from you either, does she?"

Jeffer laughed. "Treefodder, no!"

Clave said, "I really wanted to ask them some questions before we tackle the firetree."

"We can't wait," Jeffer said. "Let's go see what we can scavenge. This is the most interesting thing that has happened to us in fourteen years."

"It's bound to bring changes."

"Like what?"

Clave grinned at Jeffer. "They've already changed your home life. You can't sleep in the Scientists' hut and Lawri won't leave."

"I've got the children too. I'm living in the bachelors' longhut with my three kids and Rather. Look, I want to go *now*, before that burned tree drifts too far. Anthon?"

"Ready," said the jungle giant.

Clave nodded, reluctantly. "Just us three? Stet. We'll round up some kids to run the treadmill. And let's take those wings along. I want to try them."

The tree still burned. Fire had eaten six or seven klomters in from the midpoint along the lee side, progressing alongside the waterfall channel, where there was partial protection from the wind. The flames streamed east like the mane of a skyhorse. At the midpoint there were only red patches glowing in black char. In the center of the burn was a prominent uneven lump. Jeffer eased the carm toward that.

Clave said, "I don't understand why it hasn't come apart."

Anthon nodded uneasily. Jeffer said, "It's a short tree. With a tuft missing it's even shorter. Tide would pull harder on a grown tree, but that thing could still come apart while we're on it. I don't *ever* want to go through that again."

Anthon asked, "Why do trees come apart?"

"They do it when they're dying," Clave said.

Jeffer said, "When a tree drifts too far away from the Smoke Ring median, it starves. It saves itself by coming apart. The tide takes half of it out, half in. One half falls back to where the water and fertilizer are. The other half . . . dies, I guess."

"I still don't see any bugs," Clave said. "It's the bugs that eat a tree apart, isn't it? The tree isn't getting fed, so the bark lets the bugs get inside—"

"I don't know everything, Clave."

"Pity."

They were close enough now to make out black lumps at the center of the charred region. There: a shape like a huge seed pod split open from inside. There: a thin shell of char, a bell shape not unlike the fire-spitting nostrils at the carm's aft end. A ridge of white ash joined the bell to the split pod. Beyond: several fragile sheets of charred wood, the remains of an oblong hut with interior walls.

Clave reached for the wings he'd bound to cargo hooks. "Scientist, can you hold the carm here? We'll go see what there is to see. If the tree breaks in half, you'll still have us tethered."

Jeffer stifled a protest. He ached to explore that ruined structure, but—"I can handle it. Take lines too."

The sun would be dead east in a few tens of breaths.

A stick protruded from the butt end of each fan-shaped wing. After some experimentation they settled for lining the stick along their shins and binding them with the straps. The wings tended to hang up on things even when folded. Clave and Anthon wriggled through the airlock and flapped into the sky.

Jeffer tapped the white button. "Prikazvat Voice," he said.

The carm said, "Ready, Jeffer the Scientist."

Clave and Anthon fluttered erratically through the air. Suddenly Anthon moved purposefully toward the blister of charred machinery, moving easily, as if he had always been a bird. Clave moved after him, fighting a tendency to veer left.

They swept away the white ash that lay between the bell and the tank. The ash enclosed them in cloud. When the cloud dispersed, they had exposed a length of tube and a loose webbing of metal strands around it.

"Kendy for the State. Hello, Jeffer."

Jeffer didn't jump. "Hello, Kendy. What do you make of all this?"

"You'd know more about the injured plant than I. I've been studying the machinery." Within the bow window the metal strands and the enclosed pipe began blinking, an outline of red light. "These, the pipe and the chicken wire, are metal. The ruptured tank—" another blinking outline "—appears to have been a large seed pod. The cone is half of a similar seed pod. The ash around the pipe appears to be wood ash.

"We're looking at a steam rocket, Jeffer. Your invaders used a wood fire to heat the pipe. They ran water through the pipe and into the nozzle. Very inefficient, but in your peculiar environment they could move a tree with that. Slowly, of course."

"Why would they pick an injured tree?"

"Ask them. Did any survive?"

"One's dead. Five more are in bad shape. My wife won't let me near them. Wait a few days and see."

Clave and Anthon flew along the split in the great tank. They reached the cluster of black oblongs at the other end.

The Checker said, "Their wounds won't become infected. We didn't bring disease bacteria."

"What?"

"I was thinking aloud. I want to talk to your invaders. Take them on a tour, Jeffer, when they're ready. Show them the CARM."

"Kendy, I'm not sure I want them to know about you."

"I will observe only."

Clave and Anthon were flapping back to the carm. They carried blackened cargo, and they no longer wore tethers. "Company coming," Jeffer said.

"Jeffer, you've concealed your contact with me from the rest of your tribe, haven't you?"

"I haven't mentioned it to them yet."

"I'll keep my silence while others are aboard. Play the game any way you like."

Clave and Anthon returned black with soot. They untied the now-clumsy wings, then wiggled in, pushing armfuls of blackened salvage ahead of them. Clave crowed, "I love it! It's really flying!"

"You never did like tide, did you, Clave? How's the leg?"

"It never gets any better." Clave flexed his right leg. The misshapen lump on his thighbone bulged beneath the skin and muscle. The compound fracture he'd suffered in Carther States had healed, but in the jungle there had been no tide to tell the bone to stop growing. "It feels like I strained it. If I have to fly any distance I'll use just one wing."

They set to mooring their loot along the walls. Two tremendous hooks, wood stiffened with metal. A meter's length of metal band with tiny teeth along one edge. A hardwood tube had kept its shape if not its strength; the remnants of charred plastic hose clung to one end.

"Weapons and tools," Clave said. "There was wire twisted together like a harebrain net, but it was burned through in too many places. Nothing else worth taking except the pipe. We've got to have that pipe. We moored the lines to it, Jeffer. Let's pull it loose."

"It must be important, given that you've moored the carm to a tree that's about to come apart. Why? Just because it's metal?"

"I've got a vague idea what this setup is for," Clave said. "We could duplicate everything except the pipe, in theory anyway. The pipe isn't just metal, it's starstuff, something out of the old science."

"Why do you say that?"

"We couldn't find a seam," Anthon said. "It gleams when you rub away the soot. Clave, I'm not sure I like any of this. Jeffer's right, that tree could come apart and throw us spinning across the sky, and for what? Wings, sure, those are wonderful, but the rest of this is just weird!"

Clave the Chairman said, "Pull that pipe out, Scientist."

Anthon fumed and was silent. Jeffer said, "Strap down. Let's hope the tethers hold."

Under attitude jets the carm shuddered and lurched. Then six meters of metal pipe two hundred ce'meters across pulled loose in a cloud of ash.

When Anthon and Clave went out to retrieve it, Jeffer went too. They watched, grinning, while he thrashed and spun; and suddenly he was flying, kicking stiff-legged across the sky like any swordbird.

They bound the pipe up against the hull and took the carm back to Citizens' Tree. The burning tree continued to drift west and in.

Lawri kept the citizens away from her hut for five days, a full waking-sleeping cycle. That became impossible when she sent Rather for food. Rather came back with waterbird stew, and Clave, Jeffer, Gavving, Minya, Debby, Jayan, Jinny, Mark, Jill, and a host of children. She kept them outside while the strangers ate. Then she and Jeffer pulled the hut's entrance apart. It could be rebuilt later.

The man named himself: Booce Serjent. He shaped his words strangely. He named the others: his wife Ryllin, and their daughters Mishael, Karilly, and Carlot.

"We've delayed the funeral until you're strong enough," Clave said. "Can you make yourself discuss funeral practices?"

Booce shrugged painfully. "We cremate. The ashes go into the earthlife tanks. What do you do here?"

"The dead go to feed the tree."

"All right. Chairman Clave, what has happened to *Logbearer*?"

"I don't understand."

"*Logbearer* is our ship. You saw a burning tree? The fire started around *Logbearer*, in the middle."

"We went there. We brought back a metal pipe and some other stuff."

"You saved the main feed pipe! How?"

"We used the carm. It's an old starstuff relic, still working. We use it to move the tree."

Booce smiled and sighed and seemed about to drift off to sleep.

Lawri asked, "What are you? Carlot said *loggers*."

"Let him alone. I'm awake." The older woman sounded tired. "I'm Ryllin. Yes, we're loggers. We take lumber back to the Clump and sell it there."

Chairman Clave asked, "You mean there are men in there?"

Ryllin's laugh chopped off as if it had hurt her. "More than a thousand. With children, near two thousand."

"Thousands. Huh. And you move trees. Don't you have trees in the Clump?"

"No. The tide's wrong."

"How do you move a tree?"

"You cut off one tuft. Then the wind only blows on the other tuft. Booce generally takes us west, so of course we want the log to go east. So we cut the in tuft. The wind pushes just on the out tuft, so it pushes the tree west, and that slows it down. The tree drops closer to Voy and speeds up—"

The children and some adults were looking confused. *We taught them this!* Lawri thought angrily. *West takes you in.* Pushing a tree against the Smoke Ring's rotation—west—would drop it closer to Voy. Lower orbits were faster orbits. The tree would move east toward the Clump.

"—But of course we need the rocket too," Ryllin was saying. "A rocket is a tank of water, and a nozzle, and a metal pipe with a fire around it. You run water through the pipe. The steam sprays away from where you want to go. Without the pipe there's no *Logbearer*. You understand reaction effects?"

The citizens looked at each other. Children understood the law of reaction before they could speak!

Ryllin said, "Well, when you get to the Clump you sever the other tuft and work the log to a mooring with the steam rocket. Then you have to sell it. We've done it all our lives. But the pipefire got away from us . . . Lawri? I'm tired."

Gavving said, "Sell?"

"Forget it, Ryllin. Everybody out," Lawri ordered. "Chairman, can you move them?"

The citizens drifted away in clumps of heated discussion.

Four sleeps after reaching Citizens' Tree, all of the Serjents were on their feet. Various citizens volunteered to lead them about. They moved tentatively, slowed by healing burns and unaccustomed to tide. They listened intently, and spoke in vowel-twisting accents and strange words . . . but for Karilly, who huddled close in the circle of her family, silent.

Booce and his family came back tired. Their new home was primitive, and roomy, and oddly beautiful. The citizens had managed well with so little.

Lawri the Scientist looked them over and judged them well enough to attend a funeral.

Chapter Four

THE IN TUFT

from the Citizens' Tree cassettes, year 7 SM:

INTEGRAL TREES

. . . These integral trees grow to tremendous size. When such a plant reaches its full growth, it stabilizes by tidal effect. It forms a long, slender trunk tufted with green at both ends: tens of thousands of radial spokes circling Levoy's Star, each scores of kilometers long.

Like many plants of the Smoke Ring, the integral tree is a soil collector. The endpoints are subject to tidal gravity. And wind! The tufts are in a perpetual wind, blowing from the west at the inner tuft and from the east at the outer tuft. The tide-oriented trunk bows to the winds, curving into a single, nearly horizontal branch at each end, giving it the appearance of an integration sign. The tufts sift fertilizer from the wind: soil, water, even animals and plants smashed by impact.

Free-fall conditions prevail everywhere except in the integral trees. The medical dangers of life in free fall are well known. If **Discipline** *has indeed abandoned us, if we are indeed marooned within this weird environment, we could do worse than to settle the tufts of the integral trees . . .*

—*Claire Dalton, Sociology/Medicine*

Foliage framed half a world of sky.

The treemouth faced west, at the junction between branch and trunk. Spine branches migrated west along the branch, carrying whatever their foliage had picked up from the wind, to be swallowed by the conical pit. Citizens came too, to feed the tree. The treemouth was their toilet, their garbage disposal, and their cemetery.

Lawri the Scientist had described all of this in advance. Booce tried to tell himself that it made sense; it was reasonable in context; it only took getting used to.

Wend had been placed at the lip of the pit. She'd had time to ride the spine branches halfway into the cone of the treemouth. Booce was glad that he could not see her better.

Burning was cleaner. Reducing the body to ashes burned away memories too . . .

How was Karilly taking it?

Karilly was the quiet one. She obeyed orders, but rarely showed initiative. She almost never spoke to strangers. A good child, but Booce had never really understood her.

She hadn't been burned. All of them had watched Wend die; how could it be worse for Karilly? But she hadn't spoken a word since the fire.

Chairman Clave spoke, welcoming Wend into the tribe. Lawri spoke of a citizen's last duty, to feed the tree. Ryllin spoke her memories of her lost daughter. Karilly cried silently; the tears sheathed her eyes in crystal.

Older citizens ate first. Booce saw his daughters hanging back—they had learned that much already—while a Citizens' Tree girl-child filled his bowl with waterbird stew from a large, crude ceramic pot. He lurched away across the woven-spine-branch floor of the commons, following his wife, trying to keep his bowl upright.

"You think of the tide as something to fight," his wife said softly. "Think of it as a convenience."

"Hah."

"Tide gives you a preferred direction. Something to push against. Look." With the bowl held in one hand, Ryllin leapt one-legged into the air and spun in a slow circle before her feet touched the floor again. She hadn't spilled a drop.

"Moving isn't unpleasant in a tide, it's just different. These, ah, *citizens* make us look clumsy, but we can adjust, love. We *will* adjust."

"Stet. I've climbed trees all my life. . . . Company."

They were surrounded by children. A pudgy half-grown girl said, "How do you move a tree without a carm?"

Booce said, "Let's sit down and I'll tell you."

A dozen children waited patiently while Booce and Ryllin nested themselves in foliage. Then they all settled at once.

Booce thought while he ate. He said, "You need a rocket. My rocket was *Logbearer*, and it was my father's rocket before me. To make a rocket you need a rocket."

One asked, "How did anyone build the first rocket?"

Booce smiled at the dwarf boy. "The first rocket was given by *Discipline*. It had a mind—the Library—and the Admiralty still has that, with more knowledge in it than you'll find in your little cassettes. Anyway, you've got to have a rocket so you can get to the pod groves."

A woman of Booce's own size settled within earshot. Booce pretended not to notice. "The biggest pod you can find in the pod grove becomes your water tank. You cut another pod in half and it's your rocket nozzle. You run the pipe into the stem end. You wrap sikenwire around the pipe to hold the firebark. You light the firebark. You pump water through the hot pipe and it turns to steam and goes racing out the nozzle, and that pushes you the other way."

The pudgy girl (though all the children looked a bit pudgy, well fed and compressed by tide) asked, "Where does pipe come from?"

"I don't know. *Discipline*, maybe, if there ever was a *Discipline*." The children snickered. Booce didn't know why, so he ignored it. "There's a hundred and twenty meters of pipe in the Empire, so they tell me, and forty-eight of that makes up the pipes in eleven logging ships. *Woodsman* carried a spare pipe, but they're richer than we are.

"So. A rocket is one and a half pods, and a pipe, and some sikenwire, and the hut complex at the other end of the tank. You need big hooks for towing, saws to carve up wood, and crossbows, because you've got to find your own food. A trip takes a year or two. Most of us travel in families.

"Now you find a sting jungle. The honey hornets live in the sting jungles, and there's nothing so big they can't kill it. You need to cover yourself all over to get at the nest. Honey is sticky red stuff, sweeter than foliage.

"Now you pick a tree. If it's more than forty klomters long, the wood'll be too coarse and you'll be forever coming home. Thirty's about right. You moor your rocket at the midpoint, but you don't use it yet. You paint a line of honey down the trunk to one of the tufts. Then you gash the bark in a circle above the tuft, and paint honey along that. You know the bugs that eat a tree apart if it starts to die?"

Heads nodded. The Serjents had been told of the death of Dalton-Quinn Tree. Children must hear that tale early.

Booce said, "The bugs follow the honey down. They eat the honey above the tuft. Then they're stuck, because they've eaten all the honey. There's nothing left to eat but wood. After a few sleeps the tuft drops off."

There were sounds of dismay. "We don't use occupied trees, you know," Booce said gently. "The tree would die anyway when it gets near the Clump. Integral trees want a straightforward tidal pull, straight through Voy."

The pudgy girl asked a little coldly, "How many trees have you killed?" Booce saw that she was almost an adult. Her height had fooled him: the tide had stunted her growth.

"Ten."

The dwarf (an adult too, with beard beginning to sprout) asked, "Why do you cut off the tuft?"

"To move. You know the rule? West takes you in, in takes you east. I want the tree to move east, back to the Clump. So I cut the in tuft. Now I've got a west wind blowing on the out tuft, and nothing at the in stump to catch the wind. The tree accelerates west. It drops toward Voy. Things move faster when their orbits are closer to Voy, so the tree moves east. After a while I'm in from the Clump and still moving. That's when I need the rocket. I have to cut off the other tuft, then fire the rocket to move the tree into the Clump."

The dwarf boy asked, "What then?"

"Then I sell the log for what I can get, and hope nobody else brought a log in at the same time. If there are two of us competing, we might not get enough to pay us for the work."

Most of the children looked puzzled. The dwarf asked, "What went wrong this time?"

Booce's throat closed up. *His* decision! With some relief he heard Ryllin say, "We were in a hurry. We thought we could get more water for the rocket. So we set the rocket going before the tuft dropped off. That started a fire. Wend was trying to get out of the huts when the water tank—well, it got too hot and—"

Booce jumped in, hastily. "The water tank split open. Wend got caught. Carlot and I were burned pulling her out of the steam. We were steering the log for that pond out there, and your tree moved in front of it, so it was the closest. So we made for it. And you found six of us clinging to the trunk like tocs in hair, and—and Wend was dead, and the rest of us were ready to die, I think."

The adults had all been served. The children drifted toward the cookpot. Booce ate. He'd let his stew get cold.

Likely he would never see the Clump again. It was as well. He and his family would be paupers there. He had never owned anything but *Logbearer* itself, and even that was gone. But was it really beyond belief that these people could build another *Logbearer*?

When all the adults were eating, the children drifted into line at the cookpot. Rather was just ahead of three tall and dark young women, and just behind his brother Harry.

"Take Jill's place," Rather told Harry.

"Why should I?"

"Beats me. Will you do it?"

"All right."

The favor would be repaid. Rather would take Harry's place at the cookpot or in the treadmill, or show him a wrestling trick; something. These things didn't need discussion. Harry stepped out of line and talked to Jill where she was serving stew. Jill served herself and Harry took her place.

The blond girl joined Rather. "What's that for?" she asked; but she seemed pleased.

"I've been listening to the old ones. Now I want to talk to the girls. Come along?" If they wouldn't talk to a dwarf boy, maybe they'd talk to a girl.

They followed the Serjent girls as they made their exaggeratedly careful way across the commons' wicker floor. The refugees settled slowly into the foliage, keeping their eyes fixed on their bowls. Stew still slopped over the edge of Carlot's bowl. "The hole's too big," she said.

"You just need practice.—I'm Jill, he's Rather."

"How do you eat when you're at the midpoint?"

Jill and Rather settled across from them. Rather stripped four branchlets for chopsticks. Jill said, "I'd take a smoked turkey along. What do you use? Bowls with smaller holes?"

"Yes, and we carry these." Carlot produced a pair of bone sticks, ornately carved. "You're lucky. You've always got . . . spine branches?"

"These are branchlets. The spine branches are the big ones."

The third girl, Karilly, had not spoken. She was concentrating fully on her bowl.

Mishael said, "You seem to be happy."

Rather found the comment disconcerting. "What do you mean?"

"You, all of you. You've got your tree and it's all you need. Lumber from the bare end of the branch. The clothes you wear, the cloth comes from branchlet fibers, doesn't it?"

"It's foliage with the sugar washed out."

"And the dye is from berries. Water comes running down the trunk into that basin, and you eat foliage and catch meat from the sky. And there's the carm. Without the carm you'd have to build a rocket to move the tree."

"Right." Rather thought, *We don't know how to do that. The carm is all that keeps us from being savages. Is that how they see us?* "We had to leave the tree to get our lines. And the adults keep talking about earthlife crops. They couldn't bring seeds and eggs with them."

"You could buy them in the Market if you were rich enough."

Jill said, "We don't know those words. Rich? Buy?"

Carlot said, "Rich means you can have whatever you want."

"Like being Chairman?"

"No—"

Mishael took over. "Look, suppose you want earthlife seeds or pigeons or turkeys. Stet, you go to the Market and you find what you want. Then you've got to buy it. You need something to give the owner. Metal, maybe."

"We don't have much metal," Rather said. "What are the people like? Like you?"

"Sometimes," Carlot said. "What do you mean? Tall? Dark? We get dark and light, short and . . . well, mostly we're about as tall as me, and the men are taller."

"No dwarves?"

"Oh, of course there are dwarves. In the Navy."

"What do you think of dwarves?" He hadn't meant to ask so directly; he hadn't realized how important the question was to him.

Carlot asked, "What do you think of my legs?"

Rather blushed. "They're fine." They were hidden anyway; Carlot was wearing the scarlet tunic and pantaloons of Citizens' Tree.

"One's longer than the other. My teacher's got one leg longer than mine and one leg like yours, and it never bothers *him*. And the Admiral's got an arm like a turkey wishbone. I've seen him. We're all kinds, Rather."

It was Mark's habit to eat near the cauldron, where others might find him. Rarely did he get company. This day he was mildly surprised when Clave and Minya settled themselves across from him. They plucked branchlets and ate. Presently Clave asked, "What do you think of the Serjents?"

"They're doing all right."

"That wasn't what I meant," Clave said, while Minya was saying, "What will they do to Citizens' Tree?"

"Oh." Mark thought it over. "Half of you came from the in tuft of a broken tree. You were from the out tuft, Minya. Three from Carther States. Lawri and me from London Tree. London Tree used to raid Carther States for copsiks. Fourteen years we've been living here, and nobody's killed anyone yet. We can live with the Serjents too."

Clave said, "Oh, we can live with them—" while Minya wondered, "What do they think of us?"

Clave snorted. "They think we're a little backward, and they'd like to talk us into going to the Clump."

Where was this leading? Mark asked, "Are you thinking they want the carm?"

"No, not that. Not impossible either . . . Have you talked to Gavving or Debby lately?"

"They don't like my company. Neither do you, Minya."

Minya ignored that. "They're trying to figure out how to build a steam rocket, starting with just the metal tube they brought back!"

"Uh-*huh*." Mark saw the point now. "They can build us a machine that moves trees around. They can tell us why we should all go to the Clump. So you're a little nervous, Chairman? We could lose half the tribe. Lawri keeps saying there aren't enough of us *now*."

"And what do you want, Mark?"

Mark would have wished for a wife or three, but he saw no point in telling Clave or Minya that. "I want nothing from the Clump. We're here. Twelve adults, twenty children, happy as dumbos in Citizens' Tree. We shouldn't be announcing that all over the sky. Even if the Clump doesn't keep copsiks, maybe somebody out there does. Things aren't perfect here, but they're good. I wouldn't want to wind up as somebody's copsik."

Clave nodded. "That's what I'm afraid of."

Minya said, "We worked so hard to make this our home. Gavving knows how close we came to dying. How can he risk what we've got?"

"We seem to be agreed," Clave said briskly. "Well? What do we do about it?"

Lawri and Jeffer were missing dinner. Lawri had led her husband east along the branch, beyond the region of the huts. In a dark womb of foliage and branchlets, they were making babies.

Resting, relaxed for the first time in many days, Lawri plucked foliage and put it in Jeffer's mouth. He talked around it, indistinctly. "Does this remind you of being young?"

She lost her smile. "No."

He leered. "Little London Tree boys and girls never snuck off into the foliage—?"

She shook her head violently. "It isn't like that for a girl in London Tree. When boys get old enough, they don't need us. They go to the in tuft. Copsik women belong to any male citizen. Jeffer, you know that much!"

"I should. That's how Mark got Minya pregnant, before we got loose."

She changed position to lie along his length. "If he did. Any man can father a dwarf."

"Even Rather doesn't believe that."

"Bother him?"

"Yeah . . . But women had children in London Tree, didn't they? And married?"

"Yes, if we were willing to act like copsiks ourselves. How else could we compete? I would've been some man's copsik if I wanted to make babies. So I never made babies."

Jeffer looked into her eyes as if seeing her for the first time. "Are you glad I came?"

She nodded. Perhaps he couldn't see her blushing in the near-darkness.

"Why didn't you ever tell me?"

That was a stupid question. Knowing how she needed him, he'd use his advantage to win arguments! "This wasn't what we came to talk about."

"Did we come to talk?"

"What did you find on the burned tree?"

"We didn't keep any secrets. —That's right, you weren't there when Booce was telling us what we had. Well, we got a pot full of charred stuff—honey, he said—and a metal thing for cutting wood, and hooks . . . miscellaneous stuff. And the metal pipe. Everything else that burned— I've forgotten what he called it all, but it can all be replaced, except the— what did Booce call it? The sikenwire."

"I want to go to the Clump," Lawri said.

"Me too. Clave would never let both Scientists go." Jeffer kissed her cheek. "Let's wait till the last minute and then fight about it."

"What about the sikenwire?"

"We'll think of something. Do you think Clave will let us take the carm?"

". . . No."

She felt him shrug. "Okay. We go as loggers?" She nodded (their foreheads brushed) and he said, "I'd guess Clump citizens will all look like jungle giants. We should have a few. Anthon and Debby'll come. A couple of the Serjents for guides. Defenses . . . we wouldn't want to risk the carm in the Clump, but we could take the silver suit."

"Wrong. A lot of citizens don't want anything changed. Clave thinks we're too close to the Clump already. He wants to take us farther west. Mark agrees with him."

"Yeah, I've talked to Mark. Treefodder. Without him we can't use the silver suit . . . Lawri? Clave wants to move us west?"

"What are you thinking?"

"We don't know enough yet. Forget it. Look what you missed when you were a little girl . . ."

Whatever the disagreements now roiling through Citizens' Tree, there was at least this bone of consensus: they all wanted to fly.

The Serjent girls were willing. From branchwood sticks and from cloth that was made on the looms below the branch, they made wings. Karilly worked quietly and skillfully and without words. Mishael and Carlot explained as they went, and corrected the mistakes of the children who emulated them. The work went fast. Citizens would wear their old tunics and pants for half a year longer, for cloth was not made quickly; but twenty-four wings were ready within twelve days.

Jeffer took Mishael, Minya, Gavving, and eight of the older children to the midpoint via the lift. Other children ran with zeal in the treadmill, knowing that theirs would be the next flight.

Jeffer had chosen with some care. These were the children who had not shied back from crossing to the pond on the day of the firetree. Yet there had been lines to cling to then. Today there was only bark, and some of them clung to that.

Rather flew, and was instantly in love with wings. Jill looked like she was facing death, but when wings were bound to her ankles and Rather was already in the sky, she flew. Mishael served as instructor. Jeffer learned how to kick, how to turn. When the sky was filled with winged adults and children, the rest gulped hard and loosed their hold on the bark and flew.

They were in the sky for one full circle of the sun. The adults had their hands full herding them back to the lift. Arth made a game of it, fleeing across the sky until Jeffer and Gavving closed in on him and pulled his wings off. The sun was rising up the east before they had the children rounded up.

Then Jeffer sent the others down without him. He told Minya, "I want to do some maintenance. Start the lift again after you're down."

"Kendy for the State. Hello, Scientist."

"Hello, Kendy."

"How are your refugees?"

"Four of the Serjents recovered. One of the girls, Karilly, looks okay but she doesn't talk."

"Shock. She may recover. When may I see them?"

"Kendy, I wanted to give Mishael a tour of the carm. The Chairman vetoed that. He's afraid they'll try to steal the carm."

"Nonsense. What do the rest of your tribe think?"

"We're split down the middle. Half of us want to go see what's in the Clump. They've got a place . . . the Market? . . . where we could get anything we want. The Serjents told us about it."

"And?"

"The Chairman is scared spitless of the Clump. He thinks we're too close now. Some of the others feel the same way. Jayan and Jinny, of course, but Mark and Minya too. Even the Serjents don't all want to leave. Mark's asked Ryllin for permission to marry Karilly, and she gave it."

"Good. How do you feel about this, Jeffer?"

"I want to see the Clump. Booce told me they've got something they call the Library, but it sounds like a carm autopilot. I want to scan their cassettes. Kendy, I'm doing what I can. I just took some of them flying. They like that. Maybe they'll start wondering what else they're missing."

"I remember Clave. He leads his citizens where they want to go. Call a council. Force your citizens to make a decision."

"What good does that do us?"

"If you lose the vote, you'll know where you stand. Then make Clave set a date for moving the tree. Decide what you need and who you need. Is there any chance you can talk Mark around?"

"None."

"The Serjents told you how to go about setting up a logging enterprise. Tell me."

The children slept on, exhausted by their flying. Gavving was making an early breakfast on a slice of smoked dumbo meat. He said, "The Admiralty has earthlife plants."

"We've lived without them for fourteen years," Minya said sleepily.

"We lived without lifts and the carm for longer than that. It was because we didn't *know*."

"The Admiralty has never touched us. We wouldn't know it exists, except that Booce tells us so. But you want to know more. Aren't these matters more properly discussed in council?"

Gavving looked closely at his wife. "You looked like this fourteen years ago, when you were trying to kill me. The whole tuft is like that. There hasn't been fighting like this since the War of London Tree!"

"I haven't forgotten London Tree. We made a home here. Any change is for the worse."

"Dear, are you sorry they came?"

"No!" Minya said with some force. She was fully awake now. "There aren't enough of us. We all feel that."

"Lawri the Scientist talks about the gene pool being too small—"

"We don't need that gibberish. We can *feel* we're too few. Now we have three more women, even if Ryllin is too old to host a guest, and they're *different* from us—"

"They are indeed!"

"Well, that's good!"

"Suppose they want to go home?"

"They can't," Minya said flatly.

A child stirred: Qwen. Gavving lowered his voice. "Suppose we built them another rocket. Suppose some of us wanted to go with them."

Minya stopped to sort words through her head. Gavving waited patiently. Presently she said, "They'd have to be crazy. We'd have to be crazy to let them go. Gav, have you forgotten London Tree?"

"No. I haven't forgotten Quinn Tuft, either, or Carther States. *They* didn't make citizens into copsiks, and neither did your people."

". . . No. But we attacked you the instant we saw you."

"True."

"Do you remember being lost in the sky, clinging to a sheet of bark and dying of thirst? We faced dangers we can't even describe to our children, because they were too strange! We fought hard for Citizens' Tree!

And now *both* Scientists want to cross a thousand klomters to the Clump shouting 'Here we are!' Why do you want to risk what we've got?"

"They've got things to trade. They've got wings—"

"We've got wings."

"We picked jet pods, when we could find them. All this time. And it's so *simple*! Minya, what would you have given for a pair of wings, when we were stranded in the sky? Everything in the Smoke Ring can fly except men, and all it takes is spine branches and cloth! They've got a rocket that moves a tree, and it isn't stolen starstuff, it's made mostly from things they find in the Smoke Ring. What have they got in the Clump? What haven't we seen yet?"

She put bitterness in her laughter. "A thousand people and a drastic need for copsiks, maybe."

Gavving sighed. "Stet, you don't want anything changed. What should we do? They're *here*."

"Make them welcome," said Minya. "Teach them how to live in a tree. Get the girls married. Make them part of us. Gavving, Mark intends to marry Karilly."

"Karilly's sick in the mind. She isn't getting over it."

"Sure, and Mark's a dwarf. He's needed a wife, and none of us would touch him. I never did feel *sorry* for the copsik runner, but . . . but he's willing to take care of her. And I think you ought to marry one of the other girls."

Bang! Gavving stared. *This* was a woman afraid of changes? "I am married."

"Clave has two wives. Anthon did, until Ilsa died. I'm getting too old to make babies, dear."

"You don't mean—"

"No!" She hugged him. "But it won't give me a guest to carry."

"You're serious? Okay, who?"

She hesitated. Then, bravely (he thought): "I would have thought Mishael. She's the oldest. Gavving, she showed me how to fly. I like her."

"Have you mentioned any of—"

"No, you fool! A woman doesn't ask a woman to be her wife!" And when he laughed she smiled, weakly. Gavving saw how difficult this was for her. Minya must have thought long and hard about this.

"There's room to extend the hut," she said. "We'd have another pair of hands, adult hands. The children are growing up, they're not as much fun anymore—"

And if some of us marry Serjent women, we'll have their loyalty when the Admiralty comes to us! Logbearer *can't be the only ship in the sky.* Gavving wondered if his brain was working in the service of his seeds. Minya had not referred to Mishael's alien beauty.

And if we do visit the Clump, his brain ran on, *we'll need guides. Booce or Ryllin would have to go. With their daughters among us, we'd have their loyalty—*

Chapter Five

THE SILVER SUIT

from the Admiralty cassettes, year 3 SM:

We were chosen for this. No citizen leaves Earth orbit until the State has learned his tolerance for free fall. One in ten thousand have the genetic quirks to survive months or years of free fall without softening of the bones, without failure of the digestive system, without the terror of falling.

*We served the State by flying to the stars. When the drive was off we played at flying, while cramped in a seeder ramship with barely room to flap our arms. Here is real flight. Of **course** the Smoke Ring seems an incredible dream come true—to **us**.*

—Sharon Levoy, Astrogation

"Kendy for the State. Hello, Jeffer. It's been more than thirty days."

"I was busy. We got our council. It's over."

"How did it go?"

"We lost."

"Who sided against you?"

"Clave. Jayan and Jinny. Minya. Mark."

"Five out of ten. If you count the Serjents, twelve."

"Thirteen. Mishael's old enough, and married too, but she acts like a junior wife. She won't make Minya *or* Gavving angry. Gavving doesn't want to fight with Minya. The Serjents don't think like citizens yet. Anthon won't get into the arguments. I'm not really sure where he stands. The rest of us want to see what's out there, but we don't all want it enough. Debby loves arguing, but she's not very good at it. We didn't give Clave any trouble at all."

"You're disappointed. Don't be. Did you think that flying would bring them around? People tend to side with authority, and authority tends to protect its own power. Clave is the key. Clave has everything he wants in Citizens' Tree."

"Kendy, do you see us as savages?"

"Yes. Don't take that too seriously, Scientist. I would probably see the Admiralty as savages too. I want to educate you all."

"Then educate me, Kendy. I can't just take Booce and Ryllin and go off into the sky. We—"

"You must go, Jeffer. The wealth of the L4 point is almost irrelevant. It takes many people to hold a civilization together. There are too few of you here to be more than savages!"

Jeffer didn't react to the insult, barring an increase in infrared radiation from his cheeks, neck, and ears. "We'd need things Citizens' Tree can't spare. Lawri's on my side, but we can't both go. The tree needs a Scientist. We'd have to take the carm too. We—"

"Take it."

"You're not serious. Dalton-Quinn Tree died because we couldn't move it. I won't see it happen to Citizens' Tree."

"Bring the carm back when you're through with it."

Jeffer paused to think. (Kendy never did that. It was another reason to distrust Kendy: he seemed to *leap* at his answers, without forethought.) "We might lose the carm."

"You can build a steam rocket. Jeffer, I'm drifting out of range."

"We've got *one* pipe, and we need that to be loggers. Without the pipe, Citizens' Tree couldn't build a steam rocket. I wouldn't have *believed* that so much could change in twenty sleeps. Kendy?" The signal dissolved in noise.

Kendy returned to his records.

For twenty State years CARM #6 had been taking pictures, not just through the CARM cameras but through the fish-eye lens on the pressure suit too.

Here: the squirrel cage that ran a muscle-powered lift, and the lines leading up. Far too much footage of that.

Here: fire burned in a great bowl of soft clay. The silver suit moved around the edges of the fire, poking it, or adjusting sheets of bark that had been set as vanes to channel the wind into the burning wood. The look of the clay began to change.

Here: less fire than smoke. What looked like enough spaghetti to feed Sol system's entire State government had been spread leeward of smoldering wood. The pressure suit moved around and within the mass, turning it and loosening the strands—vines—with the handle of a harpoon so that the smoke would cure them. These were the lines that now served Citizens' Tree.

Ingenious. A poor way to treat State property; but they were making use of local resources too.

The platform around the cookpot was of boards tied with line. It had always been flimsy, and that didn't matter much in Citizens' Tree's low tide; but over the years the lines had loosened. Jayan and Jinny complained about the way the platform lurched while they tried to make dinner. So Rather and Carlot had been sent to repair the platform.

Rather enjoyed the work. It called for muscle rather than dexterity. He lifted one end of a new branchwood plant into place. He called, "Hold this," and waited until Carlot was set. Then he bounded down to the other end and hoisted that.

Carlot giggled.

Rather began to tie the planks. One loop of line to hold it, then he could work on a more elaborate mooring. He asked, "What's funny?"

"Never mind," Carlot said. "Are you going to tie this for me?"

"I thought I'd just leave you there. You make a good mooring, and decorative too."

"Oh." She held the planks in place with one arm while she reached out. Her right leg was twenty ce'meters longer than the left, and she usually reached with that. Her long toes grasped a coil of line and pulled it to her hands. She tied a temporary binding.

In the twenty-two sleeps since their arrival, all of the Serjent family had become dextrous in Citizens' Tree tide.

Rather wrapped a dozen loops of line around the plank ends, then began tightening them. Heave on a loop, pull the slack around; again. From the opening beyond the treemouth the wind blew steadily, drying sweat as fast as it formed.

Carlot called from her corner. "That's as tight as I can get it."

Rather was finished at his end. He jogged down to Carlot's end (ripe copter plants buzzed up around his feet) and began pulling in slack. She'd left a good deal, of course. Carlot was agile, but not strong. He asked, "What got you giggling?"

"Just the way you scurry."

Rather's hands paused for less than a second, then continued.

"You did ask," she said defensively. "You have to go running back and forth because you can't reach as far as—"

"I know that."

"Did you make this cauldron yourselves? I wouldn't have thought you could do that here. It's big enough to boil two people at once."

"Hey, Carlot, you don't really *eat* people in the Empire, do you?"

She laughed at him. "No! There's a happyfeet tribe that's supposed to do that. But how did you make it?"

"The grown-ups found a glob of gray mud west of the tree. Maybe it was the middle of a pond that came apart. They brought some back. We took all the rocks in Citizens' Tree and piled them in a bowl-shape, out on the branch where we couldn't do any damage. I was just a kid, but they let me help with the rocks. We plastered the mud over the rocks. We got firebark from another tree and piled it in the bowl-shape and fired it. It took a dozen days to cool off, and then it was like that. We did it twice—"

"You're cute," she said solemnly.

Carlot was a year older than Rather. An exotic beauty was growing in her. Half her hair had been burned off, and she had cut the rest to match. Now it was like a skullcap of black wire. She was two and a half meters tall, with long fingers and long, agile toes, and arms and legs that could reach out forever.

Carlot affected Rather in ways he wasn't quite ready to accept. He said, "Put it in the treemouth. When do I get to be overwhelmingly handsome?"

"Cute is good. If I weren't your aunt—"

"Treefodder."

"Are you not my nephew?"

Rather studied his work. "I think we're done. —It's an Empire thing, is it? You don't make babies even with relatives of relatives? Fine, but you've got a thousand people in the Empire! At least that's what your parents say. We had ten adults and twenty children when you came. I won't get much choice about who I marry."

"Who, then?"

He shrugged. "Jill's a half year older than me. All the other girls are younger. I'd have to wait." The subject made him uncomfortable. He looked up past the treadmill and along the trunk, to where a handful of citizens were trying their wings. "I wish I was up there. You've been flying all your life, haven't you?"

"I *should* be there, showing you people how to fly. This damn fluff,"

Carlot said. Long sleeves were sewn loosely to her tuftberry-scarlet tunic. She pulled one away. The green fur along her arm had turned brown; the patch had shrunk. "How's yours?" She touched his cheek. The patch felt half numb and raspy; it ran from his face down his neck and across part of his chest. "It's drying up. Ten days, it'll be cleared up."

"Too treefeeding slow."

"We just have to stay in the shade for a while. Fluff needs sunlight."

"Yeah."

From eastward, his first mother's voice called above the wind-roar. "Rather!"

Rather bounded toward Minya across the floor of braided, live-spine branches. Carlot gave him a good head start, then bounded after him. Her asymmetric legs gave her an odd run, a pleasure to watch: bound-BOUND, boundBOUND, low-flying flight. Soon she'd be faster than Jill. She reached Minya a good six meters ahead of Rather, turned and flashed a grin at him. She lost it immediately.

"—Crawled too far toward the treemouth, and now he can't—" Minya stopped and began again. "Rather! It's the children. Harry and Qwen and Gorey went crawling around in the old west rooms. Gorey went too far, and Harry and Qwen can't reach him, and he can't get out."

"You can't get to him?"

"I didn't try. Rather, we don't know how long it was before Harry came to get us."

"Oh." Harry would have tried to rescue Gorey himself, then spent more time working up the nerve to tell his mother. And Gorey was only five! "I'll need some kind of knife," he said.

"What?"

"I'm no narrower than you are, First Mother. I'm just shorter. I may have to cut through some spine branches."

The wind didn't reach Mark's long hair and beard. They held the sweat like two sponges. The slab of hard branchwood strapped to his back massed as much as he did. He scrambled up the slope of the treemill, panting, trying to stay higher than Karilly and seven children. With a weight on his back, Mark was the equal of any two adults.

The treadmill was six meters across and four wide, a fragile wheel of branchwood sticks. Water running down the trunk helped to spin it, but runners were still needed.

It was getting easier; the treadmill was spinning faster. The cages must be almost passing each other. "Out!" Mark panted. "Runners, out!" Seven laughing children jumped from both sides of the treadmill, until only Mark and Karilly were left.

Above was a sudden glare as the sun passed into view.

Karilly's dark skin shone with sweat; she breathed deeply as she bounded uphill alongside him. He knew she could understand him. "Karilly. When the up cage is at the top it . . . doesn't weight anything. It takes all of us . . . to lift the down cage. Right now . . . the cages are next to each other. I can run by myself. In a little while . . . the down cage will be falling. I'll have to get out. Use the brake. Slow it down." She watched him as if she were listening. "So you jump out now."

Then he saw that she was afraid.

"Okay." He let the cage carry him around. Inverted, he scrambled down the other side. "I'm slowing it. Can you get out now?"

Karilly scrambled out.

Twenty klomters over his head, Lawri and her student flyers must be wondering what had gone wrong. Mark started the cage spinning again, letting his body do its accustomed work while his mind drifted.

Long ago and far away, there had been civilization.

London Tree had had stationary bicycles to run the elevators to the tree midpoint, and copsiks to run the bicycles. Citizens' Tree was primitive. They had London Tree's carm, of course: a thing of science dating from the day men came from the stars. Otherwise they must build everything.

Mark had shown the refugees how to build a lift. Mark had wanted to make bicycles, but the Scientists had built the treadmill instead. They kept the silver suit next to the treadmill with its helmet open. Citizens at the carm could call for the lift through the radio in the suit.

Below him he could see the hollow space of the commons, and two children bounding east. The tall, dark girl was far ahead of the smaller boy, who moved in slower, shorter steps, as if tide were heavier for him.

His son. His size proved it. Mark would not have wished that on him; yet Rather would be the next Silver Man. Mark wondered if the citizens would appreciate their fortune. In the short lifetime of Citizens' Tree there had been no need for an invulnerable fighter, and the silver suit had become a mere communications device.

Had it not been for one stupid, stubborn act, Mark would still be a citizen of London Tree. But he would never have seen the stars, and he would never have seen his son.

The treadmill was spinning by itself. Mark jumped out. He set the branchwood slab down. He looked up along the trunk, but he couldn't see the down cage yet. "We'll let it run for a bit."

If Karilly could talk, would she still smile at him like this? He took her hand. "Lawri wanted you with them. You were afraid to go up, weren't you?" He had known a London Tree citizen who was afraid of falling. It was instinct gone wrong. If such a woman were born in a place like Carther States, would she be afraid all the time? Until the added terror of a fire pushed her over the edge.

"Lawri wanted me up there too. I wonder what it's like. Flying."

But the silver suit caught his eye. *No.*

His business in London Tree had been war. Were there copsik runners in the Clump? Karilly would know. "I wish you could talk. The Scientists can't marry us till you can say the words. The key word is *yes*. Will you try? *Yes*."

"Mark!"

He jumped. "Debby?"

She called from below. "Yeah. Shall we relieve you?"

Mark swallowed his irritation. "The empty's coming down. You want to brake when the sun's at about eleven."

"We'll do it." Debby and Jeffer climbed up to join them. "Hello, Karilly." Jeffer said, "You didn't go flying? You should try it."

"Not me. I'm the Silver Man. I fly with the silver suit. Come on, Karilly." Maybe somebody would need muscle at the cookpot platform.

The tunnels ran through the tuft like wormholes in an apple. Unused tunnels tended to close up; but passersby ate from the foliage as they passed, so the tunnels in normal use stayed open. One such tunnel ran past Rather's home.

At its west end Rather could have circled the hut with his legs. This was the oldest section. As the spine branches migrated west along the branch, eventually to be swallowed by the treemouth, enclosures tended to shrink. The newest sections were the largest.

This disappearing section had been small when new. It had housed only Gavving and Minya and the baby Rather. Other children had come, and Gavving wove new rooms eastward, faster than the treemouth could swallow them. By now there were seven children, and a new wife for Gavving, and a far bigger common room; for the Citizens' Tree populace was growing too. The original rooms had disappeared into the treemouth. These that he was passing now, wicker cages alongside the tunnel, were still less than Rather's height. The children tended to claim these for their own.

Rather found a deformed door. As he crawled inside he heard Minya saying "Keep going, Carlot. Go to the common room and get my old matchet off the wall and bring it back. Hurry."

Harry, eight years old and Rather's height, was crying into Mishael's chest. Rather nodded to Mishael. "Second Mother. Which way did he go? Straight west?"

Mishael, seven years older than Carlot, had Carlot's dark, exotic beauty in fully developed form, and legs that caused even Rather to stare: long and slender and perfectly matched. She'd cut her trousers into loose shorts, odd-looking in Citizens' Tree. The low roof cost her some dignity. She had to crouch. She looked uncomfortable and annoyed. "Straight on in. And he's stopped talking. I think he's mad at us."

Rather said, "You know this is no big deal, don't you? It happens all the time."

"I *don't* know. Rather, I still get the shivers in your crawling huts! Your parents just don't understand that. And poor Gorey, he is frightened."

"Sure. Carlot's coming with Mother's matchet. Send her after me. I need it to cut my way through." It didn't feel odd to be speaking thus peremptorily to his second mother. Mishael wasn't that much older than Rather; she was new to all this, and it showed.

Rather crawled west.

Memories tried to surface around him. His parents' bedroom: he'd lived in a basket, in a corner too small for a baby now. The private dining area, and ghosts of wonderful smells: were they in his nose, or in his mind? The common room, and too many strangers: he'd cried and had to be taken away. The spaces were distorted and tiny, a green-black womb. The spine branches were still growing. He tore them away with his fists; tore through an old partition.

He didn't like this. His past was too small to hold him. "Gorey!"

From west by north, Gorey yelled piercingly. He sounded more angry than frightened. How had he gotten *there*? What had been a kitchen wall had crumpled and grown half a meter thick! He must have found some way around—

"Rather?"

Carlot, behind him. He reached far back and took what was pushed into his hand. "Thanks." He pulled it to the level of his face, turned it with some difficulty and pushed the blade farther.

"Can you get to him?"

"One way or another."

For years the matchet had been no more than a part of the wall. He'd never really looked at it. The handle was long and a bit too wide for his short fingers. The blade was sixty ce'meters of black metal, tinged red by time. Time and use had serrated the edge. It had once belonged to a Navy man of London Tree.

In this restricted space he must use it as a saw. He didn't try to cut the wall. He cut branchlets west of him. He turned starboard, still sawing through miscellaneous branchlets. "Gorey?"

Cautiously, doubtfully: "Rath?"

"Here. Give me your hand. Can you reach me?"

"I can't move!"

Rather saw a thrashing foot. He pulled on it experimentally. Gorey was pinned between a spine branch and a smooth dark wall: the main branch itself. He must have tried to crawl between them. Rather wriggled forward. He sawed the spine branch half through, reached farther and broke it with his hands. Gorey wriggled out and wrapped himself around his brother and clung. Presently he asked, "Are they mad?"

"Sure they're mad. How did you get here? Hide-and-seek?"

"Yeah. Harry said he was gonna catch me and feed me to the triunes, so I kept going. Then I was afraid the treemouth would get me and I got *really* scared."

"Harry wouldn't get that close to a triune family. You know that."

"Yeah, but I was mad."

"You'd starve to death before you reach the treemouth. Here, grab my foot and follow me."

The boy's fingers were long enough to overlap Rather's ankle. He was already taller than Rather. They crawled out, with easier going at every meter.

In the common room Rather's mothers greeted him as a hero, while Gorey was scolded and petted. Rather took it with what grace he could. He wondered if Carlot was laughing at him; but in fact she seemed to think he had done something actively dangerous.

It made him uncomfortable. He was vastly relieved when Gavving poked his head through the door. "Treadmill runners!" he called. "Rather?" And Rather was rescued.

Harry and Carlot came with them. As they neared the treemouth Gavving said, "Harry, Carlot, why don't you see if they need help with the laundry pot?"

They split off, Harry grumbling.

Rather followed his father up through the tunnels toward the tread-mill. His nerves were prickling. Something odd was going on. "Father? Do they really need treadmill runners?"

"No," Gavving said without looking down.

The treadmill was at rest. Debby and Jeffer lay in the foliage nearby, eating and talking. They sat up when Gavving appeared. "Got him," Gavving said.

This must have something to do with the Serjent family; and the con-ference before the last sleep, from which children were barred; and the ar-guments that divided half the families in the tree. *Do my mothers know about this? Would they approve?* Rather asked instead, "Should we have brought Carlot?"

"No need. Rather, we have to find out something." Gavving pointed at a short, faceless fat man made of silvery metal. "Try that on."

"The silver suit?"

"Yeah. See if you can get into it."

Rather looked it over. This thing had a fearsome, quasi-scientific repu-tation. It was a flying fighting machine, stronger than crossbow bolts, stronger than the airlessness beyond all that was known. Rather had never before seen it with its head closed.

Jeffer instructed him. "Lift this latch. Take the head and turn it. Pull up. Turn it the other way."

The head came up on a hinge.

"This latch too. Now pull this down . . . now pull it apart . . . good."

The suit was open down the front, and empty.

"Can you get in?"

"Where's Mark?"

"Debby?"

"No problem. We relieved him and he took Karilly to the kitchen."

"Father . . . wait. Listen. I'm the only boy in the tree with two mothers and two fathers." Rather plunged on despite the sudden hurt in Gavving's face. "We've never talked about this, but I always knew . . . sooner or later I'd . . . does Mark know what you're doing with the silver suit?"

"No."

"What's it all about?" Four big adults could make him do whatever they wanted; and it didn't matter. They needed his cooperation, and he didn't know enough to give it.

Jeffer the Scientist said, "It's about seeing what's outside Citizens' Tree.

It's learning about the Smoke Ring, what we can use, what we need to be afraid of. Or else it's about staying savages until someone comes out of the sky to teach us the hard way."

"We're going to the Clump," Gavving said. "We'll be safer if we can take the Silver Man."

"Uh-huh. Mark doesn't want to go?"

"Right."

They watched as Rather tried to get into the suit. He had to get his legs in first, then duck under the neck ring. He closed the sliding catches, the headpiece, the latches. The suit was loose around his belly, snug everywhere else. "It fits."

Jeffer closed the helmet on him. He rotated it left until it dropped two mi'meters, then right.

Rather was locked in a box his own size and shape. The suit smelled faintly of former occupants, of exertion and fear. He moved his arms, then his legs, against faint resistance. He turned and reached and plucked a handful of foliage . . . good. He could move. He could move like a normal man.

The air was getting stale . . . but Jeffer was already turning the helmet, lifting it. The adults were smiling at each other. Gavving said, "Okay. Get out of it."

Getting out of the silver suit was as difficult as getting in. Rather said, "Now tell me."

"Some of us are going to visit the Clump. Do you want to come with us?"

"Who's going? How long will it take?"

"Me," said Jeffer. "Gavving. Booce and Ryllin. Anthon and Debby. The Clump is all jungle giants. We need people that size."

"How does the Chairman—"

"He'll try to stop us."

"Father, I don't really like the thought of not ever coming home."

Gavving shook his head. "They'll want the carm back. They'll want us back too. Citizens' Tree isn't so crowded that they can afford to lose anyone who breathes. They'll want to know what we learned. They'll want what we bring back. Half the citizens are on our side anyway; they just don't want to buck the Chairman."

"You're taking the *carm?*"

"We are." Gavving clapped him on the shoulder. "Think about it. We've got two sleeps to get ready. Whatever you decide, don't mention this to anyone, particularly your mothers."

"Father, you'd better tell it all." Rather didn't consider whether he had the right to ask. Clave wouldn't like this; Minya wouldn't like it; and if he agreed to this—it was only just coming to him—if Rather agreed, then *he* was the Silver Man.

Jeffer said, "It isn't just the wealth of the Clump Admiralty. It's—"

"Tell me *what* you're going to do."

They told him.

Chapter Six
THE APPEARANCE OF MUTINY

from *Discipline's* log, year 1893 State = 370 SM:

Medical readouts showed that the inhabitants of CARM # 6 lied to me. They reacted strongly to accusation of mutiny. I lost my chance to question them in detail. They may have mutinied against legitimate holders of the CARM. Heredity will tell.

It's a bad habit. I will break them of it.

—*Sharls Davis Kendy, Checker*

Clave pulled himself out of the elevator first. Wings were tethered next to the cage, and he pulled one free and tied it in place along his left shin. "This was a good idea, Gavving. Wings aren't much use in the tuft."

"Oh, we'll keep some there too. Hunters used to carry jet pods. Wings are better. But there's no point porting them up and down every time someone wants to fly. What are you doing?"

"Fixing this." He chopped with his matchet at his other wing. When ten ce'meters were gone, he tied the wing to his right shin. He felt distinctly lopsided.

Jeffer and Gavving were also winged now. The three flapped out toward the carm, spurning the convenient handholds the bark afforded. Clave's flight wavered, then steadied. He'd been right. This was easier on the warped muscles in his thigh.

Jeffer was first through the airlock. "Prikazyvat Voice."

The carm's deep voice said, "Ready, Jeffer the Scientist—"

A woman's voice broke in. "Jeffer, it's Lawri. I think I want to join you."

"Come on up. Bring something to eat. We'll be running the main motor for maybe two days."

"Will do. Lawri out."

"What was that about?" Clave asked.

"Lawri doesn't trust me with the carm." Jeffer laughed. "Now we refuel the beast."

Clave sighed. "Pump?"

"Right. You pump while I do a checklist. Otherwise we'll lose the pondlet when we go under thrust."

Some pumping had been done, but megatons of water still nestled against the trunk. Clave ran the hose from the carm to the pondlet. The pump was a wheel and a tube and piston, all carved from hard branchwood. Clave braced his back and arms against the bark and kicked the wheel around with his feet on the spokes. "Help would be appreciated," he grunted.

Gavving joined him.

The pump leaked. The pond didn't dwindle fast, but it dwindled. They broke to drink thirstily, then resumed pumping. The sun had dropped from zenith to nadir—which at the midyear was not behind Voy, but north by three full degrees—when Jeffer poked his head through the airlock. "Stop! The tank's full!"

Clave tossed his head to shake some of the sweat out of his hair.

"Come inside." Jeffer ushered them forward to the front row of seats. "Strap down."

He tapped, and vertical blue dashes appeared in the panel below the window. Four clusters of four each at the corners of a square, and a larger dash in the center. He tapped the central dash.

The sound within the cabin was like the roaring of wind at the treemouth. Clave felt a featherweight of tide and knew the tree was in motion.

Jeffer told them, "We're already placed right, with the motor aimed west. We thrust eastward. That puts Citizens' Tree in a wider orbit, so we slow down and drift west, away from the Clump."

Clave wondered if he wanted to watch from outside. "Is it dangerous out there?"

"Could be. You don't want to fall into the flame. Anyway, the view's better in here." Jeffer's fingers danced, and the carm window sprouted five smaller windows. "The ventral view got ruined when we fell back into the Smoke Ring—"

"Jeffer, you don't lecture this much unless you're nervous. What's wrong? We've moved the tree before."

Gavving laughed. It appeared that he had a touch of nerves too. "Remember how twitchy we were then? Merril was sure we'd break the tree apart and kill ourselves."

Clave shrugged. He went aft and braced himself in the airlock.

What remained of the pondlet stretched itself out from the trunk, then broke into one big drop and a line of little ones. The mother pond they'd robbed twenty-two sleeps ago drifted west. The sun passed Voy and began to climb. A fat triple-finned bird, dead west by a klomter or three, suddenly went into an epileptic seizure, split into three slender birds, and scattered. Clave was late in understanding what he'd seen: a triune family suddenly washed by the invisible heat of the carm's exhaust.

Clave went in and strapped down again.

He had been anticipating Lawri's arrival for some time, but the carm's roar covered her entry. He turned to see her halfway up the aisle . . . and Debby behind her. And Ryllin. And Booce and Carlot. Clave fumbled to release the buckle that bound him to the chair.

It took too long. He was between Jeffer and Gavving, with Lawri behind him. He sighed. "What's it all about?"

Jeffer's fingers danced. The board went blank. He said, "We can fight or we can talk. Or we can talk and then fight, but there's only one of you, Clave. Cripple me and Lawri flies the carm."

Call for help? If he could get past Jeffer to use Voice, the elevator would still take a day to get up . . . forget it. Voice connected to the silver suit, which Rather was now pulling headfirst through the airlock.

It would have felt good to hit somebody. Clave said, "I'll be good. Now what's it all about?"

"We're going to visit the Admiralty," Jeffer said.

Rather and Booce were moving things inside: two smoked turkeys, a huge amount of foliage, water pods.

"All of us?"

"Not you, Clave. Lawri's staying too. Citizens' Tree needs a Chairman *and* a Scientist."

"How did you decide—"

There was a bit of an edge in Lawri's voice. "We knew one of us would have to stay. Now I've missed my time of blood. I'm hosting a guest. I wondered why the copsik was being so affectionate."

"You should all be staying. You're taking the carm?"

"The carm, the silver suit, and the pipe from *Logbearer*."

They all looked very serious. The background roar prompted Clave to ask, "Are you planning to set the tree moving first? Or was that a lie too?"

"We'll give you a day's thrust," Jeffer said. "No more. I won't be here to decelerate you, and I want to be able to find you again."

"With what? Would London Tree have let you keep the carm? The Admiralty won't either!"

Patiently Gavving said, "We've talked that over. We won't take the carm into the Clump. They'll never know it exists. Jeffer will hide the carm somewhere. The rest of us will go in as loggers, with Booce and Ryllin to show us how."

Clave's mind was racing. "Now listen to me. Will you listen?"

"Yes, Chairman."

"First, are you all volunteers? Rather, how did they suck you into this?"

"They can't go without the silver suit," the boy said.

"Oh, they'd go. Wouldn't you, Jeffer?"

"Yes."

"I'm going anyway," Rather said.

He didn't look like he'd change his mind. Rather didn't even bother to argue, though the boy was good at that. Clave knew how *he* would enlist a fourteen-year-old boy. Put him in the silver suit, call him the Silver Man, offer him status and adventure . . . "Carlot?"

"I'm going home," the girl said defiantly.

"Debby?" But a glance told Clave he'd lost that battle. Debby was fiercely happy. He hadn't seen her like this since the War of London Tree. "What about Anthon?"

Debby said, "I never told him. Jeffer, I did get him talking. He likes Citizens' Tree just fine and he doesn't want any changes. Have you noticed how fat he's getting?"

"Too bad," Jeffer said.

Clave said, "Stet. I accept that you're going to do this. I've heard your speeches, and you've heard mine, and the treemouth can have them both. But don't you see that this will tear Citizens' Tree apart? It's mutiny. Hold it! I mean it's mutiny the way you've planned it. If we don't fix that, Citizens' Tree will never recover. It's got to look better than it does."

The mutineers looked at each other.

"Here's how it's got to be," said Clave. "First, I'm going. Gavving isn't. You said it and you're right. The tree needs a Chairman and it's Gavving."

Gavving said, "That's silly. You're—"

"I'm the treefeeding Chairman, and if I go the expedition is official. Besides that, I've got to see to it that you return the carm and the silver suit. The citizens would be crazy to settle for less. I hereby appoint you my Chairman Pro Tem until I return."

Coolly Gavving asked, "Anything else?"

"Yes. You don't get both Booce and Ryllin. One of them stays. There has to be some reason for the Serjents to bring us home."

"We can't do that," Ryllin said. "Booce takes care of *Logbearer*. I take care of business. I do all the buying and selling. Anyone who sees one of us in the Clump will expect to see us both."

Clave was massaging the lump on his thigh. Sometimes that helped him think. *Think!* "The citizens you deal with, the . . . merchants? If they deal with Booce, what will happen?"

Ryllin said, "My husband is very good with machinery, not so good at trading. He did much better after he had the good sense to marry me. But *Logbearer* understands him, he—"

"Without you they'll get a better trade?"

"Damn right they will," Booce said bitterly. Then: "Yes, they will."

"They'll like that? They won't be too curious about where their luck comes from?"

It was Ryllin who nodded. "It's all right, love. Think of a story. They'll want to believe it."

"But we're missing three daughters too!"

"The house. They must have finished building our house by now. The girls and I are with *Logbearer* or we're at the house, wherever you're not. Maybe I'm somewhere in the Market buying furniture. That was the whole point of this last trip, we were going to—we were—" She turned away suddenly.

Emotional displays weren't needed here! Clave said, "We're not hiding anything but the silver suit and the carm. Otherwise we can tell any story we want. What's next? Gavving, Lawri, Ryllin, you back each other up when you go back to the tuft. Whoever's asking, the Chairman had to be talked into this, but I did agree, and I put the fine details in."

Rather called from aft. "Jeffer, the pipe's moored to the hull. We've got everything else, but it all has to be moored."

"Go ahead. I'll check you later. Gavving, are you willing?"

"Treefodder. Well, it'll probably keep Minya from killing me . . . Clave, will this work? Is it enough?"

"Only if we come back. We come back with the carm and something else too. It almost doesn't matter what."

"Stet. I'm the Chairman Pro Tem."

Jeffer killed the main motor. "Somebody go out and get our lines untied."

Rather went. Debby joined Booce aft. They began mooring what remained of the cargo: two big hooks, spare clothing, sacks of undyed cloth, harpoons, crossbows.

Lawri said, "Jeffer, let me show you something." She eased up next to him and tapped at the controls, whispering. Her shoulder blocked Clave's view. Clave's mind still raced, seeking flaws . . . he was looking for holes in a harebrain net! There was no way to make mutiny smell sweet.

"Are we bringing the spitgun? No, of course not." The weapon Mark had been carrying when he was captured was now in custody of the Chairman. "Gavving, it's in the older part of my hut, what used to be the common room. If you don't have the spitgun, you're not the Chairman. Get it before anyone notices."

Rather scrambled back through the airlock. Gavving, Ryllin, and Lawri left. Jeffer let them get well clear before he pulled away on the little jets.

The tree receded. Three tiny citizens fluttered toward the elevator dock. A cage had nearly reached the dock. One of the occupants was shrieking and waving its fists.

"Somebody must have found Mark," Debby said. "Relax, Clave, we only tied him up."

"Yeah. But if I'd known a rescue party was coming . . . skip it. You'd have closed the airlock in their faces. I hope you treefeeders can find something worthwhile in the Clump. It's *my* reputation on the line now."

Section Two
THE LOGGERS

Chapter Seven
THE HONEY HORNETS

from the Citizens' Tree cassettes:

> *Year 384, day 1590. Jeffer, Scientist. We have departed Citizens'
> Tree to explore the fourth Lagrange point, with attention to resources
> and population. The mission as outlined is revised as follows: Chair-
> man Clave now leads. This expedition has become an approved activity
> of Citizens' Tree. I now turn the log over to Chairman Clave.*
>
> *Clave, Chairman. Crew consists of Jeffer as Scientist and Captain,
> Citizens Debby and Rather, Booce and Carlot Serjent as guides, and
> myself. Priority at all times will go to protecting the carm and other vi-
> tal property of Citizens' Tree. No knowledge is worth gaining unless it
> can be reported to Citizens' Tree.*

Carlot was watching over their shoulders. "You use—"

"Prikazyvat End log," said Jeffer.

"—the same dates we do?"

"Why not?"

"Well, how do you know?" Carlot demanded. "Years, you just watch
for the sun to go behind Voy, but what about days? We sleep a couple of
days out of five, right? But maybe you lose count—"

"Who cares?" Clave said. "Who knows how many days there are in a
year? It depends on where you are."

Jeffer summoned up numbers on the panel. "The carm logs a standard
day, about four and a half per sleep. We used to keep marks on sticks in
the Scientist's hut. How do you keep time?"

Carlot said, "The Admiralty posts the time."

Booce laughed. "They must get it the same way! The Library looks a lot like this panel, Jeffer. Like somebody ripped out this part of the carm."

"Keys like this too?"

"I wasn't close enough to see. They don't let ordinary crew near it. Let's see . . . in the crossyear ceremony Radyo Mattson did the talking, but there was a Navy officer standing in front of the Library, and his hands moved . . ."

And Kendy watched them all.

The CARM autopilot heard everything. Every ten hours and a little, it squirted its records at *Discipline*. Kendy sorted the conversations for what he could use.

Two CARM autopilots separated for five hundred and thirty-two years and eleven months were both keeping Smoke Ring time, with *Discipline*'s arrival set at zero. Interesting. The mutineers must have adjusted them after it was certain that they would never return. They had severed relations with the past, with Kendy, with Earth, with the State itself.

Yet they used *mutiny* as an obscenity. Puzzling.

The CARM flew east, airspeed seventy-one kph, partially fueled, carrying water that would become fuel. Solar collector efficiency was running at fifty-two percent, the collectors partially shadowed by the old pipe moored to the hull.

It was a liquid oxygen pipe ripped from a CARM. Many CARMs must have been dismantled when they stopped working. The Admiralty "Library" was certainly the control panel from a ruined CARM; but was it still functional?

The cabin interior was offensively dirty. Kendy detected traces of old meals eaten aboard; feathers and bird shit from the turkey roundup ten years back; the black clay that had returned the same trip; and mud repeatedly expelled from the water tank. Dirt was not dangerous, only aesthetically distressing. Kendy foresaw no problems other than those of microsociology.

He was on course.

Humankind was scattered. No telling how far they had spread through the Smoke Ring. They had settled cotton-candy jungles and the tufts of integral trees; he knew of four tiny civilizations outside the L4 point. But the Admiralty seemed to be the densest gathering, the most numerous, the best organized: the political entity most suited to become the heart of an expanding empire.

It would not resemble the State at first. Conditions were fantastically different. Never mind. Give them communications, gather them into one political group. Then shape it.

He must know more. Hearsay from a family of wandering loggers wasn't good enough. The Admiralty "Library," *that* would tell him how to proceed next . . . but he already knew that he must eventually contact the officers themselves.

Somehow the CARM must be moved into the Clump.

Jeffer had seemed to have matters well in hand. The effects of mutiny on Citizens' Tree did not concern Kendy . . . but Clave had ended a mutiny by joining it! Now he must persuade Jeffer and Clave both. But Kendy couldn't talk to Clave. Exposing Jeffer's secret would lose Jeffer's trust.

It was precisely the kind of problem a Checker enjoyed most.

For now Kendy watched six savages in a recording made over the past ten hours. They had much to teach him.

Booce speaking: "We own—owned our own ship. I suppose that made us richer than most. I inherited *Logbearer* from my father, and I made my first trips with him. Ryllin was another logger's daughter, and she was used to the life. We had four daughters and a few lost ones out of maybe twenty pregnancies, all while hauling logs. I've become a good maternity doctor . . ." The cassette ended.

Men had changed in the Smoke Ring.

Pregnancy was easy in low gravity. Women became pregnant many times during their lifetimes.

Infant mortality ("lost ones") was high, perhaps around sixty percent; the natives seemed to take it for granted. *Discipline* had carried no diseases. Yet the growth of bones and organs was altered by altered gravity. Some children could not digest food. Some grew strangely, until their kidneys or livers or hearts or intestines would no longer work because of their shape.

The environment was user-friendly for those who survived childhood. Kendy's citizens came in odd shapes. Kendy caught a reference to Merril Quinn and learned that she had died six years ago, in early middle age. Merril had had small, withered legs. She had fought against London Tree, and not as a cripple.

Distorted children had wandered through the CARM to be photographed. Ryllin Serjent had an awesomely long neck, quite lovely and graceful and fragile looking. Carlot's legs . . . Kendy wished he could see her walk or run.

They matured more slowly. Carlot claimed fourteen and a half years; she would be twenty by Earth's reckoning. But she looked no more than fifteen.

Men had not evolved for the Smoke Ring. Infant mortality must have been ghastly among the original crew. Five hundred years of natural selection was taking care of that. As with the cats a few generations back: the near future should see an impressive population explosion.

Kendy would guide the civilization that resulted. He had been right to move *now*.

The CARM was coming back into range. Kendy's telescope array picked it up falling east and out, slowing.

In present time, Booce and Carlot and Rather were on watch while the others slept. The CARM moved through a patch of thin fog. Fog didn't block the CARM's senses. Kendy noticed the anomaly some time before the crew did.

He saw birds of unfamiliar type. They had lungs (the CARM's sonar could see the triple cavity), but they had retained part of what must once have been an exoskeleton: an oval of hard sky-blue shell covered one side. Fourteen of these birds, each about the mass of a boar pig, were strung in a line across the sky. They were folded into themselves, fins and wings and heads folded against that oval of shell. Sky-blue blobs, cool in infrared, comatose or dead.

Booce had noticed now. He shook Jeffer awake. "A whole flock of dead birds. What killed them?"

"Nothing that can touch us with the airlock closed." Jeffer's fingers danced. "Outside air's okay, nothing poisonous. Well, *treefodder!*"

"What?"

"The temperature. It's *cold* out there."

Kendy had already found the source of the cold.

The present-time transmission showed Jeffer easing the CARM alongside one of the big birds. The other crew were in and around the airlock. Debby sent a tethered crossbow bolt into the bird. It twitched. She loosed another . . .

. . . while Kendy set a blinking light around the image of the pond.

Only Jeffer was there to see it. He said softly, "Stet."

They had pulled the bird aboard. Clave said, "Well, it's dead now."

"I've got something," Jeffer said. "Clave, there's a pond in that dense cloud. Do you see anything odd about it?"

"No life around it. That cloud's awfully thick for being so small. What does it mean?"

"I don't know."

Ice. The pond was a core of foamy ice within a shell of meltwater. Ice was rare within the Smoke Ring. The pond was huge now, several hundred thousand tons, but Kendy guessed that it had been bigger yet. A tremendous pond must have been flung out of the Smoke Ring by a gravity-assist from Gold. In the near-vacuum of the gas torus it would have boiled and frozen at the same time, and later fallen back, reduced by evaporation, reduced further by reentry heat. Now it cooled the sky around it as it melted. Kendy could hear the *pings* as bubbles of near-vacuum crumpled within the ice core.

"I don't like it here," Booce said. "It's too strange."

"Your wish is granted. Strap the bird down and take your seats." Jeffer waited while they did that, then fired the aft attitude jets. The CARM surged away.

Carlot pointed into the aft view. "Look!"

The shieldbirds tumbled in the CARM's hot wake. One by one they fluttered, then spread a rainbow of wings and tails and fluffy feathers. They basked in the heat, catching as much of it as they could. Now their shells were no bigger in proportion than a warrior's shield. As *Discipline* moved out of range, the birds were lining up and flying west, putting distance between themselves and the melting glacier.

"There's no point picking out a tree till you've got honey," Booce said. "You can find a tree a hundred klomters from the Clump and still go half a thousand klomters to find your sting jungle."

Their catch was moored by cargo hooks, divested of skin and guts and some of the scarlet meat. Booce was holding raw bird flesh sliced thin and rolled around a stalk of lemon fern. He used it to point into the dorsal view. "And *that* is a sting jungle. The green dot, straight out."

"Stet." Jeffer tapped attitude jets to life. The carm turned. Carlot squeaked and grabbed Rather, startling him awake. Booce dropped his meal to snatch at a seat back.

Jeffer hid a grin. These sophisticated Admiralty folk found the carm as unsettling as Jeffer's own citizens did.

He aimed the carm east of Booce's green dot. East takes you out . . . "Half a day and we'll have honey. What else do we need?"

"Some way to collect it," Booce answered.

"We'll put Rather in the silver suit. No treefeeding insect will sting him through that!"

"Right. Better than armor."

"Tell us about the Admiralty," Clave said.

Booce closed his eyes to think. Then: "You're lonely out here. There's too much space. Everything is dense in the Clump. Think of a seed pod, and think of the Admiralty as the shell. There are more people in the Market alone, any time of day or night, than you've ever seen.

"We pull the logs back to the Clump over the course of a year or two, and we arrange an auction in the Market. Twice we've been attacked by happyfeet bandits. Once we got back just as another log was being docked, and we got half what we expected for the wood. But over the years we put enough money together to buy my retailer's license. This was going to be our last trip. We were going to settle in the Clump, and I'd work the wood myself and sell finished planks and burl, while Ryllin set about finding good husbands for our daughters. That was the point: they're reaching that age . . ."

Clave asked, "Can we really make the Admiralty believe we're loggers?"

"We'll *be* loggers," Booce said. "Rebuilding *Logbearer*'s no problem. We should have more weapons in case happyfeet come by, and it all has to look like Admiralty gear . . . and we still won't look like a typical logging family. But we don't have to, because I've got my retailer's license."

"What does that mean?"

"It means we don't have to sell the log straight off. The Navy ships will escort us in and give us a berth. I can set up shop in the Market and sell wood, and hire anyone I like; which means that the rest of you can be workers hired off a happyfeet jungle, or bought as copsiks. Some of the happyfeet keep copsiks. The Admiralty doesn't, so you'd be free if I bought you."

"Free, but not citizens."

"Right."

"Why can't you have hired us off a tree?"

Booce thought about it, and smiled. "You have a gift, Clave. Tell as much of the truth as possible. Debby, you're from Carther States, directly. You were stranded in the sky, you made your way to a tree, and now you want to live in a jungle again. Okay, Debby?"

Debby's lips were moving as she silently repeated the details. "Stet."

"We'll have to say Citizens' Tree is close to the Clump. Otherwise we got home too fast, and we'd have to explain about the carm."

Clave nodded. "So then we sell the log. How?"

"Set up in the Market and announce an auction. Buy your earthlife seeds with the money and go home. The Admiralty'll take half in taxes—"

Clave exclaimed, "Half?"

Jeffer said, "Taxes?"

"Taxes," Booce said, "is the money the Admiralty takes to run itself. Everybody pays, but the rich pay more. A good log is wealth. For the price of the carm you could be very rich indeed."

"The carm is what makes us what we are. We won't risk that," Clave said.

"Then don't take it into the Clump. The Navy won't want something that powerful floating around. They'll pay well, but they'll buy it whether or not you're selling."

Jeffer tapped the forward jets awake. They were pulling near the sting jungle.

Certain mooring loops fit the silver suit too perfectly, as if it were their specific purpose. Four sets. For four suits?

Jeffer pulled it loose. "The silver suit is yours, Rather. I'm going to teach you everything about it."

Rather had seen the silver suit as a mark of rank. He hadn't thought of it as an obligation. "Did Mark show you how to work it?"

"I've watched him. Lift this latch. Take the head and turn it till it stops. Pull up. Turn it the other way. Lift. Now this latch. Now pull this down . . . pull it apart . . . good."

The suit looked like the flayed skin of a dwarf.

Legs first, then arms. Duck under the neck ring. Rather closed the sliding catches, the latches. "Do I have to close the head?"

"Cover yourself. You don't want to be stung," Booce said. "Those little mutineers can sting a moby to death."

Rather closed the headpiece. He said, "The air's getting stale."

They couldn't hear him. He couldn't really suffocate this fast, could he?

Jeffer lifted the headpiece. "*Listen* first. Put your hand here." He guided Rather's fingers to a row of square buttons on the outside of the neck ring. He pushed one (colored lights lit below Rather's chin), and another (air jetted inward from all around the neck ring). He used Rather's fingertip to roll a small wheel back and forth (the air jets grew weaker, then stronger). "Close the helmet."

Rather did as Jeffer had shown him. Air from the neck ring hissed around his head.

Clave was saying something inaudible. Jeffer guided Rather's fingertip to another tiny wheel, and suddenly Clave's voice was a roar. "—use up the air? Does that thing have to be closed? We're not going back out of the Smoke Ring again, are we?"

"Let's hope not. Rather, you're leaking. Close that flap at your chest.

The way Booce talks about honey hornets, you don't want anything open."

Rather felt it out, then used finger pressure to close a snap he'd missed.

Now he was being shown little wheels on his chest. He moved the left one experimentally. His left foot kicked upward and he was wheeling in the air, banging his head and elbow, snatching for a mooring loop while his other hand rolled the wheel back to zero. He banged both knees before he could stop his spin.

Clave and Debby were helpless with laughter. Jeffer had jumped clear. "Leave those alone while you're inside! You fly with those. Now I'm going to walk you out the airlock. Play around with the jets. If you get in trouble we'll come after you."

Rather braced himself in the airlock, feeling imprisoned. The sting jungle was a fat, fluffy ring half a klomter across, dark green around the outside, slowly rotating. The inner rim flamed in orange and scarlet. Rather, looking out through the airlock, saw motion there like jittery fog.

Clave and Booce eased him into the sky.

They couldn't have any idea what the boy was going through, Kendy thought. How would they? None could fly the ancient pressure suit. Rather would have to be an agoraphile and an acrophile both.

Kendy had explained the pressure suit with diagrams and pointers; but had he shown Jeffer how to replenish the suit's oxygen and fuel? Replay that memory . . . no. Do that soon, if it wasn't already too late. What Kendy was watching was already two hours past.

But the CARM was in range again, and in present time the boy was aboard, and out of the suit, and still alive. Kendy kept the tape running:

Debby and Clave hovered a safe distance away. The boy floundered. He was all over the sky, spinning, faster . . . slower, tilting himself back and sideways to slow the spin . . . learning to move arms and legs to change his attitude. He found the throttle dials and turned both jets to minimum. He circled the CARM, then arced off toward the green doughnut that Booce had made his target.

Jeffer spoke through the suit radio. "Not yet, Rather. Come back. You don't have anything to carry the, the, Booce?"

"Honey."

"The honey. Booce, what does he need?"

"That's what the sacks are for."

Rather oriented toward the CARM, increased the thrust, doubled on himself for two seconds, then arched backward as he fell toward the air-lock. Fire sprayed from his ankles, arcing forward. Nice, Kendy thought. Of course he wasn't a complete novice. He'd flown with those giant swim-fin fans.

The boy left his helmet open (but didn't turn off the air jets!). Debby began strapping twelve coarse sacks to his back, got yelled at, and strapped them to his chest instead, where he could reach them. She used several loops of line. The savages were never without line, Kendy recalled. Good practice in a free-fall environment.

In present time Rather was leaving the airlock again, and the signal was fading. Kendy waited.

The great green torus became landscape as Rather came near. It was darker than integral tree foliage, and fluffy, finely divided to catch as much sunlight as possible. Scarlet and orange peeked over the curve, be-coming clearer. Orange horn-shapes, rocket-nostril shapes, quite pretty. Thousands of them.

The jittering mist cleared too: not steam roiled by wind, but myriads of particles swirling round the blossoms, dipping in and out. Now the motes abandoned the horn-shapes and streamed toward Rather.

They were all around him, a humming black cloud of rage.

"Scientist? I'm in the center. I can hardly see. The honey hornets are—"

"Look for red," said Booce's voice.

Orange and scarlet. Orange horns the size of drinking gourds, and scarlet of another shape. Rather jetted closer.

The honey hornets came with him. Thousands of thumb-sized birds: tiny harpoon for a nose, invisible blur of wing behind. He could hear the angry buzz through his helmet. "I've got a red thing . . . Booce, it's a kind of a sloppy polyhedron half a meter through, covered with lots of little triangle holes. It's growing between these horn-shapes."

"Those are flowers. It didn't grow there, it's attached. Did you take a knife?"

"No. Wait a breath, there's a matchet on my leg. It must be Mark's."

"Cut the honeypod loose and put the sack around it. Tie the neck shut."

Rather swung the matchet behind the scarlet polyhedron. The silver suit made all movements stiff. Presently the honeypod was floating loose. Rather pulled a sack free, opened the mouth, and swept it around the honeypod.

"Got it? Tie the bag *shut*. Done?"

"Done. There's sticky red stuff all over my gloves."

"Stet. Now keep doing that till you run out of sacks. Don't lick the honey."

"With my helmet closed?"

"Don't *ever* lick honey. It's suicide."

Chapter Eight
THE HONEY TRACK

from the Citizens' Tree cassettes, year 1426 State:

GOLDBLATT'S WORLD

Goldblatt's World may have begun life as a Neptune-like body in the comet cloud around the paired stars. In Goldblatt's scenario, the body was captured some millions of years after the supernova event. The collapsing core of the supernova, spewing its outer envelope asymmetrically due to a trapped magnetic field, may have picked up a skew velocity that nearly matched the velocity of the proto-Neptune. Robbed of its orbital velocity, Goldblatt's World would fall along a drastically eccentric orbit, passing very near Levoy's Star. Extreme Roche tides would warp the orbit into a circle within a few scores of passes.

It seems likely that Goldblatt's World's orbit and the associated gas torus have been contracting for all of their billion years. Meanwhile Levoy's Star has been cooling—since neutron stars no longer undergo fusion—maintaining a relatively stable balance of temperature in the Smoke Ring.

Note that the Roche Limit is never an absolute. It varies as the density of the orbiting body. A gasball world may be within its Roche Limit, and this one probably was. But the rock-and-metal core is dense. Goldblatt's World would have been well outside its Roche Limit after the gasball lost some of its gas and the eccentric orbit became more circular.

The planet is now no more than two and a half times the mass of Earth. . .

—Sam Goldblatt, Planetologist

"You see the problem? Too much of it is gibberish," Jeffer told the children. Rather and Carlot were nodding, but their eyes were glassy. "You can look up some of the words. You can guess a little. Goldblatt's World is Gold. There's a file on Earth and Neptune and the rest of the solar system, but it's hard going. Roche tides, Roche Limit—that seems to be a balance point between tide and some other force, maybe the same force that changes your orbit if you pass too close to Gold. Fusion is power: it makes the sun burn, and *Discipline* ran on fusion. Oort cloud, magnetic field, supernova—Lawri and I never figured those out."

He turned to Booce. "The kids need this, but I hate to make you sit through it again at your age—"

Booce's eyes were glassy too. "No, no, no. This is all new to me."

"Didn't you have classes? There's the Library—"

"For officers' kids only," Booce said brusquely. "Go on with this. What's eccentric?"

"That's a round path that isn't a circle. It goes out and in. Booce, am I committing a crime if I teach you and Carlot these things?"

"But I want to learn!"

"Shush, Carlot. It's never come up before," Booce said. "You're not showing us the Library, after all."

Carlot demanded, "Scientist, what's the point in stopping *now?*"

Jeffer laughed. He tapped, and the window was restored. The Clump was nearer now, and a score of parallel dashes lay across the carm's path. "You're right, Carlot, but the lesson's over anyway. We're getting too close."

Debby answered with a raspberry.

"Booce?" Jeffer said. "Any special favorites?"

"The smallest, I'd think, but let's have a better look." Booce disengaged his seat tethers and moved aft. "Jeffer, would you open those doors?"

"Will do." He did. "Booce, don't you trust the windows?"

"I prefer my eyes. Swing us around, will you?" He braced himself in the airlock. Others of the crew had followed him.

Jeffer began the maneuver. In the forward view, now moving into the port view, one of the trees had begun blinking: a green halo going on, off, on, off.

Nobody was near. Jeffer whispered, "Why?"

Now a point far in along the trunk was doing the blinking. Then that stopped—

An arm stabbed past Jeffer's ear, and he had to repress a shriek. "There," Booce said, pointing at one of the trees. "Thirty klomters, and it seems healthy."

"What about this one, Booce?" Jeffer tapped the tree that had blinked at him.

"Nothing wrong with it. It's bigger, twice the mass. Take us longer to get it to the Market, but of course there'd be more wood too, and there's the carm . . . Why that one?"

"A hunch. You've got no objection?"

Now Clave was behind him too. "Jeffer, are you playing dominance games?"

"I—"

"I'm the Chairman, you captain the carm, Booce is the logger. Booce chooses the tree."

Jeffer repressed a sigh. "Yes, Chairman. Booce?"

Booce pointed to Jeffer's selection. "That one."

Ten klomters above the tuft, the wood of the trunk had grown to enclose a node of foreign matter. Jeffer saw Booce catch his daughter's eye as Carlot was about to speak. She held her silence.

At the tree midpoint Jeffer nosed the carm against the trunk. He ran the attitude jets while his crew pounded spikes into the bark to mark a rectangle the size of the carm's bow. The carm drifted while they chopped out a dock with matchets.

Even on this younger tree, the bark was a meter thick. They made life easier for themselves by chopping along cracks. The five of them lifting together could rip great mattresses of bark away from the wood beneath, then saw off sections. Booce and Carlot used the saw, then let others take over until they got the hang of it.

Booce and Carlot rejoined Jeffer in the carm. Booce said, "They seem to be doing all right."

"But it's *scarred*," Carlot objected.

"And how much wood will that cost us?"

She shrugged. "Five percent? And weren't we in a hurry to get home?"

Booce was smiling. "Exactly. Jeffer, why this tree?"

"You'll be painting a line of honey down the trunk, stet? Have a look at that scar."

"Can you tell me what I'm supposed to find?"

"No, I can't."

"Jeffer the Scientist, Citizens' Tree gave us shelter and a place among you. We're grateful. I will not quarrel with any decision you make. You won't need to test it again."

Jeffer could feel his ears and cheeks burning. "If that scar isn't more interesting than you expect, you can count on it that I won't make a fool of myself twice. Stet?"

"Stet. I won't raise this subject with the Chairman, ever."

"You are kind. What's next?"

"The honey line."

In the cabin the roar of the main drive was like a great beast heard far away; but outside the airlock the roar was deafening. A translucent blue flame reached out from the carm's main rocket nostril. Warmth backwashed against the bark.

Carlot's eyes were big with fear. Rather pulled at her arm to set her kicking toward the in tuft, and followed, with Booce following him.

They stopped where the noise had decreased somewhat. The rough bark itself absorbed sound. Booce screamed, "That noise is beyond belief! What is that damn carm, a ship from the stars?"

"Jeffer says it rode here on the starship. My father never saw *Discipline*." What Rather said would be true whoever his father was. "But he's seen the stars. They're real."

"I'm afraid of it. I admit it. Look, the noise is scaring the bugs out of the bark! Let's get to work."

Booce used a branchwood matchet to open a hole in one of the honeypots. The interior was partitioned; the cells held red, sticky honey. Booce used the blade to paint it on the bark.

"You'll find a few hornets still in there," he told Rather. "They try to sting through the sack if you give them a few days to get restless, and then they die. But don't count on it. Don't let one get at you. Now you paint dabs a couple of meters apart. Closer, you waste honey. Farther apart, the bugs lose their way."

Rather had thought he was a climber, but this was different. He had problems keeping up. He was almost lost among the sacks he was carrying. Booce and Carlot climbed head-down; they would have left him behind if Booce had not been stopping to paint the trunk.

They took a breather when the sun was at nadir and the shadows had become confusing. The sun was passing closer to Voy as the year waned.

A day later they took a longer rest. "This is the part I like best," Booce said. "We're usually in too much of a hurry. This time your carm is already pushing us home. We can take our time, do what we like!"

"Like what?"

"I'll show you as we go." Booce began tearing up sheets of bark greater than a man, mooring them edgewise against the bare wood. When he had them arrayed he set them alight.

The smoke tended to stay where it formed. Booce moored a four-kigram slab of shellbird meat in the cloud. They broiled smaller steaks on their matchets, closer to the fire, and ate them still hot.

"The smoked meat will keep till we're down," Booce said. "But there are other things on the trunk. You've never climbed?"

"When we were children we did a little climbing, but just on the lower trunk. We weren't supposed to go more than a klomter up. If you fell, the foliage would catch you. Any higher, we rode the elevator."

They slept carefully tethered in cracks in the bark. Sometimes, for moments, the roar of the carm could be heard above the wind. A dark cloud had formed above them and was gradually drifting down.

The bugs of the tree had found the honey.

They breakfasted on smoked bird. Then Carlot did the painting while Booce carried the food.

The sun circled them, once and again. Always they stopped when the shadows were pointing straight out. Water was beginning to flow sluggishly in alongside their path. "Bugs like it damp," Booce said. "The bark's wet enough for them around the midpoint, but not lower down. You have to paint down the east side, alongside the waterfall, or they won't come. Also the trunk blocks the wind. You don't want the bugs blown away."

There was fan fungus like so many pallid hands reaching from the bark. Carlot showed Rather how to tear the red fringe off before eating the white interior. It was bland, almost tasteless, but went well enough with the strongly flavored smoked meat.

With lunch came entertainment: a gust of roses on the wind. The stems were four meters long. Dark-red blossoms fragile as tissue paper pointed straight toward Voy, soaking up blue Voy-light. Rather had never seen the like. He and Carlot watched the roses blowing east until they were out of sight.

Rather took his turn painting. Booce kept a close watch, but it seemed simple enough. A dab the size of a baby's hand; the next dab two meters lower.

A dark cloud flowed after them down the trunk.

The wind grew stronger, though the trunk blocked most of it. The growing tide made climbing easier for Rather. The water flowed more strongly. It was cleaner than pondwater, cleaner than the water that reached the basin in the commons. It tasted wonderful, and painting was hard, thirsty work.

In two days, Rather's arm was one long cramp.

He was too tired to help with dinner. Booce managed alone. He found shelled things hiding in the bark and pulled them loose. Roasted, their white flesh made a fine meal.

Again they wedged themselves along a wide crack in the bark, with Carlot between the men. There were dangers on the trunk.

Rather's aches kept him awake. He presently noticed Carlot's feet stirring restlessly. "Carlot?"

He would not have spoken twice, but she answered at once. "Can't sleep?"

"No. My father told me about climbing *up* a tree. When they got to the top the tree came apart."

"That's one reason we don't just chop off the tuft or burn it loose. This is easier, but it also gets the bugs away from the midpoint. When the tree dies, they're not there to eat it apart."

"How do you get rid of the out tuft?"

"Oh, some of the bugs won't follow the honey. They'll be breeding while we travel. When we get close to the Clump we'll paint another trail out."

"Why are you awake?"

"Tide. I have trouble sleeping in tide." But her voice trailed off raggedly. He stopped talking, and presently slept.

After breakfast Booce said, "There's something I want to see on the west side of the trunk. Leave the gear here."

Climbing was easy if you didn't have to paint too. In less than a day they had half circled the trunk. Above them by a quarter klomter, the bark bulged like a wave surging across a pond. They climbed toward that.

"Jeffer wanted us to look at this," Booce told them. "Something must have hit the trunk while it was younger. The wood's grown around it."

The wood bulged to hide it like some secret treasure. Rather was almost inside the crater before he could see anything. Carlot, ahead of him, had stopped. Booce was at his shoulder. Rather heard him gasp.

Carlot said, "Metal!"

"I must apologize to Jeffer," Booce said. "Metal indeed! The tree may consider it poisonous; see how reluctant the wood is to touch it! But the Admiralty won't think so."

Rather asked, "We want this?"

"We do. Secret auction, I think." Booce was deep into the crater, running his hands over the reddish-black surface of the metal. "Six or eight thousand kilos. No point in trying to move it. We'll have to show it to the Navy anyway, unless . . . hmm."

Carlot looked at her father. "We don't want to attract attention."

"Exactly. I have to think about this. Well, my merry crew, I think we've earned a holiday."

They climbed back around the trunk, taking their time. Booce knew just where to find the shelled burrowers. After lunch they spent a day tethered in the now strongly running waterfall, first washing each other and squeezing honey out of their clothing, then wrestling. They still got some painting in before sleeptime.

In twenty days they had reached the wild tuft.

Rather had never appreciated foliage before. It had surrounded him all his life. He gorged, savoring the taste and texture. "You love it too," he observed. "Carlot, Booce, why don't you live in a tree?"

"Oh, there's foliage in the Clump too," Carlot said. "All kinds. Rather, I can't wait to show you!"

They slept in foliage. Rather slept like a dead man, from exhaustion and the familiar sensation of sleeping under tide, in a womb of soft foliage. He woke early, feeling wonderful.

Carlot lay not far from her father. Her face was grief-stricken. She thrashed in slow motion, unconsciously trying to hold herself against the tide.

Rather took her hand, gently. "Hey. Nightmare?"

Her eyes opened. "Oh. Rather. I was trying to get to Wend. She was screaming and trying to fly with just her bare feet—" She shook her head violently and sat up. "Something I have to tell you."

"Okay."

"When we were swimming. Father noticed you were up."

"Up? Oh, *up*. You're very pretty," Rather said a little awkwardly.

"We can't make babies."

"We can't? Hey, the jungle giants and the London Tree citizens didn't have any trouble. I'm a dwarf, but—"

Carlot laughed. "*Father* says we can't. He wants me to marry another logger. I think he wants it to be Raff Belmy, from *Woodsman*, but definitely another logger. I thought I'd better say something before . . . well, before you got to thinking."

"Thinking. Well, it's too late, then."

"It's all right, then?"

"Sure. Go back to sleep." The truth was that Rather was almost relieved. Carlot with her clothes off made his head swim and his blood boil: an uncomfortable feeling.

And Booce didn't want his daughter to love a dwarf savage. Should he resent that? Somehow he didn't.

Breakfast was more foliage. Then Booce gave Rather the matchet. "Pry the bark off. We want a complete ring of bare wood half a meter across. We'll paint along behind you."

Three and a half days later he was halfway around. The bark was soft, easy to pry loose, but the trunk must have been a good two klomters in circumference. They returned to the wild tuft to sleep and eat. Rather was one vast ache, but it still felt good to be sleeping in tide, in foliage.

After breakfast Rather was still on the matchet. The Serjents seemed to share Citizens' Tree's faith in a dwarf's superior strength. He finished the job before they slept again. They were ahead of schedule. Jeffer would not bring the carm down for them for another six or seven days.

From the base of the trunk they watched a moby attack the bugs descending along the honey track. Mobies normally skimmed clouds of bugs from the sky for their food. This was a tremendous creature, mostly mouth and fins, riding the wind toward the trunk and the bug-swarm at a hundred meters per breath. It realized its mistake just in time. It thrashed madly, gaping, irresistibly comical, as the wind hurled it toward the tree. Its flank smashed loose a shower of bark as it passed.

The bugs descended like a cloud of charcoal dust. They reached the ring of painted bare wood and spread to north and south. The cloud condensed, growing darker, swarming a few ce'meters out from the bark.

"Carlot. Do you like it on the tree?"

She nodded, watching the bugs.

"Booce? I've watched you. You like it here."

"I love it."

"Then how can you kill trees?"

Booce shrugged. "There are plenty of trees."

Chapter Nine

THE ROCKET

from *Logbearer*'s log, Captain Booce Serjent speaking:

Year 384, day 1280. Ten degrees west of the Clump. We've found a grove and chosen a short one, 30 klomters.

Day 1300. Refueled in a raincloud. Everything's wet.

Day 1310. Anchored at midpoint of tree.

Day 1330. Ryllin and Karilly must have laid the honey track by now. Bugs are following them down to the tuft. I'll take **Logbearer** *in to pick them up. We're all eager to return to the Admiralty, but there's no way to hurry the bugs.*

Day 1335. Ryllin and Karilly are aboard. From the in tuft they spotted a pond 50 klomters west and a little in. The women argue that we can fire up the rocket and start our return without waiting for the bugs. The pond will let us refill the water tank. It would gain us twenty to thirty days.

Now it's my choice. There's a risk, but I've never yet held out against the women. I'll give up early, save time.

Day 1360. The bugs have reached the honey band around the in tuft. Ordinarily I would be down there supervising, but I can't do that while we're under acceleration.

We maintain staggered watches against happyfeet. If they find us we can ready **Logbearer** *for independent flight in half a day. The rocket is hot and running.*

Day 1370. I'll stop feeding the pipefire soon. Let it burn out before the bugs cut the tuft loose. I can guide us into the pond on the last of our steam.

If the rocket runs dry it'll teach the girls caution. We'll still fill the tank before we reach the Clump. You always bump a pond or two when you're moving.

Day 1380. A mature tree is drifting to block our path. Dammit. Maybe it'll move past.

No further entries.

The carm picked them up on the branch and returned to its dock with the cabin half filled with foliage. Rather suspected that they would not eat foliage again, nor sleep in decent tide, for a long time.

He heard the argument when Clave wanted to restart the motor. "There's no point," Jeffer told him. "We'd be using fuel to fight wind. We're doing fine."

Booce added his voice to Jeffer's. "We'll sail even farther in after the tuft severs. Leave us something to breathe!"

Had anyone else seen Clave glance aft? Clave had taken less than a breath to read the faces of his crew, but Rather had caught it.

Not so long ago, far away in Citizens' Tree, Gavving had spoken thus to his eldest son: "You're a citizen now. Watch Clave during a meeting. He leads where we'll go. He always has. You don't have to go Clave's way just because Clave says so . . ."

The motor stayed off.

The tree moved ponderously west and in. Its westward motion slowed over several days. The days were shorter, and Voy had come nearer. The smallest children learned never to look directly at Voy; but Rather could tell. In the corner of his eye the violet-white pinpoint was more intense, closer and *smaller*, with less sky to blur and distort it.

It took six days to make a sleep; then seven. Time whirled around them until they stopped caring. The journey had become more important than their destination.

The crew lived on the bark, all but Jeffer. They found the carm too strange. Even Rather left the carm after a few sleeps. He had learned that he liked strangeness; but he sensed that Jeffer saw him as an intruder. *The Scientist captains the carm.*

Debby and Booce disappeared down the trunk to monitor the progress of the bugs. They returned with smoked dumbo meat and two cured skins, which Booce shaped into armor that looked remarkably like the silver suit. "We won't use it this trip, but it's standard gear. The Navy will expect us to have it."

A grove of integral tree sproutlings passed Voy-ward of the tree, the first the citizens had ever seen. They were a few scores of meters long, tufted only at the out end. "The seeds drop away, out and in," Booce told them. "After they sprout, they have to sail back to the median. They'll grow the other tuft when there's enough to feed them."

The day came when Carlot called her father and pointed outward. "Isn't that a pod grove?"

Backlit by the sun, the cluster might almost have been a miniature tree grove hundreds of klomters out. "Small . . . yes. Too far, though."

"Why?" Debby asked.

"Well, it'd take too long to . . . I'd forgotten the carm. Let's ask Jeffer."

Jeffer summoned up his windows-within-windows. "Sure, we can get there. Clave, want to take a trip?"

"Can we find our way back? The tree looks big when you're tied to it, but from six hundred klomters away—"

"Trust me."

Forty plants grew in a loose cluster, all much alike. From a fibrous cup that faced west, a long, limp leaf trailed eastward, waving sluggishly in the wind. A thick vine reached a hundred meters out from the boll, ending in a kind of collar. Each collar held a brown egg-shape.

"Those are jet pods," Debby realized suddenly. "We used to ride them in Carther States."

Booce directed Rather to one of the largest plants. Carlot and Debby hung back. Rather the Silver Man circled the pod, cautious in the face of a new thing: a fibrous brown egg as big as the common room in his father's hut. There was tide enough to pull the vine taut. Smaller pods grew in a spiral around the stem end, ranging from fist-sized to man-sized. Replacements, he surmised, that would grow after the ripe one dropped away.

Satisfied, Rather wrapped his legs around the stem for leverage and swung his matchet.

The sound blasted his whole body. The sky spun round him. Tide was pulling him apart. His fingers and toes felt like they were inflating as spin pulled blood into them.

Against the tide that was pulling him rigid, Rather forced his legs vertical to his torso, pulled an arm against his chest, and fired the ankle jets.

The spinning sky slowed. He aimed his feet against the spin and brought it to a stop.

Battered and deafened, he pulled his helmet open to hear what Booce was shouting at him.

"That one was ripe! Try another plant!"

Rather jetted toward the grove. Booce guided him from a distance. "No, that one's stunted. We want a big one."

"Aren't the big ones likely to be riper?"

"That's why we use armor! Try there—"

The pod exploded, blowing him west and away, while seeds *spanged* off the silver suit. The spin was less this time; the blow had been more direct. Rather opened his helmet. "I think I had more fun on the tree!"

"It's too wet here. The pods like to spread their seeds when there's water around. Try that one. *Close your helmet!*"

Rather seriously considered telling the alien merchant to go feed himself to the tree. But he was already moving toward a third vine. *There isn't any other Silver Man,* he thought. He swung viciously at the base of the pod. *And what am I, if I'm not the Silver Man?*

The pod dropped out and away. Carlot and Debby flapped after it.

The next one didn't explode either. Rather chased the seed pod down, with Booce chasing him. They braced their shoulders against the pod and started back. They were near the carm when Rather's jets died.

He fiddled with the throttle wheels. Nothing.

"Booce! Don't leave me!"

"What's wrong?"

"The suit won't move!"

Booce laughed. "Are we going to have to put wings on that thing?"

"Can you push me—"

"Can and will. Here comes Debby. I'll push you and the ladies can have the pods." Booce seemed indecently cheerful, and Rather was a long time understanding why.

Booce had found a flaw in Citizens' Tree's intimidating science.

"You ran out of fuel, that's all," Jeffer told him. "See that little red light below your chin?"

"It was on when I started out. I don't know what it means."

"Means you're out of hydrogen. There must be a way to refuel the suit. I'll search the cassettes. If I can't find anything we'll have to ask Mark, after this is all over. Calm, now! We've got pods and we've got honey. Maybe we won't need the silver suit again."

A forty-klomter-long tree is hard to lose from six hundred klomters away. Jeffer had no trouble bringing them home.

Booce attacked the first pod gingerly, hacking at the stem with the matchet, flinching back at each blow. At the sixth blow the pod suddenly spewed foggy air under terrific pressure. Booce threw himself into the sky. He flapped back, staying well clear.

He opened the other pod in the same cautious fashion. Then he and Carlot sawed it in half. The inside was lined with fist-sized puffballs, each with a dangling tendril. Booce scraped these away.

He sawed the stem off the first pod, leaving a small hole. He shaved the edges until the hole was just smaller than the metal pipe, and quit for dinner.

They resumed work after breakfast. It took four of them to shove the ends of the pipe into the holes in both pods.

Clave asked, "Now how do you get water in there?"

"Punch a little hole in the other end of the tank. Put the pipe in a pond and suck. You need good lungs to be a logger."

"We're too far in to find many ponds."

"I know. Usually we fuel *Logbearer* before we go to work on the tree. But, dammit, we've got the carm, and there'll be a pond somewhere, and *Logbearer* is whole again! Except for the lines. And cabins. We'll need wood to build cabins."

"We'll go for wood after the next sleep," Jeffer said. "The out branch, I think. The in branch may be about to fall off."

"No. Another thirty days at least."

Carlot said, "Father—"

"Don't trust that," Booce said instantly. "We'll use the out branch."

"You're the logger. What changed your mind?"

Booce sighed. "I was guessing. I don't *really* know when the in branch will fall off. Jeffer, there's likely to be a shock when the branch tears loose. Stay aboard the carm. Stay strapped in when you sleep. Leave the motor off."

"Stet. Will the rest of you be okay on the trunk?"

"As long as we keep our wings handy. Always have your wings in reach . . . always. But you should be in the carm in case we need rescue."

The steam rocket still required attention. Booce and Carlot festooned the water tank with lines and wove a braid of lines around the bow end. "We'll moor the cabins here. Other than that . . . I still don't know what we're going to use for sikenwire. There has to be some way to hold the coals in place."

Clave had a suggestion. "We could arrive crippled. Get a push from the carm to drift the log into range, then signal for help somehow. Tell the Navy we lost our sikenwire, got home by luck."

"Mmm . . . maybe. I'd look like a fool, but maybe. I just don't want to be in too much of a hurry." He stopped abruptly. Then he said, "Ryllin and the girls, they—*we* were in a hurry to get back to the Admiralty. We started the rocket running before the tuft dropped off."

"What's—?"

"Did I tell you you're rich?"

"I don't know what it means," Clave said.

"That wart on the trunk is thousands of kilos of metal. With metal you can buy anything that's for sale in the Market. It also makes us a target. Someone might try to steal it."

"Good news and bad news."

"Right. We'll set up shop to sell the wood, and take our time selling the metal. No hurry."

Food had grown short again. Debby and Clave flew in along the trunk until they found a covey of flashers. With the trunk as a backstop they fired their full complement of arrows and shot half a dozen of the small birds. It took them six days.

They built a fire on the trunk to cook the birds. *Logbearer's* crew was ready for a feast.

Booce was the exception. He ate little. He was uncharacteristically silent, his eyes on the fire, until Carlot said, "Dad? Twenty, twenty-five days?"

"About that," Booce said. Then: "I guessed last time. I should be in the tuft watching the bugs."

"Dad, you couldn't warn us from down there anyway."

"I could start climbing ten or fifteen days early . . ."

"Dad—"

"I'm glad we don't have the rocket running. We were running the rocket when it happened."

The silence stretched. Debby asked, "What happened?"

Booce told it.

Booce was fast asleep when the cabin's yielding wooden wall slammed into his face and chest. His grunt of surprise was lost among feminine shrieks. He was reaching for his wings before his eyes were fully open.

The women were a flurry of action around him, snatching for their wings, moving out. Ryllin reached the door, looked about her, then immediately turned toward a violet-white glare that hadn't been there when they'd gone to sleep. Carlot and Karilly followed. Wend hadn't found her wings. She was near tears as she searched.

Booce left her. Nothing terrible could happen to Wend aboard *Logbearer*, and this would teach her *always* to know where her wings were.

He saw it all at a glance:

Logbearer was moored against a vast wall of bark, the east side of the trunk. Coals in their retaining net burned bright orange along the middle length of the pipe. The nozzle cone pointed east toward the Clump. Some meters from the cone, live steam condensed into a white stream klomters long.

The Clump was a distant whorl of white-and-gray storm, with the misty white tube of the Smoke Ring converging beyond and below it. The eye might follow that white line down the sky . . . and where the tree converged to a point, there was Voy.

The glare-white pinpoint had been masked by the in tuft when Booce went to sleep. The in tuft was gone. It had torn loose days before Booce expected it. Freed from its weight, the tree had lurched outward. Booce had guessed as much; now he could see it.

In toward Voy, a fluttering black silhouette was haloed in blue light.

Mishael had been outside on watch. The lurch had torn her loose. She was far in along the trunk, flapping out-and-east to bring her out, just as she'd been taught. But he'd never taught her to lose one of her wings!

Ryllin and the girls flew toward her: foreshortened black silhouettes. They made slow progress. In-and-west would have taken them straight in, but the west was a wall of black bark.

Booce followed slowly. Mishael seemed to have it under control.

With the in tuft gone the center of mass was higher on the tree. Tide was pulling Booce away from the tree, and in. A new breeze announced that the tree was under sail, accelerated by the wind on the out tuft. He kick-flapped to adjust. Ryllin and the girls had nearly reached Mishael. Karilly looked up and flapped to turn. She was shouting at him. The wind tore her voice away. He tried to hear. She kicked toward him, screaming—

Booce turned toward *Logbearer*, too late.

The lurch and the breeze and Booce's inattention, these had caused the disaster. A flurry of coals had been jarred loose from the sikenwire cage. Irradiated by the pipefire, the bark had been drying and warming for tens of days. It had been ready to ignite.

Under normal circumstances an integral tree is in equilibrium with the wind. A steady gale blows at each tuft, and no wind blows at its center. Air must move past a fire to keep it burning. But a tree under sail is moving, and there is wind. Coals reached the bark and blazed up.

Booce flapped hard toward a *Logbearer* already embedded in flame.

He hadn't panicked then. There was a hose, and pressure in the water tank, for the fire would be heating it. He would use the hose to spray water and steam on the fire. Booce breathed deeply as he flew, hyperoxygenating. He'd hold his breath while he worked. The danger was that he might breathe flame.

Wend crawled gingerly through the cabin door. Her feet were wingless, her eyes and mouth wide in terror. She saw Booce, gathered herself, and leapt toward him, into the sky.

The water tank ruptured.

Booce saw Wend blown outward in a wind of live steam laced with boiling water. He flapped to catch her, hearing his own howl. She was flying past him. He stretched impossibly and caught her bare ankle, and felt the scalded skin slide loose beneath his hand.

There were comforting hands on Booce, on his shoulders and arm and ankle, for touching was the way of Citizens' Tree. Rather hung back, uncertain, reluctant to take such liberties. Booce was a mature adult.

Where was Carlot?

Booce was hoarse, for he had been shouting, howling; but he sounded almost calm now. "Everything's blurred after that . . . Lawri the Scientist was feeding me foliage and I couldn't remember anything. It all came back a bit at a time."

Rather eased away from the cookfire and flew toward Voy. Behind him Booce was speaking mostly to Debby, who was rubbing his temples.

"It never happened before . . . not to us. Sometimes a logging concern just disappears. We wonder why. We never find out. For Ryllin, for the girls, I should give it up. But logging's all I know . . ."

The memories must have been too much for Carlot. If she wanted to hide . . . a crack in the bark? Bark walls would muffle the agony in her father's voice. She might have gone in any direction . . . but the cracks ran out and in. Try *in*.

Rather coasted above the bark. He didn't mind being seen. She'd have kept going until she couldn't hear the words.

"Go away."

He somersaulted and kicked air to stop himself. "Carlot?"

No answer. It had come from his left, from the north. There: scarlet showed in a crack. He said, "I wouldn't have found you if you'd kept your mouth shut."

She was pulled into herself, like the shellbirds around the ice pond. Her wings were on her back. He fluttered into the crack beside her but didn't touch her. "It must have been bad."

"It was bad."

He tried again. "Want a hug?"

"I want Wend back."

"You have to learn to think of her as a lost one."

"She was fifteen!"

("She wasn't even two!" Jill had wailed after a sister sickened and died. Ilsa had hugged her daughter frequently. When Ilsa died at thirty-one, it, had been no better for Jill.

(Age didn't matter. Touching helped.) Rather worked his fingers into her hair and began a scalp massage. She didn't move. He said, "I've had brothers and sisters die. We all have. You forget."

She'd removed her sleeves after the fluff died. The skin of her arms was smooth and richly dark, and she suddenly wriggled about and had him in a deathgrip.

Rotating, they drifted in the sky. Rather still wore his wings; his instincts told him to return to the tree. He held her.

She wasn't sobbing. Presently she pulled her chin off his shoulder and kissed him.

He asked, "Better?"

"Yes. I don't want to go back."

"Will you be all right here? Shall I stay?" Half a dozen finger cactus drifted east, less than a klomter distant. A windborne finger cactus could be lethal. These were only drifting, and drifting away at that . . . but you never stopped *looking* for danger.

Carlot hadn't answered. He said, "Your father might get upset if we stay here too long—"

"Father's made mistakes before."

"He tells you who to make babies with, though. Mishael had to ask, and she's older than you."

"Do you want to go?"

" . . . No."

"I thought hard before I took my clothes off in front of you."

He remembered swimming in the waterfall, and laughed. "I noticed. But Booce was there."

She freed him, and all the muscles in his body jumped. *Loose in the sky!* But he had wings. Carlot drifted, rotating away from him . . . donning her wings? No: she pulled her tunic over her head, then rolled her pants off and balled them up together.

He looked. *Now* she was tying her wings to her ankles. Her clothes too. Nudity was not strange to him, but this was different. Carlot was long, one and a half times his own height. Her breasts were perfect cones, an abrupt break in the long smooth stretch of her torso. Rather resisted the urge to touch her. He spoke hurriedly, before he could lose that fight. "Now, what would happen if we really did make a baby? Could you still marry anyone you want to?"

She said, "It's all right. We just have to watch what time we do this."

"Yeah?" Rather had never heard anything about how *not* to make a baby. "When can you do it?"

"Now."

"I've never done this before." He swam toward her.

"I'll show you. Take these off."

Chapter Ten

SECRETS

from the Citizens' Tree cassettes, year 31 SM:

> *FISHER PLANT is boll-shaped, 100–300 meters in diameter. It can extend a long water-inflated root into a passing pond, for fertilizer as well as water.*
>
> *FISHER JUNGLE may be considered a large (400–700 meters) fisher plant with a sting. May attack big birds as well as ponds. Prey are brought into the jungle to rot.*
>
> *FINGER CACTUS—The newly budded form looks a little like a green potato, with eyes. Fingers sprout from the eyes, and branch and re-branch, until an adult in flower may bear 20–30 fingers. Each finger is tipped with a spine. Any creature that comes too near may be speared; and then roots grow into the victim. Later in life, fingers bud new finger cactus.* **Dangerous.**

Rather woke because his eyes burned.

They were filled with tears. Blinking did no good. The tears were under his eyelids, filling them. The pain had him whimpering. He tried lifting his eyelids with his fingertips to let the water out. That hurt. Mopping his eyes with his tunic brought agony. He couldn't see!

"Carlot?" He remembered that she wasn't with him. They had not returned to the cookfire until all were asleep except Debby, on watch. She had winked at them . . . they had separated . . .

Sleep, then daggers in the eyes. He would not have wanted Carlot to see him like this. But he was alone, and blind!

"Clave? Debby? Anyone?"

Rather could feel bark surrounding him. Yell again? He'd yelled when the silver suit's jets gave out. The memory embarrassed him. He'd had gritty eyes before, when he was tired . . . but not like this! "Someone help me! I can't see!"

"Rather?"

"Debby? My eyes are on fire and I don't know why!"

Her hands were cool and rough on his cheeks. "Open them."

"I can't . . ." He got them open, just a slit for just a moment. The light was agony.

"They're bright red. I'll get Clave. Don't loose your tether."

"No way!"

The pain grew no worse and no better. It was a long time before he heard voices.

"Rather?"

"Clave! What's wrong with me?"

Long fingers held his head still; thumbs lifted his eyelids. "You're not blind. You're not dying either. It's an allergy attack. Your father used to get this way when Dalton-Quinn Tree was dying of the drought. We were too far in toward Voy. Dry, thin air and not enough sleep."

"What do I do?"

"Gavving mostly suffered. In half a day he'd be over it. Don't rub your eyes. Let me think."

It seemed to hurt less now that he knew it would go away. It hadn't killed Gavving. And if they both had the same allergy, then—*He's really my father! I should tell him! Mother too . . . and Mark?* But the pain was more urgent. "Clave, if this happens when I don't sleep, and I can't sleep because it hurts too much . . . Clave?"

His line went slack. "I've thought of something. Just relax. I'll tow you."

"Kendy for the State—"

"Kendy? Treefodder! It's been a long time."

"That's not my fault, Jeffer. Every time our orbits have matched, there has been someone else in the CARM. Where are they now? I don't find them outside either."

"They're asleep. I was too. Everyone but me sleeps on the bark. Kendy, how do I refuel the silver suit?"

Diagrams appeared: CARM and silver suit, side by side. Parts of the schematics blinked blue as Kendy talked. Jeffer saw that tanks along the calves of the silver suit were what made the legs so bulky. "Hydrogen here, oxygen here. There's hose under these little panels. The spigots are recessed, here and here, under these covers on the hull. You open them from the control panel. Bring up the schematic, then twist above these dots, this way." An arrowhead circled.

"Good."

"Remember. Oxygen line from here to here. Hydrogen from here to here. Getting it wrong may cause an explosion."

"What keeps the gases cold?"

"In a pressure suit? No, the gases are just under pressure. That's why the tanks go dry so fast." Kendy's face was back in the bow window. "Did you find six metric tons of metal ore?"

"Yes. Thanks. Booce says it makes us rich."

"Good. I see you've been building a steam rocket. Is it finished?"

"Booce still has to build cabins. We'll go to the out branch for the wood. He still doesn't know how to hold the pipefire—"

"Here's the CARM," a voice said. "Feel the airlock walls? *Treefodder!*"

Clave was in the airlock with Rather behind him. The display went blank, a breath too late.

Clave got his mouth closed. "First things first. Scientist, Rather's having an allergy attack. You remember how Gavving was during the drought? Rather, you need thick wet air. So, we'll close the airlock and turn up the pressure and humi . . . um, wetness. Do it, Jeffer."

Jeffer let his fingers dance. Close both doors, humidity up, pressure up. Pressure in his ears. He worked his jaw. He untethered himself and moved aft.

Rather's eyelids were puffy; the eyes were scarlet. Jeffer said, "It goes away after a while no matter what you do. This might help. Or not. Work your jaw to pop your ears." He turned to Clave. "Well?"

"How long has the Checker been back?"

"Since the Serjents reached the trunk."

"Why didn't you tell someone? *Me!*"

"Let's go outside."

He opened the inner airlock door and gestured Clave in. From the look of him Clave might explode any minute; but he came. They were nose to nose while the inner door closed and the outer opened.

"Keeps the pressure in," Jeffer said. "That's why it's called airlock." He kicked out into the sky.

Clave followed on mismatched wings. "You're stalling."

"No. Kendy can't reach us except when the sun is dead east, but anything that goes on in the carm, Kendy hears it later. He can't hear us now."

"He wouldn't have heard us in the Citizens' Tree commons!"

"Yeah. Clave, the truth is that I didn't trust anyone else to talk to Kendy. I don't trust Kendy, and he's very persuasive."

"Am I too fluff-brained to say no?"

"Clave . . . all right, so I was arrogant and wrong-headed. Now let's go tell the Serjents."

"Uh—"

"Hey, citizumf!" It wasn't really a shout, but Clave's long fingers closed over Jeffer's face. After a moment the palm lifted to expose an evil grin.

Clave said, "You still should have told *me*. Rather didn't see anything. Did you tell Lawri?"

"No."

"What does Kendy want?"

"He wants the Clump. He wants to know *everything* about the Clump."

"This trip was his idea, wasn't it?"

"I told you he's persuasive. Clave, we have to tell Rather about this before he talks to anyone. He already knows too much. Nobody else, right?"

"Right. Then I want to talk to Kendy."

"He comes in range every four days lately. Four days from now, when the sun is dead east."

Jeffer found Rather in the Scientist's seat, hands poised above the controls. "Freeze," he said. "Now move away."

Rather obeyed. "I was trying to open the airlock."

"Use the little lights on the doors. Rather, any citizen knows better than to fiddle with the controls. Once I nearly killed us all with one ill-considered tap of one finger. But I don't have to explain that to you. I only have to say, Jeffer captains the carm, keep your treefeeding hands off the controls. Stet?"

"Stet. Sorry, Jeffer. I've seen you open the doors, and I was feeling shut in."

"How are your eyes?"

"Okay."

He held still while Jeffer looked. Rather's eyes were pink and the lids were puffy, but he didn't blink. "From now on you sleep in the carm with me. I should have someone here anyway in case we get shaken up when the tuft tears loose."

Rather had already summoned the blue diagram of the carm's cabin. Jeffer opened his fingers over the lines that represented the airlock. The doors opened behind him. He said, "Help me get the hose linked up. Then take it outside."

Booce met them at the door. "I'll take that, Rather. We're filling the rocket. How are you doing?"

"Better."

Debby, Clave, and Carlot waited at the rocket. Booce and Rather crawled along the bark, dragging the hose after them. Booce spoke quietly. "Did you know that Carlot was a crossyear child?"

"No. What's it mean? The crossyear is when Voy crosses the sun—"

"Children born at the crossyear are unpredictable. They can go any way at all. Rather, I'm trying to tell you that you and Carlot are not to marry. She'll marry a logger."

Rather didn't answer. Carlot's expression was unreadable until the moment Booce's back was turned. Then she winked. Rather felt his face glowing.

To work. Booce forced the hose into the rocket nozzle. "Jeffer says he can fill it without anyone sucking on the end. Clave, give us a hand here. Now push. *Jeffer! Ready!*"

The three were braced to hold the hose in place. Clave said, "There's a signal Jeffer uses that tells the carm to push what's in the water tank back out. It gets rid of mud—"

The hose writhed. Water sprayed out around the join. Rather could feel the power of the water trying to tear the hose out of his hands.

They held it, held it . . . and suddenly the hose bucked loose and thrashed like a live thing. Rather dodged and was flailing in the sky. Booce bellowed, "Enough! Jeffer, it's full!"

They were soaked before the hose went limp. Jeffer called cheerily from the airlock. "When do we see a test?"

Booce looked embarrassed. "I still don't know how to substitute for the sikenwire. We've got time—"

"Yeah. Well, we've used up too much water, one way and another. I want to refuel the carm. Clave, Rather, come along. We won't be long, Booce. The rest of you can start dinner."

The three of them returned to the carm. Clave asked, "What do we do for a pump?"

Jeffer was smiling. "I've thought of something. There's a pond thirty klomters out and a little east . . ."

The sun wasn't much past zenith. A pinpoint diamond blazed next to it, out and a bit west: sunlight focused through a pond. Jeffer set the carm moving straight out.

The out tuft ran at them and past them. The pond wasn't far beyond, and not much bigger than the carm. Jeffer set the forward jets firing when they were close. They came to a stop just in from the water globule.

Jeffer opened the airlock. He told Rather, "Get into your wings and follow us. Bring the silver suit. We'll refuel the jets."

Jeffer led them outside and around to the carm's dorsal surface. Rather followed, tugging the silver suit by its limp wrist. There Jeffer took the suit from him. He watched as Jeffer produced narrow hoses from under a hatch . . .

Clave said, "Forget the suit for a while. Let Jeffer do it. Rather, you missed something during the allergy attack. What do you think happened then?"

"All I know is, you caught Jeffer at something."

Jeffer grunted. He had the hoses hooked to holes in the suit's legs.

Clave said, "You missed your chance to see Sharls Davis Kendy. You'll get it again in, what, half a day?"

Jeffer looked at the sun: past two o'clock, a few degrees out from west. "A little more than that. The thing is, this is a secret, Rather."

"Everybody's got secrets. . . . Kendy? The Checker?"

"Tell him, Jeffer."

Jeffer said, "Kendy's back. He pointed out the Wart for us. He talked to me the day we rescued the Serjents. We've talked since. I gather it costs him something, maybe shortens his life, and he still can't reach us more than once every two days."

Rather said, "The tales Mark and Gavving tell, Kendy would have killed you all if he'd known you stole the carm."

"I don't think he could have done that," Jeffer said, "but he might have wanted to. We stole the carm to get away from London Tree. We had Lawri tied to her seat, and Mark the Silver Man too. Kendy might have called it mutiny. You know some of this."

Rather said, "You were copsiks. They owned you. I never understood how you could live with Lawri and Mark after that."

Clave said, "What were we supposed to do, throw them into the sky? They earned their citizenship, Rather. When the air was leaking out of the carm, Lawri found the way to plug the leak. When Kendy was asking questions, Mark covered for us. We could have told Kendy we were escaped copsiks, but I'm not sure how he would have felt about that. Maybe Kendy's people kept copsiks."

"Kendy."

"Yeah. He—Scientist, you understand this better than I do."

Jeffer said, "Give me a minute." He was moving the hoses. "Need to refuel the legs one at a time . . ."

"Stet. Now, Sharls Davis Kendy claims to be the recording of a man. I don't understand that. Neither does Lawri. We don't even know how cassettes work, really. I wondered if he was just some madman who reached the old starship, like we almost did, and was living aboard. But it's been fourteen years, and he doesn't sound any older. He wanted to know all about us. Whether we were mutineers. Well, treefodder, we *did* steal the carm, we *were* mutineers, much as I hate the word."

"That's all in the past," Clave said.

"Yeah. Now he wants to see the Clump. Clave, remember how he talked fourteen years ago? I think he still wants everyone in the Smoke Ring to be one big happy tribe taking orders from Sharls Davis Kendy."

The dark pond blazed at its eastern edge. Rather wondered if there would be time for a swim. He was not comfortable in this maze of secrets. "Kendy isn't the Chairman. We don't have to do what he says."

"No."

"Well, we want to see the Clump too. And if he can't touch us—Why not tell the Serjents?"

"Boy's got a point," Clave said.

"You didn't tell them either."

"Maybe that was just reflex."

"Just talk to Kendy, Chairman, and then I'll point out something."

Clave merely nodded. To Rather, he said, "One more thing. Kendy hears everything anyone says aboard the carm."

Rather laughed.

Jeffer asked, "Anything else to discuss? I think I'm finished here. Now let's refuel the carm. Go back in and strap down."

"We still don't have a pump."

The Scientist's answering grin was a little mad. Clave sighed.

Jets grumbled, then died. Rather watched a wind-riffled wall of water move toward the bow window.

Clave asked, "Shouldn't you close the doors?"

Jeffer grinned and shook his head.

Clave said, "I wish to point out, *Captain,* that we're going to hit that pond."

"Yeah."

The pondlet struck. Rather sagged in his straps. Clave grunted. He asked, "Do you honestly know what you're doing?"

"I honestly do."

Through the great window the interior of the pondlet was open to view. A flock of tiny silver torpedoes sped away through the murk and disappeared through the shivering silver surface.

"The carm's hundreds of years old and nothing's hurt it yet. Now I reduce the interior pressure." Jeffer's fingers moved; the air system hissed; water entered the airlock in an expanding silver bubble.

The doors closed. Water remained inside, flowing over the aft walls, the curve of it becoming more and more concave. Waves curled and sloshed as Jeffer turned the carm away from the pond.

He grinned at them. "Now I set the pressure back to normal and turn down the humidity. That tells the carm to make the air dry by taking water out of it. The water goes to the tank. See? We can't run out of fuel now. It's something Lawri never thought of."

"It's treefeeding *wet* in here, Scientist!"

"But you don't have to pump. Next on the agenda is Kendy. Checker, when you hear this, please introduce yourself."

Clave asked, "What if he's not there?"

"He'll hear it when he runs the record—"

There was a face in the bow window.

Kendy was a dwarf. Rather had expected that, but he was still taken aback. Deepset eyes examined him, judged him, within a face like carved rock. A giant's gravelly voice said, "Kendy for the State. Hello, Chairman Clave. Hello, Rather the Silver Man. Scientist, your manner of refueling the CARM is likely to destroy it. If the impact had torn away the solar cell arrays, how would you break up water? A CARM doesn't fly on water."

Jeffer looked nettled. Clave said, "Welcome back, Kendy."

"Thank you, Chairman."

"Why did you hide from me?"

"I felt that Jeffer was better equipped to judge his political situation than I."

Clave bridled. "And I'm not?"

"If Jeffer had told you, he would surely have had to tell his wife. Do you trust Lawri's judgment?"

"I give up. Between you, you . . . stet."

"I watched your nonmutiny with some interest. You're a natural leader, Clave. You should be ruling many more than your thirteen citizens."

"Thank you, Checker. Where do you propose I find another thousand citizens, all of whom are inclined to trust a tree-living outsider?"

The language was cold and stiff. Jeffer and Clave did not trust Kendy, and Kendy clearly knew it. He said, "You need not turn a compliment into a policy statement, Clave. I can't force you to obey my orders. You can't stop me from observing through the CARM's instruments. You know that I know things you do not. Can't we work together?"

"Maybe. Thanks for showing us the Wart."

"You're welcome. Has Booce found a way to confine the pipefire?"

"Not yet."

"Even with sikenwire, the pipefire is dangerous. You do have a source of metal. You can make a firebox from the Wart."

Clave grinned. "What a good idea."

"You probably don't have the facilities to make a smelter—"

"What?"

"A smelter refines metal. It melts metal ore and burns away impurities. You shape the metal by pouring the liquid into forms. Gravity is needed, or tide, or spin. The Admiralty may have such technology, but I gather you do not."

"We do not. You'd set the tree on fire for sure!"

"But you do have a saw. It was moored in the cargo section. Use it to cut slices from the Wart."

"Kendy, you'd ruin the teeth."

"No. That saw was taken from *Discipline*. Most of the tools aboard *Discipline* were made to last. Even with trivial items, the major cost was transportation. The chicken wire must have been made in the Admiralty, but your hose is reinforced with hullmetal alloy. The pipe is hullmetal. So is the saw. You won't damage it by sawing slices from a mass of soft iron. Here—"

Kendy's angular visage was replaced by a line drawing of the steam rocket, then another line drawing: a rectangle with tabs at its edges. "Cut three of these. Use the first as a template—"

"How do we hold the parts together? Tethers would burn."

"Set the plates in place and pound on the tabs until they bend down. They'll fold over each other." Three rectangular plates formed a triangular prism. The tabs along the edges blinked green, then bent themselves over to interlock. *Logbearer* reappeared, and the three-sided box now enclosed the pipe and pipefire.

Clave said, "I'll ask Booce. You won't get much air flow to the coals."

"Mount the rocket two or three kilometers in or out from the center of mass. The wind will keep the coals alight. You couldn't make a completely closed box anyway. It will leak."

"Mmm . . . yeah. You've been thinking hard about this."

"I can solve simple mechanical problems. What will you do with the CARM when you reach the Clump?"

Clave was still studying the diagram. "We'll hide it before we get there. Take the log in with the steam rocket. Take our time selling it."

"You'll want to keep the CARM safe, but near enough for rescue if something goes wrong. Now, the Clump is more crowded than the Smoke Ring in general, but one may still think of it as mostly empty space. Two thousand people won't crowd a region the volume of the Earth's Moon! You'll find plenty of hiding space."

"Kendy, we can't steer the carm into the Clump and just look around! We'd be seen!"

"I have a better view of the Clump than you do, even if it's not a good view. If you approached from north or south of the Clump—"

"What we'll do is take the log in, then look around while we're selling the wood. If we find a safe way in, we'll take it."

"Another thing you might consider," Kendy said. "The CARM is power. There may come a time when we'll want to use that power . . ." Kendy's voice and picture faded.

"Well, that's that." Jeffer left his seat. He stretched elaborately. "Let's go out. Take some spears. We'll get us some waterbirds before we turn back."

They moved out. Clave said, "Well?"

"*Now* do you see what I mean? He wants the carm inside the Clump. He wants it bad. If he can get some Admiralty citizens into the carm, he could look them over and question them."

"He didn't say anything unreasonable," Clave said.

"Persuasive, isn't he? All right, think about this. There occurred an accident that allowed Chairman Clave to see the Checker talking to the Scientist. That happened *after* Kendy was sure he couldn't talk *me* into this."

Clave smiled. "An interesting coincidence. The carm has outside cameras, doesn't it?"

"Yeah. And Booce would like to be *rich* so that he can give up logging.

Do you think Kendy could persuade Booce to trade the carm to the Navy for metal?"

The smile slipped. "We'll do it your way. Rather, this stops with us. All of it. Now shall we get us some waterbirds?"

"I said that to get us outside," Jeffer said.

"Let's do it anyway."

Chapter Eleven

HAPPYFEET

from the Admiralty Library, year 131 SM, day 160:

> *Voice has set us the task of integrating the deserters—excuse me,*
> **wanderers**—*into the Admiralty. It will certainly take generations. Exec*
> *Willoughby admits that it may be impossible, and I've come to agree.*
> *Half a dozen cotton-candy jungles now trade regularly in the Clump,*
> *meeting at the crossyear. They obey Admiralty law, where Admiralty*
> *Navy is present to enforce it. Outside the Clump there is piracy and slave-*
> *taking. We believe that the Seekers and the Lupoff family were involved in*
> *such incidents, though they were the first to trade in the Market.*
> *We cannot bring law to thirty Earth-volumes of inhabitable terri-*
> *tory. The Smoke Ring is too huge, and we are too few and too slow.*
> *—Lieutenant Rand Carster*

Brilliant as it was, the neutron star was too small to give much illumination. Yet the sky was never dark, even at crossyear, when the sun at
nadir had to shine through the full thickness of the Smoke Ring's farther
arc. One must seek darkness in a cloud or a jungle or a tree tuft, or in the
unoccupied depths of the Clump.

Now the sun was dead east, somewhere behind the slowly roiling blotch
that was their destination. It was gloomy in the shadow of the Clump.
Masses near the white-fringed black mass seemed to blaze in contrast.

"We're better than halfway home," Booce said. "Debby, I've been looking for more pod plants. The last thing I ever wanted was to come home
with a pod for my cabin, but we don't have time to build real cabins."

"The rocket's finished otherwise?"

"Yes."

"Good." Debby had been working hard. Her tunic was off and her pale skin glistened with sweat. "Now, how do we make it work?"

"Trade secret."

Debby regarded Booce angrily. "We built the treefeeding thing. You won't tell us how to make it go?"

"Classified, Debby."

"Will you tell us how to make it stop? In an emergency, if you and Carlot aren't in reach, how do I stop it from just burning up?"

"We'll get an extra pod and fill it with water to pour on the pipefire—"

"Very *good*! Now, suppose you and Carlot both fall off the tree and lose your wings and we've got to come after you. Suppose you left the rocket going. What do I want to do?"

Booce found her persistence disturbing. "Use the carm, I suppose—"

"The carm is gone."

"They're only refueling it."

"It could be gone again!"

"Then use your wings. *Don't* try to use the rocket. That's dangerous."

Debby glared and was silent. She was Booce's height and almost Booce's age, marked by a dangerous and exotic beauty. Pale-brown skin, pale straight hair, fiery blue eyes; a face all planes and angles, with a nose like an axe head. She was the type of woman who would remake a man, who would run his life for him. As Ryllin was. And Ryllin was far away . . . and if Booce carried that thought further, Ryllin would know somehow, and Booce would regret it greatly. Booce looked at the sky to escape Debby's eyes.

He'd been watching the sky for days now. They were closing on the Clump. Matter would be thicker here, even this far in: more ponds, plant life, animals, predators, perhaps Navy craft or wandering happyfeet.

West of out, almost behind the log's remaining tuft, he found paired bright and dark dots: the pond and the carm. No sign of pod plants. Would they have to cut wood from the out branch after all? Branchwood was better . . . but it was hard work, and the cabins would be crude.

Debby was still fuming. "You know, arguing isn't the thing I do best. But Clave is going to have this out of you, because it's *stupid* not to tell us how to use the basic logger's tool. Won't the Admiralty expect us to know—?"

"No. You're hired labor."

"Right. I forgot."

The days went fast this close to Voy: nine days between waking and waking. North and west, the reddish fringe of the Clump's shadow was sliding rapidly down a tremendous wall of cloud. Storm and lightning inside, and ponds forming . . . The line of sunlight picked out a green dot, a drifting jungle emerging from the fringes of the storm.

Carlot suddenly asked, "Debby, should we know how to use the carm?"

"Yes. *Yes*, we should know how to run the carm! Treefeeding fools they are, Lawri and Jeffer both."

Booce was jolted. "Debby? You can't fly the carm?"

"Nobody knows but the Scientists. *Classified.* Lawri I can understand. But Jeffer, he stole the thing himself, and now he acts just like her! Fifteen years, almost!"

"Dad? She's right. We should all of us know all of that, and we have to start somewhere."

Booce sighed. Crossyear child! Playing around with a dwarf tree dweller . . . but the women always won the arguments. "Debby, as far as any Admiralty citizen is concerned, you know *nothing* about how a rocket works. Understand?"

"Yes, Logger Booce. Now, what is it you loggers have been concealing from us laborers?"

"Go ahead, Carlot."

Carlot considered before she spoke. "All right. Just the way you taught me. Debby, you'll have to imagine the sikenwire in a tube around the pipe. I stuff firebark inside and light it."

Debby nodded.

"The coals are just along the middle of the pipe, not too close to the ends. I wait. I want the metal to get hot. It should glow red. Hotter than that, the nozzle starts to char. That's bad. So I run water through the pipe. The metal stays dark red, and steam comes out the nozzle. You can't see it where it comes out, but it can flay the flesh from your bones, so stay clear."

Her father smiled, nodding approval. He'd taught her well.

"Now, how do I move the water into the pipe?"

Debby mulled it. "No tide—"

"How do I keep outsiders from watching me do it?"

Debby brightened. She kicked herself to the fore end of the water tank. "I'm here, right? There's a cabin, and I'm in it. And here's the plug . . ."

"Just so!" Carlot joined her. "You pull the plug. You blow in it. When the water spurts back at you, you slam the plug in quick."

"I could get a lungful of water that way."

"Sure you could. We've all done our share of choking. Father taught us this so he wouldn't have to do it himself."

"Why does it blow back?"

"I . . . Dad?"

Booce said, "The steam pushes both ways. Out the nozzle, and backward too. That churns the water so more water comes down the pipe. After the rocket settles down, it's thrust that pulls the water through. The back-pressure holds it from going in too fast. You can let the rocket run till the water's almost gone."

Carlot said, "You've got to let the pipefire die before the tank's empty. Otherwise you'll char the nozzle and the tank both. It's a mess if you have to throw water on a pipefire."

The storm was definitely reaching out to enfold the tree . . . and the jungle was closer too. Booce pointed. "Carlot—"

Carlot looked. "Happyfeet?"

"Maybe. Debby, what have we got for weapons?"

"Harpoons. The rocket, I guess."

"Not enough. All right, ladies. Maybe it's just a loose jungle, and even if it's happyfeet they may not have noticed anything, but I think we should hide."

"*Hide?*" Debby was outraged. "Booce, that's not much of a jungle. Carther States was twenty times that size."

The jungle was closer now, a fuzzy green ellipsoid with a shadowy slit in it, as if foliage had been shorn away to form a window into the interior. Booce said, "A jungle that size can hold a family of twenty or thirty. Debby, a tree is big. We can vanish into cracks in the bark and never be seen. I . . . think we've got time. Help me take the rocket apart."

"Booce, it was tough enough putting it together!"

"You think I like this?" But Booce and Carlot were already tugging at pipe and nozzle, and Debby perforce joined them.

"The pipe is . . . priceless. We . . . can't let happyfeet . . . get it." Booce gasped in the thin air. The nozzle jerked loose and tumbled along the bark with Booce wrapped around it. His voice drifted back. "The rest they can have. We'll hide the pipe in some crack and guard it. Now we *really* won't have time to make cabins."

They pulled loose the pipe and water tank. The green puffball was closer yet, and a line of vapor trailed behind it. The vapor trail became a curve . . .

Debby said, "It's dropped five men. Winged. Now it's going away."

Nozzle and tank floated, slowly rotating. Now Booce was free to look. "They're making for the Wart."

"We can't let them have it!" Debby cried.

"Well, the truth is, we can," Booce said. He was pushing the pipe ahead of him, kicking hard. Carlot and Debby flew to help. "Maybe the carm can take it back for us. If not . . . we don't need the Wart to reach the Clump. Those five that were dropped are after *us*."

The log was far east, drifting in the fringe of a storm complex. Rather found it before Jeffer did: shadow backlit by the sun.

Jeffer chased it down. The carm arced over the top of the out tuft, moved in along the east side of the trunk. The dock came into view: a rectangle of bare wood, ragged around the edges. Rather felt the pull of the forward jets and heard pondwater slosh toward him. Water had spread along the carm's walls and was creeping forward.

He wasn't actually getting used to this, was he?

"Where's the rocket?" Clave sounded merely puzzled.

Where they had built the rocket, there was nothing. Wait . . . there, drifting loose, a pale-brown bell-shape: the nozzle. There, some distance away, a brown ellipsoid trailing lines. Where was Carlot? Where was anyone?

"What happened here?" Clave demanded. "An explosion?"

Had there been a fire? Rather found only the small black scar of the cookfire. The arrangements around it were undisturbed.

Jeffer said, "We can't search the whole tree. Where's the sun?" Straight east. "We won't get Kendy for another day."

"Take us in," Rather said.

Jeffer looked at him. "Why?"

"Just a guess." Carlot had gone in, last sleep.

Jeffer swung the carm toward Voy and fired the jets. They skimmed above the bark. The fog was around them now.

Jeffer played with the controls. "There," he said suddenly. "Five men." But what showed in the window was an abstraction, orange blobs on red-and-black.

"We're seeing by heat," Jeffer said. For an instant the normal view returned: fog sliding along black bark. Then the red-and-black was back. "Didn't Booce say something about happyfeet?"

"Find our people," said Clave.

"Mmm . . . there." Three orange blobs in a line. By normal light they became three human shapes lined along a crack. "And the rocket pipe, I think. Rather?"

Rather quickly disengaged his seat belt and moved aft. He pulled the silver suit out of the water and slid his legs inside. Clave said, "Good. Get the rest of it on and go join the others. Take some harpoons. They won't have weapons. Jeffer, how did they get here?"

"Good question. I don't see anything that could have brought them. Something could be around the other side of the bark."

Rather waited while Clave bound six harpoons against the silver suit's chest. Air on; voice on. "Can you hear me?"

His voice blurted from the control panel, and Jeffer jumped. "I hear you fine."

"Let me out."

The bark was half a klomter distant. Rather used his jets. He thrilled to the pull of thrust along his body: blood leaving his head, abdomen settling toward his feet. Not quite a comfortable sensation, but one few others could share.

Behind him, the carm accelerated south around the curve of the trunk and was gone.

Carlot and the others had seen the carm; they waved.

Two klomters toward the blue blur of Voy, a hundred meters out from the tree, green-clad men emerged from the fog. They flew along the bark, peering into cracks as they passed. At this distance Rather could see only that they were five jungle giants, and armed.

They saw him. Their legs stopped moving, though their motion continued. Closer now. One was a woman. . .

Then they were kicking again, turning back toward the storm that was reaching to engulf the tree.

He could catch them. They couldn't know about the silver suit. His tanks were full. Rather fired his boot jets; his course became an arc.

He could catch them. Then what? Kill them? Rather's parents had both killed. They didn't like talking about it. When they did, old anger distorted their faces. Yet this was the Silver Man's duty: from time to time, he killed.

One of the intruders looked back, and then all five were kicking madly, doubling their speed.

His arms were full of harpoons, hampered, while Debby and Carlot and Booce had no weapons at all. Rather swung back toward his crew.

He thumped into the bark not far from Booce. Carlot was looking at him oddly. He opened his helmet and said, "It's me. Five of them almost found you. What happened?"

"Happyfeet," Booce said. "A small jungle, steam-powered. Lupoff family, from the look of them. They want the Wart."

Rather thumbed his personal Voice on. "Silver Man calling the Scientist. Jeffer, they want the Wart. Go for that."

Nothing.

"They can't hear me. Booce, I'll guard you on the surface, but I don't think they'll be back. They looked like they were running."

Booce grinned. "They thought you were Navy."

"What?"

"Skip it."

Rather settled himself on the bark above their heads. Helmet closed. The invulnerable warrior (and Carlot had looked at him as at some alien bird). But the happyfeet warriors were gone from sight.

The storm enclosed the tree. The fringe of it was a fine mist, just beginning to obscure vision. *I wish I could use those other kinds of light Kendy sees by. And the ventral camera's almost blind . . . hydrogen low, oxygen low, water volume low but increasing. We should have built a pump by now. Hey*—"What's that?"

Clave looked. "Jungle. Small. Just opposite the Wart."

Now Jeffer spotted green dots around the puckered bark. Men, and one was pointing toward the carm.

The voice of Kendy startled him. "I'm scanning in infrared. I can't see anything human outside of the Wart area. Take the CARM closer. Give me a view."

Jeffer accelerated in. He asked, "Did you just come into range?"

"Yes. I'm running the record of your approach. You should have killed the invaders on the east side. They could attack your people."

As the carm approached, the jungle jetted away on a trail of steam: north into the storm, then around the trunk, steam spraying in a wide curve. It was hidden before the carm arrived.

Jeffer brought the carm to rest a quarter klomter from the wooden crater. The happyfeet had been digging around one side of the Wart. Elongated men hovered around the block of black metal.

"Ten," said Kendy. Rings of red light blinked scientifically on the bark, haloing men Jeffer had already spotted, pointing out others. Three interlocked rings circled bare wood. "Four in the open, three between the bark and the Wart, three more in a crack outside the crater."

"We'd better follow the jungle," Clave said. "They could find the rest of us while we're busy here."

Jeffer turned in his seat, but Kendy spoke first. "There's time."

"They're too many to fight anyway," Clave said.

"Nonsense. Spray them with rocket exhaust. Jeffer, have you been shown the throttle for the main drive?"

"Yes." Jeffer didn't know the word *throttle*, but Lawri had shown him how to control the push of the rockets. His fingers danced.

The carm moved toward the Wart. The happyfeet waited, blurred by fog, spears ready. "Brace yourself, Clave." The carm swung around, still approaching the puckered bark, but stern foremost.

Men left the Wart, swimming hard. Others appeared from the bark beyond. Spears flew. The dorsal camera watched a bulbous-headed spear strike the hull and explode in a puff of smoky flame. Authoritative thumps could be heard through the hull.

Jeffer tapped the main drive on.

It felt like suicide. He'd nearly died the last time he did that. The carm surged forward. Jeffer felt his chest sag, his cheeks pull backward in a dead man's grin. But his arm was rigid above his face, fingers almost touching the control panel.

It worked! Moving his fingertip down along the green bar reduced the main drive's thrust to something he could handle. *Throttle.*

A nearly invisible blue washed across ten happyfeet warriors. The invaders burst into vivid yellow flame. They were comets, the flame streaming back from them. Explosions sent bits of men flying—

Clave cried, "Treefodder, Jeffer! Stop!"

Jeffer tapped the drive off. (Hydrogen, oxygen: both quite low. The Wart receded.) "Clave, they attacked us. They've got exploding harpoons."

"They couldn't have *moved* the Wart with us on their tails! We only had to take it away from them!"

"All right, Chairman." Jeffer turned to look at Clave. "Now tell me what they're doing to Booce and Debby and Carlot."

"It's time to learn that," Kendy said. "Time to move, Jeffer. I've lost sight of the jungle from *Discipline*'s position. It circled half around the trunk and was approaching the point where you dropped Rather. We'll have to get there fast, before I'm out of range. The invaders here are harmless enough now."

They were. Some were still writhing, some were motionless, but all were burned black. Jeffer set the carm moving. It was too early to feel guilt.

———

They were in the cloud now: a thick, swirling fog, growing thicker. Jeffer could see the tree only as a wall of shadow. Kendy said, "Turn starboard. You need not steer so wide of the trunk, Jeffer. I have infrared."

The carm moved around the trunk in a great curve. Lightning flared suddenly aft.

"I have the jungle in view, straight out by five point six kilometers. Straight out, Jeffer."

"I can't see."

"Ventral. Two degrees more. Good. Accelerate. Cut! Rather has the jungle in view. Silver Man, come in."

Rather's tinny voice spoke from the control board. "I see a big shadow, but no detail. They can't see us either."

"They've found you somehow," Jeffer said.

"You're near," said Kendy. "Swing one-eighty degrees."

"I won't—"

"Citizen, I don't know where the men are! What else can we do but attack the jungle itself? Swing around." There was something strange in Kendy's voice.

Jeffer turned the carm. He half hoped Clave would countermand the order, but Clave said nothing.

"Main drive." Kendy should have sounded excited. He only sounded *loud*.

Jeffer tapped the button. The carm surged. His face tried to crawl around to the back of his head. A yellow light bloomed in the mist behind him, and he heard Rather's gasp. He killed the drive, but the yellow light remained.

The harsh bass said, "Done. I'm losing range—"

Clave said, "You kill too easily, Kendy."

Kendy's voice was becoming blurry. "Citizens, you're missing the point. This was a mobile jungle. These happyfeet may have contacts in the Admiralty. They've seen the carm and the silver suit."

"Men aren't honey hornets, Kendy!"

There was no answer.

Rain drifted across the carm's main window in drops the size of fists, carried by eddies in the wind. The wood outside was black with water. Inside the cabin it was soggy enough. Jeffer's segment of pond had spread a film of water across all the walls and the cradles.

Warm, dry air blew from vents fore and aft, thrusting the water away from it. The citizens clustered around the aft jet.

Next time I'll pump the water, Jeffer thought. *Got to build a pump.*

Carlot said, "We saw that huge shadow come out of the fog. It was scary enough. Then five . . . well, they could have been birds for all I could *see*, except that they were flying toward the jungle and thrashing at both ends. Waving their arms, I guess. It was the bandits who ran away from Rather. The jungle stopped to pick them up."

"They were Lupoffs," Booce said. "I know their clothing. I've met them in the Market. A big family, three jungles, and they'd colonize if they could buy another firepipe. They're crowded."

Clave said, "So?"

"If the Lupoffs find out what happened here, you'll have two jungles hunting you."

"They won't find out." There was no triumph in Clave's voice. Jeffer shuddered.

They were warm enough, dry enough, if they stayed in the air jet. But the storm splashed rain across the bow window, and through the rain came the yellow glow of the burning jungle.

"I wouldn't mind killing a bandit or two," Booce said. "I've been robbed once or twice. It's the scale of the thing that bothers me. There must have been forty citizens in that jungle, not counting children."

Clave jumped toward the fore end of the cabin. After a moment, Jeffer followed. The fore air jet was as dry as the aft.

Clave said, "I'd had enough of that."

"Forty people," Jeffer said. "There just isn't any way to make them stop talking about it."

Clave's voice was a hoarse whisper. "Persuasive, is he? Nobody but you can be trusted to talk to Kendy, right? You burned them while they were trying to rescue their citizens!"

"They attacked us."

"With spears. So?"

"What was I supposed to do? They were threatening *our* citizens!"

Clave sighed. "I'm not blaming you. And if I am, I shouldn't be. But Kendy—" By the flick of his eyes, Clave had remembered that Kendy would hear this. He began pronouncing his words with more care. "Tree-feeding Kendy killed them like a hive of honey hornets, because they were in his way. Because they might talk to the wrong people!"

Silence and discomfort. Debby came to join them. "Wet," she said. "What did you do to get it so wet?"

Jeffer didn't answer. To Clave he said, "I felt much worse when I killed Klance the Scientist to steal the carm. He wasn't expecting it. These citizens were. They were making war."

"Right!" Debby said enthusiastically. "When London Tree raided us, I used to wish we could capture this thing and set their whole tree burning. The bandits aren't the same, but by the State, we finally did it!"

"Don't do it again," Clave said. Jeffer nodded.

CIVILIZATION

Chapter Twelve
CUSTOMS

Year 384, day 1992, by heliograph:

> *Station Two to* **Gyrfalcon.** **Swallow** *reports large incoming log east of Admiralty. Master unidentified. You will rendezvous for customs duty if convenient. Location of log at day 1990 was two-nine-oh degrees flat, five degrees north, two-eight-oh klomters radial. Acknowledge.*

"Rice, did this just come in?"

"Yes, sir. I was scraping the hull when I saw the light blinking near the Market. Took the message and came straight in, but I don't know how long the helio was blinking."

Petty Mart Wheeler thought it through. *Gyrfalcon* carried six crew; *Swallow,* two. The Navy preferred that civilians notice the big armed ships. In the act of paying customs they should remember what they were buying. So.

"Where are we?"

"I'll find out, sir." Spacer Rice turned toward the instrument closet.

"No, not you. Bosun Murphy, take our position." This was not an urgent mission. He'd use it as a training exercise.

The dwarf nodded cheerfully; her flame-red hair swirled around her. Her short but powerful legs shot her across the cabin to the instrument closet. She chose what she needed and went out.

The long hair would have to go when she reached higher rank. Pity. But dwarves were rare, and Bosun Sectry Murphy must be trained quickly . . .

Through the hatch Wheeler could see a blue light, tiny and intense: a

Navy heliograph, reflected Voy-light blinking near the east limb of the
whorl. Red hair and a squarish feminine face suddenly blocked the view.
"Petty, we're at two-sixty-five flat, six south, two-forty klomters."

"And we've got better than half a tank, right?" Murphy nodded. "Get
on the heliograph. We'll rendezvous with the log. Jimson, Rice, get us
ready for a burn."

The thick, disordered sky made Rather dizzy. If he fell into that he
would be more than ordinarily lost. He climbed with care. Clave and
Debby trailed him.

There had been hard work followed by a long climb. They were all
tired. Rather's fingers and toes were starting to cramp. But the rocket was
in sight, a hundred meters out . . . if that direction was still *out*.

The log was rising through the Clump's eastern fringes. Wind slapped
at Rather from ambush, here, there, everywhere, as if he were embedded
in a flock of terrified turkeys. Clouds ran in peculiar directions, not east-
west, not flattened spirals, but shallow in-out curves. A line of small green
puff jungles flowed in an arc that was not tidelike at all. Confronted by
such strangeness, Rather's bewildered eyes sought the one unchanging
reference point.

Voy burned blue-white and steady . . . twenty-five degrees east of the
stump of the in tuft! Choppy clouds blurred the sun. Shadows pulsed,
blurring and sharpening. Overlaid on those, Voy's faint, sharp blue shadows
lay in skewed directions. Children learned not to see Voy-shadows. Voy-
shadows told nothing, for they never moved, never changed, never distracted the eye.

The tree had turned; the trunk was pointing *wrong*.

Booce and Carlot waited at the rocket. Debby called, "Booce! How
can you stand it?"

"The tide? I grew up in it. You'll get used to it. The happyfeet do."

"The shadows are making me sick to my stomach," Debby said.

Rather's own stomach was queasy. "Carlot—"

"We're almost home." There was no mistaking her joy. She *liked* it
here. "Look, we've got the pipefire going."

"I'll start the water." A smaller pod had been carved into *Logbearer's*
new cabin. Booce crawled inside. "Tether yourselves."

The rocket cone pointed east. Rather poked his nose into the small
hatch. "Booce, are you slowing us again?"

Booce's voice echoed. "What? No, tide's different in the Clump. We'll push west, straight toward the Dark." He pulled a wooden plug from the water tank. He inhaled, put his lips to the hole, and blew.

Rather withdrew his head to watch the completed rocket in action. Yellow-white coals glowed within the iron firebox that had given them so much trouble. The iron glowed dull red. A fourth pod nearby was filled with water in case the plates didn't hold together.

At the nozzle end of the rocket—"Nothing's happening."

His answer was the sound of Booce inflating his lungs. Then the rocket went *Chuff!* and sprayed steam.

"It's going, Booce," Rather said, and looked in.

Booce's face dripped with water. He was coughing and choking while he pounded the plug in with the heel of his hand. His glare was murderous.

CHUFF, CHUFF, Chuff chuffchuffchuff . . . The rocket settled down. A row of cloud-puffs became a steady stream jogged by the play of capricious wind. Rather felt no acceleration. It would be gentle, with so great a mass to be moved.

Carlot came up behind him; her long fingers found his hand and enclosed it. "Father? Shouldn't we—"

Booce sounded like his throat was still full of water. "Yes, go play lookout on the west face, you two. Watch for Navy and anything we might hit."

The maelstrom revealed itself to them as they circled the trunk. Flying was a continuing wonder to Rather, but Carlot did it better. She kept darting ahead, then circled to urge him on. At a vantage point on the west face they doffed their wings and rested.

The Clump was a whorl like a tremendous fingerprint. Inward, matter thickened. There were puzzle trees, distorted cotton-candy jungles, the much smaller puffballs that Carlot had pointed out for him ("fisher jungles"), and greenery that was totally unfamiliar. Ponds took odd shapes in the distorted tide. The sky was thick with birds: skyhorses, triunes, and a thousand tiny red and yellow darts converging on a puff jungle. Everything moved in arcs, tighter near the center of the whorl, and darker. The center itself was almost black, but motion could still be seen there.

The triune families were hard to spot, but two had turned to observe the passing log. They were fat sky-blue cigar-shapes with wide triple fins: male and female and child, linked along their bellies. Three slender blue shapes flashed violent-orange bellies as they converged on the red-and-yellow bird-swarm: another triune family, separated to hunt.

A thin stream of cloud cut across other patterns of cloud-flow. Rather spotted it in the moment before Carlot pointed. "There. Navy."

"How do you know?" Rather saw only a dark point at the end of the line of cloud.

"It's coming toward us. Customs. They'll make a burn and intercept us in a day. Oh, *treefodder*."

Rather laughed. She'd borrowed his curse. "What?"

She showed him.

Far in toward the Clump's dark center, in the thick of moving matter, was a broad, flat ring-shape with a pebbly inner surface . . . angular structures in pastel colors . . . blatantly artificial. Could it really be as big as it looked?

He judged its size by an even larger natural object nearby: a tree with one tuft missing. The log was smaller than their own, Rather thought. At its midpoint he could make out a rocket-shape, cone and tank and angular cabin.

Carlot said, "I know that rocket. *Woodsman*. Dad won't like this. They could just as easily have been out another damn year." She looked into his eyes. "We won't have much time together. The Belmy family owns *Woodsman*. Dad wants to marry me to Raff Belmy."

"Will you do it?"

"Shut up." She pulled him against her by the slack of his tunic. "I don't want to think about it. Just don't talk," she breathed into his ear, and he obeyed. It crossed his mind that Booce should be told of these things. But there would be time . . .

Gyrfalcon found the log easily: bigger than average, with both tufts severed. It was making its burn: a wavery line of cloud behind it was beginning to arc over. The rocket would be behind the trunk.

"Instruments," Wheeler instructed. "Rice, get us a rendezvous track. Murphy, the neudar. That dark blemish in the wood—"

"I see it, sir."

He waited and watched. His crew moved well, Bosun Murphy in particular. She hadn't yet used the neudar under field circumstances. She moved slowly, but without mistakes. That would reflect well on Wheeler.

"The blemish is dense. Metal," she said. "Kilotons."

"Now the rocket."

"I can't see anything—"

"Behind the midpoint."

"Oh! I can look *through* the wood!" She tried it. "Mmm . . . something . . . metal, not much. Our own iron rocket nozzle would show a mark like that."

"Rice?"

"We need a burn, Petty. Fifty degrees planar, zero axial, a hundred breaths of burn and we'll go just past."

"Give us the burn, then all hands suit up. Spacer Rice, you're in the cabin, on instruments. Murphy, on the pump."

Gyrfalcon carried a glass alcohol tank and a pair of water tanks. Its valve system had been rifled from the hulk of an ancient Cargo and Repair Module. On long voyages, standard practice was to spray water into the alcohol flame as working mass. Water could be replaced in domains beyond the Admiralty's reach. Alcohol generally could not, though some of the happyfeet tribes carried alcohol distilleries for trade with the Admiralty.

Wheeler and Jimson tethered themselves carefully at the steering platform above the motor. Murphy began to pedal. Pedals could be extended, but a dwarf on the bicycle always delivered more power. Wheeler put his hand in the airflow to test it, then started the alcohol flame. He checked his crew's handholds before he increased the flow.

Thrust pulled at his skin and his bones. He ran water into the flame. Thrust rose again, and heat bathed the inner surfaces of his straining legs.

Rice called down from the cabin. "Cut it!"

Petty Wheeler reached below his feet for the alcohol valve. The roar died to a hiss: water on a hot surface. Next, the water valve. *Gyrfalcon* fell free.

The log was nearer; the plume of acceleration was gone. Using the binoculars, Wheeler found a pair of human shapes on the near side.

"They're not giving us much attention," he said.

Murphy took the binoculars. Presently she said, "They'll have time." She looked until he took them away.

The Navy ship was bigger and more elaborate than *Logbearer*. It arrived in a wave of warm steam and paused a hundred meters from the center of the midtrunk. Four men emerged and flew toward them.

Logbearer's crew waited outside the cabin.

"They're fast," Debby said.

Booce chuckled. "Never try to outfly the Navy. Navy wings are different, and the men are picked for their legs."

They were closer now. Rather suddenly gripped Booce's arm. "Booce, they're wearing silver suits!"

"*Ah!* Rather—"

Rather eased his grip. "Sorry."

"Well, *watch* that. It's only Navy armor.".

"But it looks—"

"Just armor. There are three vac suits in the Admiralty, and we aren't important enough to see one. Incidentally, they'd love to make it four."

Closer yet. The armor didn't cover them. All wore helmets: head-and-shoulder pieces with an opening for the face. Some wore additional plates. And one was a dwarf.

Their wings! They pointed a little forward, as the foot did; they folded on the forward kick and snapped open on the back-kick. *The Scientist should see this,* Rather thought.

They left their wings on even after they touched bark.

The dwarf was a woman. Red hair showed around the helmet before she lifted it. Pale skin, pointed nose, and pointed chin; hair like flame streaming from a tree afire. Her chest plate stood several ce'meters out from her chest. She was five or six years older than Rather, quite lovely, and Rather's height.

She caught him looking and smiled at him. He forgot that he could move. Her eyes were blue, and they danced.

He was blushing, and Carlot had caught it, and Rather looked away in haste. And watched a long, long man kicking toward them.

The globe helmet was much larger than his head, with an opening for his face . . . like the silver suit's helmet with the faceplate missing. Separate curved pieces protected his thighs, back, upper arms, and hips. Those were wood painted in silver; but the head-and-shoulder piece was of hammered metal. Wide nose, dark skin, black cushion of hair: he might have been part of Booce's family.

He recognized Booce (and ignored his crew). "Booce Serjent? You may remember me: Petty Wheeler. Welcome home."

"Good to see you again, Petty. You'll remember Carlot—"

She smiled brilliantly. "Good day, Petty Wheeler."

"Oh, yes. You've grown, Carlot."

Booce said, "These others are Clave and Rather Citizen, from Citizens' Tree, a few hundred klomters west of us. Debby Carther we hired before we left."

Meeting strangers was outside Rather's experience. Booce had told him what to do. He said, "A pleasure to meet you, sir," and held out his hand.

"Pleased." The Navy man's handshake was strong for a jungle giant. "I'll speak to you later, Rather. Clave, Debby, a pleasure. Booce, do you have anything to declare?"

"Yes. One log, forty klomters or thereabouts. If you want to measure it yourselves—"

"No, we'll just take half the manifests as you sell it off."

"And the Wart," Booce said complacently. "Our one bit of luck, and a happyfeet tribe almost made off with it."

"That mucking great chunk of metal halfway in?"

"Heh. You've found it already? We haven't measured that either, but it's thousands of tons. Petty, we'd like the Wart classified. We won't get so many thieves that way."

"All right, but if happyfeet attacked you—"

"I don't want to file charges. They got away, but we hurt them, and I don't want them to know who. They might want to come after us with friends."

"That attitude makes life difficult for the Navy, Booce. We'd rather chase them down. You're sure? . . . All right. We'll want our taxes in metal."

"Fine. I want to keep that makeshift firebox until I can buy more sikenwire. It's not pretty, but it works. Barring that, I'll sell the entire lode to the Navy right now, if you can tear it out and tow it home. Take it off my hands," Booce said.

Rather couldn't help himself; he stared. *But what if he takes you up on it?*

Petty Wheeler laughed. "I don't have alcohol to tow it and I can't authorize that kind of expenditure. But we'll inspect it now, and I'll send a team to cut our share loose after you're moored."

Petty Wheeler's crew began searching *Logbearer* inside and out. Rather's momentary impulse was to stop them. But Booce showed no surprise . . . and of course there was nothing aboard *Logbearer* to be found. Meanwhile the Navy officer turned to Rather and said, "Rather, wasn't it? You should consider joining the Navy."

"Why?"

The man smiled. "The pay is good, particularly for a tree dweller, if you can get in. We'll shape you up and teach you things you should know, like how to win a fight. You'll be holding civilization together. The personal advantage is, you're the right shape. You noticed Bosun Sectry Murphy? Short, with red hair—"

"Yes?"

"She'll be wearing a vac suit within six years. Guardian is the highest rank there is, unless you were born an officer. You could do the same."

"I'll have to think about it."

"Talk to her yourself. Ask Booce, for that matter. Booce, we'll fly down and inspect your Wart. Would you like to ride with us?"

"I'd be delighted." Booce looked around at his crew and added, "We'd *all* be delighted."

Gyrfalcon's hull sported handholds everywhere. The Navy men spaced *Logbearer's* people high along one flank. There were shelves for feet and straps to circle a waist (or just under the armpits on Rather). "Fighting vessel," Clave whispered to Debby. "They can cover the hull with archers."

Three Navy worked aft, around the motor. They ignored the civilians.

Something green was trying to grow on the wooden hull. Fluff, maybe. The wood had been scraped recently. Rather noticed that much before the rocket fired.

If Wheeler was trying to impress a barbarian dwarf, he succeeded. The rocket roared and spat flame. Rather felt his blood settling into his legs. The log's rough bark surged past, accelerating. Aft, Wheeler and Murphy used toothed gears to point the nozzle. In a way it was more impressive than the carm. You could *see* how it all worked.

The roar of the motor would cover his voice (and the fear in it). Rather asked, "Why don't they let us inside?"

"Classified. Nobody knows what's in a Navy ship," Carlot said. "We haven't seen the whole crew, I'm sure of that. Rather, I noticed you staring at the, um, red-haired woman?"

Rather told a half-truth. "She looks short. I mean, it's surprising, because she's the same size I am. Mark never looked short."

Carlot seemed to relax. "Well, no. He was bigger than you when you were growing up."

Wheeler moved the nozzle ten degrees to port. The ship slewed around, spraying flame. He swiveled the nozzle starboard; the rotation slowed and stopped, and *Gyrfalcon* decelerated. It eased to a stop less than a hundred meters from the blister in the trunk.

"The bandits almost had it torn loose," Wheeler observed.

Booce nodded.

The same four Navy personnel accompanied them to the Wart. Three set to examining the blister that had grown up around the metal and the matchet-chewed wood that extended far back behind it. The fourth sought out Rather. "Petty Wheeler said you might have questions to ask me," said Bosun Murphy.

Rather was not really thinking of joining the Navy. He didn't say so. "I don't know enough to ask good questions."

She smiled enchantingly. "Ask bad ones. I don't mind."

"What are the vac suits? Why are they important?"

"They're old science, as old as the Library. They're invulnerable," she said. "The highest fighting rank is Guardian, and that's the rank that wears the vac suits. There are supposed to be nine Guardians. We've got eight. This—" She rapped her helmet, then the plates on her thighs. "—It looks like this, but all over. You'll get as high as Petty just because you're the right shape, and then you find out if you actually fit into a vac suit."

"Do you?"

"I don't know. I haven't got that far yet." She looked down at her protruding chestplate unhappily. "Maybe I won't fit. I'd still keep my rank as Petty. Understand, you have to be qualified, you have to be trained. It's just easier if you're the right size."

"Training. What's it like?"

"They'll put you through exercises. You may think you're strong— you're a tree dweller? I can see the muscles. But Petty Wheeler could tie you in knots. After you've been through training you could tie *him* in knots. I could, I think, and you're stronger. Your people, do they use polar coordinates to find themselves?"

"No."

"They'll teach you how to find yourself in the sky. You'll learn how to count, if you don't know—"

"I can count."

"You'll learn how to work a rocket, not a steam rocket but a Navy rocket. They teach you how to obey too. You want to go in braced for that, Rather. A superior officer tells you to fly, you fly, wings or no."

It sounded unpleasant. "Where do the Navy ships go?"

"Mmm . . . Where do you come from?"

"Citizens' Tree. A little west of the Clump."

"You're not likely to visit your family. We don't see many tree dwellers. We send ships outside the Clump, but not often, and never more than a few thousand klomters. Mostly we cruise the Clump itself. We collect taxes, of course—"

"Yeah."

"We fight the wildlife. Dark sharks and other things. Citizens find a drillbit nest, or honey hornets, they call us and we burn it out."

"Triunes too?"

"Oh, no, the triunes got the idea fast. They never attack us. Some of them like us. There's a guy, Exec Martin, he hunts swordbirds with triunes. Nobody knows how bright they really are, but they can be trained."

"Why do you burn honey hornets? Booce says they're valuable."

Her expression soured. "Honey is contraband. Put just a tip of a fingernail's worth on your tongue, you dream wonderful dreams. Then you
can't stop. Use a little more and you die in ecstacy. Some people will pay a
lot for that."

Honey is suicide. Rather hadn't realized that Booce meant it literally. He
thought it over, then said, "But it's their choice—"

She shook her head. "Not my decision. Then there's detective work,
and riot control, and rescue work. We don't specialize much. You learn to
do all of that, but first you learn how to fly a ship."

"What happens to cadets who fail? Murphy, what happens to *dwarves*
who fail?"

"Nothing. I mean, they're out of the Navy, of course. They hire out or
they build a business, maybe they go diving in the Dark for mushrooms
and fan fungus, or they go logging. Hell, what does a logger do if he fails
at something?" She looked closely at him. "What's the matter?"

"I'm having trouble with this. There're more people here, so there's
more places for people, right? If you can't hunt or do earthlife farming,
you just try something else?"

Murphy nodded brightly. "Next question?"

Would we see each other if I joined up? May I call you Sectry? "Thank
you, Bosun."

"Any time," she said, and sprang away. She coasted parallel to the bark,
toward Wheeler as he emerged from behind the Wart.

"It's big," Wheeler called. "Booce Serjent, you've made your fortune."

"Recouped it, anyway. The first thing I'll do is rebuild *Logbearer.*"

"Yes. . . . Well, I've seen enough. Eight thousand tons or so. Those
scars on the metal—"

"We used the saw to get the slabs that make up the firebox. It worked
better than I'd hoped. It's a good substitute for sikenwire, and the saw's
not damaged."

Wheeler nodded, satisfied. "Can we lift you back to your ship?"

"No, we need to cover this somehow before we reach the Market."

"I think you're worrying over nothing. How could anyone steal anything this *big?*"

"With saws. . . . Well, you may be right."

They watched *Gyrfalcon* steam toward the Clump interior. Something
bright twinkled at the bow. "He's calling home," Booce said. "They use
mirrors to bounce Voy-light where they want it."

"What happens now?" Clave asked.

"Wheeler thinks I sawed off more metal than just those plates for the firebox. He'll watch to see if I sell it on the black market. He could have bought the Wart on the spot, but he thinks I'll give him a better price if he waits. A few days after we dock I'll get an offer. It'll be too little, and I'll boost them a bit and then take it so I can stop guarding the metal—"

"What do we do *now*, Booce? Jeffer must be going crazy waiting for us to call in."

"We're still being watched."

Gyrfalcon was tiny now. Its steam trail was dissipating. Clave asked, "Can they still see? Have they got something like the carm windows?"

"A box they hold to their eyes. Clave, we'd like some way to disguise this mucking great chunk of metal."

So *Logbearer*'s five crew swarmed over the Wart, taking their time, just looking at it from all angles, as if there were some way to hide a conspicuous pucker in the honest wood of a tree. The sun crept from zenith to pass north of Voy. And presently Debby said, "Booce, you've seen more trees than any of us. What kind of a thing causes this kind of scar?"

"Something hits the tree . . . could be stony, it doesn't have to be metal. I've seen this kind of gap with nothing in it at all, just chewed wood healing over. I never did figure it out."

Debby wondered, "Ice?"

Booce's face went . . . stupid? Mouth agape, eyes drifting. He said, "Heh. Yes! A chunk of ice could smash a tree, then melt."

"Still doesn't do anything for us. What else? Disease? Is there something that builds nests? Or the tree bugs could chew just in one place—"

"Sure, a honey pod could hit a tree, and the bugs would chew a huge hole . . . give me a breath, Debby." Stupid again: thinking. "We can do it. Twenty days to reach the Market. Okay. We need a fisher jungle that's got termites, and we need to look like we've been through a disaster, but we've got that already. I *never* thought I'd come home with a pod for *Logbearer*'s cabin!"

"What do you need from us?" Clave asked.

"Stay here, talk to Jeffer. The rest of us will fly up the trunk. This is *nice*. If Wheeler wonders why we're still hovering around the Wart, he'll see us hiding it!"

Rather swallowed his protest, because Clave was saying, "You don't need Rather. I want him."

"Stet." Booce had his wings on. "Come, children."

Chapter Thirteen

THE TERMITE NEST

from the Citizens' Tree cassettes, year 5 SM:

THE LAGRANGE POINTS

Matter tends to collect in the fourth and fifth Lagrange points (L4 and L5) of Goldblatt's World. These regions appear less turbulent than the storms around Goldblatt's World itself, but we have postponed exploring them in depth.

We inspected only L4. The more or less stable region is 600 km across. Mapping the equipotential tide curves gets us nested crescents. What shows to the eye is a misshapen whorl dwindling east and west into the arc of the Smoke Ring proper.

The whorl is green around the periphery, darker and browner near the center, where accumulated matter becomes thick enough to block sunlight. Tide-stabilized plants don't thrive here. We've found familiar life-forms—triunes and cotton-candy jungles—but also some specialized life-forms not seen elsewhere.

Deep radar indicates solid masses within the dark inner region. None are large.

We have wondered why the Clumps never condensed into one large body. Perhaps life itself acts to remove matter from the inner regions. The fisher jungles' roots disrupt large ponds. Saprophytes feed in the dense core, then fire spore packages away into the Smoke Ring. Birds are forced out by famine or population pressure . . .

It made his head hurt.

Jeffer ate as he read. When he reached the end he doggedly scrolled back to the beginning. His students had found it bewildering. So did Jeffer, but he had an advantage over his students. He had Kendy.

If Kendy would call!

Today he had hunted the sky. He'd returned to the dead fisher jungle trailing a sizable shieldbird. A small fire near the carm had cooked his catch. He was getting good at it. Sandwiching the meat between two of the shieldbirds' bone plates cooked it tender without scorching it.

He almost choked when the carm suddenly spoke. "Jeffer? This is Clave. Jeffer, can you hear me?"

Jeffer swallowed hard and said, "Prikazyvat Send to pressure suit. And about treefeeding time too! Are you alive?"

"Jeffer, we couldn't get to the helmet. The Navy searched *Logbearer.* Even after they left they were watching us. Where are you? Are you hidden?"

"Clave, I found something good. Do you remember Booce's description of a fisher jungle? A green puffball a klomter across, with a long coiled root. It reaches out to put the root in a pond, but there's poison on it and it can attack life forms and kill them and draw them in to rot—"

"Right. They're not supposed to live outside the Clump."

"Maybe so. This one's fifty klomters from the Clump fringes, and it's dead. The axis trunk is hollow. There's a Navy ship coming this way. It's not likely they'll want to sniff around a fisher jungle, but I've got the carm moored inside the hollow anyway. When it goes away I'll tether it above the root so the carm can get some sunlight. Where are you? I can't see anything."

"I'm in the dark. I'm in that channel we chopped past the Wart. We haven't moved the silver suit yet."

Jeffer remembered extending the work done by the happyfeet. His back and shoulders still ached. "We should have let the happyfeet do more of the carving."

"It was worth it. Booce was right. The Navy knows if you're carrying metal. This Petty Wheeler citizen knew about the Wart, but he didn't look for anything behind it."

"What's the Clump like?"

"Crowded. We'll have the log moored in twenty days. Booce has a way to hide the Wart. He's afraid of thieves, and we can't use the silver suit to win a fight, because—"

"No, of course not."

"—Because they'd recognize it. Jeffer, they've got *three* silver suits. It's a mark of high rank. Dwarves are in good shape if they join the Navy, and Rather's had an offer."

An offer? "Rather, you there?"

Jeffer heard Clave's distant yell. Presently Rather said, "Here."

"You had an offer to join the Navy? What was said? What did you tell them?"

"I didn't take the Petty seriously. The idea is to learn something about the Admiralty, buy some earthlife seeds, and get back to Citizens' Tree!"

"We want to know about the Navy too."

"I learned a little—"

Clave interrupted. "How serious are we? Booce, what has the Navy got that we want to see? I'm not so eager to see the inside of a Navy rocket that I'd feed one of my—"

"The Library! The cassettes! What's on the Admiralty cassettes?"

"All *right*, Jeffer. What makes you think Rather could get to any of that? Booce might know, but he isn't here to ask."

Jeffer finished the shieldbird meat while he thought. "Ask him when you get the chance. Now, I'm getting terminally bored here. Are you free to move the silver suit into the rocket?"

"No. It's too easily recognized," Clave said.

"How about just the helmet?"

"We'll have to ask Booce, but . . . I think not. Let's get Kendy in on this. Are you in contact?"

"He said he was changing orbit. He'll be back in another day. Clave, I wish you could give me some kind of a view."

"I'll think of something. Jeffer, Rather's waving at me."

"Scientist out."

"Clave? You'd better see this," Rather said.

"What? I was talking to Jeffer." Clave crawled out of the cavity behind the Wart. "Oh."

From out of the crowded sky came a shapeless thing colored a dead yellowish brown. Its outline was fuzzed with a jittering motion that caused the optic nerves to twitch. It was coming straight at them, and *Logbearer* was behind it.

"Get out of its way, Rather, it's going to hit! Got your wings?"

They fled. The thing fell toward the Wart with a faint, frightening buzzing sound. Myriads of black flecks swarmed around it, insects much smaller than honey hornets.

It struck the crater around the Wart and deformed like soft mud.

Logbearer bumped the trunk more softly. Debby emerged from the hatch in the forward pod. She stared hard at the intrusionary mass. She called, "It's going to stick."

Booce answered from inside. "Stet. Spread the honey."

Debby waved at Booce and Rather, but that was all the attention she gave them. She began spreading red sticky honey around the rim of the crater.

The swarm of insects followed her. When she closed the circle, most of the insects had migrated to the honey.

"Done!"

"Good. Get aboard. Clave, Rather, I've got to moor this thing. Want a ride?"

Clave bellowed, "Booce, you get out here and answer some questions!"

Booce's head popped out. He thought it over, then flapped to join them. He looked indecently self-satisfied.

"It's a termite nest," he said before Clave could ask. "We'll say we didn't have any choice, it was the only tree around and we had to get back to the Clump because . . . I'll think of something."

"Uh-huh. The honey?"

"Encouragement. When the termites run out of honey they'll eat wood. They'll bond the nest to the Wart."

"What about the silver suit? Were you just going to leave it?"

"Where would it be safer?"

"Jeffer's all alone in the sky. He'd go crazy!"

Booce's grimace told it all. Clave said, "He's the Citizens' Tree Scientist, and he is *not* a crazy murderer. He was in a fight with our lives at stake, Booce, and he used what he had. It was more powerful than he thought it was—"

"He used it twice."

"Booce, if you've ever been a happyfeet bandit yourself, tell me now."

Booce was astonished, then amused. "Oh, really! No, I'm *not* protecting my own kind. I'm *not* defending bandits that prey on loggers. Granted they'd generally rather attack some tribe of helpless savages. Your suspicions are right there, Clave, but it doesn't mean I *like* bandits. I wouldn't have burned a whole damn tribe either!"

"Uh-huh. You would have sent them away without hurting them so much. How? Describe the procedure in detail."

"I can't do that. Jeffer hasn't told any of us how to fly the carm! Clave, the Scientist is not to burn any tribe, ever again. I'm telling you, not him. *You* are to stop him."

"I'll tell him. Now what?"

"Oh . . . we'll leave everything but the helmet where it is. Jeffer's scientific eyes are in the helmet, right? Those little windows in the forehead? We'll moor it in the nest. He'll have a view. We'll be spending enough time around the Wart; we'll talk to him then."

The CARM with its cameras was hidden in a dark place, the pressure suit was in another, the incoming recordings were days old, and in present time Jeffer wasn't present. Kendy skimmed the recordings. He was learning more through *Discipline*'s own senses.

Logbearer was easy to follow: forty kilometers of tree with tufts missing and a metal mass off-center, now rounding the starward limb of the L4 whorl. Maintaining contact wasn't going to be easy here. *Discipline*'s new orbit had twice the period of Goldblatt's World, with periVoy falling north of the L4 point. Tilting his orbit out of the Smoke Ring allowed his instruments to penetrate less of the garbage in the Clump; but the log and the CARM and all of Kendy's citizens would be circling that center on long kidney-shaped paths.

At least he wouldn't have to burn more fuel. If he could establish relations with the Admiralty, his present orbit might suffice for hundreds of years.

Savages in a thriving civilization would find trouble sooner or later. Patience. Some emergency would force Jeffer to bring the CARM into the L4 point. Then he must open the airlock to the Navy . . .

One problem at a time. Wait. Learn.

Jeffer entered the cabin before Kendy passed out of range. There was fresh pink blood on his tunic and more on his hands.

"Kendy for the State—"

"Hello, Kendy. How can we—"

"Jeffer, if Rather has an offer from the Navy, I want him to accept."

"You would. Rather didn't sound too enthusiastic. Neither am I. How can we get away with not hiding the silver suit?"

"An excellent question." Kendy was using light amplification, but it only showed him iron ore and chewed wood. Clave and Rather had departed the hiding place. "If the Navy has pressure suits, they'll recognize yours. I thought of disassembling it, but they'd know the helmet too. We would ruin the camera if we tried to dismount it, and the electrical source is in the helmet."

"So?"

"Patience."

"Feed your patience to the tree, Kendy. I've got a cryptic entry under 'Lagrange Points'—"

"I've had three hundred and eighty-four years to learn patience. You are almost out of range. Can you feed yourself there?"

"Sure. There's hand fungus, and flashers living on the bugs, and some other things. In a way it's like learning to hunt all over again . . ." The link was lost.

A chance to examine the Admiralty's military arm from inside! But Rather wasn't *enthusiastic*. And Kendy would have to talk Jeffer around before his arguments could even reach the boy.

Patience . . .

Chapter Fourteen

DOCKING

from *Logbearer's* log, Captain Booce Serjent speaking:

Year 384, Day 1700   This trip we need not fear happyfeet.

I fear Jeffer the Scientist. I fear the secrets we hide from the Admiralty and the secrets the Scientist keeps from me. But I owe a major debt to Citizens' Tree.

Day 1710   We've found a simple way to hide our empty crew member. May I never have the chance to thank the happyfeet for making it possible.

Day 1780   We've gone for more pods. One has become our cabin, one stores extra water in case a fire spreads. Returning with a pod for **Logbearer's** *cabin grates in my soul, but it will surely hide the wealth we carry.*

Day 1810   Making paints gave more trouble than I expected. The colors are still poor, but will suffice. We've painted the honey hornet logo across **Logbearer's** *cabin. Now we'll see what can be done about my crew's wings.*

Day 1996   Entered Admiralty space. **Gyrfalcon** *has registered log and metal for customs. Assessment to follow.*

Day 2000   Log nearing Market. Metal concealed from all but Navy. Conditions optimal.

Day 2015   Docked. Sent the crew off with Carlot. Would have gone with them if I could. I never dealt with tree dwellers before. I can't guess how they'll react.

I miss Ryllin. I never in my life had to weave so many threads at once.

A fat, baby-blue torpedo cruised slowly along the Serjent log, moving closer to where Rather and Carlot stood watch. Suddenly it split along its length, and four slender blue-and-orange triunes dove on some tree-dwelling life-form.

Rather pointed. "Four?"

"Sometimes triunes have twins."

"I've never heard of that."

"You never saw one of those either." She pointed out a triangular shadow. "That's a Dark shark. They don't usually come this far skyward. They're dangerous. All teeth, no brain."

"Skyward?"

"Dark, skyward, spin, and antispin. We use all the normal directions too."

"How do you keep it all straight?" Rather reached to wrap his legs lightly around her waist. She did not respond.

A ball of green fluff stretched a quarter klomter of curly tail toward a passing sphere of water.

Booce, Debby, and Clave were around the log's horizon, ready to use the rocket if anything came near. Carlot and Rather kept watch from the east. "We can still keep our eyes on the sky," Rather pointed out.

Carlot pounded his kneecaps with her fists, briskly. "Who's watching *us?*"

"I don't mind triunes watching. Maybe I even like it."

"What about the houses?"

"Houses?"

"You'd say *huts*. Look—"

Beyond the Market, beyond Carlot's pointing chin, six cubes were strung along a spire of wood with a rocket tank and nozzle at one end. "That's Captain-Guardian Wayne Mickl's household," Carlot said. "He's one of the richest officers."

"It isn't close."

"That one is."

A structure floated against the Dark, a cube festooned with platforms, extrusions for tethers, water pods, and other things for which he had no name.

"That's the Hillards, I think. And that puff jungle is the Kerians."

The sky was full of puffballs. The one Carlot pointed out bore a big *K* with other letters within, too small to read. Carlot said, "Crew live in those if they're too poor to buy wood. Usually they clip a logo in the foliage."

Rather laughed. "Okay, I'm convinced." Another puff jungle was marked with a slender figure eight. "If you're rich, you build with wood?"

"Yes."

"Your family has a house."

"We find our own wood! I'll show you if it comes around. It wasn't finished when we left, but I know the design."

"We're poor, aren't we? Citizens' Tree is poor."

"You live poor. The carm makes you rich, except that you can't use it . . . and there's your share of the Wart, once Father sells it. Rather?"

"Speaking."

"I think I'm going to marry Raff."

Rather turned to look at her. The sudden black emptiness in his belly was entirely new to him, yet he couldn't feel any surprise. He got his lips working. "Would you be better off if I went somewhere else?"

She was having trouble meeting his eyes. "I haven't seen Raff in three years. Rather, I think he'd be happier if he didn't know we've been . . ."

"Making babies. I won't announce it."

"All right. But I wouldn't push you into the Navy just to get rid of you! Don't ever think that! I don't know if it's a good idea or not. I don't think for Citizens' Tree, and I don't do your thinking either. Don't give up the idea just to stay near me."

"I have no intention of joining the Navy." Rather turned back to the sky. He was still on watch.

Now that he knew what to look for, the sky danced with structures. Puff jungles were everywhere, more of them toward the Dark, and some were marked. There were wooden cubes and clusters of cubes, elaborately colored in bright primaries. He could pick out wind-curdled lines of steam crossing the Dark.

He said, "People change in three years."

Carlot said, "Sure. Maybe we won't like each other. We'll see. I'm telling you, Rather, if we get along I'll marry him. Belmy was the first of the logging concerns, and it's the most powerful."

The helmet had been in place in the termite nest for some twenty hours. Kendy ran the record through his mind, classifying, deducing, making notes. When he reached present time he went back to the beginning.

His mental model of the Admiralty was shaping up nicely.

There were more new plants than new animals. Animals showed the same modified trilateral symmetry here as they did in the Smoke Ring proper. There was a clear absence of tide-stabilized plants: hardly surprising.

The buildings were interesting. Everything less primitive than a carved-out cotton-candy plant was built in rectangular solids. It was as if they still built to resist gravity . . . but not quite, for addenda sprouted at any angle, and openings might appear in any of the six walls. They looked like Escher had designed them.

Some houses had a big square fin sticking out from one corner. The Clump was turbulent. In infrared Kendy could see little whirlwinds, "dust devils" with no dust in them. A house would tumble and keep tumbling without that fin.

Unless it was attached to some larger structure.

Why was there only one Market? It didn't look difficult to construct. Houses were scattered through the outer Clump. Most would have no neighbors at all most of the time. There was no need for such isolation. It was inefficient and lonely.

The tree's attitude changed continually. The view through the helmet camera wavered with it. Kendy was getting only glimpses of the Market, but he could integrate them.

Many of the structures were moored by concrete to the Market frame. Too bad. Kendy would have liked to offer them concrete. If he ever got their attention he'd have to have something to offer, some bit of knowledge to make their lives better. He knew the pattern that would make them a thriving, Smoke Ring–girdling State in a hundred years; but there had to be something quicker.

Electricity? The Clump never had true night either. How did they light their houses?

He recognized a glass tank from one of *Discipline*'s seeding missiles, emitting a sharp spike in the light spectrum: chlorophyll. They'd made it into a hydroponics tank. The faceted hemisphere nearby was an old survival tent sheathed with wood, with transparent facets left open. Other structures on the ring were made from Smoke Ring materials: mostly wood, but one was a cotton-candy jungle tethered to a mast.

A building beyond the Market sported a broad picture window: the windscreen from a CARM. Otherwise, no glass anywhere. No sand?

Crew drifted among the buildings like leaves in an autumn wind. Half-grown children flew in groups tended by one or two adults . . .

I've got to know more. Can I find a way to move the helmet into the Market?

Booce was in position at the rocket, with hot coals ready, and Debby and Clave to watch and to steer. The sky was thick with debris. One might hope that Carlot and Rather would keep to their watching . . . but at least they'd have their chance to talk.

A Navy ship had them in clear view. Supervising, to make sure that the log came to rest a safe distance from the Market. A larger rocket pulled free of Belmy's log and steamed toward *Logbearer*.

Booce and his damaged tree would arrive in a blaze of publicity.

He was returning like a beggar.

But of course there was the Wart . . . and the silver suit behind it. He would have liked to lose that. The worst the Admiralty could charge him with was "concealment of vital resources," but that was a heavy charge. Was it worth the risk, to be able to talk to Jeffer the Scientist?

Not that he had a choice.

He was almost home. The Belmy log was ahead of them, eclipsing the Market. The tuftless end looked chewed. Belmy had sold some of his wood.

Woodsman was prominent in the sky, arriving nozzle-foremost. There was no mistaking that elaborate superstructure, four cubes surrounding the water pod, each painted a different color, each bearing the small black *B* logo. Handholds everywhere, and a steering platform around the nozzle, with a carved rail. The nozzle was mounted a little out from the rest so that replacement water pods could be inserted easily. Hilar Belmy was coming to greet him.

"Almost time," he said, and saw Clave and Debby nod acknowledgment. Booce pushed his coals into the firebox. The fire would need time to catch. "Belmy docked his log behind the Market, of course. We're going to have to dock behind him. Then it gets unpleasant."

Debby asked, "Why not dock just ahead of the Market?"

"Because that's where the Admiralty docks its ships."

"Booce, if you're expecting a fight, you'd better tell us now. Also, what weapons—"

"Bloodthirsty woman. No weapons, no fight. It's just . . . I'm coming in behind Hilar Belmy with a fuel pod for my cabin and a log damaged in two places. Checker only knows what Hilar will think. He'll change his mind when he finds out about the Wart, but . . . That log still has one tuft."

"So?"

"Why on earth would Hilar Belmy leave one tuft on a log?"

Clave asked, "Why didn't we?"

"Wind. You can bring a log to its mooring with one tuft on, but it's tricky. It usually means you ran out of honey or bugs . . . hmm?"

"What?"

"Just a passing thought. *Hello, Hilar!*" His crew stared. They had never heard so cheerful a sound from Booce Serjent.

Woodsman vented steam, decelerating. Two men rode the platform above the nozzle. They were tall: taller than Booce. Their necks were long, like Ryllin's; there was a great-grandmother in common. Black hair, gray hair, otherwise nearly identical.

The black-haired man waved joyfully. Booce couldn't tell Belmy's sons apart, but that must be Raff, and Carlot would be waving back.

Gray hair was Hilar. He looked good: sturdy, prosperous, a few kilos more massive than his son. "Booce! I thought I'd offer you a tug. How . . . Did you have some trouble?"

"That we did!" Booce's shout became less effortful as Belmy's rocket drew closer. "Hilar, thanks for the offer, but I'll bring her in myself."

"Stet," Hilar Belmy shouted back. *Woodsman* slowed and stopped fifty meters from the trunk. "Join us after! I want to talk business."

"Stet." Booce dropped his voice. "Now let's do this *right*. Debby, stand by the water pod. Clave, I'll need you to help me turn the rocket." *Logbearer* looked ready. The firebox was dull red; white light glowed through the cracks. The plates had never fit exactly, but they didn't seem to be coming apart. *Logbearer* was tilted nearly parallel to the bark.

Booce entered the cabin. He blew into the flow port (**CHUFF** CHUFF chuff chuffchuff . . .) and emerged panting. "Clave, not quite yet . . . now."

They heaved against *Logbearer*'s fuel pod, tilting the rocket in its bark nest to keep it pointed straight toward the Market. Condensing live steam drew a line across the sky. *Woodsman* stood well clear. The log turned as it approached Belmy's log; and the rocket turned in counterposition, and the log's sluggish motion slowed, slowed, stopped.

Booce dove into the cabin. He knocked the plug loose from the flow port and jumped away. Warm water globules followed him out. "I've spilled the water. Debby, hose down the firebox. We're in place."

The firebox hissed. Globed in invisible water vapor, the coals went out immediately. The gap between the two logs remained constant.

"And *that* was a nominal docking," Booce said in satisfaction.

Carlot and Rather came around the curve of bark. Booce called to them. "Well done, my crew! I'm crossing to *Woodsman* to see what Hilar wants. Carlot, why don't you show these people the Market?"

Carlot reached him well ahead of Rather. "Speak to you in private?"

They flew clear of the others. Booce asked, "Have you been making decisions?"

She nodded, jerkily. "Raff probably expects to see me."

"Then you decide whether to take him along. Will Rather behave himself?"

She hesitated. "It's not a good idea."

"I'll make your excuses to Raff. Blame everything on me."

Clave and Debby followed Carlot. Rather hung back a little. Flying too close to Carlot would be uncomfortable now.

They passed close to *Woodsman*. It was Rather's first good look at Raff Belmy. He was dark-haired and tall, three meters or close to it, with long arms, long symmetrical legs, stiff black hair, and a short beard. His neck was like his father's: long and graceful, but the lines of muscle showed strongly. If you liked tall, Raff was a good-looking man. He waved energetically as they flew past, then ducked into a cabin. There must have been hasty conversation in there. When Raff Belmy emerged he did not follow them.

"I'd have liked to talk to Jeffer first," Clave said softly.

"Let him wonder," Debby answered. "We'll have plenty to tell him when we get the chance."

They passed the Belmy log, and the Market was huge in their sight.

The wheel was ten to twelve klomters in diameter, and a hundred meters broad. The inner surface was partly covered with . . . houses? They surely weren't proper huts. They glowed with color. Most were cubes and oblongs, but there were other, stranger shapes: a faceted hemisphere, a wooden cylinder, a larger cylinder as transparent as the carm's bow window.

Carlot shouted back at them as they flew. "We learn all about the Market in school. It started out as a beam carved along the entire length of a log, three hundred years ago. The Admiralty ran it through a pond to soak it. Then they used tethers to bend it in a circle. Before that, the Market was only shops tethered together."

This tremendous made thing . . . this was wealth. Rather felt the fear and the awe of any savage approaching a civilized city.

People were flying to meet them.

"The older shops are funny shapes. Balls and geodesics. That glass cylinder is the Vivarium. Vance Limited grows earthlife there." Carlot noticed that all three of her charges were dropping behind. She turned in a half-circle and rejoined them. "Are you all right? Tired?"

Rather answered for the others. "It's a little frightening. Who are those people?"

"Friends. Traders. I'll introduce you. Raym! Crew, this is Raym Wilby—"

He was an older man, a jungle giant with pale skin and dark, curly hair and beard. He shouted at the sight of Carlot, bounced into her a little too hard, and wrapped her in his arms. As he examined her companions the wide, goofy smile was lost to a look of comical amazement. "Carlot? Shorts?"

She rebuked him. "Raym, these are some of the citizens who saved our lives when our tree caught fire. Hey, John, hey, Nurse!" Others were arriving. Carlot squirmed loose; clasped hands or toes; chattered introductions. John and Nurse Lockheed were brother and sister, and looked it, with angular faces (shaved, in John's case) and white-blond hair. Long-headed Grag Maglicco was in the Navy as a Spacer First. Adjeness Swart was small for a jungle giant. Her hair was black and straight, her nose curved and sharp. She worked in the Vivarium, Carlot said.

Half a dozen others reached them and Rather started to lose track. Raym would be thirty to forty years old; Grag would be a little younger. The rest were around Carlot's age. Jungle giants all, and expert flyers.

Carlot told her tale as they flew toward the Market. Other strangers joined them and she had to start over. Now there were a dozen jungle giants among them, and all were strangers to all but Carlot. She stuck to her father's story, and made no mention of Wart or carm or silver suit.

The citizens were uncharacteristically quiet. There was too much to see, and they were surrounded by as many strangers as there were adults in Citizens' Tree.

Debby was finally ready to admit that it had been a mistake. She wanted to go home.

She hadn't been with Anthon in hundreds of days. Booce was afraid of his wife, Jeffer seemed to be married to the carm, and Clave . . . the best she could tell, Clave was vastly enjoying his vacation from his wives. She was in a sexual desert.

She had other reasons for being on edge. The Market covered a quarter of the sky. No bigger than a small tree, it was obtrusively a *made* thing, made by the ancestors of this crew.

They didn't look that powerful. They flew a little closer together than Debby found comfortable. Easy to guess why: they'd been flying all their lives. Raym Wilby was chattering to Rather. "The bugeyes, they get whistling drunk when the fringe blooms. You just reach out and pop 'em in a bag—" Debby tried to follow it, but she couldn't. The Lockheeds stayed together, off to one side. Maybe they were shy?

Adjeness Swart flew alongside Debby. Cheerfully she called, "How do you like the Market?"

"Impressive."

"Your first visit to civilization?"

"We like to think we've got a civilization too," Debby said. *We must be gawking like fools.*

Adjeness laughed and waved around her. They had passed the rim of the Market and were crossing the central gap. "If you've got anything like this, the Admiralty would like to know it." And as Debby was throttling the urge to tell this smug Clump dweller about the carm, Adjeness asked, "How much can you see of the Admiralty from your tree? Why haven't any of you come here before?"

"Some didn't want us to come at all. We didn't know what we'd find. Maybe things we wouldn't like. Excuse me." Debby kicked hard to reach Carlot.

Chattering companions surrounded Carlot. Debby tried to ease inconspicuously among them, just to listen . . . but she hadn't counted on Admiralty manners. The locals drifted away from Debby and Carlot and left them to talk.

Carlot looked at her questioningly. Debby said, "I'm afraid I'll say too much."

"Adjeness?"

"Yeah. It isn't just the questions, it's her treefeeding superior attitude. Carlot, I feel so *small.*"

"Can't help you there, but . . . go fly next to Raym. He won't let you talk at all." Carlot held her voice low. "Raym Wilby is an old Dark diver. It's gotten to his brain."

"What's he doing with us?"

"He's an old friend of Mother's. I'd hate to have her see him now! I could get rid of him, but it's more trouble than it's worth. Either I'd hurt his feelings or it'd take forever."

"Stet. What's a Dark diver?"

"Ask him. Or just listen."

Debby dropped back. Raym was telling Rather, "It isn't the dark that bothers you, it's the thick. Your eyes get used to the light in there. It's kind of gray, and the colors bleach out. I never heard of a diver getting wrecked unless he was a damn fool, because things don't move fast in there. But you can't move fast either. You drift. Sometimes you get lost, you forget which way is out. You come out never knowing how many days you were in."

Rather asked, "Why do you——?"

"Credit. On a bad trip you only come out with mud, but Zakry pays high for mud. A good trip, you can come out with your hull covered with blackbrain or walnut-cushion or fringe." Raym grinned, and Debby realized what it was that bothered her about Adjeness's toothy smile.

Rather said, "This makes you——"

"No. You never hold on to it."

"——Rich?"

Teeth. Raym was an older man, yet he still had half his teeth. Adjeness must be Debby's age, but her smile was all teeth, with only three or four gaps. The rest were youths: no teeth missing at all.

Angular huts surrounded her. Debby fought vertigo. Down in all directions; no tide. The Admiralty crew were forming a line as Carlot led them toward a huge transparent cylinder. They had flown all their lives. Their grace made Debby feel clumsy.

Debby eased into line behind Rather. The starstuff cylinder had an opening at one end. Debby brushed it with her wings as she went through. None of the others did.

Chapter Fifteen

HALF HAND'S

from the Citizens' Tree cassettes, year 80 SM:

We've found a fungus with important medicinal properties . . .

W*oodsman's* door had been braced hospitably open. A guest need only grip the rounded edge as he flew past, set his wings in the racks, and swing himself in. Booce entered an atmosphere rich with blackbrain tea.

Jonveev Belmy was a small woman, not much more than Clave's height. Booce had watched her auburn hair turn gray over the years, but it was still long and thick. She was busy at a turning cookglobe. She stretched a foot to meet Booce's hand.

Her grip was strong. "Booce, I'm so sorry about Wend. Is Ryllin all right?"

"She's fine, Jonveev. We're doing business with Citizens' Tree, and that's where she is now." He wondered what Jonveev was thinking. Her concern was real, of course; but she had never dealt with Booce himself. In business matters Ryllin and Jonveev did the talking.

Jonveev swung the big globular teapot round her head to settle the water, then quickly opened the spigot. Steam puffed. Hilar wrapped the teapot in cloth and passed it to Booce. "I never saw a log come home like that. Do you want to talk about it?"

Booce sipped and swallowed. He liked his tea hot, and this was just off the boil. He savored old memories as much as the powerful, bitter taste. He said, "Not a lot—"

Hilar waved it off. "Oh, then we'll—"

"I have no wish to drive you crazy at this time."

"Tell us a story," Jonveev said.

He told it long. Carelessness and bad luck; the fire; Wend dead, Karilly mute with shock. "There was a tuft tribe waiting to rescue us. They helped rebuild *Logbearer*. We found a tree." Booce hesitated. "We were only half a thousand klomters from the Clump, Hilar, and we might've had to go halfway to Gold to find a better choice. It was big and it was close and we wanted to go home."

"I never saw termites on a tree before."

"A new breed, maybe. They're dying now. They haven't done that much damage, and it's a lot of wood."

"That it is. We have a problem," Jonveev said.

The tea had come round again. Booce sipped and passed it on. "I notice you managed to sell some of your wood."

"Some. Then the whole Market saw you coming and the orders dried up. I could have sold at a loss, but Jonveev thought—"

"I thought we might reach an agreement," she said. "The merchants can't whiplash us if one of us announces that his wood isn't for sale."

Booce smiled. Such things had been done. "We'd have to give them time to believe we mean it. Thirty sleeps or so. That'll cost one of us."

"We're willing," Jonveev said. "We'll want something in return, of course."

"Speak further." He sipped. The bitter taste of blackbrain fungus was the taste of civilization and hospitality and homecoming. He wished with all his heart that Ryllin were here. If Hilar was tiptoeing round the edges of a risky venture, Ryllin would have known at once.

Jonveev said, "Booce, we'll agree not to sell our tree until the next midyear. What I want is a loan at reasonable interest. Or I'll offer you the same deal."

Booce was silent.

"The loan would be, say, ten-to-fourth chits. Enough to keep one of us going for nearly a year." She affected not to notice Booce's sudden mirthless smile.

"I don't have that much on hand. And you, I suspect, don't need that much—"

"We'd need it if we don't want to shortchange some of our other concerns. But we can float such a loan and recoup it by selling our wood. On the other hand, whatever you're doing with . . . what was it, Citizens' Tree? It's bound to bring you money, but not soon, stet? But you have a house that's never been lived in."

The tea caught in his throat. Booce swallowed carefully, managed not to sputter. He said, "Ryllin would wring my neck."

"Well, then, you can't do it," Jonveev said instantly.

On second thought . . . he could put the house up for sale, to buy time. If he set the price high, buyers would hang back and wait, because the Serjents were supposed to be broke. If the Navy bought the Wart metal soon enough . . . he'd have to take a lower price, but he'd be able to keep the house.

But what did the Belmys have in mind? What would a loan do for them? It would be eating interest—"What interest?"

"We'd pay fifteen percent until the next midyear, or take the same."

That was high but not out of line. His first niggling suspicion began to look like the truth. "I'll sleep on it," he said.

Wickerwork ran around the inside of the glass bottle and across the center; wickerwork everywhere, but you had to look twice to see it beneath the plants and mud. The mud was at the interstices, held in place by nets. Plants grew from the mud, bearing red and yellow spheres and cylinders. Leafy vines strangled the wickerwork, the mud, and everything else in sight.

It was a jungle with curving corridors through it. Debby felt a sudden terrible homesickness for Carther States . . . but the jungle of her childhood was drab compared to the Vivarium.

The old man who watched from within one of the openings was an elderly, undersized jungle giant. In the humid warmth he wore only a loose pair of short pants. His knees and elbows were knobby; his skin was yellow-brown, and there was something funny about his eyes. He watched the growing crowd in some surprise. He said, "Late, Adjeness."

"Zakry, these are customers," Adjeness Swart said firmly. "They've been living without earthlife since Checker knows when."

"*Have* they." The yellow man brightened. "Well, we can't have that. Carlot Serjent, how good to see you! Adjeness, why don't you show the crew what they've been missing?"

Carlot and the yellow man disappeared into the greenery. Adjeness Swart said, "Clave told me that. No earthlife crops. Is it true?"

"Almost," Debby said. "We've got turkeys."

Raym Wilby guffawed. Adjeness was suppressing a laugh. "Turkeys, stet. Try this." She reached into a jungle of vines and plucked forth a red sphere. She sliced it apart with her knife and offered wedges around.

It was juicy. Its taste was strong. Debby chewed and swallowed, trying to decide if she liked it.

Rather plucked a slender yellow spike from the muck. Adjeness intervened. "Not that, Rather. You have to cook that. Try this. Don't eat the skin." The sphere Adjeness sliced up for him was orange outside and in. Rather bit into a wedge, and his eyes got big.

Being back on Earth would be like this, Debby thought. Alien. She recognized almost nothing.

There were people darting among the plants. They glanced incuriously at the intruders, then went back to what they were doing. Some sprayed water at the mud globules or the plants themselves. One was pushing a plant ahead of him; muddy pale appendages waved naked at one end. An older man floated slowly along an aisle, turning as he flew, to see in all directions.

Debby tried a slice of the orange sphere. The sweetness, the wonder of it almost paralyzed her. "Treefodder!"

"That's an orange. This—"

"I can see that." Debby reached at random. "What's this, a yellow?"

"Plum. Not quite ripe."

It was bitter, sour. Adjeness gave her a dark-red spheroid from another part of the plant cluster. "This should be better."

It was.

"You wouldn't want to spend all your funds on fruit," Adjeness said. "You'll want legumes too, but they have to be cooked. Let Carlot take you to Half Hand's Steak House before you make any final decisions. Unless you're really rich? Then you can buy everything."

Clave said, "I'm not sure what we can afford. I haven't heard any prices."

Adjeness nodded. "Here. Eat everything but the center, and you can eat that if you want to. Apple."

Rather asked, "Clave, did you eat like this in Quinn Tuft?"

"No. Hey, corn! We had corn before the drought. Here. Strip off the leaves. Now the silk too." He smiled, watching Rather bite into it. "Just the outside, and it's supposed to be cooked."

"It's okay this way. Leave the white stuff?"

"Stet."

Raym's hand sneaked into a bush as if without Raym's knowledge. Three red objects each the size of his thumb went into his mouth all at once. Debby was nearly sure Adjeness had caught it. She only smiled.

Carlot and the slant-eyed man emerged from a leafy wall. Carlot's voice was just slightly ragged. "Crew, Zakry Bowles is our host here. We'll go look at the prices after we know some of what we want. How are you doing?"

"Carlot, it's wonderful!" Rather burst out. "Oranges, plums, I think we want everything in sight. Zakry, can you eat everything here?"

"Almost. Every plant has something you can eat growing on it some of the time. These potatoes, you can't eat what you see. The root's down there in the mud. You don't eat the inside of an ear of corn—"

"Clave told me."

"Or the pit of a plum."

"Oop."

"What did you do, swallow it? It'll come out all right in the end. Let me show you what else we've got—"

Bean vines grew mixed with the corn. They seemed to want to take over everything. "We stopped growing tobacco long ago," Adjeness said. "Only the officers had fire handy, and they weren't buying enough. This is lettuce." Lettuce was leaves. It wasn't as sweet as foliage. Strawberries were as startlingly good as oranges. Squash looked like jet pods. Zakry was enjoying himself.

They went back to the entrance to examine a list of prices. Clave memorized the numbers he was interested in. "Why so much for strawberries and bananas?"

"Strawberries keep dying. I don't have bananas. Can't grow them here at all. They need tide. The Navy buys them off some tree dwellers east of here, when they get the chance. Clave, you haven't established credit yet—"

"Credit?"

Zakry Bowles spoke slowly, enunciating. "You haven't shown that you can pay. But you can pick out what you want now, then come back later, pay me and collect it."

"What we want is stuff we can grow in a tree."

They discussed that at length. Rather joined in; there were things he would not go home without. Debby eased over to Carlot. "What's got you upset?"

"He won't give me credit. We came in with a pod for our cabin and the Belmy log already in dock. Well, Dave Kon owes me money. I'll go see him. Excuse me."

Zakry was urging something else on them: a greenish-yellow fruit with an obscene shape. He showed Debby how to remove the peel. Clave laughed when Debby bit into it, but it was good. Carlot was talking to the Lockheeds, and they were nodding.

She came back. "I have to talk to Dave Kon. You'd be bored—"

"You're leaving us?"

"Stet. Stay with the Lockheeds. I'll meet you at Half Hand's Steak House."

Half Hand's was across the Market.

They flew through rain. Droplets flew from the edges of their wings. Rather breathed through his nose; from time to time he snorted out water. Debby and Clave were doing the same. The locals had donned masks of gauzy fabric, except for Raym, who breathed in the rain as if he cared not at all.

Half Hand's was a faceted dome adjoining a smaller, less symmetrical structure. You could see through some of the facets on the big dome: they were starstuff fabric. The rest was gray concrete. One six-sided facet had been cut away, and a wooden door hinged into the opening.

Grag Maglicco, the Navy man, suddenly asked, "Have we all got sticks?" He assessed the blank looks correctly. "Go on in. I'll join you, couple of breaths." He swerved aside, headed for an angular hut twenty meters along the wheel.

The inside was concrete too: concrete troweled over a structure of starstuff, outside and in. The concrete bore paintings of intriguing complexity and a variety of styles, but Rather caught only glimpses of these through a wall of citizens.

Half Hand's was full. Men, women, and children made a hemispherical shell around the newcomers, their toes clinging to two-meter poles protruding from the concrete. There were no foothold poles in the windows, so those stayed clear.

From an open hexagon on the far side drifted smoke and cooking odors. Nurse Lockheed led them that way. She called through the opening. "Half Hand?"

A man came out of the crowd behind her. "Hi, Nurse. You got money?"

"No. Put it on the Serjents' tab. I have a party of eight."

There was nothing wrong with Half Hand's hands. He was a jungle giant, mostly bald, and his arms and legs were corded with muscle. He said, "Serjents? I heard—" Full stop. "Sure, I'll give the Serjents credit. What do you want?"

"Let's see the kitchen."

"Nobody sees the kitchen." Half Hand was peering past Nurse Lockheed. "Shorts?"

"Tree dwellers. They've never seen anything like your kitchen."

"Nobody sees the kitchen."

"I did," Nurse said.

Debby pushed her way forward. "Half Hand? I'm Debby Citizen—"

"Pleasure," he said gravely.

"I wonder if you'd be interested in a description of a kitchen in a tuft."

Half Hand studied her; nodded. "Just you. Nurse, the special's moby."

"How old?"

"Eight days ago, shipful of Dark divers took a moby. Special is moby till we run out. Sausage cost you three times as much. No turkey today."

"We want vegetables, lots, all kinds. Couple of kigrams of moby too, not too rare."

"Moby's ready now. Vegetables soon. You, Debby, you cooked in that tree?"

"Some."

Half Hand beckoned her in.

Rather could feel the eyes. With a conscious effort he *looked*. Of the forty or so diners, only a dozen or so were watching what was happening at the kitchen entrance. Even those concentrated more on eating: their right hands kept pale wooden sticks in constant motion. The eye-pressure still made him flinch.

Grag Maglicco rejoined them. He passed out pairs of sticks of pale wood, no bigger than the branchlets a tree dweller was used to.

A woman brought them a two-kigram slab of meat, black on one side, pink on the other. John Lockheed took it on his knife. He flapped toward the wall, pushing the meat ahead of him. Diners edged aside to give him room or to avoid getting grease on their clothing.

Nurse had to urge them. "Come on."

There were too many people.

But Clave followed Nurse, and Rather followed him.

There was room. Nurse talked to some of the locals around them. John carved chunks from the meat and passed them, knife to sticks. Moby meat was *good*. Tenderer than swordbird, richer than turkey.

Grag's own sticks—like every Clump citizen's—were ornately carved. Some were wood, more were bone. Grag caught Rather looking. He showed Rather his own bone sticks. "You carve them yourself. Circle would mean I'm married. Spiral means I'm looking. A bird would say who I work for.

Outline around the bird would mean I own the company. What I've got is the rocket, 'cause I'm Navy. You'd want a honey hornet, for Serjent Logging. Change lifestyle, start new sticks."

John Lockheed pointed out a clump of customers to Clave. Tall men and women, a dozen or so, and a few infants; isolated, clustered close as if for protection. Peculiar footgear, thick-heeled sandals with toes protruding. "They're happyfeet. Half Hand should make them check those shoes at the door," John said. "They're for fighting, for kicking."

"Lupoffs?"

"Yes. Why?"

"No reason," Clave said.

Gourds of red liquid passed among the diners. One came within reach, and John took it. He drank, then passed it to Clave. "Fringe tea. Don't take too much."

It went from Clave to Rather. Its taste was bitter and sweet, not unpleasant. John stopped Rather from passing the gourd to Raym. "Too much in his blood already." Raym grinned and nodded.

Debby and Half Hand joined them; they made room. Debby said, "He's got four citizens doing the cooking, all women. There's a major fire against the back wall, held in by sikenwire. The kitchen's got maybe twenty windows in it, and Half Hand closes some of them to get the breeze he wants, keep the fire going and the smoke out. He's roasting a slab of moby the size of two men. It's black on one side and raw on the other, and he slices off the charred side.

"There's also . . ." She waved a hand and a foot as if trying to describe without words. "I thought it was a ball of hard stuff like the Vivarium. Inside, a froth of water and live steam, and cut-up plants."

"It's a bag," Half Hand said. "Keep it turning, the vegetables cook even. Draining the water is the tricky part."

"I saw them do that. They open the bag and throw the whole glob of cookwater at the lee windows and catch the vegetables in a net."

"Ho! Vegetables are ready then." In fact three jungle-giant women were already flying around the dome's curvature, passing out what they carried.

"We use an open pot," Debby told Half Hand. "Tide keeps it in, whatever you're cooking. We cook meat and vegetables together. If you don't keep stirring it, it all bubbles out."

"M'shell!" Half Hand waved one long-toed foot in a half circle, and the nearest of the kitchen women came toward them. She served red and yellow and green vegetables into small-mouthed bowls. Half Hand said,

"We serve only earthlife plants. A man wants foliage, he gets it at home. Meat's different. We take what we get. Nothing turns up, Sanchiss has a turkey farm Darkward."

The vegetables: some were good and some were not, and some you couldn't decide right away. Clave was making notes as he ate. Food that wasn't eaten went into a wooden barrel. From time to time one of the women replaced the barrel.

Grag Maglicco was asking Debby, "Has Booce been wondering where his house is?"

"He hasn't done anything about it yet."

"Well, we saw Serjent House a few days ago. It was twenty degrees spinward of the Market and maybe fifteen klomters skyward. Doesn't look like anyone's disturbed it. Can you remember to tell him?"

"Stet. Tell me something else?"

"Sure."

Debby waved around her. "I'm surrounded by teeth. How can so many of you keep most of your teeth?"

Grag fished in his tunic and produced a stick like a third eating stick, carved in the same way, with a tuft of bristly vegetable matter at the end. "Scrape your teeth after you eat," he said, and grinned at the tree dwellers' dubious looks.

Another gourd of fringe tea came past. Rather was thirsty; but nobody was taking more than a mouthful, and he didn't either. He passed it to Grag, who drank deeply and sent it on.

"Why do they call you Half Hand?" Debby asked.

"My great-square grandfather was Half Hand. Stuff that moved the old carm sprang a leak, froze his hand. Grandfather was Half Hand too. Got bit while he was Dark hunting. Now me. Soon or late, I lose it." The idea didn't seem to bother him. "Raym, sell me some walnut-cushion?"

"Not this trip. Next time."

"I need it. Goes good with potatoes. Green beans too."

"Next time for sure," Raym promised.

Nurse Lockheed laughed and said, "He can't. He doesn't have a ship."

Carlot was shocked. "Raym? You lost your *ship*?"

Raym nodded without looking at her.

Half Hand quietly moved off toward the kitchen. Nurse reached out and lifted Raym's chin. "Tell them the story, Raym!"

It was the last thing Raym Wilby wanted. Some of the locals were looking embarrassed. Clave was quick enough to catch it. "If it's story time, I'll tell you about the breakup of Dalton-Quinn Tree."

Raym's ship was forgotten as Clave talked.

Rather knew the tale too well. What he noticed was the rise in the noise level. Half Hand's was turning boisterous. Clave's words were just perceptibly slurred, as if he were sleepy; yet he was animated, frenetic, as he relived what had been the end of the world for him and for Rather's parents. Rather himself was feeling strange.

Half Hand was back. "Look out the window or go outside," he said. "See something."

"Water," Rather said clearly.

"What?"

"Water, not fringe tea. Does something to my head."

"Oh. Get you water, stet. *M'shell!* I'll fix it. Tree dwellers shouldn't drink too much fringe. Get to a window, boy. Thank me later."

The nearest window was crowded, but Rather managed to get his head into the grouping. He watched three kitchen women carry garbage barrels outside and fling their contents across the sky. Nothing happened for a time. Rather continued to watch. He felt as if he were dreaming. Fringe?

He dreamed that triunes abruptly converged from all directions, splitting into individuals as they came. Rather shouted: not a warning, just an incoherent yell.

The women heard. They looked at him in the window and laughed. Slender blue-and-orange torpedos dove among them. The wind of their passage sent them tumbling. In twenty breaths it was over. The triunes moved away, regathering their families. The garbage had vanished. The women kicked to stop their spinning—and not one had been touched by the predator birds.

All the strangers around Rather were laughing at him.

The only good thing about it (he decided as he returned to his pole) was that nobody else had gone to a window. Grag and Debby seemed mostly interested in each other, but the rest were held spellbound by Clave's storytelling. He spoke of the foray into the Carther States jungle—

He was on the verge of describing the London Tree carm! "Clave?"

"Me, I didn't notice most of this, what with my broken leg. Yeah?"

"Drink some water. This fringe is strong."

John Lockheed said, "Yes, you're not used to it," and passed Clave the water gourd. Clave drank, and drank again. Rather was given a gourd, and he couldn't understand how he had become so thirsty.

Then Carlot was there and it was all right, and Rather was free to go to sleep.

———

Kendy saw them streaming toward the log like a covey of brightly colored birds: young men and women stretched like taffy. Wings patterned in primary colors flapped behind, making them seem even longer. Each pattern was different. Birds must find each other in the sky.

The helmet microphone picked up giggling and snatches of talk. Some flew with skewed clumsiness, drunk on alcohol or other recreational chemicals. Kendy ran the record again, but the noise factor was too great; the words wouldn't come clear.

They passed out of the helmet's view and were gone.

Chapter Sixteen

HIGH FINANCE

from the Citizens' Tree cassettes, year 926 State:

CHECKER
*Officer responsible for the attitudes and emotional well-being of the
citizenry, and for their benign relationship to the State.*

Booce started tea when he saw them coming. He looked them over
as they entered. Nurse Lockheed had the giggles. Her brother was
furious.

Booce smiled at them. "Half Hand's?"

"Right. Fringe tea." Carlot wasn't happy.

"It was strange," Debby said. "We ate . . . well, we tried everything.
Clave made a list—"

"I hope we can afford it all," Clave said. "Where'll we grow it? We'll
have to plant the out tuft and make the lift cables twice as long."

The teapot went among the half-dozen Clumpers who had returned
with *Logbearer*'s crew. In a dozen breaths it was empty.

"Jonveev was kind enough to lend me some stuff," Booce said. "The
teapot, some blackbrain, some cookware. Carlot . . ." He frowned. She
should have brought supplies from the Vivarium and the Market shops.

She handed him a translucent blanket-leaf folded lengthwise. There
was food within: vegetables, a slab of cold moby meat, and a baked sweet
potato. "Half Hand gave us credit."

"That'll be breakfast. Jonveev fed me."

John Lockheed sensed what was happening. "Many thanks, Booce, and we'd best be going."

Raym showed his astonishment. "We just got here!"

"Raym, *now*. Come on, Nurse. Booce, we're sorry about your trouble, but it didn't ruin a good evening. It's good to see you back safe. Carlot—" He stretched his toes to clasp hers. Then the whole covey of Clumpers moved out into the rain, shooing Raym and Nurse ahead of them.

"Now why did they do that?" Clave asked.

"They know we have to talk about money. You don't do that in front of strangers," Booce said. "All right, Carlot."

"Zakry won't give me credit. We'll have to forage the trunk for food. I went to Dave Kon. He still owes for a klomter of wood from our last trip. He wouldn't pay me. He offered full payment if we'd sell him a klomter off the new log at two times ten-square. I turned him down."

"Right. That mutineer thinks we can't afford to hire a judgment! See, Clave, the Admiralty won't convene a civil court unless both sides can prove that they can pay court costs. Loser pays. But the Navy knows we have the Wart! One way or another, we'll get money or credit. Carlot, I think I know what Hilar has in mind. Burl."

Carlot thought it over. The tree dwellers watched with no sign of comprehension. She said, "Risky. Nobody knows how."

"Hilar can afford to take the chance. He brought his tree in with the tuft still on. He asked for a loan and offered decent terms. Usually the tree dies, but sometimes—"

Debby suddenly said, "I remember. The idea is to let a tree grow without tide. The wood's supposed to twist into knots?"

"Right. But trees aren't really built for that. I wonder if Hilar knows something? If he can get money to live on, he can grow his burl while we sell our wood. He'd like to get the money from us, if we had it."

"We should be asking Jeffer about this."

Booce grimaced. Then: "Sorry. Debby, you're tree dwellers, you *should* know a lot about them, but you've never seen a tree growing outside of tide."

"You wouldn't grow burl yourself, stet? Belmy's not a fool or he wouldn't be richer than you, stet?" Booce bridled, but Debby went on. "He knows something you don't, something about burl. Jeffer the Scientist knows a *lot* we don't. Let's ask."

"Burl," Jeffer said musingly, watching the faces in the bow window. Debby was hiding anxiety. Booce had asked his question with some belligerence. This had been her idea, not his. *Are you any good at all? Prove yourself, Scientist!*

Blue lines of print scrolled across the faces.

Integral trees grow well in a wide range of tides. Low atmospheric pressure kills them faster than low or high tide. In dense air and very low tide they might survive. In free fall they die. Otherwise we would find trees growing naturally in the Clump.

Booce was talking. "Hilar thinks he's got me by the seeds. He offered me a loan if I withdraw my tree from sale, but he's not serious. It'd break me. I'd be paying interest, and no way to get it back. Of course he doesn't know about the Wart metal."

"Do you really need to know if he can grow burl?" Jeffer said. "Booce, you're satisfied that he's *trying* it. You only need a short-term loan till you can sell your metal. The Belmys aren't your enemies, are they?"

"No, they're friends. Who would I talk to if I couldn't talk to other loggers? But Hilar would *love* to have me carving the dumbo on my sticks, and all the loggers want to be richer than, say, the architects. Jonveev won't loan me money unless she thinks I can pay it back. Or if I've got some kind of collateral . . . hell."

A tree should continue to grow if there is sufficient tide to pull water and nutriment into the treemouth and to work the internal veins within the trunk. Spin the log, Jeffer.

"Tell them about the Wart," Carlot was saying.

"I didn't want to. I guess . . . I've got to. It'd be better if I knew *exactly* what Hilar's planning."

"He'll spin the log," Jeffer said.

"What? What for?"

"Spin tide, Clave. It's a scientific thing. Here, pick up that pot or whatever and throw it round and round your head. Arm's length . . . like that, stet. Feel the pull? Like tide, isn't it? Belmy'll use his steam rocket to start the log spinning, not enough to tear it apart, just enough to keep some pull inside the tuft. The tree needs tide to move its food around—"

"By the State, I believe you're right."

"But the, uh, growth patterns would still be screwed up, with Voy going round and round and weird Clump tides going every which way. I've never seen burl, but isn't that what you want, Booce? Grain that doesn't

grow in straight lines? He'll spin it just enough to keep water and fertilizer in the treemouth."

"Yes. Okay."

Losing contact.

Hilar and Jonveev waited, wearing polite smiles, until Booce had finished talking. "Burl," Hilar said. "It sounds interesting but risky."

"Hardly cost-effective," Jonveev said.

Booce said, "There are other values. It would be indecently lucrative if it
worked. You'd have done something nobody else could." They did not comment, and he went on. "Let's assume, just for talking purposes, that you've
been considering a burl tree. Who else would you let in on the secret?"

The Belmys looked at each other.

"You'd need masses of tree food. Mud, say, from deep in the Dark.
Would you buy it from Zakry? Or haul it yourselves, with *Woodsman*?"

Jonveev sighed. "All right, Booce. What have you got in mind?"

"*Logbearer* could haul the mud to feed the tree. The whole Market
knows that my last trip failed. They won't be surprised when *Logbearer*
becomes a Dark diver. Let them think I'm looking for fringe and blackbrain while I haul mud for Zakry."

"Mmm," said Jonveev.

"One thing more. I've got eight kiltons of metal buried under the
termites."

Their faces were quite blank. After a moment Jonveev said, "That's not
portable money. You still can't offer us a loan, not until you sell it."

"An excellent point. Hilar, Jonveev, what I want is this. First, you do
your damnedest to turn that half tree into burl. Second, I need a loan—"

Hilar was laughing.

"A short-term loan to let me spend money like an old Dark diver while
I wait for the Navy to buy my metal. I'll pay twenty percent to the
crossyear, and I need ten-to-third chits. I'll pay part of it back in mud at
the same price Zakry pays. The rest at the crossyear, and I'll hand you
another five times ten-to-third. That'll save any project you had to shortchange. It's not a loan, though. It buys me half the burl."

"*Half!*" Jonveev exclaimed.

"So."

Caught! Jonveev Belmy laughed and said, "We hadn't thought of spinning the tree. But can you really afford to risk that many chits? You're
moderately rich now. Why not stay that way?"

"I like the odds. I've got some crew who think it might work, and they're tree dwellers. I think *you* think it'll work, and that helps."

"Two-fifths of any burl, and we want five times ten-to-third chits. We'll get you your loan, but at forty percent to the crossyear. Mmm . . . I'll hand you our cash on hand and give you the rest in ten days."

Booce said, "I'll pay thirty percent to . . . to ten sleeps past the crossyear. The Navy might just hold me up for that long. And classify this. If the Navy knows I took a loan, they'll know I'm still under pressure. I want them to *move*."

Hilar laughed. "Where else could it have come from?"

"I'll visit the house before I start throwing money around. They'll think I had it in the house."

And all of this was reported in garbled form, through Clave and then Jeffer, who had never dealt with finance, to Kendy, who never had either. But Kendy had sketchy records of the capitalistic societies that had died with the formation of the State, hundreds of years ago.

It was a hell of a way to run a civilization. These people *needed* him.

Jeffer, seated before the CARM camera, asked, "Do you understand any of this?"

"Yes, but it would be difficult to explain. What matters is that your citizens will have their earthlife seeds."

"Yeah." Jeffer stretched unself-consciously. "That's good. We'll have to talk fast when we get back to Citizens' Tree. The seeds'll help, and we'll carry fresh food too, something they can eat right then. Are you getting what you wanted?"

What Kendy wanted was still beyond his reach. He said, "I've learned some things."

"Tell me."

"The Admiralty is self-sufficient. They're a successful culture, but the crime rate must be high. Otherwise they would need fewer Navy ships, and the houses would have more openings." Kendy displayed the picture the pressure-suit camera was sending from the Clump. Small green outlines flickered as Kendy pointed out ships, then the few but massive doors on nearby houses. "They've settled the outer shell of the Clump, but they only venture gingerly into the dark center. Their infant mortality rate must be as bad as yours. When they add up their population they don't count children, any more than you do."

"I never noticed that. Hmm . . . London Tree didn't either. Is it because so many children die?"

"Yes. Wait a thousand years and the death rate will have diminished. There's nothing else to be done."

"I never thought there was. While I've got your attention, Kendy, I found a listing on the Clump. Lagrange points, it's called. What do these words mean? Equipotential, saprophyte— Something's happening."

A steam rocket emerged from the fog and rain. It came to a halt fifty meters from the helmet camera. "Navy," Jeffer said unnecessarily. "I wonder . . . that's Booce. And a silver suit!"

"I see them. An equipotential is the curve on which some force or energy level is everywhere equal. It might be gravity or tidal force or magnetic force. A saprophyte is a family of plants that don't use light. We'll see some if Clave can take the helmet into the Dark."

Four men flew toward the camera: two in Navy armor, one standard-issue pressure suit, and Booce Serjent. The pressure suit was better kept, cleaner and shinier, than the Citizens' Tree suit. There were big Navy-style fins at the ankles. The design painted on the back was repeated on one shoulder and on the fins: a broad green ring with a blue dot at the center.

Kendy tried to make contact with the suit radio. He found nothing. Either it wasn't on, or the frequency had wandered over the centuries.

The helmet was thrown back on its hinge despite the rain. The face inside was a rounded Anglo face, without the soft elfin look of most Smoke Ring citizens: a "dwarf" face, shaved, sprouting an Earth day's worth of dark shadow.

The "dwarf" looked around him. "This was clever, Booce. Do you have torches?"

"I'm sorry, Captain-Guardian. We can make some up."

"No need. How do I get through this muck?" The dwarf had no accent.

Kendy gloated. No accent! He spoke exactly as a State citizen would have. The officers must learn their speech from the Admiralty Library!

They were drifting out of view. Kendy switched to the fish-eye lens. He and Jeffer watched the Captain-Guardian take his wings off and tether them to lines on his chest, shin-sticks uppermost. The two lower-rank Navy men pulled up an edge of the termite nest. The "dwarf" squirmed in. Sudden yellow light flashed through the hole.

Jeffer asked, "Does that light come from the pressure suit?"

"I'll show you how to work the helmet light. Later."

The "dwarf" popped out of the hole. "There's a respectable store of metal here. We'll have to wait for the Council to convene before we make an offer per kilton delivered. Unless you're prepared to accept an immediate offer of, say, two times ten-to-fifth chits for the whole chunk?"

"I can get two or three times that on the Market."

"Perhaps. If we come to an agreement I can give you payment within ten days."

"No, thank you, Captain-Guardian. I'll wait. Maybe I can earn some money Dark diving. Can I offer you tea?"

"You wouldn't want to have to sell your new house. Two and a half."

"No. I should point out that you've been seen coming here. There's a happyfeet jungle in dock, and they might guess what that means. Also I'll be expected to hire an exterminator. I can't hide the metal much longer."

The Captain-Guardian snorted and waved to his escort. They departed.

Booce waited until they were well away. Then he moved face-on to the camera. "Jeffer?"

"Here."

"That was Captain-Guardian Wayne Mickl. Officer by birth, but his effective rank is Guardian. Keeping him happy is a good idea."

"He didn't look happy."

"If he's too happy, we got robbed. Jeffer, how sure are you that spinning a tree will make burl?"

Jeffer laughed. "I never tried it myself."

"Yeah. Are you all right?"

"It isn't too bad. Something like being young again, just old enough to hunt alone. I've got the cassettes when I get bored. I miss Lawri."

"Well, I'm going to move the silver suit. We can't leave it here."

"Where, then?"

"My house. I'll set it up so you can see the commons room. We can talk any time, and when I have guests you'll see them too."

"That's good," said Jeffer.

Very good. Losing contact.

Chapter Seventeen
SERJENT HOUSE

from the Citizens' Tree cassettes, year 6 SM:

*Sharon Levoy speaks of the archetypal rebellious computer, HAL 9000, from Gillespie's opera **2001**. Carol Burnes claims **Frankenstein** and **Faust** to be older and more appropriate images. One-upmanship is alive and well in the Smoke Ring. One and all, they expect me to tell them **How It Happened**.*

For the record: I don't know what's wrong with Kendy.

—*Capability Jasper Gray*
Cyberneticist, **Discipline**

Debby was in a hurry the next morning. It seemed she'd arranged something at Half Hand's: she was to meet Grag Maglicco for flying lessons. Booce drilled her to make sure she wouldn't get lost in the sky, then sent her on her way.

The rest shared out the meal from Half Hand's for their breakfast, then got to work. They fueled and fired *Logbearer* and set it steaming along the trunk. A half turn brought the rocket to a halt opposite the Wart.

Clave, Carlot, and Rather swarmed out and attacked the termite nest with matchets. When *Logbearer* blocked the Market, and floating chaff and chips of bark and wood blocked most of the sky, Clave and Rather ducked into the nest. Clave retrieved the body of the silver suit, Rather the helmet. Booce had kept the rocket hot. He jetted water into it, and away they went.

Secrets. Rather was starting to get the knack of it.

Half the termite nest had been scraped away, not by a hired team but by amateurs. What would the Market think? *Booce must be hurting for money. His crew has exposed damage to the log: a gaping, ugly hole behind the termite nest. They've quit in disgust.* Unlikely that anyone else would pry into that bug-infested darkness.

The house had drifted about the sky since its completion a year and a half since. Debby had relayed Grag's message: it was fifteen klomters skyward and some degrees to spin from the Market. The house was closer than it had been when Grag spotted it, but it was still a three-day trip.

The house was five cubes arrayed around a concrete core. A small puff jungle grew on the roof. The main door was a huge slab of wood five meters long by four wide, half a meter thick. Booce set massive triangular braces to lock it vertical to the doorway. Mountings covered the inner surface: tethers for wings and cloaks, and coils of line, and big knobs to serve as moorings for winches and pulleys.

They tethered *Logbearer* to the door. In its shadow they moved the silver suit and helmet inside.

Secrets. What has been seen? Logbearer *flies to Serjent House. The crew stays for some hours while Booce inspects his new home and shows it off to visitors. Presently Booce will be spending money.*

Navy: *Booce has retrieved funds from some hiding place. He can outwait the Navy to sell his metal.*

Belmy House: *Booce came as misdirection.*

The Market: *Any hiding place in Booce's house must be empty now.*

"Where do we put it?" Rather held the helmet like a severed head.

"Look around," Booce said. "Something will occur to you."

The citizens smiled at each other. They began to tour the house.

Doorways led from one section to another through the star-shaped concrete core. There were only two ways to move. Rather had to squeeze past Clave circling the other way.

The house was roomy: as big as a Citizens' Tree hut, though much harder to build. The public room was lined with handholds and with hooks for outer garments and weapons, and a rack for a teapot.

The outer wall of the kitchen had long slots in it for ventilation, a concrete fireplace with a bellows attached, and racks for wood and cookware. Rather found Carlot making tea. He asked, "You already know?"

She nodded brightly.

The sleeproom: tethers and some wiry foliage padding four of the walls.

What was this next room? Curtains fixed across both interior doors, handholds and tethers mounted next to small windows with hatches over them . . .

Ah. This was the treemouth. And the fifth was a storage room, with another oversized door and moorings for tethers, but nothing stored yet.

Rather returned to the public room.

Debby was moving slowly around the perimeter. She seemed more cheerful than she had been lately. "Hi, Rather. Grag brought me back. I gather we're looking for some secret hiding place. Any luck?"

"Not yet. Booce, how do you get rid of the treefodder after you feed the tree?"

Booce stared. "*What?*—Oh. The wind floats it away and fisher jungles gather it in. Now you know why everyone doesn't just tether his house to the Market. Find anything?"

"I didn't see any hiding places. I've never seen a house before."

"You were all somewhere else, so I searched here," Debby said. "Nothing. Booce, are there holes in the concrete?"

Booce laughed. "I could have done that. Access through the walls? Well, any burglar could tear the core apart and all he'd find is concrete and two chunks of sporing fringe buried along the hub. Meanwhile, what do you think of my door?"

"Thick. Like you're afraid someone might kick his way through."

"We tend to make them massive. Not just for burglars. It has to stand up to rough treatment when you're moving heavy stuff."

Clave shook his head in disgust. "We'd know who our thief is. We'd kick him into the sky. Booce, your trouble is, you've got too many people in the Clump."

Booce was taken aback. "I never thought of it that way. Anyway, let me show you what I did—"

When the door was fully open, one could slide aside a panel in the edge that faced the hinges. The half-meter thickness of the wood had been hollowed out. The silver suit went in easily. The helmet was barely small enough.

"Now we need a hole," Booce said.

"Kendy for the State. Jeffer, would you rather sleep?"

"Mpf? No. Hello, Kendy." Jeffer stretched. "If I didn't want you waking me up I'd sleep outside." He looked at the view in the bow window. "Oho!"

It was dark, but Jeffer could make out Clave's anxious face. His voice sounded faint, distant. "Jeffer? Talk to me, Jeffer."

"Prikazyvat Relay to pressure suit. Scientist here."

"What do you see?"

"You. And a ragged border. What did you do?"

"You're looking through a hole in a door. Booce ripped a hook out. From here it looks like he just put too much tension on it."

"Good enough. I take it we can talk. Rather, you there?"

Rather floated into view, smiled, and waved. Others joined, until five citizens floated in a star with their heads inward.

Booce said, "I've made a deal with the Belmys. Jeffer, would you like to learn something about the Dark?"

"You mean the Clump interior? Sure."

"That's good, because I've agreed to bring back some mud for Belmy's burl tree."

"You're going? All of you? *Logbearer?*"

"Ah . . . no. I think I'd better stay here. I've been weaving financial threads into one very complicated net. Carlot, you can handle *Logbearer* alone, stet? And I gather Raym Wilby is at liberty. He can guide you." Carlot was nodding eagerly. "Oh, and Hilar hadn't thought of spinning the burl log, but he's going to try it."

"Sounds good. Carlot, will you take the helmet so I can see these marvels?"

Carlot looked to her father, who said, "Why not?"

"Good. Rather, tell me about the Navy. Take your time."

Rather talked. Kendy guessed that the boy wasn't hiding anything, but he kept jumping back and forth. Kendy printed questions across the bow window; Jeffer solicited descriptions of Petty Wheeler, Bosun Murphy, Navy armor, the Navy ship, Murphy's description of Navy life, Wheeler's offer . . .

"Is this standard, Booce? Anyone can join the Navy?"

"Not just anyone. They wouldn't have Carlot because of her legs. Otherwise . . . well, any savage could join, but he might not get beyond Spacer First until they've watched him for years. The Navy wants loyalty. They take more men than women, and they won't take you if you're too old to be trained."

"Loyalty?"

"If you're loyal to your tribe, you're not loyal to the Navy. Navy above all, even family."

"The question is, if Rather goes in, can he get out? Booce?"

Booce mulled it. "Up to a point. It would be . . . convenient if Rather let Petty Wheeler make his pitch. Rather, the Navy could put certain kinds of pressure on me until I talk you into doing that. They want the Wart, but they can slow things down for me, and we don't want the Navy taking a *hard* look at us."

"No," Clave said.

"But when Wheeler interviews you, he might learn that you're simply not suited to Navy life. I can help you to help him reach that conclusion."

Carlot said, "He could get out later than that. Rather, my cousin Grag says they treat you like a copsik in Basic, but after that you're supposed to think you're better than the citizens. They do think they're better than us, and they don't take just anyone. When you're ready to leave, just do something wrong. Or get sick and stay sick. Tree dwellers do get sick in the Clump. They'll bounce you out."

"You think I should do this?"

She shrugged unhappily. "Whatever you want."

Jeffer said, "I'd really like to get him into the Library."

Booce shook his head. "No dwarf gets beyond Guardian unless he was born an officer, and even then . . . well, Wayne Mickl is officer and dwarf. They need him as a Guardian, so he'll never *use* his higher rank. Guardian is the lowest rank that can reach the Library, but they can't use it because they aren't taught to read. And you wouldn't be a Guardian for years, Rather."

Jeffer jumped on it. "But he *could* reach the Library. And Rather *can* read, and I can teach him how to use a carm keyboard!"

Rather was feeling trapped. He knew how to talk to Jeffer the Scientist, but how could you argue with a door?

"I hate to pass up the chance," Clave said. "Rather, you're reluctant. How do the rest of you feel? Debby?"

"It feels like we're selling him as a copsik. I'm against it."

Thank you, Debby!

Clave stared at her. Then: "Rather, does it feel like that? I wouldn't *do* that. We're just talking now—"

"They want his loyalty, stet, Booce? They've been doing this for going on four hundred years," Debby said. "Maybe they can *get* his loyalty—"

Clave snapped, "Treefodder, Debby. London Tree was keeping copsiks for about that long. When the chance came to bust loose, they did it!"

"Not all of them, Clave!"

". . . Uh-huh. Booce?"

Booce said, "We're talking about power, Navy power, and it cuts two ways. If Rather was Navy, the Serjents would see a certain friendliness emerge. I'd love to put a son in the Navy."

"Carlot?"

She spoke to Rather, not Clave. "If you can stand it. Remember what I said about Basic. They worked Grag's tail off . . . hey. You're stronger than Grag. You lived in a tree. You just might give them a shock."

"We know you can fit a silver suit," Booce added. "Even Bosun Murphy doesn't know that."

"I'm scared."

Clave just nodded, but Jeffer snarled like static. "Oh, Rather! We're *here* already! Back in Citizens' Tree, that was the time to be scared." Pause. "What are you scared of?"

"It's all too strange." Rather was suddenly, unbearably homesick. This wooden house, all angles—

"It'll keep being strange. Nobody fooled you on that."

"Scientist, I came here *looking* for strange. I wouldn't *be* here if it was going to be just like Citizens' Tree—"

"Then—"

But Rather had the words straight in his mind now. "I followed you here, but the idea was to face the Admiralty in the company of my friends and my elders! And my father. Are we all going to join the Navy now? Is that what we're talking about?"

Clave said, "Jeffer?"

The door said, "I'm for it, of course, but the boy's got a point. It's his risk, not ours."

Rather wasn't finished. "You're asking me to swear to something that isn't true. I am *not* loyal to the Navy. If you thought I was, you wouldn't like it."

Nobody wanted to answer.

"You can feed your secrets to the tree. I will not join the Navy. But I can go talk to Wheeler, if you think it'll help. I'll do that."

"I go with him," Debby said firmly.

"And Booce, you tell me how to look unsuitable." A black depression was settling over him. He felt rejected by all of his companions save Debby; but Carlot wanted him out of the way. For Raff Belmy.

Chapter Eighteen
HEADQUARTERS

from the Citizens' Tree cassettes, year 384, day 2050:

Jeffer the Scientist speaking. Candidates are considered unsuitable for the Navy if they are sickly, or undependable, or easily lost or distracted, or loyal to some entity other than the Navy. They may have unacceptable motives for joining. If a family member accompanies, candidate may be reluctant or may need supervision.

Acceptable candidates would presumably have opposite traits. Data are as acquired from Booce and Carlot Serjent.

Headquarters was a pillbox: a short, wide cylinder, blurred to Rather's weeping eyes. The rim was dark wood. The nearer flat face was concrete covered with a variety of doors, platforms, winches, coils of line . . . and a broad strip of glittering stuff very like the hull of the carm. Two rockets were moored near the hub. A third, larger, was being winched in nozzle-foremost.

Debby looked back. Rather was far behind. When she stopped flapping, a gust of wind caught her wings and turned her on a random axis. She sighed and flapped back to rejoin him. "I wish I could help," she said.

Rather made himself laugh. "I did it to myself. Debby, you fly better than me."

"I watched the crew when we went to Market. Keep up a steady kick. Don't try too hard. If you kick with all your might the wings just bend and don't take you anywhere."

"What I need is longer legs."

"Longer *wings* might do it. Try the Navy wings too. Now, what door did Carlot say?"

"I can't tell. Pick one."

"No, I—"

"Debby, *pick one at random*. I don't *mind* if Wheeler thinks I got lost."

"Oh. The one in the middle, with the guards. We'll ask them."

It was big and round and rimmed in scarlet paint. The four guards wore helmets and torso and leg armor and carried harpoons. Debby back-pedaled to stop within a meter of the harpoon points. She said, "Looking to join up."

One smiled and said, "I hope they take you, beautiful." His harpoon pointed. "That one, just next to the rim."

"Thanks." She rejoined Rather. Half blind, he'd been afraid to fly close to sharp spears. "It's over there.—Lovely beard on that one. Like golden-wire plant, and *clean*. The crew keep themselves cleaner than Carther States people ever did. Maybe I'll see him again."

"Jeffer'd like that."

"He would, wouldn't he. He probably likes my seeing Grag too. I won-der what they're guarding?"

The door they sought was a rectangle with curved sides, marked in print along one edge: RECRUITMENT.

The room within was sizable, but of the same odd shape. A man made marks on thin white sheets fixed to a slab of sanded wood. His pants and tunic were blue with Navy markings. No armor. He ignored them for a bit, then looked around. "Yes?"

Rather pointed to the wooden rectangle. There were clips along the edge, and stacks of paper leaves in the clips. "What would you call that?"

The man frowned. "You never saw a desk before? What do you want?"

"Petty Mart Wheeler wants to interview me for recruitment. I'm Rather Citizen."

"I'll see if he's available." The man kicked against the table and disap-peared down a corridor. Lack of wings didn't hamper him: he touched the wall and disappeared into a doorway in one smooth flow.

Debby smiled at Rather. "Easily distracted?"

"That's why I did it, but look at how the grain of the wood curls around! I think it must be burl. How did they get it?"

"There had to be burl somewhere or Booce wouldn't know it was possible."

When the desk man reappeared, Rather was mopping at his eyes with his tunic. The man said, "Come with me."

Debby said, "May I come too?"

"I'm afraid not. Would you be his mother?"

"Stepmother. I really think I ought to be with him."

"That's not permitted."

The office was small, a cube with two curved walls. Petty Wheeler was at a desk, lightly gripping the rim while he talked to another man . . . and that one was Rather's height.

Their talk stopped. Wheeler said, "Rather, good to see you. This is Captain-Guardian Wayne Mickl."

Mickl nodded but said nothing. He seemed relaxed and disinterested. Wheeler said, "We want to ask you a few questions. You probably have questions too—"

"A hundred. Um, whereabouts is Bosun Murphy?"

"Mpf? Last I saw of her she was on her way to the Purser's office. After that she'll be on leave. . . . Why?"

"I thought I might see her before I go."

(Booce had told him, "Try to talk to Bosun Murphy. Your interest in the Navy comes straight from your seeds. If you see her, make a pass."

("What's a pass? Do you mean propose marriage?"

("No . . . yes. That's got just the right touch. All seeds and no judgment.")

Wheeler asked, "Rather, is there something wrong with your eyes?"

"They get this way sometimes."

"When?"

"Lack of sleep. Dry air." His eyes were clearing up now, but they still hurt. To Wheeler they must appear pink and weeping. He was sniffling too.

Wheeler took writing implement in hand. "Where were you born?"

"Citizens' Tree, year 370. It's a tree sixty klomters long, six or seven hundred klomters west of the Clump."

"What's your height and mass?"

"One point nine meters. I don't know my mass."

"We'll weigh you on the centrifuge. How did you know the year?"

"The Scientist keeps track. Was I off? This is 384, isn't it?"

"That's right. Put your arms straight forward, fingertips touching. Now your legs, big toes touching." Wheeler made a note. "Symmetrical. How much do you know about the Admiralty?"

"Not much. We tasted some of the food you grow and had a wild dinner at Half Hand's Steak House." Wheeler laughed at that. Rather went on, "The Serjents told us a lot. I've seen houses and the Market. The ride on the steam rocket was—well, I've never been through anything like it."

"Scary?"

"No, not that." He knew instantly that he should have said *yes*.

"Why do you want to join the Navy?"

"I came to find out if that was true, Petty. And you asked if I had questions."

Petty Wheeler stiffened a little. "Well?"

"I've seen the ships. They're all over the sky. I think I ought to ask, if I become a Navy man, will I in fact be riding one of those ships?"

"More than one, I expect. Over the years you'll fly every style."

"Will I be flying them, or just riding them?"

"You've given this a lot of thought."

"Yes sir. Once I thought I'd be a hunter for Citizens' Tree." No need to mention the silver suit. "When I joined Booce and went logging, that was a big jump. I didn't know what I'd find here. The Market, it's frightening to think such a thing could be *built*. So many people!"

Wheeler was smiling, nodding. (In the corner of Rather's eye, Wayne Mickl was clinging to a wall tether, merely observing.) "Daunting, is it?"

Rather nodded.

"The ships, the Market, Headquarters, we built them all. And more. We built a civilization," Wheeler said gently. "Now that you've seen it, how can you not be a part of it? Yes, you'll fly a ship before you're much older."

"I want to know whether I'll be able to visit Citizens' Tree."

"Mph. The answer's yes, but I don't know how often. We'll want to contact Citizens' Tree at once. Set up some form of trade. There'll be visits, and you'll be useful as an intermediate."

It was the right answer, Rather thought, except for two things. The tree was in the wrong place; and if the Navy did find it, the citizens would have to hide the carm every time the Navy came visiting.

So Rather only said, "That's good. I'd hate to be cut off from my family." (Booce had said, "They want your loyalty. They won't like it if you're loyal to your family, your tribe, *me*—")

"How often do you get these allergy attacks?"

"Usually just when the air's too thin. I had them while we were moving the log; we were too far in. It's like knives in my eyes. I haven't been getting enough sleep lately. It happens then too."

"Would you describe yourself as sickly?"

Rather told himself that nobody would come to a recruitment office if he considered himself sickly, and said, "No. It's just something that happens. A day later I'm fine. It's almost over now."

"I see. All right, Rather. Go ask Able Jacks to put you on the centrifuge. We'll get in touch with you through Booce Serjent."

Debby and the desk man were ignoring each other. Debby seemed nervous.

"Rather! How'd it go?"

"Fine. Are you Able Jacks?"

"That's right."

"You're to take me to the centrifuge. What's a centrifuge?"

"I'll show you."

The wicker structure resembled the treadmill that ran the elevator in Citizens' Tree. It was wider: twenty meters across. Rather was instructed to cling to the rim and wait. Two ratings spun it up, timing it with a handheld device. The wheel rolled eccentrically with his mass to throw it off. A rating measured the divergence of the hub. "Your mass is eighty-one kilograms," he said.

They locked the centrifuge in place and made him run.

Pushing himself round the rim gave him the sensation of tide. They had him run as fast as he could. It made him dizzy; the tide became fiercely strong. Then they made him slow down and run at a measured rate, until his legs burned and his eyes blurred. He would have stopped then if he had not noticed Bosun Murphy watching him.

He waved. The motion almost sent him tumbling. She didn't respond. But she watched, and he ran.

. . . It came to him that he was *rolling* around the centrifuge. He'd blacked out.

A rating snatched at his ankle and pulled him out. "Take a rest. Here." He handed Rather a towel, and Rather, gasping for air, mopped a sheath of water from his body.

Murphy said, "That was quite a performance. I could win bets on you."

"I grew up in a tree."

"I know."

There was no animation in her voice, her face, her body language. *Navy thinks they're superior,* Carlot had said; but that wasn't it. "Bosun, are you all right?"

"I'm a little down," she said. "Call me Sectry, Rather. I'm not on duty."

"Does *down* mean something like *miserable?*"

"Yeah. Guys, are you finished with him?"

"He's all yours, Bosun. No need to be careful, he ain't fragile."

Sectry Murphy flashed them a fleeting smile. To Rather she said, "I can't picture the Petty rejecting you after he hears about that performance."

Treefodder. Booce hadn't thought to tell him to hold back on a stamina test. "What's got you down?"

"Not here, stet? I need someone to talk to, not Navy. I just came from the Purser's and I'm ready to tie one on. Want to join me?"

"I'm with Debby. My stepmother."

"Stet. Let's go get her. How does Half Hand's sound?"

Rather was coming down the corridor. There was a woman with him.

Once upon a time Debby had seen Rather and Mark talking in the Citizens' Tree commons. Both dwarves, but they hadn't looked at all alike: Mark's face nearly square, Rather's nearly triangular . . . She remembered it now, because Rather and the dwarf woman looked *right* together, though they were clearly from different branches of humankind.

And both, in different fashions, looked worn out. Debby asked, "What happened to you?"

Rather said, "Centrifuge. They ran me to death. I could have lifted an elevator all the way to *Discipline.* Debby, you remember Sectry Murphy—"

Clasping toes felt odd: Sectry's reach was so short, her toes so stubby and *strong.* "Hello, Sectry. I take it you're off duty."

"Right. On our way to Half Hand's. Join us?"

"Sure."

Sectry led them in. "The place is nearly empty," she said.

It wasn't. There were a good dozen people scattered around Half Hand's. But windows were clear, and Sectry led them to one. "It's nice to have a view," she said over her shoulder.

Rather flinched. Debby grinned; she'd seen Rather watching Sectry's kicking legs.

"Grab a pole, someone will come. You hungry?" When one of the women from the kitchen appeared, Sectry said, "Fringe tea and sausages for three, Belind. You two should try the sausage."

"Stet," Rather said. "What's got you down?"

The false gaiety ran out of her, and Debby saw pain. "I've been trying on pressure suits. I don't fit."

Debby said nothing. Rather said nothing.

"They don't let you try the suit till you qualify for Guardian in all other respects. So they got me into the small one and I couldn't breathe." Murphy wasn't wearing armor now. Her breasts stretched her tunic tight. Debby had never had trouble feeding her children, but her own breasts didn't have that *vulnerable* look. "I could have faked it, but the suits aren't all quite the same size. So I tried the bigger suit. My feet wouldn't reach the toes. There are controls in the boots. My fingers don't quite reach either."

"That leaves one," Debby said.

"The large? It's in use. It won't fit. If my damn toes were longer! I'm out. I can't be a Guardian."

Belind was back.

Sausage was a tube seared around the outside, delicious inside: ground meat with bits of plants added. Fringe tea Debby knew from last night. She still had a trace of the morning headache.

The situation felt uncomfortable, and Debby was rehearsing excuses to leave. She asked, "Are you going to stay in the Navy?"

"I think so. I'll never get further than Bosun, though."

"You'll be flying. More exciting than guarding the Library."

"As a Guardian I could spend some time making a home! Get married, carry some guests!"

"Don't they mind Navy people making babies?"

"You go to half pay when you're showing, but you've got a mate working . . . and even if you don't, Navy pay is good." Sectry drank deep. She hadn't touched her sausage.

Rather asked, "Sectry? Why would someone like the Captain-Guardian be interested in a recruit?"

"Wayne? That's easy. If he can get enough dwarves at Guardian rank, he can move up to Captain. He's got the rank but not the duties. Him, he'd be better off if he *couldn't* fit a pressure suit."

Debby took the rest of her tea in two gulps. "I've got to be going. Thanks, Sectry. I shouldn't have come in. I'm supposed to be buying stuff at the Vivarium, now that we've got money."

"Well, remember you're on fringe," the redhead said. "Watch the prices."

"I'll be careful."

Outside, Debby let herself smile.

How would Rather handle it? Let Sectry believe that he'd come to the Navy only to get close to a lovely dwarf woman?

It might even be true.

A sheet of rainwater clung to the window. A blurred puff jungle drifted past.

Rather had finished his sausage. Sectry passed him half of hers. When Belind came past she ordered more fringe tea. She asked, "How do you like the Clump?"

"It's mostly strange. Too wet, for one thing. I think I could get tired of boxes. Huts in a tree aren't like that. Sectry, why did they build Headquarters round?"

"It was built to spin."

"Spin?"

"The early officers, they thought we'd need tide to stay healthy. They gave that up early. They couldn't dock a ship while Headquarters was spinning, and it tended to wobble. So they stopped the spin and they built the exercise room, centrifuge included. Those early Navy men must have been *monstrously* strong. But it turns out we don't get sick. We still use the exercise room, though."

The fringe tea was fizzing in his blood. Sectry Murphy seemed to glow. His mind was trying to follow a dozen paths at once. It suddenly seemed very natural that the early men would move a tree into the Clump, spin it, try to settle the tufts, get the benefit of tide *and* the clustered resources of the Clump . . . and produce the burl that later generations hadn't been able to duplicate.

At the same time there was a strangeness in what Sectry had said . . . and then he had it. "How do you know all that? Booce told us about the Library. He said only officers' children are taught there."

"Wayne told me."

"Oh."

"We were together for a while. I never thought he'd marry me, I'm not an officer, but when he . . . What I was saying, he told me a lot of history. The Library used to be part of a starstuff rocket. We've never built anything like it."

"What does it look like? Where—"

She shook her head; her hair spread around her like a flaming halo. "I never saw it myself. I'd like to. I wonder if I could talk my way past the guards . . ."

Guards. *That* door.

Voices and vision were turning strange. Sectry glowed; she was the Smoke Ring's most beautiful living thing. Rather took a firm grip on his equilibrium. Offering to make babies with a high-ranking Navy officer now seemed presumptuous beyond insanity. Carlot had warned him: she might be badly offended. Yet he'd never seen a woman like her.

"Then he married a woman three meters tall and thin as a feather-snake. She's got a face that would scare away a drillbit, and when she carries a guest she looks like a line with a knot in it. But she's an officer."

"Money."

"Mmm? No. Rank."

"Money," Rather said distinctly, "is why Carlot is going to marry Raff Belmy." He was losing control of his mouth.

"Oh. The dark girl, Serjent's daughter?" A smile flickered and vanished, but Rather caught it. "That's rank too."

"You saw us."

"Yeah." The smile was back.

"Do you have rank?"

"I'm a Bosun. Crew."

"Do I have rank?"

"No. What's this all about? If you want rank you join the Navy. Then you're crew."

"Would you marry me then?" His mouth was running away with him. Fringe.

She laughed. She was trying to stop, and ultimately she succeeded. "We just met. How old are you?"

"Fifteen."

"I'm twenty-eight. Where do you want to live?"

"Citizens' Tree. Any tree."

"Carlot probably wants to live in the Admiralty."

"To the treemouth with Carlot."

"I do too."

"Make babies with me," his mouth said.

She thought it over, while Rather tried to think himself invisible. She said, "Right."

A score or so of puff jungles were in view. Some bore logos. They chose one that didn't, and circled it to be sure. "Quietly now," Sectry said.

"Nobody here but us flashers."

"If we scare flashers out, some meat eater might come after them."

He wiggled through the foliage in her wake. Nice to have a view. The puff jungle was hollow in the middle. A thousand flashers edged warily away, flashing blue and yellow wings at them.

They balled their clothes and threw them at the flashers, causing great excitement.

The birds perched in a shell around the hollow, watching them. She was just his size. She knew more than Carlot: delightful things. There were moments in which Rather resented that knowledge. Others in which he was shocked. His body knew things his mind hadn't dreamed.

They rested . . . running hands and toes across the sweat-slick contours of stranger's flesh, learning each other. *Smooth muscle. Hair red everywhere. Fingers and toes stubby like his own. Either of Sectry's breasts fit nicely into his two hands.*

"We could go back and forth," she said. "Live some in the Clump, some in your tree."

"Do you mean that?" As the fringe died out of his brain he began to wonder what he had committed himself to.

"Who knows? Don't ever make decisions when you're on fringe." Suddenly Sectry wriggled out of his arms. She snatched up her wings and eeled through the foliage and out. Rather followed, curious and horny.

Only her head poked into the sky. Flashers wheeled there, and something much larger circled thirty meters away. Sectry asked, "Want to see something funny?"

A wedge with teeth. "Get back." He pulled at her ankle. She had donned her wings. "That's a Dark shark. Carlot showed me."

"We try to keep them out of the Market region." She thrust herself into the sky, naked; waved her arms and yelled. The Dark shark froze. A window came open in a nearby cluster of cubes. The beast charged.

Rather didn't have his wings. He called, "Sectry! Dark sharks aren't funny!"

The long limber torso whipped back and forth too fast to see. The narrow triangular wing was a rippling blur. Sectry turned and kicked hard. She dived into the foliage, whooping, pulling Rather after her.

They were in the hollow center.

"Are you nuts?" he bellowed, and she laughed. Then the Dark shark burst through in a shower of leaves and splintered wood.

All Rather could see was teeth. His own wings were out of reach. He set his feet against a branch and watched the predator. Which way to jump? Flattened head and the forepart of a thrashing torso, three big crescent eyes, a thousand pointed teeth . . . the eyes beginning to show panic. Sectry couldn't stop laughing.

The beast was stuck.

Rather asked, "You do this a lot?"

"Sure. We don't like Dark sharks." She wrapped her arms and legs around him and laughed into his face.

The predator snapped its teeth at them, raging and impotent. Sectry murmured in his ear. "Gives it a kick, doesn't it?"

Debby was tired. She was flying blind, pushing bags of about her own mass, with no more than the strength of her legs. From time to time she stopped to look past her burden. The Serjent log grew larger.

Logbearer had dropped Debby and Rather near Navy Headquarters on its way to the Serjent log. Now Debby found the rocket moored near what had been the out tuft.

Two days' time had wrought wonderful changes.

A skeletal cylinder perched atop the fuel pod. Men were all over it, placing planks, driving pegs into wood. Booce floated nearby, watching contentedly. When he saw Debby coming he donned wings and kicked to join her.

"No problems?"

"No problems," she said. "Zakry wanted money. I just went down the list and paid him what I had. Here, there's some left. I don't think I got cheated. I've only got half the seeds here. We're supposed to get the rest within five days. Where do we store all this?"

"Not in *Logbearer*. There'll be paint fumes."

They lined the seed bags along a crack in the bark and ran tethers across them.

More men approached, pushing a cylinder of wooden beams. Debby watched as they maneuvered the lumber toward *Logbearer*. She called, "Ho, Clave! Learning a new trade?"

Clave joined them. He smelled of hard work. "I'm learning it, but I don't like it. Too nitpicking. Every board has to be just the right size, just the same thickness."

"I got the seeds."

"Good. Booce, isn't this a bit of a luxury? Don't we have other concerns?"

"Like selling my wood? This'll show off its quality! I'll paint my logo, but I'll leave most of the wood bare. I'll cruise past the Market and anyone can see I've got a good tree."

The hired crew were fixing panels on the long cylinder. Clave, rested, resumed work. Some of the panels were on swivels: windows. The sun swung behind the Dark; the day turned gloomy. When the sun reappeared, passing within a degree of Voy, one whole flank of *Logbearer* was finished.

A shadow flapped out of the sun and became Carlot with her arms full of gear. Debby flew to help her. Carlot was pushing cooking utensils and a slab of smoke-blackened moby meat. She asked, "Where's Rather?"

"I left him in Half Hand's with Sectry Murphy."

"Mmm."

They stored the gear near the bags of seeds. "We'd better do our cooking here tonight," Carlot told her father. "That paint's awful stuff." Booce agreed.

Carlot asked, "How did Rather do? I keep forgetting we want him to *fail*."

"Yeah. The way Sectry Murphy was acting, he made some kind of endurance record on a big wheel. *Somebody* should have thought of that."

"Me," Booce muttered.

"Might not matter. They seem to want him bad."

The cabin formed with remarkable speed. Now men were pegging crossbars across the bow . . . for pushing against a log? Two men produced gourds; wind brought a noxious chemical reek. Booce excused himself and went to supervise while they painted the finished flank of *Logbearer*.

Carlot asked, "What was he doing with Murphy?"

"You remember your father said—"

"Yes, and I said she might be seriously offended. He didn't actually make a pass, did he?"

"Not while I was there. She's in a rotten mood. They put her in a pressure suit and she didn't fit."

"That's bad."

"She wanted to blow her mind out on fringe tea, and she wanted company. I left them alone. Treefodder, Carlot, if he does get Murphy mad at him, what'll she do? Keep him out of the Navy!"

". . . Yeah." Carlot began setting her gear up for cooking. She worked with furious energy.

Debby watched. Presently she asked, "Carlot, are you going to marry Raff Belmy?"

"I don't know. I just spent a couple of days with Raff aboard *Woodsman*. He seems—he takes it for granted we'll be married. He's so sure, he hardly mentioned it."

"So? It's what you told Rather."

"I know. Where *is* he?"

There were beams left over from the making of *Logbearer*. Clave brought them an armload. Carlot arrayed them and started a fire.

Booce paid off the hired crew and they departed. His own crew went to inspect the altered rocket. Booce was exuberant. Clave was proud. Debby made appropriate noises. *Logbearer* had been repaired in just four days.

The paint was well done, she thought. She wasn't qualified to judge woodwork. The cabin was as big as the pod, roomy for half a dozen. Booce and Clave began the finishing touches: setting knobs and moorings into the hull, outside and in. Booce wanted particular patterns . . .

The fire was going well: a dim globe of heat, nearly invisible while both Voy and the sun bathed this side of the log. Carlot sliced the moby meat into two slabs. She set sliced vegetables between the slabs, locked them together with wooden pegs, and tethered it all within the fringe of the flame.

A distorted blue-fringed black man-shape swam across Voy.

"Rather! Where have you *been?*" Carlot shouted.

He reached the bark. "I'm in deep trouble," he said. "Where's the Chairman?"

"Working on the rocket. What kind of trouble?"

"Carlot, maybe you can tell me." Rather looked bewildered, a little frightened. "I'm afraid I've gotten myself in deeper than I wanted."

Section Four

THE DARK AND THE LIGHT

Chapter Nineteen

THE DARK

from the Citizens' Tree cassettes, year 54 SM:

*We've had serious arguments about why Kendy cut contact. Maybe something just burned out some circuits. Mass does constantly rain out of orbit onto Voy—make that Levoy's Star, my apologies to Sharon. A big infall would cause big magnetic storms, maybe big enough to burn out **Discipline's** computer, and the thick Smoke Ring atmosphere would still shield **us**. I hate to think so. I liked Kendy.*

That sounds crazy. A computer program . . . I can't help it. Kendy had less imagination than the turkeys. I tried telling him a joke, once and nevermore. But I admire dedication, and Kendy had as much dedication as a man can stand. I'm going to leave this in.

—Dennis Quinn, Captain

Booce had bought a small pump. Rather was working it to fill *Log-bearer's* fuel tank. A Navy ship was doing much the same on the other side of the pond. Water had to be shared, this close to the Market. Greetings had been exchanged, and now the two crews were ignoring each other.

Carlot said, "Raym's been running messages for Dave Kon and Mand Curts. They'll know where he is. You'll have to track him down, though."

"No problem," Booce said. "How did he lose his rocket?"

"I didn't want to ask. He's far gone on fringe spores, Dad. We want him, but I don't want him in charge of anything."

"Fine. Rather, stop, it's full."

Rather began packing up the pump and hose. "That was quick," he said, remembering how long it took to fill the carm.

"A pretty good pump for something that's all hardwood. Let's get going. Carlot, you drop me and Clave at the Market and then go on to the house. Clave, you get the rest of the seeds. I want to buy us some clothes. You're all still wearing tree-dweller pajamas."

"You'll bring Raym?"

"I'll send him to the house. If he's too fringey to find it, I don't want him aboard any ship of mine."

Rather had not found the chance to confide in anyone but Debby and Carlot. Maybe that was good. Booce seemed to take it for granted that he would stay where the Navy could find him. Rather's plans were quite different.

Would Carlot help him? He wasn't sure. The way she was acting—

The Market swarmed like a hive. When the rocket came near, a dozen citizens separated from the pattern and flew to look. Booce delayed his exit for dramatic reasons. When he emerged he was surrounded. He stayed to talk, and Carlot joined him. Clave grew bored and flapped off toward the Vivarium at the far rim. Booce took an order for a thousand square meters of wooden planks . . . and the sun crossed half the sky and was behind the Dark before *Logbearer* moved on.

Serjent House continued to drift. It was now radially out from the Market. The Dark eclipsed the sun; Voy shone from the side. Half violet, half black, the cluster of cubes made an eerie sight.

"We'll have to tell Clave," Debby said. "First chance we get."

Carlot said, "I'm still not sure about this."

Rather said, "Booce was right, wasn't he? I want to look undependable. So—"

"They'll think you had Dad's permission!"

"The Navy doesn't own me. Booce doesn't own me. Even you don't own me, Carlot, and if you're holding me as a copsik I want to know it so I can think about escaping!"

"No, I don't own you." The ship was turning, decelerating. Carlot was very busy tending the rocket, too busy to look him in the face. Her voice was almost inaudible. "But it was a fool stunt, running off to make babies with that Navy woman."

"You're going to marry Raff Belmy."

"I said *probably*. Skip it. It was a fool stunt. So tell me this. Does Clave own you? Your Chairman?"

". . . Maybe."

"So ask *him* whether you're going."

"I want to talk to Jeffer too. And one other."

"You keep hinting—"

"You'll see for yourself. You too, Debby. I am treefeeding tired of keeping secrets."

A random comet had impacted Levoy's Star. It had reached the surface as a stream of gas moving at thousands of miles per second. The neutron star had rung like a bell. There were two hot spots on the rapidly spinning body, at the impact point and the point opposite, where the shock waves had converged. The violet ion streams that normally rose from the magnetic poles of Voy, which natives called the Blue Ghost and Ghost Child, were brighter than Kendy had ever seen them. Radiation was beginning to sleet against *Discipline*'s hull.

But Kendy spared instruments for the CARM.

He ran the record as it came in. Jeffer had been idle: not much there. The house had been empty most of the time. Ah, here was something—

The motley collection of metal and plant tissue the savages called *Logbearer* bumped the wall nozzle-first. Rather, Debby, and Carlot emerged. They tethered the steam rocket to the door, close enough to block the sky. Rather said, "Jeffer. Come in, Jeffer."

Jeffer had been reviewing records from the cassettes. He set up the link. "I'm here. Hello, Debby, Carlot, Rather."

"I'm in trouble," Rather said.

"Tell me."

"Petty Wheeler interviewed me for the Navy."

"How did it go?"

The depth of Smoke Ring atmosphere was blocking most of the radiation and X-rays, and Kendy's instruments too. He could still watch events on the star itself via neudar. A plasma cloud hovered over the impact site, several centimeters high and spreading at terrific speed along lines of magnetic force—

Rather said, "Scientist, I did everything right except only two things. I did what Booce told me. I slept in the silver suit with the humidity turned low, and got there sniffling and crying. Debby came with me, and I really did need supervision. I could hardly see where I was flying. I asked for Sectry Murphy: all seeds and no brain, stet? But Booce didn't tell me not to show off my muscles, so I did."

"You're strong but sickly."

"And I'm a dwarf. If enough dwarves get into the Navy, a certain Captain-Guardian Mickl gets to act like an officer. I'm quoting Sectry. Mickl was there to watch the interview."

"Two mistakes. Did you suggest marriage to Bosun Murphy?"

Laughter, chopped off. "We got high on fringe tea. Then we dived into a puff jungle and—" Quick sidewise glance at Carlot, whose face was like stone. "Jeffer, none of us ever thought she might take me up on it. Now she thinks I'm joining the Navy and making plans to marry her. Maybe she can hold me to it!"

"This is not to your taste?"

"Sectry . . . I don't know. I don't want to join the treefeeding Navy and I don't know how to tell her that!"

"Okay, I'm thinking. . . . Rather, they already know you're allergic. Let them train you. Carlot said they don't give you much sleep in training. Stay awake even when you don't have to. Get sick a lot. They'll give up."

"I thought of something better."

"Listen—"

"No, *you* listen. I went running to Carlot and Debby. Help, I said. I'm in trouble, I said. The Navy wants me. What do I do? And we talked it over, and what I want to do now is talk to Kendy."

Jeffer's medical readings showed his shock. Kendy stopped paying attention to the impact on Levoy's Star. *Paydirt!*

"Rather? You told them?"

"I'm letting you tell them. You and Kendy."

"Kendy isn't in range yet. When he gets the record—"

Carlot said, "Kendy the *Checker*?"

"The same," Jeffer said. "Kendy made contact with us fourteen years ago . . . fifteen now. I made a mistake with the carm. Kendy told us how to get home. We didn't hear from him again till . . . well, it was just before you showed up, Carlot. He wanted this expedition."

Debby was seething. "Jeffer, you treefeeding mutineer! What game did you think you were you playing, hiding a thing like this?"

Carlot exclaimed, "You can't deal with the Checker! We know all about—"

The record was finished. He'd reached present time. Kendy printed I'LL HANDLE IT across the bow window in front of Jeffer. He sent, "We told Clave. Rather was there, so we told him too. Hello again, Debby. Carlot, it's a pleasure to meet you at last. Rather, you did the right thing."

"And I suppose you'll try to talk me into joining the treefeeding Navy! But I won't do that, Kendy. I want *out* of this."

Rather wasn't aboard the CARM. Kendy couldn't get medical readings; but he sensed truth here. Never give an order that won't be obeyed! Try something else . . . while *Discipline* moves steadily out of range. Wrap it up fast, but wrap it tight—

Kendy asked, "Rather, what are you planning?"

"Remember Booce telling me to look undependable? The Navy expects me to stay in touch. I'm going Dark diving. Carlot and Debby and Clave are taking *Logbearer* to get mud for Belmy's burl tree. I'm going with them."

"Just to look undependable?"

"It's not a crime. Sectry'll hate me, and I don't like that, but it'll get me off the harpoon."

Kendy finished putting details on his own plans. The speed of his thoughts was one powerful advantage to being a computer. It helped win arguments too. He said, "That's good, but it's not enough. Not if this Wayne Mickl wants you so badly. We need to get you out of the Clump entirely. Mmm . . . Rather, I think I may have something. Booce was planning to take the helmet with him so that Jeffer and I can see the Dark. Still true? Carlot?"

"Stet. Dad wants it out of the house."

"Good. Take the whole suit. Take Rather too. Go into the Dark. Rather, the suit's fully fueled. When you're out of sight of the Market . . ."

They heard him out, looking at each other. The silence that followed lasted only five or six seconds, but Kendy found it excruciating. Then Jeffer asked, "How long have you been planning this?"

"About thirty seconds . . . twelve to fifteen breaths. I think faster than you do, Jeffer."

Carlot's voice held doubt, not anger. "It's mutiny—"

"We steal *nothing*," Kendy said. "We won't harm the Admiralty at all. The information doesn't disappear, but I can read it, and then it becomes available to Jeffer the Scientist. Rather, Debby, don't you see? We came to learn. Clave and Jeffer won't leave until they know what to tell Citizens' Tree about the Admiralty. This way we'll learn everything we want in half a day."

Rather said slowly, "You say you can tell me how to do this."

"I've taken neudar readings. I can see the gross structure of Headquarters. It's most of a CARM surrounded by a concrete shell." The neudar shadow of the CARM was splayed around its aft end, and the back third was missing. The explosion must have pulped any passengers. It had ripped away the outer door of the airlock too. "The Library must be the control room. I'll guide you. We'll time it so I'm in contact the whole time. Even if someone sees something funny, it'll be *too* funny. He won't believe it. Afterward you take *Logbearer* home."

Carlot looked at Rather. "I don't owe you this."

"Losing contact," Kendy said. There might have been time for three words more, but what would they have been? He'd simply have to wait.

The redhead found Booce as he was returning from Market. She looked funny, flying. Her legs chugged faster than a normal woman's and made shorter strokes. She wouldn't have caught up if Booce hadn't been pushing baggage.

She wasn't breathing hard, though. She had a charming smile. "Booce Serjent, do you remember me?"

"Bosun Sectry Murphy. We met when *Gyrfalcon* came to collect customs. How do you do, Bosun?"

"I do okay. Rather's been accepted for training. I'd like to tell him."

Rather wouldn't like that. "He'll be at the house."

"I'll come. Shall I help with those?"

They kicked slowly along. Behind them the Dark moved in uneasy turgid patterns, out and east; the sun crept toward Voy; western rain clouds crawled in long curves. To fill the silence Booce said, "We've finished repairing *Logbearer*. After breakfast we cruised past the Market—"

"Moving slow. I saw it."

"Clave went for the rest of his seeds, and I picked up some clothing and toothbrushes. Can't have my crew looking like savages."

"My superiors may be wondering where you found the money."

"It's not easy. The Navy's taking its own sweet time to bid a decent price for our metal. But I've got some orders for wood, and my crew is going Dark diving."

"Did Rather say anything about . . . yesterday?"

"Not to me. He didn't seem to want to talk. It must have been a strange experience."

She laughed, then grew pensive. Presently she said, "Isn't that Serjent House?"

"Yes, but . . ." *Logbearer* wasn't there.

Booce invited her in. The Navy woman waited while he made the circuit of the rooms. He found nobody. There were no seeds: Clave hadn't arrived yet.

"They must have left already," he told her. "I stayed to bargain for wood. Clave should have come back well ahead of me." It was puzzling.

"Was Rather going with them?"

"No. He should be back soon, wherever he is."

She accompanied him to the kitchen and watched while he made tea. They returned to the common room and passed the pot between them, all in near-silence. Booce wondered if Jeffer had noticed the Navy woman. What they really needed right now was a metallic voice bellowing out of the door.

"You'd think he'd leave a message," she said.

Booce nodded. *But they'd have left it with Jeffer!*

Murphy was frowning. "Is it normal for Rather to do . . . something like this?"

Booce was quick on the uptake. "He's never done *this* before. Well, he's been worried about whether the Navy'll take him. Maybe he got terminally antsy. A trip to the Dark—" And Booce knew he was right. *If they think you're undependable*—Rather had gone into the Dark.

"—could be just what he needs," he finished.

"It's not what *we* need." Murphy rejected the offered teapot. "How long do you expect them to be gone?"

They weren't seriously hunting treasures such as fringe or blackbrain. All they wanted this trip was mud, so—"Thirty, forty days." But they wouldn't have left without Clave, so they must have taken the seeds he was carrying too. Why?

"Tell Rather we're unhappy. Booce, I've got to be leaving."

Booce hovered at the door to watch Murphy depart. He whispered, "Jeffer?"

Nothing.

Of course, they took the helmet too. He waited until Sectry was no more than a speck before he opened the compartment in the door.

The whole damn illegal pressure suit was gone.

For one magical moment he was nothing but relieved. But something was going on here, and Booce didn't like it at all.

Carlot made her burn with the bow pointed straight into the Dark. East takes you out, out takes you west. That a rocket might go where it was pointed was contrary to Rather's experience; but he didn't want to argue with Carlot.

The Market passed them at impressive speed. A few citizens turned to watch, and were gone.

Raym Wilby had never kept silence in his life. "This first part of a trip is fun, but you can still get hurt. Carlot, the tank's near dry, stet? Turn us. Cut the water flow. Go in facing sideways."

Carlot looked at him.

"See, if something comes at us, you run the last of the water in. Doesn't matter what way you're facing, long as it isn't forward. Something's ready to hit us, you change course. If it's gonna miss, you don't."

"Oh." She and Clave tilted the nozzle. *Logbearer* started its turn as she cut off the water flow. The slow turn continued as the sky began to darken.

"Birds are the worst. A pond, a glob of mud, a jungle, they don't follow you if you dodge. Everybody got harpoons? Stet. Hey, *smell* that. First whiff of the Dark. State, it's good to be back!"

Logbearer fell straight in. It was like entering a huge storm cloud . . . a granular-looking storm cloud. The air smelled of wet and rot and mustiness.

They strung line, using beams on the nose as mooring points. Raym watched and frowned and told them to put the lines closer together. "It's got to hold the mud while you make the burn." When they finished, *Logbearer*'s nose was the center of a great web. "I always string my extra clothes across the middle of the web. That way you *know* the mud won't go through and all over the cabin. You bring any extra clothes, Carlot?"

She spoke through gritted teeth. "You didn't tell me to. But *yes*, I brought extra clothes, and I don't much like getting them covered with mud."

"So wash them after. You do it when you're ready to leave. Then you use what's dirty. Look there, aft of center. Kerchiefs!"

Kerchiefs looked like a score of scraps of pink and green cloth afloat on the wind. "Those're flowers," Raym said. "Not fungus. They'll—"

"Could you spread those to hold the mud?"

"Carlot, they're not strong enough. Touch them and they shred. Hey, you don't mind dirty clothes when you're Dark diving!"

They took turns sleeping. The sky thickened and darkened over five or six days. Then Voy and the sun were hidden and it was impossible to know *day*. Rather's eyes adjusted. He saw colors emerging from the dark: blue tinges, green, orange. Behind them the murky sky was a blaze of light, suddenly bluer as Voy passed, too bright to look at.

Raym was forward, inspecting the web again. Or maybe he only liked the view.

Clave said, "It isn't the risk that bothers me. It's the fact that I'm not taking it. Feels like this should be my job."

Rather didn't answer, but Carlot did. "Oh, you're taking a risk. If Rather gets caught, the Navy'll want us all. Clave, it's not too late to change our minds!"

"Yeah. I know how persuasive Kendy is. And I think I should have been consulted." Rather started to speak. Clave snapped, "Yes, Rather, it couldn't be done. Besides, Kendy's right. It gets us everything we came for. Rather, if you don't come back in a decent time, we're leaving. I've got the seeds. We'll just burn straight out and let Jeffer find us in the sky."

"Stet," said Rather.

"And what about Dad?" Carlot demanded. "Why should the Navy believe him when he tells them he didn't know?"

"I won't get caught. One big risk and we go home."

"I don't owe you this," Carlot said, as she had said before. This time nobody answered. (But Jeffer had said, "You owe Citizens' Tree for your life," and it was true.)

"I think we've gone far enough," Clave said. "Nobody's going to see us from the Market."

Rather nodded. "But there's still Raym."

"He's easily distracted."

The rocket had slowed considerably. They were drifting, not flying. The murky sky was busy with soft, shadowy shapes. Once there was a jagged rock the size of *Logbearer*, half covered by . . . Rather stared. That had to be a fungus. But it was convoluted like the moby's brain Half Hand had tried to serve them.

Raym pointed through the net of lines. "You can eat that."

Clave said, "Treefodder! I mean literally. That's a tuft off an integral tree!"

It could have been, Rather thought. There was the curved blade of the branch. But where foliage should have been, now there was a great misshapen lump of soft gray curves. "I pushed one of those home once," Raym said. "Had to. My nets were torn up. It was all the food I had left, and I barely made a dent in it getting home. Half Hand served slices of it for the next twenty days, but he didn't pay much . . ."

Rather tuned him out.

The orange tinge ahead grew gradually stronger. Orange light shining through shadows. Rather had grown used to the wet, musty smell, but something else was in it now. "Raym, what's that?"

"I've been living with Exec ever since the accident. My son, Exec Wilby. He only went into the Dark but once—What?"

"That."

"That's the fire. Carlot, we have to turn."

Carlot jerked around. "Fire?"

Now Rather knew that smell. Fire burning in something wet and rotten.

"It's been burning down here since . . . I don't know when. All my life, anyway. Never gets much bigger, never gets much smaller. Now, don't hurry. Look around and find a pond and steer for that. We need more water anyway."

They looked. There was no mistaking the shape of a pond, of course, even in darkness. Rather found no spheroids in evidence. Carlot said, "I don't see anything!"

"There."

"But that's . . . oh." Raym was pointing to a fungus jungle, a maze of thick white threads . . . and the orange light glinted off something reflective inside. The mass, in fact, was mostly pond, but it was laced with fungus.

Clave used the bellows. The pipefire that had been estivating in the windless murk now blazed up. Carlot blew the last of their water into the pipe while Rather and Clave tilted the rocket.

The fungus jungle drifted across the orange light. *Logbearer* impacted softly against resilient fungus fingers, and recoiled.

"What kind of pump you got? Good. Boy . . . Rather, you want to pump?"

"You pump, Raym," Carlot said. "Debby, you go with him. Keep your harpoon handy."

"Stet, that's good thinking, Carlot. No guessing what's lurking in there." The imaginary horrors didn't diminish Raym's enthusiasm as he flapped away with the pump. The hose slowed him. Debby kissed Rather's cheek before she picked up a loop of hose and flew after him.

Raym disappeared among interlocked white strands that broke where he touched them.

Clave said, "Now, Rather."

They entered the cabin together. The bags of seeds nearly filled one compartment. Rather pulled them out, reached farther, and had the silver suit.

Debby saw only kicking wings among finger-thick white pillars of fungus. "Nothing dangerous yet," Raym called cheerfully. "Watch for stink-birds. Great State! Girl, get me a bag, a big one!"

Debby dropped the hose and worked her way in. "What—"

"Fringe!"

"Oh. Here." She'd taken to carrying the big bags they'd used to collect honey while logging. She passed one in. She couldn't see what Raym was doing in there, but the air had turned dusty. She sneezed.

Raym wriggled out in a cloud of dust motes. There was something shapeless in the bag. "Sixty, seventy chits' worth," he said. "I'll just take this back—"

"I've linked up the hose. What have you got?" Carlot had come at his shout.

Raym showed her the bag.

"Dammit, Raym, that's sporing fringe! Debby, get away from it."

"Yeah." Debby kicked out into the air. She was feeling dreamy . . . light-headed . . . happy. But if she'd breathed spores, Raym must have breathed more.

Keep him away from the ship! Debby pulled on the hose until she had the pump. "Raym, take this around to someplace else and start pumping."

"I'll take this back," Carlot said. "Raym, you shouldn't get near sporing fringe! Sure it's worth money—" She gave up. Raym was laughing.

Clave had stuck the helmet to a wall with a dab of glue. It watched him in stoic calm. "Try to do the circle in one sweep," it said.

"Is that how the original was done?"

"First painting was probably a template, but templates wear out. The suits must be painted over and over. Every so often the junior Guardian has to paint it. I'm guessing, of course, but the original looks a little sloppy in Kendy's pictures."

Clave pointed the brush like a pencil and moved in a single graceful sweep. The resulting greenish-white circle wasn't half bad. "Bring it close," said the helmet. "Too narrow and also a little small. Go around again and add some bulk to the outer rim. Rather, when you leave, drape a cloth over yourself. We don't want to get it dirty while it's wet . . . Stet, Clave. Now the dot in the middle. Stet, leave it tiny. Give me another look at the shoulder—"

"Raym found you something, Silver Man."

Clave jumped. "What? Carlot, don't do that."

"Rather, take it. It's sporing fringe. Bring it back if you can. It's worth money."

Rather took the bag. "What's it for?"

"If you're in trouble, throw it. Everyone around you will have a wonderful time while you get away. Make sure *you* don't breathe it."

"Oh. Thanks."

"Sure."

"I'm ready to go."

There was something more that he ought to say, something she expected, but he couldn't for the life of him think what it was.

"You get tired, I'll take over," Debby said.

"No, no, the tank must be nearly full by now." Sweat slicked Raym wherever his skin showed. He was grinning and panting and pumping his legs with the vigor of a much younger man.

The tank must be full already, Debby thought. They wouldn't let Raym stop until—

Raym stopped. "What was *that?*"

Debby turned to where he was looking. "I don't see anything."

Tiny twin flames burned in the Dark, receding.

"Huh." Raym resumed pedaling. "Hope that isn't the fire getting closer. You never know where it's gonna be. It doesn't just drift like everything else, it spreads in spots and goes out in spots—"

Carlot called from the rocket. "Raym! Enough. Let's go find our mudball."

Chapter Twenty

THE LIBRARY

from *Discipline*'s records, year 926 State:

> *Your orders are as follows.*
> *1) . . . You will visit each of these stars in turn. Other targets may be added. Where appropriate you will seed the atmospheres of proto-Earth worlds with tailored algae using the canisters you carry. The State expects to settle these worlds, spreading humanity among variable environments, against dangers that might affect only Sol system.*
> *2) The State is aware that you do not require a crew to operate.*
> *The human species is not invulnerable. There is finite risk that the crew of any interstellar spacecraft may find, on its return, that it has become the entire human race. Your crew and their genes are your primary cargo. CLASSIFIED.*
> *3) Your tertiary mission is to explore. In particular, any Earthlike world with possibilities for colonization must be investigated and reported immediately.*
>
> *—Ling Carther, for the State*

Matter was too thick in here to use boot jets. Rather used them to get clear of Raym's sight, then donned his wings. He wanted to fly straight north, along the axis of Clump and Smoke Ring both. Matter should thin out rapidly in that direction.

There were no ponds; but sometimes you could catch a glint of light from one of the fuzzy-edged fungus jungles. There were white pillow shapes, and flat white lenses streaked with yellow and crimson, and networks of interwoven pale stalks. He took care to avoid touching anything; he flew around clouds of dust or spores. The paint on him would still be wet.

Rather began to understand the beauty Raym found in the Dark.

Straight lines, rare in a tree, were unheard of here, save (rarely) for long beams of blue-white or yellow-white sunlight breaking through the murk. Where he saw these, he corrected his course to cross them. This close to crossyear, north would be at right angles to Voy *and* the sun. After what felt like a couple of days he was seeing many more. The Dark had grown rarified. Now there was room for jets.

He fired a burst of five breaths' duration.

Mist flowed past him as he coasted out of the Dark. The day brightened. Too bright. His eyes were slow to adjust.

"Jeffer the Scientist calling Rather. Can you hear me yet?"

Jeffer's voice was scratchy. Rather turned up the volume. "Reception isn't good, but I'm hearing you. I'm nearly out, moving north, coasting. The rest of us are in good shape. How long till we get Kendy?"

"A quarter day to spare. Rather, did you bring wings?"

"Yes."

"Good. You can't approach Headquarters on jets. I didn't think of it."

"I did."

"I have you located. Make your burn now. You're well north of the Smoke Ring. The air's thin, it won't slow you much, but in less than half a day you'll be back in the plane."

"I know, north and south bring you back. So. How long a burn? What direction? I'm well and truly lost."

"I'll time you. Three minutes, about sixty breaths. Can you see Voy? The Market is ten degrees west of out from you, and you have to cross four hundred klomters. You didn't actually get very far into the Dark."

By now he'd fallen into clear air, with the Dark spread out below. Rather wriggled to point his feet ten degrees east of Voy. He would move nearly at a tangent to the flow patterns in the Dark.

He lit the jets. His body tried to sag into his boots. The Dark skimmed below him, a storm with granulations in it, and sudden red and golden and purple glows where the sun shifted just right. Jeffer counted aloud and told him when to fall free.

Flying. The Dark was thinning out, but coming closer too. He skimmed through the fringes of a raincloud—

"Kendy for the State," said the familiar deep voice. "Rather, are you on schedule?"

"No problems. Expedition's in good shape. Raym will probably swear I was there the whole time."

"Repeat after me. 'There's a respectable store of metal here.' "

"There's a respectable—"

"Try to say it like I did. Listen a few times. 'There's a respectable store of metal here.' "

Rather deepened his voice and tried to spit the syllables. "There's a respectable store of metal here."

They rehearsed "You wouldn't want to have to sell your new house," and "I need to consult the Library," and "I relieve you." Rather was lethally sick of it when Kendy quit. "It'll have to do. Try to be in a cloud when you sight Headquarters. Don't make your approach without me."

"Right."

"I've displayed a neudar map of Headquarters for Jeffer. He can guide you if I'm out of range. Back in two days. Kendy out."

"Jeffer?"

"Here. Rather, you should try to sleep."

"Sleep?"

"Nothing natural can hurt you in the silver suit. Sure, sleep. You'll be less hungry. You've got no food."

"I'll give it a try."

He slept not a wink. The turning of the Clump spiral caught him up and he had to make a correcting burn. Houses and decorated puff jungles passed, none close enough to see more than a passing pressure suit. Citizens would wonder what the Navy was doing out here.

Within a layer of haze he found the unmistakable shape of the Market. Headquarters to spinward . . . "Jeffer? I have it."

"How close?"

"Forty klomters."

"Get a lot closer. Approach from the Market side if you can. Rather, it just struck me: there are two ways into the Library, and they have to guard both."

"So?"

"I don't think it was ever meant to be guarded. The Library was supposed to be free to all. Just a guess."

"What's the word from Kendy?"

"Any breath now."

"I'll come in through that cloud bank. You see it? I think there's a pond in there. I'll come around that."

"Kendy for the State. Rather, are you in place?"

The boy sounded edgy. "Ready. You missed some interesting stuff."

Headquarters was four hundred meters distant. They'd lose a few minutes crossing that. Kendy sent, "Something I should know?"

"No, just interesting. I watched two triune families arrange a marriage."

"If your helmet faced it I didn't miss it. Time to move. Just wings."

Kendy watched the guards as Rather approached. Would they expect him to have an escort? They spread arms and legs as he came near, with a hand and foot to hold the harpoon. That position had been *Attention!* for any military man in free fall since long before Kendy's birth. The door behind them was large and massive, and closed.

"Just go in unless they do something," Kendy said. "I've watched them every orbit. You won't need a password because your helmet's closed. Don't hurry. Let them open the door for you."

Checklist: Communications systems nominal. Drive warming. Course correction ready. Kendy didn't intend to burn fuel until everything else had gone right.

The guards waited until they could read Rather's insignia. One rapped the door with his spear butt. It slid open in time to let Rather pass.

"Left. There's a hall, then another door." Kendy noticed pads of cottony-looking vegetation on the far wall. "Pause. Wings off, then clean your suit. You'll be expected to. Pat, don't rub. Remember the paint."

Rather patted muddy rainwater off his suit. Kendy wished he could see the result. There were paint smears on the pad. The boy moved down the corridor.

The inner door had one guard. He starfished the way the others had. "Captain-Guardian? You're early, sir."

"I want to consult the Library."

"But that's . . . yessir." The man didn't move.

Kendy sent, "You're still carrying your wings. Tether them to your chestplate." The guard must expect that, and it would give Kendy time to think. "No hurry. Aristocrats don't hurry. Shin sticks toward your chin."

To door: no hinges visible. It would swing in. What was protocol here? Have to guess. "Open it yourself, Rather."

"How?"

"Paired handles on door and wall. Grip both. Push the door inward. No, pause—"

As Rather finished tethering his wings, the guard finished pushing the door open and moved aside. "In," said Kendy.

Rather entered. He turned at the sound of the door closing. There was no handle on the inside, though a scar showed that one had been removed.

The light source was electric. Would that bother Rather? No, he was used to electric lights in the CARM.

A man in a pressure suit waited. He held a crossbow. The bow and quarrel were both hullmetal: lengths of stiff CARM wiring, with superconducting cores. So this was how they used their heritage.

The Guardian's voice had to echo through helmet and faceplate. He sounded tinny (as Rather would; Kendy had counted on that) and surprised. "Captain-Guardian?"

"I know I'm early. I relieve you. I need to use the Library."

Rather was slow. "I know I'm early—"

"That's all right, Captain-Guardian."

"I need to use the Library. I relieve you."

"Yes, sir. For what purpose, sir? I'm required to ask."

While Kendy mulled possible answers, Rather had started to speak. Kendy listened. Rather said, "We want to locate an integral tree west of here. I want its probable orbit."

No way to read the silver man's face. The Guardian said, "Yes, sir," and rapped on the door. It opened for him and closed after him.

"Alone at last," Rather said.

The room was much bigger than the machinery it housed. The CARM control system had been remounted in a wooden cradle. There were wooden handles on its four sides. Hadn't Booce Serjent said that it was sometimes displayed to the citizens?

Cradled against an adjacent wall was a small portable fusion generator. The Library's light source was a panel running around its rim. The power cable was coiled against its side. "Rather, do you see a coil of line, thick as your wrist, black—"

"Got it." Rather moved toward the generator.

"The free end has to go into a hole in the CARM controls. At the near end, near the wall."

"There are a lot of holes."

"I'll guide you."

They played "cold" and "warm" with the end of the plug. It was taking too long. The power plant might be dead. The computer might be dead. The programs might be scrambled. There would be no second chance: Rather Citizen was probably trapped behind locked doors, with Wayne

Mickl already on his way. Once Kendy had established contact with the Admiralty, he might be able to buy Rather loose. The boy was doing his best, after all, fumbling, but doing his best—

"Just push it in hard and turn it counterclockwise. Stet. Face the controls. Tap the white key." A white cursor appeared. "Say 'Prikazyvat Voice.' "

"Prikazyvat Voice."

"State your authority," said a voice so like Kendy's that Rather squeaked in surprise.

"Say 'Rather Citizen for *Discipline*. Open contact.' Watch your accent." With another part of his attention he began beaming his signal to the old CARM computer. Voice was activated; the computer would hear. *Kendy for the State. Discipline to all CARMs. Kendy for the State.*

The computer must be trying to answer. It wouldn't be able to find *Discipline* with its navigational instruments severed. He sent, *Beam to pressure suit 26.*

"Something just started humming in my head."

"Everything's fine, Rather." The signal was being relayed. He sent, *Status?*

CARM #2 sent its tale of woe. Massive malfunctions. Internal sensors out, external sensors out, motors not responding, life support systems not responding, navigational systems not responding, power low. Records intact. Presiding officer: Admiral Robar Henling . . .

Kendy sent, *Copy.*

All?

Y.

The Admiralty Library accepted the Copy program, hummed thoughtfully, and began beaming its records.

That would take twenty-six minutes. Kendy activated the course change he'd worked out hours ago. *Discipline* was about to use a good deal of fuel. It would hold him over the Lagrange point for long enough.

The records arrived in reverse order. Common practice. Recent records were likely to be more urgent. Kendy dipped into the flow. The control board had seen little while housed in the Library room. There were glimpses of the sky during ceremonies. Records of births, deaths, marriages. It had been dismounted in year 130 SM. The CARM hadn't crashed; it had deteriorated over the years, helped by deteriorating maintenance . . .

He couldn't spare attention with so much else going on. The drive ran smoothly. Tank less than a fifth full. *Discipline* accelerated, drive swinging out to point at the stars, to hold the ship close above the L4 point against its own spin. Rather was exploring the room; his pulse and breath rate were rapid. He was bored and anxious. Jeffer, crouched above CARM #6's control board, was in similar shape. The neudar view of Admiralty Headquarters showed fog-spots clumping, then moving in two streams toward the Library.

Something was happening. Little lights brightened and dimmed on the CARM control panel. His helmet hummed. It wasn't particularly entertaining. Rather said, "Kendy?"

"It's working, Rather. Don't bother me."

"Jeffer?"

"Here."

"Kendy's busy and happy."

"You've got more than two hours—about half a day before Mickl's on duty. Nobody should bother you."

"I'm hungry enough to eat a swordbird, and may the best entity win."

"Did everything go all right?"

"I'm *scared*, Jeffer. I may never get over being scared. Why on Earth are we *doing*—"

The door opened.

Rather saw a silver suit pointing a crossbow a few degrees wide of his navel. The insignia was familiar. He and Booce had spent half a day painting it on the silver suit, from pictures taken by the silver suit's camera.

The door—

Rather's radio spoke in his helmet. "I know who you are," said the voice he'd been trying to imitate. "What I want to know is why. Let's—"

Rather leapt straight at Wayne Mickl, and fired a burst from his jets for extra force. He couldn't let the door close.

The silver man swung his crossbow aside and braced to kick, too slowly. He'd expected the jump but not the jets. Rather slammed into him. Mickl bounced away. Rather struck the jamb and, spinning, was through the door and out into a horde of Navy crew.

"I know who you are—" Wayne Mickl's voice, pressure suit #5, radio frequency badly distorted by time, and Kendy locked on it. He beamed instructions to the Library: *Record the view through pressure suit #5 cameras, one snap per ten minutes, henceforth.*

It was a nice bonus. He welcomed it, because he was about to lose Rather Citizen. A dozen Navy crew in the fish-eye view, unknown numbers out of camera range—

Jeffer bellowed, "Rather! What's going on?"

"Wayne Mickl came back. Can't talk."

Kendy sent, "Get outside if you can, Rather. Mickl's jets aren't fueled."

"I've got the whole treefeeding Navy here!" They were hesitating, but they wouldn't for long. "They'll swarm all over me like honey hornets— Hey!" Rather's hands came in view holding a bag; ripped it open and flung it. The corridor became vague and golden.

Wayne Mickl could pull the cable! Was he still in the Library? CARM #2 had a hundred years of records to go . . . a solid block of data was running now, data that must have been beamed long ago by *Discipline* itself. Kendy knew he wouldn't want to read that in full, not if it was records of the mutiny. He'd spot-check.

The other pressure suit emerged from the Library and jumped to join the fight. *Good!*

Rather's camera view shot down the corridor, through dust and bodies. Navy crew grabbed at him, clung . . . and let go. It began to look as if he might make it.

What was running through *Discipline*'s receivers was a message from the State, from Earth.

Nothing in his own memory matched. Kendy pulled it and ran it. It was brief.

Rather jumped down the corridor, arms raised to block the men who blocked his path. Impacts slowed him. A burst from the jets compensated. Somebody was riding him, legs around his hips . . . a man impacted heavily against his helmet, slid across his chest, and was gone.

The silver man jumped him. The man who clung to Rather took the force of impact. They tumbled. Rather reached the door, kicked, swung himself around the jamb and was out in the sky. A burst of jets took him clear.

He paused then.

The silver man emerged and, twenty meters away and receding, stopped to put on his wings. Navy crew emerged behind him. Two flailed; they had no wings at all. The third couldn't get his on. Fringe spores must have reached their brains.

That left only the silver man.

Rather grinned. He put on his own wings and kicked away strongly. "Kendy? Jeffer? Are you watching?"

"Jeffer here. I can't get Kendy. He may be out of range."

"Well, watch. This is going to be good."

Mickl was catching up.

Rather's radio sounded calm and a bit supercilious. "Rather Citizen, you can't escape. Your wings are the right color, but they're not Navy wings. You know I don't want to hurt you. I had the chance to kill you and I didn't. But the crossbow is all I have, and it will penetrate—make holes in a Navy pressure suit. There's a hole in one of our suits because one of our Guardians turned mutineer once."

"Don't answer," Jeffer said. "He's guessing. Don't give him a chance to test it."

Mickl was meters behind him, but the drugged Navy crew were nearly out of sight. Rather pulled his wings loose, pointed his feet at the silver man, and fired his jets.

He was head-down to the Dark. Mickl was kicking hard, falling rapidly behind. A scream of shock or frustration burst in Rather's ears; he found the volume control and turned it down fast.

The Dark was around him. He couldn't see the other silver man, he couldn't see the Market.

Jeffer spoke in his helmet: a tiny squeak until Rather turned the volume back up. ". . . due to rendezvous. I've got a ship moving north out of the Dark. Stand by . . . There's a dark blob bigger than the cabin—"

"That's *Logbearer*. They've got their mud."

"Turn seventy degrees clockwise from where you were pointed and, oh, ten degrees north. Make your burn."

Rather obeyed. Jeffer counted off twenty seconds: seven breaths. The Dark thinned.

"We've got to get rid of the silver suit," Jeffer said.

"No." I'm the Silver Man!

"I don't mean feed it to the tree! I mean don't have it when *Logbearer* gets home."

"How?"

"I don't know, and Kendy isn't answering. I don't even know what course he's on now."

"What if I don't go back? You can pick me up with the carm."

"Sure, and what does Wayne Mickl say to the Serjents? You've got to face him and lie."

Rather could see the Market far behind him. Was he in view of Navy instruments? But they'd have to find him, and he'd changed direction.

The deep voice of Wayne Mickl was small and full of the chattering sound of distance. "Rather Citizen, I will wait for you at Serjent House."

"I heard that," Jeffer said. "I've spotted you. Can you see Voy? Sixty-five degrees east, burn for five seconds. Zero north, there's no point in getting higher. You'll both be back in the Dark before you meet."

"Jeffer? Why don't you come get the silver suit?"

". . . Stet. Here I come."

Rather himself had spotted *Logbearer* now, above the plane of the Dark, foreshortened and trailing steam.

Jeffer said, "I'm on my way, but it'll take me nearly a day. If you just ditch the suit it'll fall back into the Dark."

"It's doing that now. You'll have to find it somehow. I've got an idea."

Rather flew through the Dark. He was using wings. There couldn't be much left of his fuel.

He glimpsed a man-shape through the murk.

Carlot. When he opened his helmet she kissed him breathlessly. "I thought I'd never see you again! Did you do it?"

"Yeah. All of it, but the Captain-Guardian knows, or thinks he does."

She talked while she helped him out of the suit. "Raym got too much of the fringe. He's in the cabin getting through the hangover. Debby's with him. She'll keep him quiet. We've got our mud and four tons of walnut-cushion. Two Dark sharks tried to open us up. Debby took them. Rather, I'd hate to have her mad at *me*. We've got the meat, and I'll show you tooth scars on the wood—"

"I hope they were big. I'm *hungry*." He was out. He closed up the suit, leaving the helmet open. "Jeffer?"

"Here. I'm above your position."

"I'm doing it." He closed the helmet. He turned the pressure dial high and the temperature low. The suit grew rigid. "Now I want to start a fire."

"In the Dark that won't be easy."

"Help me. That . . . fisher jungle, I guess it was." He indicated a mass of dry brush with white things taking root in it. "Help me push the legs in."

They pushed the suit into the decaying fisher jungle. The branches still had some strength. Rather got a good grip, then closed a jet key with his toe. Flame blasted through the rotting fisher jungle; the suit tried to escape. He let the jet run for several breaths before he turned it off.

"Jeffer should find that okay," he said. He was guessing and he knew it. "Then *tell* me! What happened?"

He told her some of it while they searched out *Logbearer*. The rest would wait. Clave and Debby would have to wait to hear the tale, since Raym could not be allowed to. And Rather would have his chance to eat and sleep. He was exhausted.

Chapter Twenty-One

THE SILVER SUIT

from the Library cassettes, year 200 SM:

> *Citizens may never enter the Library Room. Citizens will be given access to the Library only through officers, and then only on certain dates. . . . On these days the Library will remain available, with a Programmer on duty, until all citizens have had opportunity to ask their questions; though some questions will certainly be unanswerable . . .*

They stopped twice: once at the Market, to let Raym off with half his pay in hand, and once at a pond, to refuel.

Belmy's log was very slowly turning end-for-end. A thread of steam poured from above the tuft. As Carlot made her final burn to bring *Logbearer* to rest near the midpoint, *Woodsman* cast loose and moved toward them.

Serjent House was just visible to antispinward: west. Rather tried not to think about the dot visible alongside it. He welcomed the delay.

Debby said, "I'd like to get this over with—"

Clave shook her by the ankle. "Wrong! We went into the Dark for mud, and we're back to get rid of it. We don't know of anything urgent. We're in no hurry at all."

Carlot shouted from where she and Rather worked the rocket. "Stet! Treefodder, they always make *us* wait!"

They had it all figured out. But copter plants were launching their seeds in Rather's belly.

Woodsman eased alongside. Hilar and Raff Belmy flew toward *Logbearer.* "You'll like Raff," Carlot whispered. "*Act* like you like Raff."

"It's all right. I'd make babies with him if it'd make you happy . . . or get me away from the Navy."

Hilar introduced his son. (Treefodder, but they were big!) Raff smiled much and said little. He was shy for an adult, Rather thought. He stared at the tree dwellers, but his eyes seemed to slide aside from Rather's.

The teapot passed. Carlot asked, "How are you doing with the log?"

Hilar shrugged. "No burl yet." The others laughed. "Give it time. We have some spin. I don't think we want to overdo it. We've splashed a pond against the trunk; that gives us a water flow. How are you planning to deliver the mud?"

"I . . . hadn't thought past just bringing it here."

"Raff and I talked it over—"

Raff spoke. "Dad always says keep it simple. We'll just impact it against the tree, lee side, two, three klomters above the tuft. There's already water running down to the treemouth. Let it carry the mud too. Easy, steady delivery system."

He can talk when it's about something real, Rather thought. "Have you done a lot of logging?"

Raff's head bobbed. "I spend more than half my life in the outer sky. Sometimes I wondered what living in a tree would be like."

They were getting used to that question. Clave said, "I miss it myself. Well, you grow up shorter and stronger. Cooking's easier. Hunting's different: the wind *throws* the prey at you . . ."

Rather tuned it out. The dot next to Serjent House must be a Navy ship. He felt their long-sight devices on him. What the Navy saw must look puzzling. Let them wonder: he had an explanation both interesting and innocent.

His attention snapped back when Hilar said, "Booce has been making deals. I expect he'll pay back the loan well before crossyear."

Carlot asked, "Has the Navy bought the metal yet?"

"No. In fact, something's upsetting the Navy. I haven't heard a rumor I can believe, but . . . stay alert, Carlot. You know you've got visitors?"

"We can see them. Hilar, Raff, it's time to deliver our cargo."

It took a day and a fraction and was entirely straightforward. *Logbearer* burned toward the turning tree. Her crew dismounted the spokes that braced the web that supported the mud. Mud and lines and wooden spokes smacked the trunk hard enough to stick. Water flow was already carving a runnel in the mud as *Logbearer* accelerated away. They'd be back to collect the beams and lines after they were washed clean.

———

Gyrfalcon was not moored; it floated free a hundred meters from Serjent House. Two men working on the hull did not return Clave's cheerful wave. Rather recognized one as Petty Wheeler. They watched fixedly while *Logbearer*'s crew swarmed out and set about the business of mooring their ship.

Rather looked around the common room while they tethered their wings. One fast look and then he'd have to react:

No teapot. Not a social occasion. Booce Serjent looked angry and unhappy. Bosun Sectry Murphy started to jump toward Rather, then pulled herself back. Three long-limbed Navy men were stationed around the walls, and a fourth: silver suit, helmet thrown back, bearded dwarf-face within. Wayne Mickl.

Rather let himself break into a delighted grin. It was surprisingly easy. He wanted to reassure Sectry; he was glad to see her. He let his eyes flick from Sectry to Wayne Mickl to Sectry again. He blurted, "Am I in?"

Sectry flashed from unhappy to angry. Wayne Mickl broke into delighted laughter. "Very *good*! But, Rather, there just aren't enough dwarves to make it work. Take him."

Two of the Navy crew were on him. They pulled him loose from his handhold, set him spinning in the air. He caught glimpses of them rebounding from walls. Then one had wrapped his arms and legs around Rather's lower ribs from behind, and the other had a foot in Rather's crotch and Rather's two ankles in his hands, stretching his legs straight.

There was a wrestling trick. Jill had shown him, in the brief period when she was stronger than he was. You wrapped your arms or legs around your opponent's short ribs and tightened them. Your opponent couldn't inhale. Presently he would faint.

Rather had used it on others afterward, and been punished for it. Most of the children were smaller than he was. Jilly wasn't, but she didn't have the strength of a dwarf after they both got older. Rather had been taught not to fight. He still got angry sometimes, but he learned to control it. Sometimes he wrestled with adults. He generally lost.

The man behind him (call him Navy #1) was letting him breathe, but shallowly. The other (Navy #2) wasn't kicking Rather's seeds into his belly; but he could. Rather held the red rage in check. "Booce?"

Booce answered the implied question. "You tell me. Where have you *been?*"

"The Dark. We've delivered Hilar's mud. We've got some walnut-cushion and—"

"The Navy went through this house like a whirlwind. I told them about the sporing fringe in the concrete. I was about to show them a hiding place I made in the door. I think they'd *rather* chop my house apart, and I get the distinct impression that it's all your fault—"

"Shut it, Booce," Mickl said. "Rather, what did you think you were coming home to?"

Anger made his thoughts murky, but he'd rehearsed this part in his mind. "I thought . . . I saw Sectry and I saw you. I thought the Captain-Guardian had come personally to tell me I was in. The Navy. You know. But—"

"You must know that an officer wouldn't care that much about a new inductee."

"Well, you're *here* and . . . someone told me you're very eager to put another dwarf in the Guardian slot. What *are* you doing here, Captain-Guardian?"

"It's a mistake!" Sectry burst out.

Mickl didn't shout; he projected his voice over hers. The walls shivered to it. "Let me tell you something about mistakes. There's—"

"No, allow me." Rather reached for the foot in his crotch with both hands. He had it before the leg could snap straight, and he twisted. His rib cage closed. He stopped breathing and kept twisting. The leg buckled; Navy #2 was pulled close; he loosed Rather's ankle and Rather kicked him twice under the jaw. Now his hands were free to pull the constricting arms apart and over his head and down. Torsion pulled the legs free too, and he could breathe.

Navy #2 kicked at Rather with his good leg. Rather caught it on his foot. Reaction separated them: Navy #2 was headed toward a wall. There was blood on his mouth. Rather pulled the other's arms around behind him. They came, not easily, and Rather kept pulling until he had pulled Navy #1's shoulder from its socket.

Clave had a riblock on the third man.

Rather pushed Navy #1 away. The man turned in the air, moaning, his arm at a crooked angle.

Navy #2 had reached the wall. He jumped. They traded blows: Rather put his heel in the other's midsection, but a fist smacked solidly into the side of Rather's neck. Short arms and legs had cost Rather more than one match.

Again the blows had thrown them apart. Rather's ears buzzed; lights flared in his eyes. He was too far from the walls. He waited . . . but Navy #2 was curled in a tight ball. When a wall touched him he stayed there, winded, resting.

Wayne Mickl was pointing a crossbow at Rather. "Cut it. I'll shoot you someplace nonlethal. You too, Jonthan. Stay there. You, the tree man, let go of Doheen!"

Clave released Navy #3. Doheen was unconscious.

Panting, elated, Rather said, "Stet. But mistakes are something . . . *somebody* pays for, and that's what . . . the word is for. Or am I going too fast for you?"

"Yes. Pause a minute. J— What is it *now?*"

The men in the doorway both looked surprised. One was a Navy crewman. He had Raym Wilby in a riblock. "Captain-Guardian, this one flew up like he was coming to the house. Then he saw the ship and turned around and flew away. The Petty and me chased him down."

"Who are you?" Mickl demanded.

Raym only gaped. Carlot said, "It's Raym Wilby. He guided us into the Dark."

"Wilby, what were you flying from?"

"I . . . I just don't like N-Navy."

"Stet. Jonthan, wipe your face, then take Wilby into the storage room. Ask him about the trip. Be polite."

Doheen blinked; his eyes opened. The man from the ship took charge of Navy #1, the man with the dislocated arm. Rather heard him yell as his shoulder popped into place. Jonthan (Navy #2) wiped blood from his mouth with a cloth, then took Wayne Mickl by the elbow and towed him away. Rather noticed for the first time that Sectry had a crossbow too. It was pointed at Clave.

Mickl ignored it all. "Now, Rather, tell me about a pressure suit that looks like mine. Don't forget the crossbow."

Rather was still panting a little. He took a moment more than he needed. "Pressure suit? Booce told me. You've got three. Nine crew to use them, but you're short of dwarves." *Which ought to be a pun,* he thought; but he'd irritated Mickl enough without that.

"A fourth pressure suit invaded Headquarters fifteen days ago. You were in it."

Rather stared. "No, I wasn't. Fifteen days? I was in the Dark getting mud. Is that what this is about?"

"Rather, it's your bad luck that I'm interested in dwarves. I know where every dwarf in the Admiralty is right now. There are twelve. Ten are in the Navy. One is eighteen years old. He'll be a Petty soon. Sectry already is. The rest are Guardians. There's a Dark diver's boy, but his brain was thick with spores before he could grow a beard. And there's you."

"And another pressure suit."

"Yes. I want it."

Rather wiped sweat from his face. He was thinking as carefully as if he were innocent. The trick was not to know anything he shouldn't. This seemed safe: "Captain-Guardian, if a pressure suit got into the Admiralty without you knowing it, maybe there was a dwarf in it."

Mickl didn't answer. Rather said, "S— the Bosun and I are about the same size, but I think you're bigger. How big was that fourth suit? Would I even fit?" He was stuttering a little; he had to think every word through first. How clearly had Mickl seen the silver suit? It always looked bigger than the occupant. "Maybe it's smaller yet. Maybe it's so small that it'll fit in places you wouldn't look, a closet in a happyfeet ship—"

"Why that?"

"Happyfeet tried to rob us before we got here. They don't care much about laws. Isn't there a Lupoff ship in dock?"

"True enough, but a closet is silly. He'd suffocate."

"Somewhere else, then." *There's air in the silver suit. Am I supposed to know that? What else am I not supposed to know?* "What really happened? What is it you think I did?"

"You entered Headquarters in an unregistered pressure suit painted like mine. You got into the Library. You got rid of the Guardian. We haven't been able to find out what you did there, or whether you got what you wanted, but Voice was running when you left. When I came in you scattered sporing fringe throughout Headquarters and got away." Mickl's throat worked, and Rather saw how close he was to uncontrolled rage. "I went after you. I couldn't catch you."

"Um . . . that doesn't make sense. Booce told me never to try to outfly Navy. The wings are different—"

Mickl slashed the air with his arm. "The suit outflew me! This isn't just another pressure suit. You'd be in enough trouble if it was only that. We've *got* to have this suit. It's special."

"How?"

"Classified, you little fungus!" Wayne Mickl closed his eyes. He pulled air in through his nose until his lungs were full, then let it all out. Calmly he said, "Booce, show me this hiding place."

Booce showed him. *We wouldn't have been told this either,* Rather thought. *Secrets!*

Mickl closed his helmet. When he peered into the compartment, light blazed from the forehead. He studied the interior at length. "Ingenious."

"Maybe not. It weakened the door." Booce pointed out the hole. Mickl nodded.

Jonthan was back. A long bruise was forming on his jaw. His glance at Rather seemed disinterested. He and the dwarf officer conferred in low voices. They disappeared toward the storage room.

That left only Navy #3, Doheen. He and Clave were holding a staring contest, Clave smiling, the other poker-faced.

Booce said carefully, "Rather, there's something you should know. You're trying to tell the Captain-Guardian that you're probably innocent. It's not enough."

Rather had thought things were going well. "Raym was with us. He'd have to believe Raym was lying too. Raym doesn't have the brains."

"No, of course not. Mickl believes you now." A quick glance at Doheen, who reacted with something like a shrug. "But just in case he's wrong, he'll stop *Logbearer* from ever leaving the Admiralty, because we might be smuggling that fourth suit. He'll ruin me financially, in case I might say something to save myself. He'll hound you. It'll never be over."

"Then . . ." *What'll I do? There can't be a way to convince Mickl I'm innocent. I'm guilty!*

Admiralty pressure suits don't have working jets. No fuel. There's a suit with jets, somewhere, and Mickl wants it. He'll never settle for less.

Give him the silver suit? He'd know we're guilty then.

If I could—Ah. He had something.

I can't ask Booce. Doheen's listening, and Booce doesn't know what happened anyway. The others—

Fate and air currents had put Rather near Sectry. He moved closer. She moved the crossbow aside for him. Her face was hard to read.

"I shouldn't have left," he said.

"Why didn't you wait?"

"They tell me the Navy takes forever to do anything. I couldn't just hang around twitching, and we needed the mud."

Their voices had dropped. She said, "I was here. I turned down a flight, but I can't do that twice running. You left me for *mud*?"

It was a miserable thing to have to admit, but it was better than the truth. He nodded.

"Rather, nobody makes decisions when he's on fringe. So tell me, am I too strange? Am I too old?"

"My mother's older than my father. I like strange. I'm in the Clump because I like strange. Sectry, I don't regret anything I said or did." Which was not quite the truth. *Secrets*— "Hilar Belmy is trying to grow a burl tree."

She said, "That never works."

"Well, he's trying something new. Booce bought a piece of the tree. And he owes us."

"So it's not just mud, it's money. All right, Rather. I can understand money."

"That's more than I do. It's power, but it doesn't make you an officer. Are there un-rich officers?"

Her lips twitched. "They marry rich citizens. Their children are officers. The number of officers goes up. One day we'll all be officers."

"Why does Wayne Mickl want that suit so much? I'd think it would be the other way around—"

"It's bad for the Admiralty if happyfeet hold old science. I think Wayne's almost given up on taking his Captain's seat. The pressure suit is as much power as he'll ever have, and he takes his responsibilities—"

They were back: Wayne Mickl and Raym Wilby and Jonthan. Raym was unwontedly quiet. Mickl said, "And what were you discussing with the Bosun?"

Sectry was flustered; Rather answered first. "I was suggesting that if you did have a fourth pressure suit, you'd need twelve dwarves to man them."

Sectry tried to cover her laugh with her hands. Booce laughed outright. Doheen's mouth was rigidly straight. Mickl was about to explode.

And Rather had learned little from Sectry, but it might be enough. *Go for Gold.* Before Mickl could speak, he asked, "Does it fly better than your suits?"

Mickl's face didn't change. "Yes. How did you know that?"

"You said it outflew you. Besides, I heard something once."

"You'll tell me."

"Privately, if you don't mind, Captain-Guardian."

They took the kitchen. Mickl said, "That fringe-addled Dark diver makes you a poor witness."

"I don't know anything about your Chairman's Court."

"You'll see a court soon enough. Talk to me, boy."

"I don't know anything about your mutineer pressure suit either—"

"Then—"

"I once heard that there's a way to make little holes on a pressure suit spray fire. Then it can fly without wings."

"Go on."

"Maybe I can find a man who can do it. He doesn't have a pressure suit, so he's never tried it."

"Take me to him."

"They don't deal with Navy. They don't even come into the Admiralty." Rather visualized a mysterious happyfeet tribe, isolated and distrustful. "They sent copsiks once. The Scientists don't come themselves."

"Give me a name."

He picked one he could remember. "Seekers."

"There's no such tribe."

Rather shrugged.

"Well, what *are* we doing here, Rather?"

"What happens is, you give me your pressure suit—"

Mickl laughed.

"I take it somewhere." Payment? Not money; the Seekers might not use money. "I take fringe too, maybe twenty kilos. I take tools. I bring the suit back. They keep the fringe and the tools. Maybe the jets work and maybe they don't."

"Let me tell you why I can't give you my pressure suit," Mickl said gently. "First, it belongs to the Admiralty. Second, it alternates among three Guardians. My triad would notice. Third, turning a pressure suit over to savages would certainly be judged as mutiny, especially since—fourth—you might not bring it back. Stet?"

"Not stet. Let me think."

"While you're thinking . . . This mysterious tribe, did they ever have a pressure suit to practice on?"

"They say they did—"

"Could they have got it working again?"

This was taking Rather into empty sky. Treefodder! Maybe it was lost, or stolen, or—

"*Talk* to me!"

"I was trying to remember. They threw it away."

"What?"

"It killed three citizens."

"How?"

"The . . . silver was only for one who was worthy. One day the old dwarf died while he was using it. Three dwarves wrestled for it—"

"That sounds like too many dwarves, Rather."

It did. "I saw two myself, and I never got inside the jungle. I guess Seekers get more dwarves."

". . . Go on."

"The winner put the suit on and died. The one who lost to him put it on and died. The last one was a woman. She started to get into it, but while the—" Rather patted his skull "—this part was still open she said she heard the voice of Kendy the Checker. Nobody else could hear it. They got scared and dumped it and moved to another part of the sky."

"Sounds like the air feed went bad. What then?"

"That's when they found the Admiralty. They say one of your ships tried to rob them—"

"Nonsense."

"We say treefodder. They say you did." It *might* have happened in the past: Navy robbing savages—

Wayne Mickl was looking disgusted. He said, "It's possible. A ship low on provisions . . . this isn't helping."

"Wait. You three who trade your suit off. Are you always on duty at Headquarters?"

"No, of course not. Why?"

Rather took a deep breath. "Your fourth point: of course we'll bring the suit back. Not all of us will go. You'll keep friends of mine to answer for it if the suit doesn't come back.

"Your third point: maybe it's mutiny if you lose your chance at a pressure suit that can fly without wings, especially if it belongs to the Admiralty, which was my first point, and especially if you could get *three*! So let's work on your second point. Can you get the Admiralty's permission?"

"Admiral Robar Henling would rather give up his seeds. At his age it wouldn't—No. Just no."

He *was* getting somewhere. He had Mickl's attention. Think! "Will your, uh, triad try to track down that flying pressure suit?"

"We will. We are!"

"You can go anywhere if you think it's the right direction, stet? You're

Guardians. One of you is an officer. Nobody'll ask. Am I completely off the track?"

". . . Not yet."

"So off you go, tracking rumors of a fourth pressure suit. Maybe you find it. You close in. But there's a dwarf in it, and he sees you coming and flies away laughing. What he doesn't know is that your triad was working without a pressure suit for a while. Then it came back. Now off goes the bandit dwarf, but he's doomed, because your suit flies too and he doesn't know it!"

Mickl's grin was not quite a pleasant sight. "Were you a Teller, where you came from?"

Rather knew exactly what he meant. "Our Teller was Merril till she died. These days everyone does some telling. Captain-Guardian, I'm trying to help. I'll bring the suit back whether it works or not."

"But would your Seekers give it back?" Mickl sighed. "I don't blame you for attacking my men, and I won't charge you. We'll leave it at that for the moment. This isn't finished, Rather."

The civilians watched the Navy people fly toward their rocket. Sectry was trailing; and when he saw her look back, Rather snatched his wings from the door and jumped after her.

She stayed in the air while he strapped his wings on. A voice spoke from the Navy ship's cabin; she answered. Then she kicked away to avoid the rocket's exhaust. She did not fly back toward Serjent House.

The Navy rocket departed.

Rather reached her. He didn't have breath to speak. She said, "You're involved in something."

He shrugged helplessly.

"I don't know what's going on, but I don't want any part of it. I've decided I don't want to live in a tree either."

Rather had his breath back. He said, "We're the right size."

She shook her head violently. Teardrops flew. "Didn't Wayne tell you how many dwarves there are in the Admiralty? Rather, it was a good offer. Nobody makes real decisions when she's on fringe. I'm sorry."

"So am I." His tongue was in knots and his thoughts were scrambled. *The Scientist and the Checker, they caused this, they sent me into Headquarters! Would it be different if they hadn't? Did I mean it, that offer? How will Carlot feel about this? Or Jill?*

"I do want to see you again. After this is over, if it's ever over. You'll be going back to the tree, won't you? You won't like it here, not with the

Captain-Guardian on your tail!" She didn't wait for his answer. "Well, sooner or later there'll be a mission to Citizens' Tree, and I'll be on it. I hope this is all cleared up by then."

She flapped spinward, toward Headquarters or the Market. He called after her. "We have a rocket—"

"No. Thanks. I'll go on foot." She kept kicking. Rather turned back to Serjent House. He was going to have to do some fast talking . . . again.

Chapter Twenty-Two

LOOP

W here had it all gone wrong? A message may become garbled across fifty-two light-years of distance and interstellar dust. But this was simple, unambiguous, and *repeated*—

from the CARM #2 cassettes, recorded year 76 SM, day 1412:

> To **Discipline**, year 1435 State. Retrieve your crew and continue your mission.
>
> —*Frank Shibano, for the State*

—as if he were a wayward computer in need of reprogramming. Arrival date: Feb 26, 1487 State. Recorded by CARM #2 sixty-one Earth days later.

He'd accomplished his mission! Why this?

He had attempted to follow his new orders. Of eight CARMs he had sent into the Smoke Ring, he located three. The rest must have been destroyed, or worn out, or their sending systems turned off.

From CARM #2 he had learned of the death of Claire Dalton. Claire had died at one hundred and thirty-eight, less than two months before the message arrived. No other survivors were known to the CARMs. Many deathdates had been recorded.

Amazing that Claire had lived so long.

There had been a mutiny. Kendy had stored it in CARM #2's computer before he erased it from his own memory. Sharls Davis Kendy had mutinied against his crew. Fool, not to have seen that! Their descendants used *mutineer* as an insult!

He'd made an irretrievable mistake. But how? His reasoning was straight. His orders were unambiguous . . . weren't they?

> *1) . . . You will visit each of these stars in turn. Other targets may be added . . . The State expects to settle these worlds, spreading humanity among variable environments, against dangers that might affect only Sol system.*
>
> *2) . . . The human species is not invulnerable. There is finite risk that the crew of any interstellar spacecraft may find, on its return, that it has become the entire human race. Your crew and their genes are your primary cargo. CLASSIFIED.*
>
> *3) Your tertiary mission is to explore . . .*
>
> *—Ling Carther, for the State*

How could it be clearer?

Kendy knew how the dinosaurs had died. The State had explored the ringed black giant planet that periodically hurled flurries of comets into the solar system. The State could stop comets now. The solar system was tamed. Ten planets were better than one; cities and industrial sites on thirty moons and hundreds of asteroids were better than none; but the lesson of the dinosaurs remained. Planets are fragile.

Earthlike worlds had been found in the habitable zones of nearby stars. Green life had emerged on two. At *Discipline*'s departure they were in the process of final terraforming. On twenty-six worlds, poisonous air resembling Earth's primordial reducing atmosphere had been seeded with tailored algae. In a thousand years some would be ready for further attention. The seeder ramship program had been running since seven hundred years before Kendy's birth.

And *Discipline* had found a habitable nonplanet!

Humanity was to be spread as widely as possible.

The dangers here were not a planet's dangers. The Smoke Ring and its enveloping gas torus were dense enough to protect Earthly life from radiation from the old neutron star, and from other radiation too. Radiation sources were normal throughout the universe. A supernova explosion near Sol . . . a passage of Sol and its companion stars through a region of star-creation . . . a catastrophe in the galactic core . . . events known and unknown could cause havoc through Sol system *and* all nearby systems. But none could harm the Smoke Ring!

His own message to Earth, sent in year 1382 State, was long and detailed. CARM #2 had the record:

Sharls Davis Kendy had abandoned his crew as they explored the Smoke Ring. Three who remained aboard had been invited to take what they needed from *Discipline* and join the others. He had never given reasons; his secondary mission was CLASSIFIED. He had shut down systems aboard *Discipline* in a pattern that forced them to the CARMs.

Ah, that explained something: those three had not loved cats. Pure coincidence.

Then, the message from Earth. *Put it back the way it was.*

How? His crew was dead!

Faced with conflicting orders, he could not function at all. He would be locked in a loop of reinforcing guilt. Kendy had sequestered all data relating to the mutiny and beamed it to CARMs # 2, #6, and #7, then erased it all from memory.

How had he gone wrong? Could the message itself have been garbled? Through 200 repetitions?

> To **Discipline**, year 1435 State. *Retrieve your crew and continue your mission.*
> —*Frank Shibano, for the State*

No explanations, no elaborations. He'd been reprogrammed like a wayward computer. *Why?* He'd accomplished his mission!

Was the message genuine? Check the dates:

Kendy's own mission report, sent 1382 State.

Message from the State dated fifty-two point two Earth years later. He was fifty-two point one light-years from Earth. This Shibano had not lingered over his decision, but . . . it checked.

—Arrived fifty-two point one years after *that*. Check.

. . . Odd. Why would the State expect *any* crew to remain alive? That Claire had survived was partly due to low gravity, good conservative health habits (her mind was that of an elderly corpsicle), youth (via the body of some bright, healthy criminal), and luck. The rest must have been dead decades earlier (and their descendants called him murderer and mutineer and damaged machine).

Shibano for the State. Kendy found it difficult to consider Shibano as separate from the state, but . . . what could Shibano have been thinking? Rescue after one hundred and four years: it was insane.

Perhaps the State's medical resources had improved? Times change. Every generation of mankind has sought longer lives. Thousand-year life spans might have become common . . .

Speculative.

But times change. Goals change. Kendy's route here had been circuitous. The state that had given Kendy his orders was four hundred and fifty-five years old when he reached the Smoke Ring. Five hundred and seven when Shibano spoke. Five hundred and fifty-nine when his message arrived.

Kendy did not normally question orders. Conflicting orders could throw him into a loop. But he had been round and round this loop, while some voiceless subsystem sought desperately for a way out.

Somewhere in a pattern of magnetic fields there was a change of state . . . and Kendy the man would have laughed. A change of State, yes. Sharls Davis Kendy's State was a thousand years in the past. Dead. Somehow he must serve anyway. His own goals had been spelled out in detail; he would serve those.

Humankind was to settle varied environments. So be it. What was his present situation?

The receding Smoke Ring covered forty degrees of sky. His mind had been following a loop for just under two months! He'd missed the final stages of the explosion of Levoy's Star, the foray into the Admiralty might have disintegrated by now . . .

To work. *Discipline*'s drive had shut down without his attention. Good! He still had fuel.

He started the drive warming. His orbit was a comet's, highly eccentric. Equations ran through his mind . . . fire a short burst at aphelion. Shed some velocity by aerobraking, by dipping into the gas torus around the Smoke Ring, twice. Use Goldblatt's World as a gravity sling, save a few cupfuls of deuterium that way . . .

Glowing in direct sunlight, the Clump was green-and-white chaos in *Logbearer*'s steam trail. Clave felt good: loose and free, cruising through an uncluttered sky.

Rather crawled out of the angular cabin. His head was metal and glass. "The suit's too big, but I can wear the helmet."

Clave smiled at the sight. "Getting anything?"

"Getting. . . ? No, Jeffer hasn't called. Maybe he can't call this suit. I tried Kendy too."

"Too bad." Clave had been watching a distant brownish smudge of vegetation. Now he shouted aft. "Carlot? Could that be a fisher jungle?"

"Be with you in twelve breaths." Carlot finished what she was doing to the motor and crawled to them over the cabin. "Where?"

Clave's toes jabbed east and out.

"I don't see the root . . . right, that's what it is. I'd better turn off the motor or we'll go past. Rather?"

Rather followed her aft. Clave stayed at the bow while they worked the motor. Presently the tide behind him went away.

Closer now, the fisher jungle looked dead enough. Brown foliage and bare branchlets. Tufts and patches of vivid green: parasitical growths. The fisher root was half extended, like a dead man's hand with three scarlet fingernails. He looked for the carm . . . and found a man flapping toward him.

Jeffer pulled himself aboard, panting. "Moor to the root. Treefodder, I'm glad to see you, but what are you *doing* here? Is everyone here?" He looked over the edge of cabin and shouted, "Hello, Carlot! Rather, what . . . is that a pressure suit helmet?"

"Yes. The rest of it's inside."

They told it in tandem while they moored *Logbearer*.

"I never did quite know if the Captain-Guardian believed me," Rather said, "but he left Serjent House without taking any copsiks—"

"The Navy watched us for the next forty, fifty days," Clave said. "We weren't doing anything peculiar. Booce sold wood and hired people to cut it. We bought more seeds and some tools and stuff. We're carrying all that. Mickl kept coming around, interrupting us, trying to get Rather to tell him more about Seekers—"

"I tried not to talk too much. I built up a picture of these Seekers in my mind, and maybe I got it across. Secretive. Not very many of 'em. Too many Scientists, maybe half a dozen. They've got a cassette and reader but they don't show it to outsiders. They threw away their silver suit, but they've got records on how to maintain it. And they swear to kill anyone who tells their secrets. The citizen who told me disappeared. He was high on fringe and I was just a kid, but I had a better memory than most kids . . . That part's true anyway," Rather said. "I haven't told Mickl all of this."

"Dangerous," Jeffer said. "You'll have Mickl desperate to meet them."

"Not if I read him right. Scientist, you know the story now, and you can back me up. Give him details I didn't."

Clave asked, "Jeffer, did Kendy get the records he wanted?"

"I haven't heard from him."

"If we're lucky the treefeeder never will call back. Anyway, we must have looked innocent enough. We never did anything odd because we didn't know anything. So. Twenty days ago three dwarves pulled up to *Logbearer* in a Navy rocket. Mickl and another man and a woman, all the same size. Weird. They gave us the pressure suit and went away. We're supposed to get the jets going and pay off the Seekers. Would you like ten years' supply of fringe?"

"No. You'd better leave it here if you're supposed to."

They carried the suit and helmet into the dead foliage. Rather and Carlot set to moving their cargo while they looked about.

Entropy and parasites had eaten a deep cavity into the fisher jungle's dead trunk. The carm was there, and Jeffer's camp: rocks for a fireplace, a rack of poles for smoking meat, a midden a decent distance away. Jeffer had made a third wing for himself, a prudent move for a man alone. From the blackened look of it he'd been using it to fan his fire.

Jeffer had the pressure suit splayed like a bird's flayed skin. "Rather, did you try it?"

"It's too big for me. —And the air feed doesn't work. I got the panel open. A little wheel isn't connecting to anything, and there's a spoke with nothing on it."

Jeffer grinned. "I see."

Rather laughed. "Mickl doesn't want the Seekers stealing his silver suit! If they try it they'll find out nobody's worthy!"

"I'll refuel it. No guarantee the jets still work."

"Well, if they do work, I get the impression that Booce will get a decent offer for the Wart. Mickl never actually said so."

"Three pressure suits?"

Clave said, "Stet. We may have to do this twice more. And they're searching Dark and sky for a fourth pressure suit. They must be looking hard at where *Logbearer* went. You may want to move the carm."

Carlot arrived pushing the last of the cargo: not seeds, but tools. "You're going to love this, Scientist." She separated something out.

Jeffer took it with glad cries. "A pump! Wonderful! The carm's low on water, and I *hate* the way I filled it last time. Can I keep it?"

"Stet. We're supposed to bribe the Seekers with it. Here, this is a bellows from the Market. You anchor one end. It's easier."

"Nice. Can you stay for a couple of sleeps? I've got food and—"

"Lonely?"

It showed in his face. "You know it."

"We've got food you never tasted. Dark fungus and earthlife. You'll love it."

Their exotic dinner was nothing unusual for Rather, not any longer. What made it fun was watching Jeffer react.

Jeffer talked while he ate. "I had some trouble getting the silver suit. I found it okay, but it was right in the fire. I had to get the bow up against it and push it out along with a kilton of burning goo. I just wonder how many Admiralty citizens saw me."

"The stories won't match," Clave said. "In sixty days it won't matter at all. I've been thinking. We'll burn the fringe here: If a Navy ship comes they'll find that the Seekers had a hell of a party and then went away."

"Good. I'll have to take the carm someplace you can find it—"

"No. You find us. *Logbearer* will be returning to Citizens' Tree in due course, maybe another thirty days. Keep watch. Pick us up well outside the Clump."

"Another fifty days of this? Treefodder. And I never even saw the treefeeding Clump."

"We'll leave you most of our food," Clave said.

Carlot carefully wasn't looking at Rather. "I'll be bringing a guest. Raff Belmy and I'll be married as soon as we get back to the Admiralty. I want to bring him back to the tree. What he tells his father is up to him, but he'll have at least a quarter year to think about it."

"So you decided," Rather said. He felt he had almost gotten used to the loss.

"I'm like you. I'm tired of secrets."

"There's a plant here that grows good foliage," Jeffer offered. "Dessert."

Carlot tossed an orange sphere at him.

Jeffer's acting like a happy eight-year-old, Rather thought as he tethered himself into a foliage patch for sleep. *Being alone out here must be rough on him. Maybe all adults stay children someplace in their heads . . .*

"Rather?"

"Yuh. Carlot?"

She wriggled under the lines and was alongside him. Rather opened his mouth and closed it again. Then he said, "I don't like lying to you."

"What *now*?"

"I was going to not say, 'What would Raff think?' "

She didn't move away. Presently she said, "You don't understand us."

"Nope."

"We like to spread the genes around. Nobody talks about it in public, but you hear. A man and a woman get engaged. They make babies together. Sixty, seventy days later, they get married. Maybe the first kid looks like the rest and maybe he doesn't."

"But *why?*"

"It's the last chance. See, I'm going to marry Raff, but there are men I turned down. They're not going to just vanish. I wasn't with Raff *all* those sleeps I was away. Raff's been seeing friends too, I don't know who. Rather, it's just different. The officers say it's good. They talk about gene drift."

"Okay."

"What Raff thinks about it is, he'd rather not know. I never did wonder what Jill would think."

Jill. "We never made promises."

"Sure. But who else is there? There's nobody anywhere near her age in the tuft. Just you."

"I suppose. I wish I could have told her I was leaving."

She said nothing. Rather couldn't drop it. "I wish I could tell her it was worth it. You never wanted that raid on the Library. You were right. If Kendy's really gone, then why did it happen? The Navy'll never stop being suspicious of us, and we didn't learn anything, and I can't even tell Jill about the raid because I can't tell her about Kendy."

She stirred. "You don't want me?"

"Sure I want you. Every sleep we're here, I want you. I wanted you for keeps."

"You can't have that. When we marry, that's the end of that. Understand?"

"Stet."

Kendy had run the records from CARMs #2 and #6 over and over. He'd built up a sublibrary of sorts under RESOURCES, LOCAL USAGE.

Here: Citizens' Tree was firing mud to make a cookpot. Here: firing the laundry vat. Both had been recorded by the silver suit as it moved unharmed through the fire. One clip every ten minutes.

Here: curing the lines from the spaghetti jungle. Mark the Silver Man unharmed in the smoke.

Here: the elevator in Citizens' Tree. Here, recorded years earlier by Klance the Scientist: the London Tree elevator, run with stationary bicycles.

Here: CARM #6 changing the integral tree's orbit. Here: *Logbearer* moving another tree.

Here: Rather collecting honey. Booce's voice explaining that it was usually done with handmade armor. Here: a set of hornet armor made to show the Navy customs collectors, lest they seek for such and find the silver suit instead.

The natives used materials from *Discipline* when they had it. When they didn't, they made do. They were doing very well without Kendy.

Discipline was making its second aerobraking pass, ass-backward through the gas torus. The cone of the fusion drive approached fusion temperatures. That was hardly a danger, but the plasma streaming back along the hull had to be watched.

Velocity, Smoke Ring median: 11 kps. Velocity at Kendy's distance: 3 kps. *Discipline's* relative velocity: 20 kps and falling. *Discipline* reached perihelion and began to rise, embedded in hot plasma. The animals were frantic. Kendy couldn't spare attention for them. Nothing had melted on his first pass . . . but the gas ahead of him thickened as he rose, because Goldblatt's World was ahead.

Visual: a raging, endless storm the size of Neptune. Neudar: a core the size of two and a half Earths spun once every seven hours, carrying the storm around with it, until the atmospheric envelope trailed off into the Smoke Ring. Instruments: impacting plasma increased in temperature and density; velocity decreased. The ship was surviving. There'd been the risk that he would have to blow hydrogen ahead of him for cooling.

Goldblatt's World passed below, warping the ship's path into something nearer a circle. Now the plasma density dropped fast.

Fifteen minutes of that was enough excitement for any computer program. In an hour he'd be over the Admiralty and out of the gas torus. He'd make his last short burn then. It would hold him near the Admiralty for a good half hour.

Discipline would be glowing bright enough to see, if anyone looked in just the right direction. That might or might not be good. Kendy had taken his time returning. His long-range plans were in tatters and he didn't know what to do about it.

Chapter Twenty-Three
BEGINNINGS

from the Citizens' Tree cassettes:

Year 384, day 2250. Booce recorded our holdings before we left. He's appalled that we never asked. Bad businesspersons, he calls us. We don't usually bother to spell out who owns what in Citizens' Tree. It drives Booce crazy.

We spent a lot on seeds and food and widgets, but we still have credit—imaginary money—in some vague amount that depends on what Booce actually gets for the wood and the metal. We'll learn that when, and if, we return to the Admiralty.

—Jeffer the Scientist

The lift cage dropped. It was crowded with eight people and several bags from the carm. Lawri and Gavving, Scientist and Chairman Pro Tem, seemed distinctly uncomfortable. It wasn't hard to guess why. Raff Belmy was uncomfortable too. Carlot clung tight to his arm, possessively, protectively.

"I had some trouble finding the tree," Jeffer said.

"Your problem," Gavving answered. "After all, you took the silver suit. How were we supposed to tell you where we were?"

"Yeah, but you moved the tree, didn't you? That thing next to the lift, is that what I think it is?"

"Yes. Lawri's doing, mostly."

"Hah. Scientist, I thought you'd be twiddling your toes waiting for me to come home."

"We found ways to occupy ourselves, Scientist." Lawri's pregnancy was growing conspicuous. The formality between her and her husband did not seem unfriendly.

Gavving said, "I hope you brought something to make us look good."

The rest of them laughed; but Clave said, "Trouble?"

"Treefodder, yes, trouble! I'd have flown to a new tree if I'd been *sure* they'd let me have wings. One thing, the children are on our side. They've been crazy with waiting to see what you bring back. And Minya stuck with me."

"She did? Good," said Clave.

"She did, in public."

Clave reached into a bag. He sliced an apple in half and passed it to Gavving and Lawri. They bit, distrustfully, and continued eating. "That'll do it," Gavving said.

"Fine. Here. Don't eat the hull." He'd cut an orange into quarters.

They gnawed the insides out of the oranges. Lawri chewed and swallowed a bit from the peel, but did not take another. Gavving said, "Yeah!"

"We've got seeds," Clave said. "This and a lot of other earthlife. We'll plant them in the out tuft."

Faces like a field of flowers below the falling cage. Two meteor-trails of golden blond hair: Jill next to Anthon, she a meter shorter than her father, both scanning the faces in the lift cage. Rather knew when Jill's eyes met his, but her face didn't change.

The cage thumped into its housing. Children piled out of the treadmill, and Mark with them. Everyone in Citizens' Tree was here.

They looked short: a field of dwarves in which Anthon and the Serjent women stood out as normal. Rather had become used to giants. Children and some adults crowded around the cage. Jill and Anthon hung back, not quite hostile, but suspending judgment. Mark had that look too.

For all these hundreds of days Rather had wondered what the tribe would think of his mutiny. He'd almost managed to forget that he had never told Jill, *could not* have told her that he was going to leave the tree.

His mothers were crowding close around the lift, and Karilly and Ryllin with them. The Serjent women hugged Carlot, then Carlot's new husband. Karilly hung back a little. She was conspicuously carrying a guest. Raff beamed like sunlight at seeing someone he knew. They fell into rapid conversation, moving away, taking Karilly with them. "Damn, but I missed oranges . . . Booce had to stay? I'm not surprised, but . . ."

Karilly was silent.

Clave folded his wives into his arms and forced apples on them.

Anthon slapped an orange from Debby's hand. Rather heard: "You took this Admiralty man aboard the *carm*?" before his First Mother picked him up to hug him.

"You treefeeding fool," Minya whispered. "You fool mutineer, you. Drillbits in your brains, both of you, you and your father. He never stopped wishing he'd gone too. Are you all right?"

"I'm in good shape. Mostly." She pulled back to look into his face. He tried to look earnest. "First Mother, I'm allergic to dry, thin air. Not enough sleep does it too. It's like knives in the eyes. I go blind. It lasts for hours."

She started laughing. She said, "I'm sorry, I'm sorry," and hugged him hard, still laughing. There were tears in her eyes. She put him down and saw him smiling slyly. She said, "It'll never happen again. We'll keep the tree where the air's thick. You'd better go talk to Jill."

"Why? What's wrong?"

"Talk to her first. Then I think—"

Jeffer shouted for attention. "I here present Raff Belmy. Raff and Carlot are married by Admiralty law. The record is in the cassettes."

Over the heads of his brothers and sisters, Rather saw the judging-look fade from Jill's face. She moved forward at last. Rather said, "Harry, can you give me some privacy? Take them along?"

Harry said, "Oh. Sure." Somehow he got his siblings moving away before Jill reached him.

The judging-look was back. She said, "Rather. How are you?"

"Fine. Nobody made me a copsik. I didn't get killed. Jill, I wanted to tell you."

"Were you afraid I'd run tell my father?"

"If I wasn't, the rest of us would have been. I couldn't, Jill."

He saw her reject that. She asked, "What was it like?"

"I'll be a lot of days telling you that!" And suddenly it was a pain in him, that he couldn't tell her about the raid, ever.

"What's wrong now?"

"Nothing," he lied. "I was remembering how close I came to joining the Admiralty Navy. I got out of it though. Jill, dinner has to be something special. Is there time to cook some of this earthlife?"

"Couple of days yet."

"I'll show you what to do." Take the kids too? He'd thought he wanted to be alone with Jill, but now he knew he didn't. "Harry! Gorey! Bring those bags to the cookpot."

The Admiralty slid west below him. Kendy began his burn, then turned to his instruments.

Neudar and the telescope array caught Admiralty Headquarters as it emerged from behind the Dark. The Library didn't respond. It must be turned off. CARM #6 was nowhere in evidence. No pressure suit responded to his query.

Sharls Davis Kendy had made more than one mistake. For half a thousand years he had been frantic to begin guiding his citizens in the Smoke Ring. Now he could begin, and now he almost knew how. Opportunities would come.

A part of his attention scanned his growing file on RESOURCES, LOCAL USAGE:

Debby described Half Hand's kitchen for Jeffer's benefit.

Clave carried the helmet on a slow trip through Serjent House.

The camera viewpoint spun erratically through a cloud of children. Children had knocked the helmet off its usual perch at the lift, then played with it like a basketball. Kendy viewed the commons as a series of stills. Corridor openings, the water trap, the communal cooking area, children laughing as they bounded in slow arcs.

A series of angular Clump houses, wildly various.

Mark's hut in various stages of construction. The silver suit had been housed there for a time.

Abruptly the CARM #2 control board came to life. Kendy sent his signal. Records came back: stills of various bored Guardians in their shared pressure suits, culminating in (present time) six jungle-giant men in a half circle around the control board, wearing anxious faces and spotless new uniforms. These must be officers; and now Kendy had their insignia.

The signal disintegrated with distance.

He rounded forty degrees of Smoke Ring before he made contact with CARM #6.

The vehicle was in its wooden dock at the midpoint of Citizens' Tree. It was empty of citizens and cargo. That was *Logbearer* next to the left cage, and some smaller structure next to that. Kendy "stared": he enlarged the image and examined it in detail.

They'd built a steam rocket.

They didn't have a metal pipe or sikenwire, so they'd used ceramics. Fired mud! The laundry vat was part of it!

Records: the CARM on its way home. *Logbearer* was strapped along the hull. Booce was missing. Rather was present(!). The jungle-giant stranger matched the still of Hilar Belmy's son.

Raff Belmy's medical readings, originally ominous, settled down over passing days. Carlot must have helped to calm him down. Rather was being abnormally polite to both, and keeping his distance. The two spent considerable time out of sight aboard *Logbearer*.

Records: moving toward the Citizens' Tree midpoint. The ceramic rocket returned ahead of the CARM. It puffed toward the in tuft, pushing a huge glob of black mud, and passed out of range.

Records: "Year 384, day 2400, Jeffer speaking as Scientist. Carm and *Logbearer* are both docked at Citizens' Tree. This will be my last log entry until Kendy calls.

"Kendy, for your information, Rather got out of Headquarters safely. We refueled the jets on an Admiralty pressure suit and returned it. Captain-Guardian Mickl could have had the other suits refueled too, but he never brought them. Now he's got a pressure suit with jets. We gave him some time to play, and then we told him what to do when they run out of fuel.

"We've had no further trouble. Booce got a good offer on the metal. The Navy was carving it up when we left.

"Rather suggests that Mickl wants the flying suit for himself. It's something even the Admiral doesn't have. He's got a secret now, and we know it, and he'll need us to keep it flying. That gives us a certain edge with the Captain-Guardian if we ever want to exploit it.

"We have some wealth and some influence in the Admiralty. We got it without your help. We do not appreciate your abandoning Rather in the middle of the raid.

"I've spent as much time waiting for your call as I care to. I'll be back from time to time. If you haven't called by the crossyear, which is three hundred and ninety-one days from now, I will turn Voice off."

Nobody was near the CARM. The lift wasn't running.

The CARM drifted out of range. Kendy scanned the far arc of the Smoke Ring out of habit; he had never seen signs of industrial activity there.

The Admiralty flowed below him. The Library had been turned off again.

Their ancestors hadn't listened to him either. They'd turned off the Voice subsystems; they'd cut the fibers that allowed Kendy to fly a CARM by remote. He'd been completely cut off for half a thousand years. As he was now.

———

Rather was scrubbing his teeth and thinking about breakfast when the Silver Man came into the bach hut. He spit and said, "Mark?"

"Who else?" Mark threw back his helmet. The silver suit was filthy and stank of smoke. "I tried that. I felt silly."

"Sure, silly. Mark, I saw their teeth. The older Admiralty citizens still have half their teeth! I bet Ryllin and Mishael have been scrubbing their teeth all along." Rather remembered that this man wasn't his father . . . and didn't know it, and had a legitimate grievance. All in a rush he said, "I stole it. We thought we needed it and we did. It was *right* to go. Treefodder, Mark, you're from a bigger tree! Don't you feel cramped here?"

"Fifteen years I've felt cramped. Relax. You brought back some wonderful things. You brought back the carm and the suit and you didn't ruin the suit."

"You looked mad enough to kill when we came down."

"That was three good dinners ago. I never thought I'd taste potatoes again. I know a better way to cook them."

"You forgive me? Mark, I'm really glad."

"What are my choices? Sure I forgive you. We're firing the new laundry pot."

"Is it that late? I slept like a rock. Needed it too. These first few sleeps I just lay there wondering why one of the walls was pushing against me."

"I've spent some sleepless nights here myself," Mark said. "It's lonely in the bach hut. We built it too big. Big enough for the next crop of men."

"Maybe that's it."

"Have you talked to Jill?"

"Minya asked me that. We've talked. Why?"

"Yeah. Well." Mark sometimes had trouble finding words. "Citizens' Tree is strange. None of us grew up the way you did. There are adults and children and a big gap in between, so you couldn't tell much from just watching older children grow up. Maybe there are things we should have said—"

"I know about sex, if that's what you mean . . . Maybe I need to know more. Two women have told me to feed the tree. It hurts. What could you have told me about that?"

Mark whistled. "You started young. Well, someone could have said, 'There's only one suitable mate for you and there's only one for Jill in this whole tuft, and she thinks she owns you, and maybe she's right.' "

Rather let that percolate through his head. "Jill wants to make babies with me? Did she tell you that, or are you guessing?"

"I'm guessing. All I *know* is, when Instant Chairman Gavving told us you'd gone off with all the wealth of Citizens' Tree, Jill was madder than I was, and that took some doing. She wanted you thrown into the sky with no wings. A hundred sleeps later she was sure you'd all be killed and she couldn't see for crying."

"I'll go see her. Where is she?"

"Go easy, stet? *You* know you can find other mates. Jill doesn't."

"I don't either. Sectry wants no part of me—" He couldn't say why. Secrets. "And Carlot married someone else. You can't imagine how bad that was. All the way home, Carlot and Raff. They spent most of their time in *Logbearer*. It wasn't any better when I couldn't see them."

Mark said, "When nobody wants you in the first place, that's worse. Trust me."

"Mark, I've gotten very good at lying. I'm trying to stop."

"Good. Go talk to Jill."

"Where is she?"

"Everybody's watching us fire the laundry vat except Jill. I've got to go back and see if anything needs doing. Try the miz hut. Then the commons."

The deep voice hailed him as he entered. "Hello, Jeffer the Scientist. This is Kendy."

Shouldn't that have been *Kendy for the State*? Jeffer said, "Uh-huh. You missed all the excitement."

"Not all. A large Navy ship is moving toward your position. They'll reach you in eighty standard days."

Jeffer took a moment to absorb the shock. He should have known. It wasn't over; it never would be. There was no going back from the Clump expedition. No going back from *knowing* about the Admiralty.

He pulled himself forward to the control board. "That gives us some time to talk."

The square, hard face in the bow window had always lacked expression. It said, "A bad thing happened to me, Jeffer. I learned too much about myself. There was no way I could communicate until now."

"Lie to me, Kendy. Say there was something wrong with Voice."

Kendy said, "The glitch was in myself. I think I have it fixed. Machines go bad, Jeffer. I left you a file under HISTORY. It's selected records from the settling of the Smoke Ring. It explains some of what went wrong. Play it after I'm out of range."

"Can you tell me about it?"

"No."

"Your timing was lousy. We thought you'd left Rather for treefodder. If you ever—"

"I can't talk about it. It hurts my mind. Damage might be permanent. Do you seek vengeance against me?"

The trouble was that Kendy looked and sounded as calm as death. Kendy never showed anger, nor relief, love, pain. It was hard to believe he was hurting . . . yet he was *not* a man. Maybe. Maybe.

Jeffer said, "Well, we got home. I assume you got most of it from the log. The earthlife food stopped most of the arguments. Now all the reunited couples are busy making babies. The arguments haven't gone away, though. They're just simmering. It won't help if there's a Navy ship coming."

"It's coming. I couldn't resolve details of design. There's alcohol in the exhaust, and it's coming from the Clump. Definitely Navy. What have you done with the seeds?"

"Seeds? We'll plant them in the out tuft. Mark's talking about building an extension to the lift before anything gets ripe enough to pick."

"Cut some foliage so the sunlight can reach the plants. I can show you how to use water flow to move the lifts with less effort. You haven't mentioned the fired mud rocket."

"That's nice, isn't it? We don't need the Admiralty's treefeeding pipes."

"You don't need me," Kendy said. He knew the risk he was taking. It was acceptable. "I've been looking at records. Most of what can be done with materials from *Discipline* can also be done with Smoke Ring resources. Lifts, housing, clothing, food, domestic animals. Now rockets. The Admiralty even has a heliograph."

"No, we don't need you," Jeffer said, "but I never thought you'd know it."

"A bad thing happened to me. I don't trust my judgment anymore. My intention has always been to make a civilization in the Smoke Ring, modeled on the State that shaped your ancestors. The Smoke Ring will never be that. How can I make a State in a place where I can't even make maps?"

"Would we even like your State? Skip it. What do we do about that ship? I hope Sectry Murphy's aboard. We'll get some notion of what they want if Rather talks to her—"

"Hide the CARM in another tree. Tear out the dock too, or put the ceramic rocket there. Show them that. It's not advanced, but it doesn't need starstuff resources. It may impress them. Keep the CARM manned. There are two ways you might need it—"

"I won't burn them!"

"One way, then. You can't ignore the Admiralty. You'd really like to join as officers. You may have to show them the CARM before they'll listen to *that*. Demand officer status, but they may settle for giving it to just the Chairman and Scientist—"

Jeffer laughed. "For a man who doesn't trust his own judgment, you certainly—"

"I think fast. I plan fast. I make mistakes."

"Anything else?"

"Mark might want to join the Navy. Sound him out. See if the Navy personnel might want him. I gather they don't like older recruits, but Mark was trained in London Tree. Karilly may benefit from going back. Is she still mute?"

"Yes, but she's also pregnant and happy. I'm not sure I want to fiddle."

"I'm almost out of range. Back in two days. The code is HISTORY. Tell nobody of what you are about to learn."

"K—"

"Unless in your judgment it would be beneficial."

Kendy had *never* talked like this. "Stet."

The face faded. Jeffer didn't move for some time. Finally he tapped the white button. "Prikazyvat Voice."

"Hello, Jeffer the Scientist."

"Link to the pressure suit."

"Done."

"This is Jeffer calling anyone. Anyone home?"

"Hello? Scientist?" It was Jill's voice.

"I want to talk to my wife."

"I'll get her. She's on the branch."

That would take most of a day. Jeffer started the HISTORY file and listened to it all the way through. Then he started it again.

Lawri climbed in through the airlock. "I didn't have anyone but Rather and Jill for a treadmill team. Everybody else is on the branch. Now, what's all the excitement, Scientist?"

"Prikazyvat Voice. Run HISTORY."

Dead voices spoke. *Discipline*'s crew reported the discovery of a weird cosmological anomaly. Some of what followed was familiar from the cassettes. Some was entirely cryptic.

"How long have you had this?" Lawri demanded.

"Kendy only just filed it. I . . . I've been in contact with him since before we left for the Clump."

Lawri was coldly angry. "That was mutiny! How could you not trust *me?*"

"I'm trusting you now. Listen."

They heard a highly formalized quarrel. Some of the participants argued for settling the Smoke Ring; some were for moving on to an unnamed destination. Kendy spoke in favor of staying, then tried to terminate the argument. It continued.

There were parts of a broadcast from *Discipline* to Earth: it had been decided that they would settle the Smoke Ring environment.

There was a message from Earth: *Retrieve your crew.*

"And that's it. Kendy got conflicting orders," Jeffer said. "It tangles his mind. He can't go for new orders because Earth is too far away, and he can't make up his own mind because he's a machine, and he can't talk about it because it drives him nuts. If that's all true, he must be close to crazy all the time. The question is, what do we do now?"

Lawri said, "We can play it through the silver suit. Play it for the whole tribe. Tell everyone."

"It'll start some fights."

"Feed the—"

He rode her down. "There's a Navy ship coming. The fights'll have to be over when it gets here. Eighty days."

"Stet. Play it at dinner."

". . . Stet."

The situation was ideal in its way. They were together, but they couldn't talk. There were only the two of them to run the lift. It took all their breath. Jill scrambled over the rungs, keeping up with him. Her tuftberry-red tunic was dark with sweat at chest and armpits. Her hair was a golden halo, as interesting and as beautiful as Sectry's scarlet.

After the cages passed each other, they let the treadmill carry them round and round. Then it was time to throw their weight on the brake. The lower cage settled. Rather and Jill dropped into soft foliage and panted.

Rather found his breath . . . and found Jill watching him solemnly.

He said briskly (he hoped), "Mark says you own me. This is a thought that never crossed my mind."

"He says that?"

"Yes. He says I own you too. What do you think?"

"I think Mark doesn't have the right to say it."

He was an arm's length away. He couldn't read her expression. He said, "It's not just Mark. My parents—all four, or all three and a half, and everyone else too, including you, Jill. You all seem to know just where I fit and what I'm supposed to do for the rest of my life."

"Well, you don't take orders worth treefodder." He was not sure that was a smile. "What's bothering you, Rather? You came home on purpose. You're on the cookpot because you volunteered to cook the earthlife. You're the Teller because you've got stories and you like telling them. It gets you off treemouth duty."

"I like all of that. But I'm told where to sleep and I'm told who to marry, and everyone looked at me funny till I changed back into tuftberry red, and the whole damn tribe sent me to talk to you."

"Okay. Talk."

"Rather doesn't take orders worth treefodder. You talk. Are you unsatisfied with me?"

"You went into the sky and left me behind."

"I did."

"Is that over now? Are you back for keeps?"

"No."

"Why not?"

Rather sighed. "I like coming home. I like seeing new things too. Some of us will have to go back to the Admiralty anyway, Jill. Ryllin wants to join Booce. Then there's a whole *sky* out there! Lawri says our gene pool is too little. Fine. We'll go find some other trees and get mates there."

"Should I do that?"

Running endlessly up the treadmill, he'd had some time to think. "Maybe. Or you could marry me, but I'll take trips, and you'd have to put up with that—"

She flared. "You'd be making babies with every woman who talks funny!"

That was manifestly unfair. Rather let it pass. "Or you could come with me."

"Stet."

"That quick? Are you sure?"

"Sure."

This was working out better than he'd hoped. "Did you work on that new rocket?"

"No. Why?"

He hadn't thought it all the way through after all. "We've got time. In a couple of years a dozen kids will be ready to find mates. That's when we'll start visiting other trees—"

"I see it. I'd have to know the rocket inside out, how to steer it, how to fix anything that goes wrong, because I'm the oldest."

"You and the rest of the crew too. Can you fly?"

"Sure. Oh, all right, I don't do much flying. Rather?"

"Here."

"You seem to have a very good idea of where I fit and what I'm supposed to do."

It *was* a smile. "Sorry."

"Maybe this is what being married is like. Anyway . . . I'll go on the next trip. That'll tell us everything we need to know. Whether I can stand it. Whether citizens can stand my company aboard a rocket. Whether I'm any good. Whether I want a mate from somewhere else. Whether you do."

"Next trip will be the Admiralty."

"Stet," said Jill. She stood up. "Let's go flying."

"There's nobody to run the lift for us."

"Off the branch," said Jill. "Fly to the midpoint. Surprise Lawri."

It would do that! Rather began to understand that Jill would go where he would, and try to beat him there too. "We'll have to fly more than thirty klomters out. Can you handle it?"

"Sure. We'll go off the branch and put wings on afterward. Otherwise someone'll stop us. Come on."

Kendy had assembled the HISTORY file with some care. It was unaltered records, but it gave the distinct impression that *Discipline*'s crew had themselves decided to settle the Smoke Ring.

The population of the Smoke Ring was between two and three thousand (Kendy included children). By his original orders, Kendy must consider that they might now be the entire human race. The temptation to meddle was very strong.

He would not shape them. They were shaping themselves, and they were doing it well. For agonizing moments he had even considered severing communications entirely.

But he had things to teach them!

The Library was off when he passed the Admiralty. It wouldn't stay that way, though. Day 2791 was the midpoint of the crossyear, three hundred and fifty-odd days away. If Kendy knew his citizens, they would celebrate, and the Library would be involved. Perhaps he could reach Wayne Mickl. Kendy had a handle of sorts on the Captain-Guardian.

Meanwhile a Navy ship was moving on Citizens' Tree. He'd see what terms he could arrange.

Plenty of time. Kendy waited.

DRAMATIS PERSONAE

The Crew of Discipline

SHARLS DAVIS KENDY   Once a Checker for the State, now deceased. Also, the evolving personality in the master computer of the seeder ramship *Discipline* and its service spacecraft.

SHARON LEVOY   Astrogation.

SAM GOLDBLATT   Planetologist.

CLAIRE DALTON   Sociology/Medicine.

DENNIS QUINN   Captain.

CAPABILITY JASPER GRAY   Cyberneticist.

CAROL BURNES   Life Support.

MICHELLE MICHAELS   Communications.

Citizens' Tree

Population: 14 adults

GAVVING   Hunter; Treemouth Tender.

MINYA   Gavving's elder wife.

CLAVE   Chairman.

JAYAN and **JINNY**   Twin sisters, Clave's wives.

DEBBY   A former jungle-giant warrior, Anthon's wife.

ANTHON   A former jungle-giant warrior.

JEFFER THE SCIENTIST   Co-Custodian of Citizens' Tree's knowledge and of the carm. Married to Lawri the Scientist.

LAWRI THE SCIENTIST   Formerly the Scientist's Apprentice of London Tree, now co-Custodian of Citizens' Tree's knowledge and of the carm.

MARK   A dwarf; Custodian of the ancient armored pressure suit.

RATHER   A dwarf, Minya's firstborn. Young adult.

JILL   Daughter of Alfin and Ilsa. Young adult.

HARRY, QWEN, GOREY   Children of Gavving and Minya.

ARTH   Son of Clave and Jayan.

The Refugees

RYLLIN and **BOOCE**   Loggers. Citizens of the Admiralty.

MISHAEL   Oldest daughter.

KARILLY   Second daughter; mute.

WEND   Third daughter, deceased.

CARLOT   Youngest daughter.

Admiralty

HILAR BELMY   Logger.

JONVEEV BELMY   Runs the business end.

RAFF BELMY   Their eldest son.

RADYO MATTSON   Officer.

DAVE KON   Owns and runs the Vivarium.

MAND CURTS   Broker for goods from the Dark.

RAYM WILBY   A Dark diver far gone on fringe.

ZAKRY BOWLES   Runs the Vivarium.

ADJENESS SWART   Works in the Vivarium.

CAPTAIN-GUARDIAN WAYNE MICKL   Officer, Navy.

JOHN LOCKHEED   Teaches flying and other gymnastics to Admiralty citizens' children.

NURSE LOCKHEED   Maintenance, works in the Market.

SECTRY MURPHY   Bosun, Navy.

GRAG MAGLICCO   Spacer First, Navy.

HALF HAND   Runs the restaurant, Half Hand's.

DOHEEN   Spacer First, Navy.

JONTHAN   Spacer First, Navy.

Glossary

BLUE GHOST and **GHOST CHILD**   Auroralike glow patches above Voy's magnetic poles. Rarely visible.

BRANCH   One at each end of an integral tree, curving to leeward.

BRANCHLETS   Grow from the spine branches and sprout into foliage.

CARM   Cargo And Repair Module. *Discipline* originally carried ten of these.

CHECKER   Officer entrusted with seeing to it that one or a group of citizens remains loyal to the State. Checker's responsibility includes the actions, attitudes, and well-being of his charges.

THE CLUMP   The L4 and L5 points for Gold. As points of gravitational stability, they tend to collect matter.

COPSIK   Slave. (Derives from *corpsicle*. In the State, corpsicles had no civil rights.)

COPSIK RUNNER   Slavetaker or slavemaster.

DARK SHARK   A predator of the Clump interior.

DAY   One orbit about Levoy's Star, the neutron star. A *standard day* is an orbit of Goldblatt's World.

DUMBO   Inhabits the integral tree trunk.

FAN FUNGUS   An integral tree parasite. Parts are edible.

"FEED THE TREE"   Defecate, or move garbage, or die.

FISHER PLANT   Boll-shaped, reaches toward ponds with a long water-inflated root.

FISHER JUNGLE   A large fisher plant with sting. May attack big birds as well as ponds.

FLASHER   An insectivorous bird.

GHOST CHILD   See **BLUE GHOST**.

GO FOR GOLD   Rush headlong into danger, or disaster, or battle.

GOLD   See **GOLDBLATT'S WORLD**. Secondary meaning: something to avoid.

GOLDBLATT'S WORLD   Gas giant planet captured after Voy went supernova/neutron. Named for *Discipline's* astronomer, Sam Goldblatt.

HAPPYFEET   Mobile tribes. (An Admiralty term.)

HAREBRAIN   Smoke Ring bird, quail-sized. Harmless, edible.

HONEY   Sticky red fluid, used as a lure for treebugs.

HONEY HORNETS   Deadly insects. They secrete nerve poison.

HUTS   Dwellings. In the integral trees, huts are usually woven from living spine branches.

INTEGRAL TREE   A crucial plant.

JUNGLE   Describes almost any extensive cluster of plants.

KERCHIEF   A Dark-dwelling fungus.

LEVOY'S STAR   A neutron star, the heart of the Smoke Ring system. Named for its discoverer, Sharon Levoy, Astrogator assigned to *Discipline*.

OLD-MAN'S-HAIR   A fungus parasite on integral trees.

POND   Any large globule of water.

PRIKAZYVAT   Originally, Russian for "command." Presently used to activate computer programs.

ROCKET   Refers only to the steam rockets used by the Admiralty and Seekers.

ROSES   Long-stemmed plants averaging four meters. Dark red blossom uses Voy light. Tide-stabilized. Not found in the Clump.

SMOKE RING   The thickest region of the gas torus that surrounds Goldblatt's World in its orbit around Levoy's Star.

SPINE BRANCHES   Grow from the branch of an integral tree.

STET   Leave it the way you find it.

STING JUNGLE   Smoke Ring plant, generally houses honey hornets.

SUN   A G0 star, also called *T3*, orbits Levoy's Star at 2.5×10^8 kilometers, supplying the sunlight that feeds the Smoke Ring's water-oxygen-DNA ecology.

TREEFODDER   Anything that might feed the tree: excrement, or garbage, or a corpse.

TRIUNE   A Smoke Ring bird, large and often dangerous.

TUFTBERRIES   Fruiting bodies growing in the tuft of an integral tree.

VOY   See **LEVOY'S STAR**.

YEAR   One passing of T3 behind Voy. Half of a complete sun circuit, equals 1.384 Earth years.

Directions

OUT   Away from Levoy's Star.

IN   Toward Levoy's Star.

EAST   In the orbital direction of the gas torus.

WEST   Against the orbital direction of the gas torus. The way the sun moves.

SOUTH   To the left if your head is out and you're facing west, or if your head is in and you're facing east, and so forth. Along Levoy's Star's south axis. Direction of the Ghost Child.

NORTH   Opposite south. Along Levoy's Star's north axis. Toward the Blue Ghost.

DOWN and **UP**   Usually applied only where tides or thrust operate.

SPIN, ANTISPIN, DARK, and **SKYWARD**   Directions within the Clump. The general rule as known outside the Clump is "East takes you out. Out takes you west. West takes you in. In takes you east. Port and starboard bring you back."

About the Author

LARRY NIVEN was born in 1938 in Los Angeles, California. In 1956, he entered the California Institute of Technology, only to flunk out a year and a half later after discovering a bookstore jammed with used science-fiction magazines. He graduated with a B.A. in mathematics (minor in psychology) from Washburn University, Kansas, in 1962, and completed one year of graduate work before he dropped out to write. His first published story, "The Coldest Place," appeared in the December 1964 issue of *Worlds of If.* He won the Hugo Award for Best Short Story in 1966 for "Neutron Star," and in 1974 for "The Hole Man." The 1975 Hugo Award for Best Novelette was given to *The Borderland of Sol.* His novel *Ringworld* won the 1970 Hugo Award for Best Novel, the 1970 Nebula Award for Best Novel, and the 1972 Ditmar, an Australian award for Best International Science Fiction.

Printed in the United States
by Baker & Taylor Publisher Services